THE FOURTH PORTAL

SONG OF SAUDADE

J. A. MERKEL

ISBN: 978-1-965109-90-8
Printed in the United States of America
First Edition October 2024

THE
SEVEN
P◯RTALS

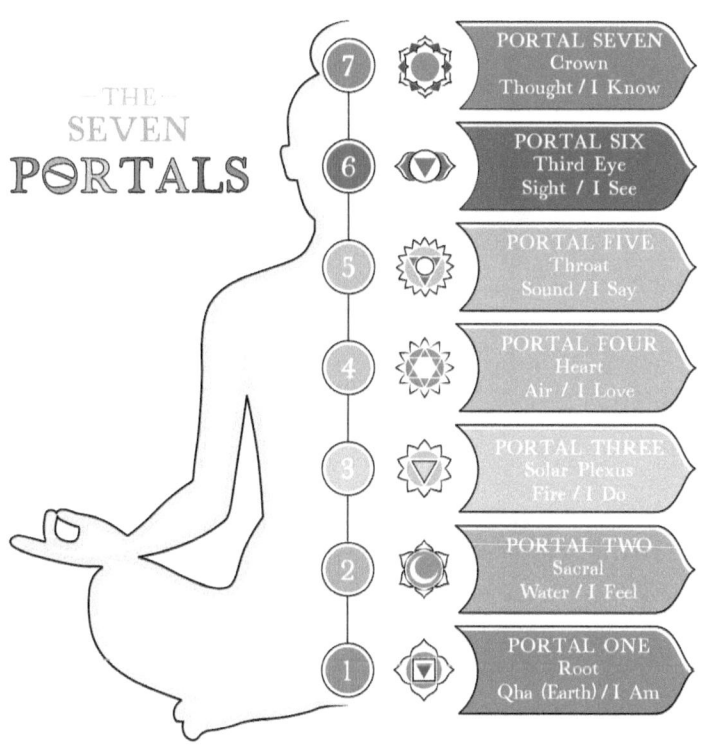

PORTAL SEVEN
Crown
Thought / I Know

PORTAL SIX
Third Eye
Sight / I See

PORTAL FIVE
Throat
Sound / I Say

PORTAL FOUR
Heart
Air / I Love

PORTAL THREE
Solar Plexus
Fire / I Do

PORTAL TWO
Sacral
Water / I Feel

PORTAL ONE
Root
Qha (Earth) / I Am

To those fighting an all-encompassing and sometimes invisible war, who love and push through the scars and pain so hard it aches, who are not fully darkened by their battles, but who, against all reason and odds, choose to keep on loving.

A scattered dream that's like a far-off memory... a far-off memory that's like a scattered dream... i want to line the pieces up... yours and mine.

- Shiro Amano,
Kingdom Hearts, Vol. 2

There is no escape—we pay for the violence of our ancestors.

- Frank Herbert,
Dune

I have learned that if you must leave a place that you have lived in and loved and where all your yesteryears are buried deep, leave it any way except a slow way, leave it the fastest way you can. Never turn back and never believe that an hour you remember is a better hour because it is dead. Passed years seem safe ones, vanquished ones, while the future lives in a cloud, formidable from a distance.

- Beryl Markham,
West with the Night

When a man is denied the right to live the life he believes in, he has no choice but to become an outlaw

- Nelson Mandela

THE ELECTRIC OCEAN
"THE GREAT SEA"

AGUAI
ARCHIPELAGO

CERULEAN
SPIRE

THE MANA CORRIDOR

CLAYH

VIRIDIAN

THE
OBSERVATORY

HEVENSPRING

THE MANA CORRIDOR

GARDENBOG

DOMINO44 MAPS

QhaHadur

DIVER'S COVE

HANIL NNELS

GELISH MAJOR

THE QUAT ZONES

ELYSIUM

EGULL'S HAVEN

SANDSTONE ISLANDS

CRIMSON PHAROS

N

NW

NE

W

E

SW

SE

S

CONTENTS

PART 3: CHANGED
THE SKIES WE NEVER KNEW

PART 4: HUNTED
THE LOVE WE NEVER HAD

EPILOGUE

PART ONE

DISPATCHED

There is a place that everyone must go, at some time, during some cycle. It may not be the same place that one's cycle-partner knows, but it will be a place, one that is always changing, just like the locations we must choose for our nation-feasts. It is under the strict discipline of survival that every QhaHadurian adheres to with undying loyalty: we go where there is life, and that is how we survive.

- from *Lessons on Survival* by the Masters

THE PLACES WE NEVER WENT

QhaHadur, The Leeg Peninsula

Nature without urge is stagnation.

- from *The Elegy of Survival*

1. FENRI THE KNOWLEDGER

7 DAYS BEFORE THE NEW CYCLE

Fenri the Knowledger was watching the second moon in the sky when she decided she had to do it that night. Underneath the glow of the ivory sickle and the greater moon beside it, the Electric Ocean pulsed with filaments of cyan blue. Storm gales touched the water's surface with stark, sudden flashes of light.

The next day would be too late, and after that, there would be no more chances. Over the collar of her skinsuit, Fenri pushed cool clouds of breath into the air. For a moment, she thought she could see her fear inside them too.

She shifted her duneboots in the sand. Tendrils of plushgrass quivered around her as waves crashed terribly against the shore. Salt and the pungent scent of seaweed stung her nostrils. The night grew misty and harsh, darker with each passing moment. She clutched at her chest as the temperature dropped lower.

"You should sleep." Fenri turned and saw Elan's shape, wide and sturdy like a barrel of limewine, outlined by the moons' light. Her mane of hair was tied in a clumsy bunch above her head, long and unkempt from their mission. "The journey home begins tomorrow."

As their team's Charge Leader and Guardian, Elan's concern for her cyclemates knew no bounds. Any of their deaths would be on her hands.

"It's tough to sleep when there's so much on my mind," Fenri said, hoping Elan would go away to let her think.

"Rest won't come easy, or for very long on the way back," Elan said. "We're behind schedule."

"Don't worry about me."

"I will always worry about you, Fenri the Knowledger. Should I not?"

Nervous heat burned Fenri's chest, and the uncertainty grew, loud as the surf around her. The moons would pull the tide higher within the next two hours. Much higher. The ocean would touch where she stood. The idea that two orbiting bodies so far away could alter the water on their planet mesmerized her. They were small and insignificant one moment, and yet utterly monstrous and destructive the next.

"That hauntaray almost stung you last week."

"It didn't."

"Because I shot it."

"I saw it. It wasn't—"

"You would have been dead within hours." Elan's voice was calm and steady. "You need to be more careful. We can't lose you now when we're so close to finishing the mission. Can't lose anyone."

You would all be free of the burden, Fenri thought. "I have made it this far. I won't be lost."

"It's good to hear you say that." Elan dipped her head in Fenri's direction, gazing at her. "Because I'm not messing up my perfect record because of your—"

Fenri flinched. The heat growing inside her pressed at her limbs, suddenly desperate to flee.

"—*condition.*" Elan's tone was flat.

They hadn't spoken about it in some time, but the topic always returned before long. They were here because of Fenri's condition. They were days behind schedule and had less food because of it. They had almost died several times because something in Fenri's body caused her random paralysis, required her to need more sleep, more food, more everything, on a planet that was starving for resources too.

But not here, Fenri thought. *Not here at the Electric Ocean. There is life. New life, and I will find it.* The memory of a greenish-purple shrub she had seen earlier that day while taking water samples swarmed her, and her mind went into hyperspeed.

The plant's dark green column as thick as her arm, the barely visible cobalt tint of the oral disc, the plum-green tentacles reaching skyward, then out, swimming—all stormed her mind in a single, whirling image. The plant was part of, or at least similar to the *Aguavi* family of plants with its thick, robust stem and tentacles, but there was something different about that one, and Fenri's mind dove deeper. The new plant was much larger, at least twice as big, and at its pinnacle was a bulb, as rare and delicious as a figvi fruit.

The plant was life itself.

An *angiosperm.*

That had further implications. Significant ones.

"Fenri?" Elan's undeniable voice snapped Fenri from her inner vision.

The plant was something new. In all her stores of knowledge, it was nothing she could place, which meant it had never existed before. If she could calculate where the tides would have taken it by now, find it, prove what it was, there would be more of it. More food. If it was what she thought it was, it would not only mean more food, edible plant food from the sea, it also meant something in the ocean was changing.

No, it was more than that.

Evolving.

But then, how was she supposed to get it by herself? They would leave tomorrow, and Fenri would never be alone long enough before Elan caught on.

"I saw something today," Fenri said. She didn't care about her condition and was tired of talking about it.

I need to convince her to retrieve it.

"You already said. It's gone. We leave tomorrow." Elan peered up at the sister moons, Kaleem and Milkali. "We've had a good cycle."

"We will return to the Masters with almost nothing."

"We have stores of food, metals, and minerals, and all of us are alive," Elan said. Under moonlight, Fenri could see her face, her dark, deep-set eyes, the curves along her high cheekbones and forehead pronouncing her middle age.

"And my ocean readings," Fenri added.

"What about them?"

Fenri clenched her fists and tried to speak, but she only tasted dry, salty air. Nothing. Elan had thrown her punch with a heavy fist, smashing into Fenri's ego. Every lesson she had ever learned told her not to react against it, to quell it. She merely wanted Elan to understand the importance of what she did.

"We need to understand the way the ocean changes, Elan." Her voice was louder than she meant it, but she didn't care. "Don't you realize how our planet is changing? We will be alive to see amazing things."

"You and I have very different definitions of amazing." Elan was as immovable as one of the Masters after a long night of drinking.

"Even Guardians should understand what I'm doing." Fenri said.

Elan laughed. "Why is it so important to you that I understand what you—what Knowledgers do? Can't we all just go about our missions without complicating things?"

Guardians never cared. Not about one logbook entry. About her discoveries, the research she provided to base. It took years, sometimes centuries to release a study with sufficient proof, but no one would ever understand anything about the planet, about themselves, without understanding the changes. Fenri said none of that. Her thoughts boiled inside her head like forgotten tea.

"We need to recover the plant that I saw before we go home," Fenri said, suddenly glad to be rid of the words clogging her throat.

"What plant?"

"I saw one today. A new species. If it means what I think it means—"

"How could you tell it was new? If you didn't get it?"

"I saw it close enough."

"Where?"

"In the water."

"Why didn't you get it then?"

"Because—" Fenri recalled the agonizing moment. Her legs had frozen underneath her, and she couldn't move. She bristled. Why should she call attention to her weaknesses? The others did that enough.

Elan waited.

"Both our moons are visible in the sky now. The tides are shifting significantly," Fenri said finally. "The ocean is evolving, and I want to find out how before it changes again. Every decision we make is the difference between our survival and being swept away from QhaHadur forever. You know this."

"I know that I was tasked with keeping you, Hasil, and Neren alive. That is my survival."

Fenri stomped away, unable to think. She left Elan alone without another word and trekked back to their camp, duneboots flicking up thick sand as she went.

Inside the baracca, Hasil sat awake. His flagelight gave their leather dome a purplish, moonlit afterglow. Outside, the wind whistled, weaving through fibers of plushgrass in strident tones. Strands of black hair fell from Hasil's forehead. He had been concentrating on something, but his face relaxed when he looked up at Fenri.

"I couldn't sleep." Hasil's voice lacked its usual luster.

"I couldn't either." Fenri sat down next to Neren, who lay tucked in the corner, half-asleep while Hasil cleaned his wound with a cloth and saline. Neren's eyes flickered in pain as Hasil applied more pressure.

Fenri looked away, pulled out her logbook and began to write.

The attitude of those who could stand to know more about what Knowledgers did angered her. Some acted as though they were nothing. Like *she* was nothing. Just some useless class of people who took pointless readings and wrote in books.

"Are you all right?" Hasil asked, his brow furrowed.

"Of course. Why wouldn't I be?"

"Because you're shaking as you write. Healers can see more than just blood and wounds, you know."

"Of course I know what Healers know. At least people appreciate what you do."

Something flickered behind Hasil's dim, unreadable eyes, like clouds passing over impossibly bright moons. The baracca rattled in the wind. "Not always," Hasil said. "Elan said something to anger you, didn't she?"

"She won't even let me stay and look for a plant. She's being unreasonable. Unfair. If she wasn't Charge Leader, she would have no say in what I do."

Outside, waves slammed against rocks like hammers trying to shatter glass.

"But she *is* our Charge Leader, and she does have a say. What plant?"

Healers were at least more reasonable than Guardians when it came to matters of knowledge. They knew about the human body, which was always evolving, so they knew the importance of research and the discovery of new plants and medicines. The plant could even benefit the Healing Circle—that is, if Fenri were able to retrieve it and study it.

"A new species. I saw it today. I couldn't move because of my paralysis. I didn't want to say anything. I didn't realize it was something new until later."

"You were going to go into the ocean?" Hasil asked. "To get it?"

"Yes," Fenri said. "It's not as terrifying as tribesmen say it is."

"You wouldn't be saying that if you worked on as many repair tables as me. There's nothing on our planet that injures or kills more."

"There's nothing that offers more answers than our ocean, the place where all life began. *Life.* Something we cannot afford to ever ignore on our planet. I need to find what I saw."

They both looked up at that moment, their gazes locked onto each other, unwavering. A breeze pushed through the vents in the top of the baracca, and Fenri could smell nothing but the damp sand in the nest of her hair, weighing her down.

"I think Elan is right," Hasil said. His voice was low, full of that serious quality he sometimes spoke with when he had bad news. Which, as a Healer, was a lot. "I know how much you cherish knowledge and the pursuit of it, but … you're not stupid enough to die for it, are you?"

Silence held their tongues in a vise grip.

"It's just a plant," Hasil continued. "It means nothing. Let the Harvesters and Divers find it. Neren is already injured. We can't afford having two of you out of sorts on the way back."

The words plunged into Fenri's chest like a dagger, and when Hasil turned away, it was the same turning of that dreadful blade, ripping through her. Hearing Hasil go against what she wanted gave it an extra layer of pain. Everyone was always against Fenri. She considered Hasil's suggestion. Allow other classes to come across the plant?

Fenri nearly grabbed a clump of her hair and pulled it out. *They won't know what it means like I do!*

Clutching her logbook, she wrote furiously. Hasil was always softer with his words. He was a Healer after all, and part of that meant helping and healing others. Fenri realized it may have been why she had come to Hasil in the first place, but somehow their exchange felt worse. Fenri wrote. She wrote about the plant she had seen. She drew what she remembered as best she could. For an hour. Another hour. The surf tumbled and ripped, like cymbals crashing and drums thumping.

Hasil slept. Neren breathed with difficulty. Outside the baracca, Fenri could see Elan under the moons, her chiseled, muscular arms hanging at her sides as she watched the tide. A knot of fear tightened in Fenri's stomach, but she forced herself to move. She lifted herself out of the baracca silently, slipped behind it, ducked down. Elan turned.

Fenri held her breath. Time stood still.

Elan did not see her. Fenri followed the ridge of the sand dunes down the bank with her gaze. Elan turned back to the ocean, and when she did, Fenri stepped over the ridge and ducked underneath its cover. She crept behind the dunes, down the beach and away from Elan and the others.

After some time, an amount of time that seemed to stretch forever, Fenri stopped. She stood up, looked out. Elan was nowhere in sight. She had moved at least a third of a hectomile, maybe more. The moons had shifted their position in the sky, allowing Fenri to track the passage of time, and the plant's path through the ocean. Based on her calculations of how the tide was moving, she knew she was close.

Her mind was racing, and her heart was thumping inside her chest with such intensity it startled her. Being alone was something new.

Fenri pulled herself from the banks of the shifting sand and stepped onto the firmer, wetter sandscape leading to the ocean. She stood taller on the dense beach.

What are you doing? You don't even know where you're going.

Always, the overly logical left side of her brain sent her messages in times of need. She knew it helped her, but the situation called for more than logic.

I know what I want. If they won't help me get it, I'll get it myself.

Anticipation surged through Fenri's chest like a sudden gust of wind filling a sail, both invigorating and terrifying her. She walked faster. The water was higher, racing its way to the bank. Fenri felt the first wave come over her ankles warm and quick. Even the ocean had a warmth to it, the air muggy and thick with twitting insects. The cells on her skinsuit activated at night, trapping heat she had created during the day to keep her warm.

The open desert beyond possessed a nightly chill, and the place they had been in for the past three months had it too, but Fenri had gotten used to it.

Of course I find something interesting on the day before we leave.

Turn back. The ocean will swallow you whole.

If I don't do this, the plant may never be discovered. It may die before we can do anything. I will miss my chance to change our world. This is what I was born to do.

And with that, Fenri walked deeper. The water rushed to her knees. As if in response to her resolve, she saw the neon flash riding on the waves. *Plankti. But so close to shore, and at this hour?* No, plankti didn't appear in open spaces, only near rocks and higher salt concentrations. And they weren't that *big.*

Fenri's heart slammed into her chest with frightful speed. She staggered as a wave crashed against her, threatening to knock her down. She stood, steadied herself. The water was up to her waist. A realization came to her all at once.

The plant was too large to be plankti, and as Fenri looked out, she saw two others bobbing in the sea, their bulbs marked by the same white-silver of the moons, an alien sheen unlike anything on the surface of their planet. The plant's bioluminescent nature gave it an eerie glow as it bobbed above the surface like a buoy.

The ocean thanks you for your blood. Your sacrifice will feed thousands.

Such as it always was. *Now the ocean is speaking to me?* A great wave formed behind the jet-black mist before her. Fear throttled Fenri, clutching all her limbs. She thought of running. Too late. The wave came up and over, barreling into her. She was thrown backward. Her breath left her as salt and sea burned deep in her nose.

Turn back.

Fenri strongly considered it.

No one is here to save you this time.

Fenri rose, and her chest was heaving, sucking in all the damp oxygen around her. The wave had turned her around, and for a moment, she had no idea which way camp was. Her mind stuttered and surged and her thoughts unraveled.

This will be your life forever. Everything, just barely. Just barely surviving. Crawling back to base each cycle. Having just enough strength to go on the next one, taking the Master's words as law every time. They won't give you what you want. Neither will your Charge Leader. And by the time you get even the tiniest sliver of your desires, you'll be old and on your way to death. You'll live on, barely. You'll never reach the rank of the Masters because you've never given them anything that's worth it. You've done eighteen cycles training for your chance away from base, and now you've done fourteen more in the field, and what do you have to show for it? A plant? Well, barely.

Stop it.

I won't stop.

You will not control me.

The paralysis had taken over Fenri's body again. If she froze, the ocean would swallow her whole, stealing her life one painful breath at a time.

Fenri closed her eyes and turned inward. Outside, the world grew quiet.

Mind before obstacle. The mind powers everything. The mind is limitless.

She waited. No other voice came. She heard the ocean, her own breathing. Fenri opened her eyes and fixed her gaze on the bobbing plant in the distance. She trudged forward. Tears carved paths down her face. She winced them away. She wanted the plant. In her mind, she knew the rhythm of the waves, when they expanded and retracted, like her own lungs. She waited.

The mind is limitless.

She ran forward. The waves pushed back, up to her chest and shoulders. They pulled back, and the water lowered to her waist. Blood pumped through her legs, pushed her forward.

She could see the glowing plant ten feet away, but there was something else too, illuminated by the sister moons.

A wave.

Bigger than any she had seen.

Now or never.

Fenri's feet left the ocean floor, and she swam. She clubbed at the sea with heavy arms as her fingers spread and clawed at everything. She needed to know what the plant was. She needed it *now* and reached out.

The wave came down and the world exploded.

Time felt simultaneously lightning-quick and infinitesimally slow. Blackness swam up her spinal cord and into her brain. She saw only darkness. Her body flipped and spun, and she became a tangled mess of limbs and salty skin. Hair wrapped around her face, strangling her.

This is death, she thought.

I hope it was worth it.

Before the wave engulfed her, her hand closed around something cold and unfamiliar.

Another thought arrived as clear as crystal: *Nature without urge is stagnation.*

Then her world snapped black.

We know how to deal with physical ailments because we understand them. Ailments of thought, or of the mind, are a different matter. They are more difficult to see, and therefore, more difficult to understand.

- from *Lessons on Survival* by the Masters

2. MASTER QI OF THE YORBAST TRIUNE

The nation-feast bustled with the long-awaited activity of homecoming as Zhao came up over the horizon, spilling its golden rays through windows and slats in the clay-baked walls of base. Where for nearly an entire cycle, there had been a scarcity of sound as Healers were confined to patients, Makers were engrossed in devices, and Engineers pored over blueprints, there was then an incredible amount of movement.

Life burst into the Chamber Hall as exhausted QhaHadurians scrambled into alcoves, casting down their terrabags, kicking off their duneboots, and gulping down cylinders of water.

Master Qi watched from the upper landings ten meters high as tribesmen stumbled home. Below, other Masters filled the tables with bowls of tamagon hearts, goblets of limewine, and gulch by the barrel. Inside alcoves, the beat of Janga drums filled the dusty air with its steady rhythm. The flutes and wind-chimes were only pleasant.

Master Qi stopped to watch the celebration, but only for a moment. There was still so much to do.

When he ducked into an alcove tucked away at the northernmost corner of the upper landings, he found Master Ghen, dressed in the traditional yellow of the Mimenza Triune, already waiting for him.

Blades of light pierced the room through a series of slats in the walls. Two pairs of sandals hid beneath a thin haze of dust and debris. In the corner, a cactusii stood on a clay stand, a dual symbol of scarcity and simplicity.

"Master Qi." The low, contralto tone pierced Qi's concentration. In the shadows of the opposite corner, another Master stood completely still, robed in the traditional brown of the Oragami Triune.

"I did not see you there, Master Yaa'ga."

The younger woman emerged from her shadowed corner. Her waist-length russet hair was tied in bunches and hung at her sides, a reminder that change was coming. In a few hours, her hair would be cut for raw material. "Hopefully you have better news for us than Master Ghen here." She gestured with a bow, and Qi and Ghen bowed in return.

Qi turned, guiding his robe around his body for better movement. His orange garb, denoting his connection to the Yorbast Triune, was the brightest thing in the room.

Master Ghen frowned, and immediately Qi saw where his companion carried the weight of his years between his eyes. Qi registered the blind frustration in his furrowed brows.

"What news have you?" Qi asked.

"There's been an infection," Ghen's tone held the experience of years, the urgency of need.

"Where? How many?" Qi asked.

"There isn't much time." Yaa'ga stepped forward. "Let's start with what is absolutely necessary."

Yaa'ga was a fairly new Master, young, spry, and intelligent, an easy selection for the Triune. Qi could not think of a Master as young as she. Perhaps she needed more time to understand pacing and prudence.

"We lost two," Ghen said. "The other two in the party are in quarantine."

"Why didn't they send a message?" Qi asked.

"They tried. They didn't know what was happening. You know how the virus works."

Qi nodded.

"Master Ghen," Master Yaa'ga said, with a nod in his direction. "You're the Master Guardian among us. You'll run the necessary tests, I trust?"

Virus L, Qi thought to himself. *It's been decades since an infection has been reported. What had they missed when creating the team? Why had the rare and incurable virus appeared now, after all these years?*

Master Yaa'ga withdrew a cubic Hive from her robe and pressed into the top of it with firm fingers. The surface flashed sky blue, beeped twice, then shot out hair-thin strings of light. Each string held bundles of data. Yaa'ga typed into the top surface of the Hive, expanding the bundles into even finer points. Qi studied the information contained in each one quickly.

"Data has just come in pertaining to the Quat Zones," Yaa'ga said.

Master Qi and Ghen squared up to give Yaa'ga their full attention.

"Past reports are finally confirmed. The satellite crawlers returned with sufficient data about heat signatures. There is Klonden, fields of it, beyond what we have seen before." Her rising inflection told Qi that she was excited by the news. He tried not to attune with it. Slowing the flow of oxygen to his heart, he swallowed the anticipation building in his throat.

"Klonden," Ghen said, his green eyes reflecting the color of the data orbs, postulating. "How much?"

"The report is inconclusive, but at least several kiloleens."

Kiloleens? Master Qi thought. *That would be enough to build and power a third base. A small one, but that number is worlds more than we expected.*

Master Qi felt small standing near Ghen and Yaa'ga with no news of his own, his presence shriveling under the shadow cast by Klonden and Virus L. But there was something. "The Quat Zones are off-limits. They're unlivable," he said.

"We don't need anyone to live there, just travel there," Yaa'ga said. "This cycle. The radiation levels have fallen in the past decade and remain in a moderately safe range for dispatch teams."

"Moderately safe range?" Qi asked.

"Project El," Yaa'ga said, ploughing forward. "You both remember, yes?"

Ghen nodded. "I suppose the time has come."

"Our planet is changing," Yaa'ga said.

"Yes," Qi agreed. "These changes must be met with prudence and moderation."

"That is why we have you," Yaa'ga said.

"Are you sure—" Qi hesitated in his own mind. He knew the members of Project El. He knew who would be sent to that terrible place. The corpses of the four who had gone there fourteen years before were crushed to dust. Qi wondered what the fallen tribesmen would say about the mission if they could. "—that this is really the best idea. The right time for it?"

"No, I'm not," Yaa'ga said. "Concerns were raised by some Masters about this particular dispatch team years ago during the Project Councils. The algorithms are rarely wrong in their calculations, but when they are, we step in to eliminate redundancies and weaknesses."

"What concerns?" But Qi felt as though he already knew the answer. He hadn't looked at the file in years, but he knew.

"The team has changed. The Digger originally meant for such a landscape passed two cycles ago. There is a Maker we consider highly capable, perhaps even more suited for the mission. The team also had a Healer assigned, but she's suffered a serious brain injury and hasn't been the same since. The slot has been filled with a different Healer who shows incredible promise."

"Those don't sound like concerns to me," Qi said.

Yaa'ga cleared her throat. "No. The other two members have not changed. The Guardian has been steady through every cycle,

Master material in time. He will be the team's Charge Leader. The Knowledger on the other hand … we haven't quite seen her potential play out as we had hoped."

Project El had been cooking in the oven for the past two decades. First, with the failed mission fourteen years ago and then the newer dispatch team. "I see," Qi said.

"We wanted to ask you," Master Yaa'ga said, "before moving forward, to give it your final blessing. This could be one of the most important missions our tribe ever makes. If there is as much Klonden as we think, a successful mission means we can repeat it. But a failure could set us back again."

"You trained her," Ghen said with hopeful certainty. "The Knowledger. Do you think she's up for the mission?"

"I remember her well," Qi said.

"The decision rests with you, Master Qi," Yaa'ga said. "We have an alternate to go in her stead if you wish it."

The muscles in Qi's lower stomach twisted.

"I was also hoping," Master Ghen began, "you'd visit the two in quarantine. To decide if they're okay to be cleared for their next mission."

"Who else has been in contact with them?" Qi asked.

"Only me," Ghen said. "They immediately turned themselves in. I sense no infection coming from them. When their cyclemates died, the virus died with them."

The drums below grew louder. A young woman began reciting a siren song.

How strange. The nation-feast hasn't even begun.

"Master Qi?" Behind Ghen's wrinkled expression, Qi thought he could see his trepidation.

He wants me to confirm what he is so sure he knows. He needs to be sure. To let the virus into our walls would unleash death on our tribe's existence as we know it.

Part of Qi wanted to run down into the quarantine chambers and inspect those QhaHadurians himself. Many years had passed since there was any danger of an infection. *And now two?*

Within the same team? Well, it did work like that, contagious as any air- or skin-borne infection Qi had ever known.

"Something troubles you," Yaa'ga said.

Qi corralled his thoughts closer to himself, remembered to smile thinly. "Yes," he said.

Yaa'ga waited.

Qi felt himself standing at the cliff of his own heart, on the precipice of change, but he could not move in any direction to stop it. The scent of new bodies flooded the Chamber Hall below, sticky with sweat, battered and bruised with injury, thirsty for liquid.

"There is always so much to do when they return," Qi said, feeling something inside him awakening. His body listened with new awareness, the sacred, tingling sensation of a portal opening. He felt pressure between his eyes where his third eye would be, the unfathomable sixth portal. A surge of power from somewhere he could not place began to stir. Perhaps finally he would gain the insight he had only played at before.

"There is this to do," Master Ghen pressed. "It is under my jurisdiction that this quarantine passes, but I require a second opinion. The perspective of a Knowledger."

"I'm honored you thought of me, but—"

"Master!" Another voice cut through the upper landing with the quickness of a durablade. "Master Qi!" A messenger stopped in front of the archway, his piercing shrill lingering in the tense silence. He bowed low before the Masters, his manners keeping him outside the alcove unless invited within. The energy of the thin boy tapped on Qi's unquiet mind.

There. The disturbance again.

Master Qi waved the messenger inside.

"I have been looking for you, Master." The boy could barely breathe but he pushed on with his message anyway. "You've been called for."

"By whom?"

"A woman," the messenger said. "She was brought in by her

cyclemates, severely injured. When she woke, she said something about a new plant discovery. Sea-shattering, she said."

"So, what, she wanted a Master?"

"She asked for you specifically."

"Strange request," Yaa'ga said. "She'll get a Healer and maybe a Master when one is available, but there's no choice in the matter."

"Who is the woman?" Master Qi asked.

"A Knowledger," the boy said, regaining his breath. "Her name was … Faeri … Fenni …" His face turned the white of an infant's tooth.

"Fenri," Master Qi corrected.

"Yes!" the boy said. "Fenri. I am deeply sorry, Masters."

Master Qi waved his hand. "It's no matter."

"Fenri the Knowledger," Master Yaa'ga said.

If it was uncommon for QhaHadurians to ask for someone by name, it was even more uncommon for a Master to recall one of their students. Holding onto a name or a connection for too long created attachment, and attachment led to much greater problems, like the virus. Regardless, memories of that kind took up too much space.

"Perhaps it will make the decision easier," Yaa'ga said.

"Master Qi," Ghen said. "The infections."

Master Qi stood and bowed to the Masters. "Recruit Master Yaa'ga to confirm your suppositions, Master Ghen. I trust your instinct. It seems I have other matters to attend to."

Energy pooled in Master Qi's root portal, the portal of qha, stability, and safety, pushing him to move. "Where is she?"

When Master Qi arrived in the healing alcoves, he found that Fenri the Knowledger, stripped of her skinsuit and lying naked, was not alone. A young girl, a student, having done no more than eighteen cycles, sat at Fenri's bedside cleaning opened wounds. When Master Qi approached, the girl looked up with sharp eyes, and Qi could see strips of neon pink staining her scalp and roots.

"Hello, Master," the girl said, bowing her head.

"What's happened?" Qi scanned Fenri.

"She had an accident at the Electric Ocean." The girl was on her feet, and Qi could see that she was slight but not weak. She did not put on weight like other students. Fenri, in contrast, held her weight well … perhaps *too* well, but Qi knew exactly why. With her bloated and cumbersome shape, Fenri appeared to have taken some water from the ocean back with her.

As if the girl could read Qi's mind, she said, "She's an Unable." It was not a question. The girl's eyes scoured Fenri's body, the same way a Knowledger's did when they were taking in vast amounts of information.

"How did you know that?"

"No one is this full or well-fed at the end of a cycle, right? They have to bring back most of their food to the nation-feast. She could only retain this much mass if she were—" As though the word were too dirty to say twice, the girl trailed off, not looking for any sort of confirmation. She pressed all the usual points, the arteries, the chest, probing for a pulse here, a heartbeat there. Qi calculated the rate by watching the rise and fall of the girl's hand on Fenri's carotid artery and counting.

Deft hands revealed a needle from somewhere, while the other searched for a suitable vein. "I heard there was an infection, Master Qi. Is that true? Did someone contract the virus and come back to base with it?"

Master Qi eyed the young Healer with caution. Her third and fifth portals, fire and sound, respectively, were unusually active for someone of her age.

"The Messenger told me but he didn't mean to, I think," the Healer said. "I'm good at reading people."

"I suppose that serves you well, does it?"

"It hasn't hurt me."

"I assure you there's nothing to worry about, dear."

"I'm not worried, only curious. About *Virus L.* Can I ask you a question?"

"You just have."

"Another question."

Qi nodded, keeping his smile straight.

"Viruses have cures. Why haven't we found one for this virus?"

"We have."

"Extermination is not a cure, is it? If that were the case, we could say that we are curing our mice farms."

Qi sensed that the young spitfire was intelligent beyond her years. She would not easily be duped, and yet, how could she ever understand the intricacies of something so complex? Something even the most trained and enlightened Masters set out to uncover. Master Qi breathed deeply, considered his training. "Perhaps we should reconsider the wording of how we talk about it."

The girl brightened, her hair and smile as light as the sun. "At least you are talking about it. Every time I ask something, I'm silenced or warned with punishment. I don't understand how it can be so dangerous to just talk about something."

There. Again, the disturbance. Qi felt it seeping into him. He looked away from the girl's gaze, from her probing questions.

Master Qi said, "You wouldn't understand because you don't know enough about it."

"Then teach me."

"I'm afraid there isn't enough time," Master Qi said. And it was as though he could hear the girl's thoughts, her voice, hanging in thin air.

Viruses have cures, and I am a Healer.

She wanted to fix things, but the virus was not something broken as much as it was its own devastating force. He did not have the time or the energy to explain that to the young girl sitting before him, so he moved forward with why he was there instead.

"Young one, I am Master Qi," he said, pausing for his voice of persuasion to settle in. "Your patient asked for me. Has she woken?"

"Not since I've been here. Her cyclemates told me she slept most of the way back from the ocean. Apparently, she wouldn't stop talking about a plant she found."

"You're still a student? You shouldn't be treating something of this magnitude alone."

"We're short on Healers as the tribesmen come home, so I'm all she gets. I hope you'll see how sufficient my training has been." The girl plunged the needle into a particularly robust vein in her patient's arm, and Fenri startled awake.

"Besides," the girl said. "With some antibiotics, bandages, and rest, she'll be ready for her next cycle in time."

Fenri gasped, gulping at the air as though she were underwater. She moved her head to look at the young Healer, then swung her gaze to the robed man before her. "Master Qi." Her voice was heavy with fatigue.

"Hello, Fenri. Are you all right? I heard you wanted to see me."

Fenri looked as though she would fly off her repair table and hug the man, but she only craned her neck upward. The black-and-blue oval covering her eye had a waxy sheen.

"Please, try not to move," the Healer said. "I'm getting you on a drip."

"Where's my plant?" Fenri asked. "Master Qi, I found something at the ocean. Where's my bag?"

"So I've heard," Qi said. "Your plant has been turned into the Masters for further investigation." He knew that Fenri imagined he was sitting there to hear about her discovery. He needed to be delicate with her. He was sitting with one of his own, one he had taught all those years ago, because of a *different* discovery.

Fenri launched into her discovery of the plant, how she had gotten it, and as she spoke, Qi intuited words before she said them. A strange idea struck him, as though he had already been there before.

When Fenri finished her explanation, the Healer said. "You're a Knowledger. I didn't know they sent them out into the field."

"Of course they do. How else can we take our readings and gather research?" She turned her gaze to Master Qi. "I don't understand how so few people know about what Knowledgers do. It's infuriating."

The Healer looked up, and Master Qi thought he saw her bottom lip curl into a smile. When their eyes met, the Healer shook it off and began to clean and bandage Fenri again.

"You don't believe me either, is that it?" Fenri stared at Qi with shards of ice in her eyes. She would not pierce a Master with her shards or sharp tongue, Qi knew, but they were there, a cold and calculating piece of her.

"I never said I did not believe you."

The Healer pressed saline into a large open wound at Fenri's knee, causing her to cry out. "Sorry."

"Our second moon," Fenri said. "It's changing the tides. There is new plant life. I don't know where it's come from, but I want to—need to—go back to study it. I'd like to go back to the Electric Ocean next cycle."

"I didn't know we could request where we want to go," the Healer said.

"When you've done as many cycles as I have," Fenri said, "you'd think you'd be granted permission to ask for things eventually."

"Now, now, Fenri. You know our ways," Master Qi said.

"Ways can be changed."

Master Qi could not, did not, believe that Fenri the Knowledger was saying such a thing. She followed rules that Guardians didn't even follow. Mostly because they didn't know about them, but Fenri knew. She knew all the rules and yet he knew that she had broken some to get to the plant.

"How many cycles have you done?" The Healer asked.

"Look," Fenri said. "I know you're a student and want to learn as much as possible, and believe me, I fully support such endeavors, but would you please let the adults talk for a minute without you interrupting every two seconds?"

The Healer half-swiveled, half-jerked her head to look at Qi. She did not blink, and Qi looked away to spare himself from seeing her half-smile again. *Is this amusing to the Healer?* There were too many things going on to think of humor.

"Why don't you leave us, dear?"

"But I haven't finished my job."

"I'll finish up here," Qi said.

The Healer shrugged as though that were the natural progression of things. She stood and smiled politely. "Thank you for talking with me, Master Qi. I hope you recover well, Fenri the Knowledger." She bowed and was gone.

Fenri did not wait for Master Qi to give his opinion. "Please, would you consider sending me back?"

Worlds of knowledge lived in the depths of Fenri's seablue eyes in that moment, their color impossibly stark against her pale skin. She wanted to know everything, and Qi lost himself in the intensity of her gaze. His own thoughts folded in on themselves.

"Fenri, I came to tell you something."

She sat up a little straighter on the table. "What is it?"

"You've been selected to go on a special mission next cycle."

"Special mission?"

"Satellite crawlers have discovered fields of untouched Klonden. We believe it's enough to build a third base."

"Master Qi, what are you saying? Where is this Klonden? We've sent satellite crawlers everywhere." The seablue of Fenri's eyes surged at the potential for knowledge that no one else had.

That was the tricky thing about a human who preyed on knowledge as a plant intakes water and light. You had to give Fenri some information but never too much. She would find holes and ask you everything until those holes were filled and her knowledge was satiated.

"There is one place we haven't gone."

Fenri froze, and time seemed to stop with her.

Master Qi had all the information he needed about Project El, but for some reason it was hard to relay it to Fenri. He could alter the dispatch missions, argue that Fenri was not fit to travel to such a dangerous place with her condition, but that didn't feel right either. Project El had gone through years of research. Painstaking detail went into selecting the team members that would finally brave the Quat Zones again. Especially since the last mission had been a complete failure.

"You want to send me there?" As much as new knowledge intrigued Fenri, even that seemed out of bounds.

Seeing her injured and battered like that brought a realness to the situation, and finally it hit Qi. He knew why his thoughts seemed so tangled, why he even considered changing Fenri's mission.

She might die there.

Qi crushed the fear that was not his to have. The projects had been decided, and Qi needed to follow the rules.

Fenri was quiet for a moment, inspecting every tear and rupture covering her body, as though the same destruction awaited her again in the field. She looked up and Qi met her gaze. For the first time in a long time, he could not place what Fenri the Knowledger was feeling, and that surprised him.

She sat up a little straighter and asked her question like it was the most important question in the universe. Maybe it was. "Who else will be going with me?"

There are seven portals residing within the human body. These portals swirl with energy and, once opened, can help us coalesce with elements outside ourselves to reach oneness. We strive to open all seven portals, save one. The forbidden fourth portal sits equidistant from portal one and portal seven, and must always remain closed. Knowledge of its power should be balanced by knowledge of its devastation.

- from *Lessons on Survival* by the Masters

3. CRAEYA THE HEALER

By the time Craeya left the healing alcove, there were twice as many people in the tunnels as before. The stream of homecomers moved in the opposite direction, their faces worn and touched red, bronze, and gold by the sun. They retired to alcoves to manage their injuries and repair their wounds while Messengers, Healers, and occasionally a Master would lead the way.

Lessonmates from Craeya's cohort emerged from other alcoves, scrubbing their hands clean with cloth. The smell of ethanol stung Craeya's senses and brought her back to all the time spent with them. They had been cutting open bodies since she was old enough to hold a scalpel. And she would be the only Healer in her dispatch mission, put with others from different classes. She would no longer train, study, or be with any of her lessonmates ever again.

"It's our way," Craeya could hear Healer Polina say.

Two figures entered the tunnel from alcoves ahead of Craeya and immediately she recognized the taller one and his lengthy, impossibly well-structured shape. The boys laughed in long, loud cackles, their voices grasping at manhood. Craeya had operated on men before. She had seen old and young in their skinsuits—their *original* skinsuits—but there was something mysterious about boys in her cohort she wanted to know beyond what her books, beyond what a naked body on the repair table could teach her.

And yet, she knew she wasn't supposed to have such thoughts.

The shorter boy left the taller boy alone, and Craeya realized she had stopped walking to watch the boy she had known as far back as she could remember.

He turned, and his eyes pulled her in so close she felt as though she was standing next to him.

Rannum.

He smirked, half-waved, and was on his way.

Craeya moved to follow.

Infection from their most contagious virus was said to be able to kill, so if Craeya had caught it, she'd know. She knew the signs, the symptoms. She had nothing to worry about. So then why did it feel like her heart would rip through her muscles and burst out of her chest, to writhe like a half-live tamagon in front of her?

According to Master Qi, there had been infections in the past cycle. Tribesmen had even been put to death. That is what violating the law meant.

Craeya quickened her pace. In a few hours, the nation-feast would begin, and the Chamber Hall would be crowded with exhausted, silly bodies, drinking gulch, and inhaling smokesticks and tilq like it would be their last time.

Craeya had been to the feast before as a child, serving drinks, replacing food and doing whatever else the Masters ordered. The evening nation-feast would be her first as an accepted adult, a tribeswoman who would finally be an equal and valued member of their society. No longer a child.

Rannum turned a corner into the Healer's dormitories, and Craeya followed. If she didn't catch up to him there was a chance both of them would be lost in the ensuing celebration, off on their missions before either of them could say goodbye.

The word filled her with dread and made her uneasy. Craeya walked on, somewhat in her own head, but soon realized that Rannum was no longer in the tunnels.

He had retired to his own changing dormitory—a place Craeya knew of, but had never stepped foot inside. She felt herself being pulled to him. Unseen energies swirled around her, pressing on her chest. Rannum was her first thought in the morning and last one before sleep took her, a weight that never truly left her.

What did it mean that she thought about him so much when they were apart? Only physically being with Rannum made the thoughts go away, but they were there again as soon as he left.

Craeya passed through the narrow tunnels. Her seasoned, wiry hands followed the curves of clay walls created long before she was born. Energy moved through them, sparking at Craeya's fingers.

She followed the faint humming in her ears, a sound that others teased her about, saying it was made up, but Craeya could *feel* it every time. She didn't care that no one else believed her. When she turned where the sound concentrated itself into an orb, Craeya stopped, noticing a hole in the tunnel wall the size of her eyeball.

She looked inside and saw him.

Rannum struggled to remove his skinsuit in the confines of his tiny changing dorm. To his right was a cot, short and long-sleeved robes strewn across it, tinged brown from dust and sandstone. He looked almost too big for such a place. Maybe it really was time for them to be out in the field with clouds as their ceilings.

Rannum's darkened olive skin was the result of carefully selected genetics. Darker skin meant more melanin and less damage from the sun. Craeya's own skin was much lighter, but she knew some traits needed to be preserved. Perhaps it made her more suited for missions at base, but she prayed that would not be the case, and Healer Polina assured her she would get to walk in the sunlight very soon.

Craeya released a breath, feeling the tension in her chest finally ease.

He's so thin!

Rannum pushed the suit past his elbow, revealing a lighter shade of olive brown. The whole ordeal was slow going.

Craeya could only see above his waist. Even with the tight skinsuit removed, she wouldn't be able to see below. She pressed her face against the hole to gain more range of motion. Nothing. Something below blocked her view. The dorm was so small.

She needed to find the changing dorm herself. Craeya touched the wall, her fingers picking up and holding the dirt in their prints. She pressed her fingers together, smudging the dirt between them. Then she headed east toward more openings, the humming in her ears guiding her.

When she arrived at the changing dorm, Rannum's bronzed back swam into view. His suit was half off, the upper part hanging off his body like a second layer of skin. From below his waist where the sun did not go, she glimpsed a slip of light pink, like the palms of his hands.

A spot of heat shot through Craeya's legs into her stomach.

Rannum's olive-colored skin looked as delicious as firenz beans themselves. So smooth. Craeya must have made some noise upon entering because Rannum turned sharply, his eyes impossibly dark and flecked with orange that spread out in concentric circles, growing like embers.

"Craeya?" he said. His torso was bare. "What are you doing here?"

Craeya eyed the muscles in his pecs—not yet pronounced at his age, but supple. They would grow.

"I think I just—" For the first time in a long while, Craeya could not find words. That same heat in her legs and stomach rushed through her body with the intensity and suddenness of fire. She did not look away. "I saw you come here," she said. "I wanted to see what you were doing."

Rannum continued to remove his skinsuit as if nothing had

happened. "You should go to the nation-feast. Everything's about to start."

"No. Everything's about to end."

Rannum reached down low to pull his skinsuit off his feet.

Craeya had seen the human body countless times on the repair table. Male. Female. She had cut into plenty of them herself. They were all dead or freshly dead, recovered bodies brought back from failed dispatch missions. Craeya and her lessonmates practiced and practiced. They worked to remove anything the tribe could use: organs that might save a life another time, skin, hair, nails, bones.

But seeing Rannum was different.

Craeya's heart pumped like the voracious beat of a newborn's, and she knew she needed to control it.

Rannum yanked the remainder of his skinsuit from his body and stood there naked. Craeya watched him. She studied the way he stood and shifted weight from one leg to the other, the muscles bulging in his quadriceps. He was thin like most QhaHadurians, but his chest was sturdy and his shoulders broad like the barrel-chested strains of their species. Her eyes dropped lower, and in that moment Rannum's eyes pierced her gaze, suddenly aware she was watching him.

"Craeya, you shouldn't be here." He scooped a robe from nearby and threw it over himself, tying it at the waist with leather string. Then he ran.

"Rannum," Craeya called, chasing after him. "I just want to talk." But she knew it was a lie. Something else propelled her forward.

Rannum entered another network of tunnels. Craeya quickened her pace. In sprinting trials, Craeya consistently got the best marks. Rannum was good, but Craeya knew she was faster. And his robe would slow him down.

She was five paces behind Rannum.

Why can't two Healers go out into the field together? Why do they have to separate all of us?

That was a question Craeya could only pose to herself. She had learned not to ask the Masters such questions anymore.

Three paces behind. She ran harder.

"Rannum, stop!"

"Craeya, you're—" Rannum stole a glance back.

One pace behind.

Adrenaline pushed Craeya onward with force. She hadn't chased like that since the Masters impressed upon them the importance of tracking, demonstrating the chemicals at work when a beast is about to claim its prize.

Craeya lunged forward and snatched Rannum by the wrist. She yanked hard, spinning him around to face her.

He looked down at her hand and smirked for a moment. Then he caught his breath and any happiness he had was gone. "What do you want? Let's just go to the nation-feast so we can eat."

"I'm not hungry."

"You will be. It's finally *our* turn. All this time spent at base, and now we can start the lives we've been training for since birth." His eyes shot to her grip tightening around his wrist. "You just gotta let go."

"You'll run again."

"I won't. Say what you need to say."

Craeya released him. "Fine. I think …" She paused to catch her breath. "It's going to be new, sure. Everyone will forget everything."

"Yes, after some time, we will forget a lot of the details," Rannum said. "We'll remember our lessons. That counts for something."

"But not each other."

"Certain memories are no good out there, Craeya. You know about the beasts. You've done a practice mission. You've seen them."

"Not really. Well, maybe one. It was far away."

"They can smell it."

"Do you know that for sure? Do you, Rannum? It's too

difficult to understand the virus from a book, it works on too many systems—respiratory, nervous, and endocrine, to name a few—at the same time. We need subjects to study it, to really understand what they say it is. We are Healers that know the human body better than anyone, and yet, there's still so much mystery around the virus. Too many unanswered questions."

"We know about emotions," Rannum said. "They create attachment. Clearly, the Masters' lessons didn't get through to you. After all these years." His thick brows furrowed together in a darkened bunch.

Craeya examined Rannum, the way he stood rooted. His body was so different from hers. The veins in his hands pulsed and throbbed with so much power. He was a mystery Craeya could not name. Rannum was so alive. He was so close to her.

"Why can't you just be like everyone else? Rannum asked. "Why do you have to cause trouble wherever you go?" Usually when he asked that it was with fondness, but his voice held the sharp edge of a knife, creating distance.

"It's just the way I am," Craeya said, but even as she said it, she knew the answer was more complicated. There were things inside her she didn't have the words for. She wasn't just curious or wild like some of the Masters used to say.

She needed to understand things by doing them.

Grabbing Rannum's wrist again, Craeya leaned forward and kissed him. With her other hand, she held the back of his head, wanting to feel another part of him. His lips were warm against hers.

In that moment, time lost meaning.

There was no nation-feast, no story endings, only the musk of sweet figvi on Rannum's lips, the pre-sweat collecting on all his pores. She could smell only him.

He pushed her off of him, breaking her grip, and stared.

"Why did you do that?" His eyes showed alarm, but something else too. Curiosity?

"There are no beasts here," Craeya said. "They can't smell

us. What harm have I done?" Her heart pounded in her chest. She wanted more.

"If you don't know the answer to that by now, then there's nothing I can say to help you." Rannum shook his head and shouldered past Craeya from where they had come. "It's time to meet our new cyclemates, Craeya. Go out to the feast and forget about this. Like I will."

Rannum wound through the tunnel, his darkened hair flickering above his robe like a beige candle petering out. She touched a finger to her lips, savoring sugars from a figvi he had recently eaten. She had felt his breath inside her, filling her up, and then it was gone.

The tunnel grew cold.

The truth of Rannum's statements struck her as she stood there unable to move. She didn't want new cyclemates. She wanted freedom, maybe. Now she had the chance to put her healing skills to the test in the field, but she wanted to do that with Rannum. Part of her never really thought it would end. A few more days and she'd be thrown into a whole new world where love, whatever that was, was forbidden. As Craeya came more to her senses, she recalled the Master's words. *Feeling love in any form is punishable by death.*

Shuddering in her own skinsuit, she thought she heard the echo of Rannum's voice calling for her, but it was only the thumping of her own heart.

Anyone reading texts about our ancestors will quickly see how different they were from us. They came from a planet with such abundant food that they sometimes became round and slow, unable to fast for more than a few days. QhaHadurians, however, have evolved to fast for weeks, relying on ketones and photovoltaic skinsuits that capture sunlight and produce Solaren, an adaptation unique to our tribe, allowing us to convert sunlight into energy. We obtain water from food sources and condense water vapor from the air, making us well-suited for our desert world. With less gravity than our ancestors' planet, we are typically taller and experience less strain on our bones, muscles, and hearts. These adaptations occurred over centuries, with countless lives lost during our accelerated transition.

- from *QhaHadur: A History and a Song*

4. LUZON THE MAKER

Luzon spread his arms wide, squinting against the glare of the sun. Wind rushed past him at such velocity it was difficult to make sense of anything. He glided lower to the ground, the jagged QhaHadurian soil coloring his vision with vibrant flashes of auburn and gold.

Steady, he thought. *One move out of line and the ground will scrape you clean.*

His left arm wobbled mid-flight. He tore his gaze away and looked to his side. His arms, there was something on them … attachments to his skinsuit? He didn't have the slightest idea how they got there. Looking to his other side, he realized his other arm had no attachment. Nothing to catch the wind.

In that moment, he faltered.

He dipped like a pawkwi suddenly shot out of the sky, the entire right side of his body failing. His shoulder grazed the ground, which cut him like a durablade cuts into meat. His head slammed into the qha with force. All he could see and taste was cold, metallic blood, filling his senses like water fills a jar.

He woke with a start.

Luzon blinked. He was not where he thought he had been. *What was that? Did I—was I ... flying?* A sudden relief that he hadn't died washed over him. He sat up and stared through the dim candlelight examining his arms. Still there as he knew them—his rough, olive-toned skin, and hairless, wiry limbs. He shook the tiredness from them. Had there been something on them? Something to make the wind catch?

Luzon had fallen. Crashed. No ... he had fallen *asleep*. He recalled the details of his past few hours. Returning to the nation-feast in one piece. Washing. Falling asleep. But he hadn't put himself here, wherever here was.

Luzon pushed himself up, inhaling the muskiness of the lonely tunnel he was in. How had he found such an eerily quiet place? He never ceased to surprise himself. Ahead, light flickered down the darkened tunnel in quick bursts, tiny tongue lashings. He walked toward the lights until he turned a corner and saw more of where he was.

Within the labyrinth he saw before him, flames danced. Thin, fleeting shadows fled and then returned.

"Hello?" he said, sensing another presence.

A voice floated back, low and raspy, from somewhere Luzon could not see. A woman's. And another voice. A young boy's. The orb of light grew larger, closer. The shadows elongated like a body standing and stretching tall.

"You'll not want to lose your place in here," the woman said. Now the voice was measured, sturdy.

Luzon walked toward the voices. They were closer. He turned at the next corner and saw a narrow pathway that slanted upward. Like some kind of ramp. Shelves built from mounds of dirt reached skyward on both sides of him. No, not mounds. Luzon looked closer. Clay *towers* stretching toward a ceiling he could not see. A growing abyss of darkness. When the voices came again and echoed, Luzon began to comprehend the vastness of where he was.

These are records. Someone wrote all of this.

"Are you lost, young man?" asked the woman. At the end of the pathway, Luzon saw the light flicker again, a small flame held loosely, giving shape to the woman he had heard earlier. At her hip stood a small boy, his hair wild, tangled; his ears were pointed like shards of glass.

"How did I get here?" Luzon's voice carried far without him having to project.

"I should ask you the same thing. No one comes here except for Masters and sometimes Knowledgers. And it's not so easy to find." The woman walked down the pathway toward Luzon, the boy at her heels. Every step was taken with care. She stood feet from Luzon. He studied her.

Her bulbous nose sat square in the middle of her round face, and her hair was streaked with flecks of ebony and ivory, like ore colored with impurities.

"You're an old lady." Luzon looked down at the boy who showed himself from behind the lady's obscure, flowing garb. He seemed to be connected to it, in sync with its every movement. There was wild fascination in his eyes when he looked up at Luzon, as though he hadn't seen another human besides the woman in years.

"Ha!" the woman snapped. "I had better be. Makes me better at what I do. If you're here, that means the cycle is almost over, and the nation-feast will begin soon."

Luzon nodded. "I came home earlier today. I don't know how I ended up here." He paused, sensing the strangeness of what he was about to say. "I fell asleep and ... saw things."

"Maybe you are like the walking dragon," the boy said.

"Walking dragon?" Luzon said.

"The boy has quite the imagination," the old woman said. "And he had better. When I join the ancestors, he'll need to be as good as I was. As good as I *am*."

"I'll never be as good as you." There was longing in the boy's tone.

"Good at what? Do you two live here?"

"Good at telling stories," the woman said. "I am Jesimene the Teller, and this is my apprentice, Gaia. You are?"

"Luzon the Maker." He didn't know if the lady was a Master in addition to being a Teller, but he closed his eyes and bowed anyway, just to be sure.

"We don't live here, but we do spend a lot of time here," Jesimene said, her lips cracking into a half-smile. "There is much for Gaia to learn, and I don't know how much longer I'll be around to tell our stories."

"A Teller," Luzon said, trying to recall. Stories he was told while taking his lessons. Other times when he was a child. Yes, he thought he remembered someone like Jesimene. "He is a Teller, and so are you. Are there more of you?"

"No. The tribe only has one Teller at a time, with one in training," Jesimene said. "That is our way."

"But there are many Makers," Luzon said.

"We don't go into the field," Jesimene said. "Our roles are on opposite sides of the desert oasis, if you know what I mean. You create. We preserve." The old woman held Luzon's gaze. "You said you saw things while you slept. What did you see?"

"In my sleep-story, I flew." Luzon recalled the strangeness of it. The sensation of flying was as real as anything he had felt while awake. The ground below him, the attachments to his skinsuit, and even crashing were all exhilarating. "It's not a memory, but I felt as though it happened."

"I thought most QhaHadurians couldn't know their sleep-stories," the boy said, looking from his Teller to Luzon.

"A long time ago, we could," Jesimene said, her eyes searching Luzon like he was some foreign creature she had never seen before. "We also flew a long time ago. Come. Walk with us."

Jesimene brushed past Luzon in the narrow pathway, parchment on the shelves fluttering in her wake. The boy stayed close behind. One of them reeked of frankincense, an oil Luzon often used for loosening joints, both human and machine. He followed the two of them, their tiny candle flame casting oblong shadows into the dark cavern before them.

"We ... once flew?" Luzon said.

"Not like in your sleep-story, no," Jesimene said. "Machines helped us do it. Giant metal hubs flying in the sky to go from one planet to another." Jesimene's voice carried a power Luzon had not heard before. He believed the words she said as soon as she spoke them. "The only reason we live on QhaHadur is because our ancestors once flew here."

Was that the reason I had the sleep-story? The ancestors did it, so I can see it in my mind?

Jesimene led them deeper. Towers of books and scrolls loomed on all sides of them, whispering at their passing as knowledge sometimes does. When Luzon looked up, he wondered how high the place went, if there was a way to reach the top by climbing. He ran his hand along one of the clay towers as Jesimene led them higher.

"Why did our ancestors fly here?" Luzon asked. "I thought they were on QhaHadur since the beginning of time."

"It may seem that way," Jesimene said. "But our ancestors came from another planet—a place filled with jasmine green fields and cerulean waters."

"Oceans, and lakes, and rivers, and waterfalls," Gaia said.

"Waterfalls?" Luzon said, hearing the strange word roll off his tongue. He murmured it again, trying to picture water falling. Did it come from the sky like rain?

"You cannot imagine the beauty of our home planet," Jesimene said.

"Why didn't they try to go back then?" Luzon said. "If it was so beautiful, why did they stay?"

"They didn't have a choice," Jesimene said. "Their flying ship malfunctioned and crashed." Her words emerged as a steamy hiss. "It was destroyed. They hoped to get off, but generations passed and there was nothing on QhaHadur to help them leave."

"It became their new home," the boy said.

"Home," Luzon said. The word in his mouth held a new weight. "QhaHadur is home. But—" He felt his heart beat faster. "Couldn't we return? I could build a ship. All the Makers, the Knowledgers, the Masters—we could build something. We could go back to the oceans and the waterfalls."

Jesimene turned, her gaze on Luzon as hard as steel. "Don't you think we've tried? Besides, it wouldn't matter. The reason our ancestors left the home planet is because it was dying. Doom had finally come for them. They escaped just in time. The planet is gone and there is nowhere else to go."

"There must be other planets," Luzon said. "There must be other places to go."

Jesimene continued her path upward. "If there is, no one has ever been able to take us there. Not a Knowledger. Not a Guardian. Not a Maker."

"Why don't the Masters talk about this?" Luzon asked. "Why doesn't anyone speak of other places? If what you say is true, then there must be other, better places, like where we come from. Have the Masters given up on leaving?"

"You think it's an easy thing to leave a planet?" Jesimene croaked. "The problems are not easy ones. One must consider other gravities, other atmospheres, other weather patterns. Our own planet doesn't have the resources to help us leave."

As Jesimene spoke Luzon felt something inside him wanting to leave his body, lifting him. "Is that why we have a Teller?" Luzon said finally. "Someone who remembers other places? Someone to tell us we can't go anywhere else?"

A scowl inhabited the boy's face where a smile had once been. "The tribe needs a Teller just as much as it needs any Maker or Seeker or Digger."

"Why, Gaia?" Jesimene's expression was stoic.

"Because there is no one else to remember. Stories help

people understand the world. They help people realize what is bad and what is good and how they should act."

"Without a Teller, QhaHadur would lose its history," Jesimene added. "Without a common past, common ancestor, common story, we would crumble into dust like the planet we once came from."

"We learn from the ones before us," Gaia said, "From their mistakes."

"What?" Luzon said.

"Our ancestors used to love each other," Gaia said.

"Love," Jesimene said. "Yes. Love eventually would have destroyed them all. Had they not defeated the virus, closed that portal once and for all, we would not be standing here today."

"Beasts would have ruled the entire planet," Gaia said.

Jesimene reached the top of the landing. Below, tiny flames twinkled, scattering flecks of light into the darkness before them. Shadows quivered like a thousand moths. Luzon looked down the narrow trail from where they had come. Towers stretched skyward like bedposts on both sides of them. He sensed the immensity of where they stood, of every record ever taken, signposts of their planet's shared past.

He looked at his skinsuit where he had once seen the attachments. Looking from Jesimene to the boy, Luzon wondered if his sleep-stories had brought him there.

"I want to fly," Luzon said. "I've already seen it."

Jesimene said, "No human has ever been able to master flight. Our ancestors flew on ships once, but no Maker has been able to replicate that."

All Luzon could see was the ground, his own certain death speeding in front of his face, and then him crashing. He could do it, if he could just understand the mechanics.

"This will lead you back to the nation-feast," Jesimene said, peering over the ledge down into the abyss.

Luzon followed her gaze, saw the ridges carved into the wall forming a ladder going down. He took one step forward, brushing loose pebbles off the edge. He faltered and threw his body backward. His heart pounded.

"Aren't you coming?" Luzon said.

Jesimene only stared.

Gaia looked up at her. "You're going to tell a story, aren't you?"

"Perhaps," Jesimene said. "There is an old story about a walking dragon that I feel compelled to tell, but now may not be the best time."

Luzon reached into his memories, tried to remember the old lady. So many things he once knew were gone thanks to the effects of tilq. Still, there was something strangely familiar about her.

"No life is wasted on QhaHadur," Jesimene said. "Sometimes those we think are useless are the ones we need the most. Don't ever forget that."

Luzon couldn't tell if she was talking to the boy or to him, but he nodded anyway. He climbed down, setting his foot onto the first rung, and looked up.

"If you ever want to know more about what I've told you," Jesimene said. "Come find me."

"I will," Luzon said, and he meant it.

"And another thing. I wouldn't tell anyone about your sleep-stories until you know where they lead. Now hurry. I'm sure there are people looking for you."

Before Luzon could ask what she meant, the old lady was gone, her bulbous, billowing robe flowing behind her, the boy at her heels.

On a planet as barren as QhaHadur, still there are pockets of life, fabricated realities where conditions are tightly controlled. These places are not great in size, but they suffice. One might think that QhaHadurians could duplicate these areas, grow food as abundantly and systematically as in orchards, and live in contentment never to leave base again. But one cannot forget about QhaHadur itself. Even with conditions near perfect, she has her own mind and will claim what she likes. She has lived this way for thousands of years and offers no explanation.

- from *QhaHadur: A History and a Song*

5. MASTER QI OF THE YORBAST TRIUNE

Master Qi had ordered the messengers to find all four members of Project El and tell them to report at sixteen hundred hours, so he was happy to see, five minutes ahead of schedule, two of them already waiting for him when he arrived in the Terrarium. Tucking his Hive and the information it offered into the folds of his robe, Qi walked toward them.

Vague slivers of light slipped into the vast, high-ceilinged space through convex windows. The scent of limewine, of freshly squashed limenz ready for batching and fermentation, filled the pungent air. Master Qi had not been in their sole greenhouse and growroom for some time, and he faulted himself for it.

The vast growroom stretched before Master Qi, its far end disappearing into a hazy twilight. Thousands of plants, their forms alien and luminescent under the artificial lights, choked the air with a thick, humid scent. The jungle of cultivated life hummed with the quiet industry of photosynthesis, and Master

Qi could feel the aridness through his thin kelester robe. He swallowed a dry lump in his throat as his gut clenched in anticipation for liquid.

Limewine by the cup, Qi thought. *And very soon. I could use a few moments of peace and stillness. Ancestors know there will be so much to do these next three days.*

The Healer's loud, vibrant tone traveled through the Terrarium as Qi approached, filling the space like fire, hot and quick. "How many cycles have you done?" she asked.

Luzon the Maker, according to the reports Qi had just read, was the man she spoke to. He'd lived through twenty-five cycles, and was the third youngest member of their team.

Luzon looked around the gardens, entranced, gradually resting his gaze on his companion. Qi was surprised to learn he recognized the young girl standing before him. She was the one who'd sat at Fenri's bedside and healed her.

Aha ... so this is Craeya the Healer.

"This will be ... five or six, I think." Luzon scratched his back as he looked at Craeya, his head cocked to one side.

"Five or six? You don't remember which?" she asked.

"Pretty sure it's six," Luzon said.

"I think it'd be easy to remember. It's not a very high number."

"You do as much tilq as we did, and you'd have a hard time remembering how many times you did something identical in nature over and over again too." Luzon paused, his face growing warm with revelation. "Maybe it was five."

"Appetite suppressant, memory masker, emotion stifler," Craeya said. "I know the effects of tilq. I thought knowing how many cycles you've done would take up too much space in your brain to be wiped out by tilq. If there's any space left."

"Says the tribeswoman who still hasn't done a cycle in the wild." Luzon smiled. "Tilq is essential to our survival. Knowing how many cycles we've done is not."

"Well, it's a good thing, because by now you'd be dead—"

Qi cut in. "Hello there. I am Master Qi." He brought both

hands to his chest. "Luzon, it's nice to meet you. Craeya, nice to see you again."

Luzon and Craeya turned in unison.

Craeya smiled earnestly. "Hi, Master Qi. Where are our other team members?"

"They will be here any moment," Qi said.

"Will we be going to the Electric Ocean?" Craeya asked. "I heard that Knowledger discovered a new plant species. Has anyone confirmed that?"

Qi's mind wandered to Fenri, and he wondered how his feisty little Knowledger was faring. By the end of three days, she would be in much better health, but Qi wished she were there. "Not the Electric Ocean. Why don't we wait for everyone to arrive before I explain everything?" He didn't want to have to repeat himself, and he knew that once they started getting answers, they wouldn't stop asking questions. Especially Craeya the Curious.

Qi had read both their reports. Master Yaa'ga and others were concerned about Fenri and her performance, but after he met Craeya, he thought maybe she was really the one they needed to keep an eye on. Many of her portals were opened, at least a little bit, and her fire and sound portals were growing stronger by the second. Her fourth portal sat idle between them, but Qi felt a strange energy emanating from that area.

"Then where?" Luzon asked. "Maybe we'll see some mountains?"

Master Qi envisioned maps in his brain, all the potential paths and trips, lines appearing as crystal-blue lights, like his Hive activating, appearing in his bank of memories. "Well, not exactly—"

"Wait." Craeya faced Luzon. "Are you one of those Mountaineers?"

"I'm a Maker."

"So you make things, right?"

"That's the idea."

"Hasn't everything already been made?"

"You're a Healer. Do you feel the same away about medicines?"

"No, but I need to heal in real time. I guess I thought Makers mainly stayed at base to work."

They both turned to Master Qi as if he would have the answer.

She is comfortable in her skin. Comfortable when she talks to Luzon. When she talks to me. Perhaps too comfortable.

Qi recalled what he had learned in the past day about her. Craeya the Wild Card they had called her, for her unexplained behaviors, her boldness, even at such a young age. Not everything was traceable. She was an epigenetic mix of her own making and didn't seem to model all the behaviors leading to survival.

Craeya tugged at a strand of her hair, the vibrant and unnatural pink fading at the tips, a testament to her scientific misstep and an experiment gone wrong.

Yes, a wild card indeed, Master Qi thought. *The Guardian will need to be made aware of her propensities.*

"Luzon is an exceptional Maker," Qi said, feeling the smallest tug from Luzon's sixth portal, characterized by sight, intuition, and insight. "Fast, but also clever. He makes things that don't fit together, fit together." The Klonden flashed in Master's Qi's mind. *We will need his hands when they return with the Klonden. There will be much work to do.*

"If something doesn't fit together, there is no reason to force it," Craeya said.

"What doesn't fit together?" The words belonged to a new voice in the gardens. Qi turned to see the specimen that was Pau the Guardian, walking at a brisk speed, all business, his third portal, fire, surging into the room with untold power, but lacking shape. He was dressed in a beige robe down to his knees, and tied tight at the waist, showcasing a lean, cut frame that wasted nothing and made use of everything. His large, bald head, recently shaved for its hair, stood atop his towering frame—all six feet, four inches of him. He'd been alive for twenty-two cycles.

The Terrarium cooled as Zhao sank into the darkness. It was

night. Lights flickered at the edge of the room as a shadow grew and crept closer to them.

Master Qi lifted his arms in greeting. "Pau, hello!" His presence was good news for the mission. Frankly, the only good news Qi could truly put his trust in. He wished he had known Luzon and Craeya better before the mission was set.

Pau stopped before Master Qi and bowed. "What's this about?"

"Don't bother asking," Craeya said. "He won't tell us anything until everyone is here." Craeya sighed, looking up at Pau. "Which class are you?" You're tall."

"I'm a Guardian. Your Charge Leader for this cycle."

"Charge Leaders are decision-makers in moments of doubt," Qi said.

It will only boost his power more. The reward system in his Guardian-trained brain will remain underactive even if his endorphin levels spike.

The personality profiles run on Charge Leaders made Pau an easy selection. Just four cycles under his belt and already he was ready to lead. In fact, with the exception of Fenri, the team was uncannily youthful.

"Where is the fourth?" Pau asked. "Everyone needs to be here before I can brief."

Where *was* Fenri?

Master Qi could taste the limewine on his tonguebuds. He swallowed his own saliva, the memory of the tangy, bitter flavor alive in his mouth.

"She will be here any moment," Master Qi said. He thought of Fenri resting in her bed, life coursing back into her, and he wondered if she would be ready to leave again in three days.

In nervous anticipation, Qi tapped his foot against the ground.

He slowed his breath, held his foot still, and thoughts, thoughts he could not share with his present company, spilled into him like the sudden pouring of water.

Their planet was changing. Now, pieces were in place to make many things change at once. Fenri's discovery appeared to be unregistered, but would it mean anything significant? Maybe. Their second moon, Milkali, had revealed itself after centuries of lurking behind their larger moon, Kaleem. The effect had changed their tides.

If there really were enough Klonden to build a third base, their way of life would begin to shift. They'd need to dispatch many more tribesmen to build and fill it, and near the Electric Ocean of all places. There were already plans in place, a research unit dedicated to its development. Soon, very soon, his people would need to overcome their fear of the monstrous, unknowable sea, of those glaring twin moons that slung waves around with open-handed slaps.

And yet, Fenri had braved her own storm and gone into the water.

Presently, Qi heard her announce herself, her voice strained.

"It's you," Craeya said. "How are you feeling?"

Luzon and Pau looked between the women to register the exchange.

Fenri took a deep breath. "I feel fine. Thank you," she said, but Qi sensed her hesitation, the battles she fought in her own brain. Qi knew the thought process of Knowledgers too well sometimes.

"This it?" Pau asked. "This is the team?" When Qi nodded, Pau said, "Good. Before we go, I need all of you to rest well, take care of all your injuries—"

"You're an Unable," Craeya said. "Won't that be a problem?"

Even when Fenri was healed and she had done fourteen successful missions in the field, she still could not escape her affliction.

"No—" Fenri started to say.

"An Unable?" Pau said. "So what? I don't make any special exceptions or accommodations. She'll get the same amount of food we all do."

"I have no doubt in Fenri's abilities in the field," Qi said. He looked at Fenri and held her gaze. "And since you're all here, it is time to learn about your mission. It is important. And very dangerous. But you've been chosen because of what you can do." Qi launched into the explanation of where they'd be going, how they were to do it, and what they were expected to bring back.

"The Quat Zones," Pau said.

"Klonden," Luzon said.

"How dangerous are we talking?" Craeya asked.

"The last mission went down there fourteen years ago," Fenri said. "Radiation levels were extreme. No one returned."

"Yes, well," Qi said. "The radiation levels have dropped significantly since then. I have full confidence that you will return. All of you. Still, Master Yaa'ga and I agree that it would be wise to send you into the Zones with a guide."

"A guide?" Fenri asked. "As in a *fifth* team member?"

"Yes," Qi said, immediately registering the distaste on Fenri and Pau's faces, grinding against their logical, analytical inclinations. Craeya might not like it if she understood what extra bodies meant. Luzon didn't seem to care if their team had four or forty people in it.

"Well, where is he?" Pau asked.

"Already waiting for you," Qi said. "We sent him a message. You'll rendezvous with him in the Clayhaze about ten days from now, and he will guide you into the Quat Zones."

"I have no trouble guiding," Pau said. "Who is this?"

"He's a Planeteer that has been roaming the planet for almost two cycles, and no offense but, he understands QhaHadur in a much deeper way than any of you. He has a sort of … vision that is born of raw ability. Without him, you will be lost."

"A *Planeteer.*" For the first time, Fenri's excitement sparked in her seablue eyes, like streaks of moonlight piercing darkened clouds.

"His name is Stone," Qi said. *Someone who knows things even Fenri doesn't.*

"Okay, but back to the Klonden." Craeya said. "What is it?"

Fenri's eyes locked with Qi's, and he knew that she was computing its possibilities. "It's an extremely rare base metal with uniquely changing properties," she said. "Malleable, durable, widely versatile in its uses."

"Due to the levels of radiation," Qi said. "We'll need to recover as much as possible in the next few cycles. We're sending you to test the area's safety, and to retrieve as much as you can.

"Now, Pau will be your Charge Leader. Luzon the Maker will provide a useful repertoire of talent. Craeya the Healer, even though it is only her first cycle, will undoubtedly impress all of you with her healing abilities and physical prowess. And Fenri the Knowledger will—"

"Master Qi," Craeya said. "Wouldn't it be helpful to have a Seeker or a Digger for this mission?" Qi did not know if Craeya's slight was intentional or not.

Even still, shame flushed in Fenri's cheeks, red as magma, and Qi heard her fight the blockage in her throat to speak. "Yes, Master Qi. You could still send me back to the Electric Ocean, where I would be much more useful—"

"We are not playing this game now, are we?" Pau seemed to grow taller as he glared down at Fenri.

Qi saw the situation spiraling out of control. Teams were meant to be healthily at odds so as not to form attachments, but this situation was not ideal.

Pau said, "If you have any doubts or apprehensions about each other or the mission, let's get them out now."

"I think that's what we're doing," Craeya said.

Qi drew power from his belly and spoke so they would *listen*. "This is your team, and this is your mission. Fenri, I know you think the Electric Ocean is better for you right now, but you are wrong. We must follow the way of the planets and what they tell us. This mission is not wrong for you. It is only right." And Qi truly believed that with all his heart. He would not allow Fenri to back out.

For a moment, everyone was silent. Qi, regaining control, continued into the quasi-calm.

"Every class has its uses, Craeya. Over the next 320 days, you will need each and every one of you more than you know to stay alive. Fenri will be your compass. Knowledgers know the biology of the planet in a special way and are intimate with what makes it up and how it moves."

The others stared back at Qi.

"So that's it, then? We can eat now?" Craeya asked.

"Find a Planeteer, enter the Quat Zones, bring back some Klonden," Luzon said. "How hard could it be?"

"Please see your respective mission Masters for your weapon, material, and nourishment allotments."

"I want an ElectroMoleculizer," Craeya said.

"We don't have any EMs to spare this cycle," Qi said.

"Give me one from the Healing Circle. There are plenty in there."

"They've been allocated," Qi said, but not as confidently. Craeya's eyes cut into him like the tips of knives.

"If one of us takes damage that is rooted beyond the dermis," Craeya said. "How am I supposed to heal that?"

"Not everyone gets an EM," Qi said. "And this is just your first cycle, Craeya."

"Not every team is going to the Quat Zones," Craeya said. "And more of a reason to give me one. Please, Master Qi. You said yourself how dangerous it will be."

Master Qi doubted his own resolve. *They are going to the Quat Zones after all. I can redistribute one EM I suppose, even if they are exclusively reserved for more experienced Healers. No doubt that Craeya will use it well.*

Master Qi nodded. "Very well. You will have an EM, Craeya."

She smiled, and she and Fenri exchanged a heated glance.

"Off all of you go," Qi said, looking to each of them. "Pick up your allotments before the nation-feast begins and then try to enjoy yourselves. On day three, you will begin your mission. No delays under any circumstances."

The members of Project El left the Terrarium promptly. Master Qi watched each of them go while the room marinated in its moonlit glow. Limewine was on his mind. Qi went to leave. He saw a figure at the entrance, her back to him.

Fenri the Knowledger! So much potential, and yet, you are unaware how to use it. Craeya, on the other hand—a different kind of intelligence, and some would argue not nearly as fully-realized as Fenri, and yet look at how she gets what she wants!

Even then, Fenri hung at the precipice of the exit, undecided about what to do.

"Fenri?"

She spun and the words spilled from her mouth. "If you won't let me go this time, let me go to the Electric Ocean next cycle. I know I can discover more than just fields of Klonden."

There was a hunger in her eyes Qi had not seen before. "I can't discuss future cycles with anyone but the Masters. So much can change from cycle to cycle. I cannot promise something that cannot be promised."

"No one knows about the Electric Ocean like I do. The colors, the planktii, the new plant species. All of it. I can venture further. If we can build a submership, I would go further!"

A draft swept from behind Master Qi, lifting his robe to his ankles. He was observing a determined Knowledger he had not seen before. "Fenri, I—"

"You've already changed your mind once today. You can do it again."

"Listen," he said, trying to find a way to give them both what they wanted. "Return to me alive, with Klonden, and I will allow you to research the Electric Ocean next cycle."

"You won't regret that decision," Fenri said, breathless.

"I believe I won't." But his mind drifted to other matters. Craeya. If she could so easily persuade him to do something he had never done before, what else could she do to get what she wanted? "There are other dangers, Fenri. Other blockades on the senses. Sixth and seventh senses that are not easily accessed."

"You're speaking about the portal system."

"Yes, and no," Master Qi said. "I am speaking of dangers, old and new. Pau will need your help more than he knows."

"My help with what?"

"With upholding our laws. Craeya the Healer is unlike many QhaHadurians in how she thinks. Her emotions can flare like wildfires. If you are to return to us alive, you must be aware of this. Take care of Craeya. Above all else. She is whip-smart, extremely active, and young. She will learn much from you. Watch how she works, her decisiveness. You will also learn from her."

Fenri searched Master Qi's face, waiting to hear if he had finished. She blinked slowly. "If that is your wish."

In all the years that Qi had known Fenri the Knowledger, she had always done as the Masters had said. "Fenri," he began. "In this cycle and the next, you have the power to effect great change. We are careful about change as you know."

"Sometimes stagnation is preferred," she said.

"What would you do if the planet was yours? If you had the ability to make decisions that affected the entire tribe, what would you do? How would you carry us forward?" He paused, saw the way her eyes blinked in quick succession, processing information, how her mind was already mapping out an answer from A to Z in the Knowledger way. "You know you won't be doing missions in the field forever. And we will continue to appoint new Masters."

"Master Qi—"

Qi observed her in the denial phase. *I'm not good enough to be a Master,* is what he read from her face. Her expression fell, then rose again.

"Someday, we will search the planet less and less. We will have more than we need here, and we won't have to leave. The beasts will live in peace, and so will we. The planet will finally be ours in all the ways we want. We won't live in fear or in scarcity."

To make our lives easier, Qi thought. *And yet, she cannot quite name the thing she wants.*

"As you go into the Quat Zones, I want you to think about how you would do this. Think of specifics. How do we achieve that? You don't have to give me an answer now." Master Qi placed a gentle hand on her shoulder, felt a spark of energy pass between them, then he pulled away.

Fenri seemed to take Master Qi's words as a strict command and didn't protest. "As you wish, Master Qi." She lowered her chin to show respect then turned and was gone, out into the tunnels.

So measured. So methodical. If Fenri could see the inner workings of her own mind and separate herself from them ... there is no end to what she could accomplish.

There is a sameness on QhaHadur that keeps us alive. As a civilization, as a tribe, as a people, it is one of our greatest accomplishments. No one strays from the collective thought too far left or too far right. What would happen if we did? I do not want to know.

- from *Confessions of the Masters, Volume I*

6. PAU THE GUARDIAN

Pau had never been below the lower alcoves before. Apparently his past cycle had been so good that he was allowed to go. He walked lower and deeper as tongue-sized flames licked out at him on both sides of the elongated tunnel. Cool air blew from openings he could not see. His slip-sandals moved silently through the dark as the scent of matured qha came up from beneath him.

Pau breathed a sigh of release. The calm away from the sun-scorched days and the bone-chilling nights was much needed, and his cycle Master had spoken the word with such reverence.

The Dark Room.

He knew vaguely of the place that was meant to provide relief. He couldn't refuse such a rare offering. Scarcity was everywhere and going to the Dark Room was a boon. Curiosity jolted up his spine for things he had not had before. For the moment, he was free from his duties of keeping his team alive, and the weight of constant responsibility had been lifted off his back.

He looked at his slipwatch. Already six hours he'd been back at the nation-feast. He'd washed, had a full body massage, and been given necessary fluids, salts, and medicines. Then he filled his belly with enough nuts, seeds, and tamagon jerky to hold him over. He felt at the peak of his existence, standing on the top of a mountain looking into the infinite space below. No one could bring down his mood or energy.

His teammates for the next cycle flashed in his brain, and he felt his blood spike in a hot moment of worry, but he breathed through it and pushed the thought away.

He treasured his arsenal and grounded himself by reciting what he'd bring on the mission: his Guardian belt with all its stunners and sprays; his stretch-rope; his gauntlets, sword-chain, and grappling claws for fighting; and his sand-spirals for gliding across the sand at faster speeds.

His body settled into a sort of calmed synchronization.

All the troubles and dangers of the past cycle fell away into the darkness behind him. There was only what lay ahead. His solar plexus tuned into a low-frequency vibration of hyper-control.

Breathe. The breath controls everything. Control your breath and you control your next step.

The end of the tunnels loomed ahead, an arched door crammed between claystones. He thought he could hear voices. A man and a woman. Pau's heartbeat thumped quicker. The reaction threw his mind into unease.

There's danger, it told him.

But there wasn't. There wouldn't be any beasts down there. *You're safe down here. You're home.*

Even still, the place was strange. Pau stopped in front of the door, peered down at his slipwatch—a necessary addition for when he couldn't tell time by looking into the sky at Zhao or the twin moons. He was a few minutes early. He'd received very little information about the Dark Room, only that it would help him in achieving deeper levels of relaxation.

Pau wondered what he would have to do inside. How quick it would be. Where the female was. Perhaps she was entering from the other end. Would he have to wait for her to arrive?

Pau took slow, even breaths. It wasn't a beast battle, but he found himself thinking of it as one. He tried to keep his mind from asking too many questions, but that thought only made his heart beat faster.

Again, the voices. Pau pressed his ear to the door to listen. Muffled groans and moans. No speech he could make out. Then, a sudden moment of silence.

The door opened with a quick thrust, throwing Pau back. A man emerged, and the sweet scent of fresh honey-Q rolled out of the room with him. His musk, a combined cocktail of sweaty male and female, leaked from his pores and filled the tunnel. The air grew heavy with heat.

Pau's hand went straight to his belt where his durablade would be. No. Only a leather string tied his robe together. He had left all his belongings back in his resting alcove. Before he could curse himself, the man's scent brought Pau back. *Sandalstone.*

Pau glanced at the stranger.

Jet black hair buzzed short on an oval head. A sickle scar cut deep across his cheek. His eyes were two different colors; one eye was dark brown, making one side of his face look darker than it was, and the other eye was stark, electric blue, wild like their ocean. Pau took him in, using other senses, probing as he always did. First with his nose.

An intense, blissful energy radiated from the man in quick, smiling bursts. He threw his hood up and revealed a wide, toothy grin. "That was different," he said.

Pau stared. He didn't expect to cross paths with anyone. "Is she in there?"

The man laughed. He seemed so relaxed, so delirious—a state Pau had trouble reading.

"She left. You'll meet a different mate."

A mate? We aren't breeding now, are we? This is only for release.

"You're a big fella, aren't you?"

Pau moved to go inside.

"Enjoy it while you can. You may never get to again. Not even in your mind."

Pau opened the door wider, shut it behind him, silencing the man. The scent of sandalstone lingered.

On the other end of the room, a single ray of firelight pushed its way inside then disappeared, and Pau heard a door close. He could not see the female, but he could feel her. Her careful breathing. Her undeniable presence. The feeling of *other.*

What came next, Pau had no idea. They weren't supposed to talk to each other. Did he initiate, or did she? He could save his cyclemates from death countless times, and immobilize an Alpha beast with the right tools, but he didn't know how to act in the Dark Room.

"Hello? It's me ..." The woman's voice was particularly feminine. Her footsteps were light against the ground. She took another step forward. Pau's heart beat faster, and he grew hard.

He heard the kelester fabric brush against her skin as she disrobed.

"We don't have a lot of time," the woman said. "I'm told I can lie down or you can."

A lump formed in Pau's throat. He found it difficult to speak. And yet the woman seemed so confident. As though she had been there before.

"I'll lay ... down," Pau said.

"It's lie."

"What?"

"Come. There's a bed on the floor here."

Pau untied the string holding his robe together, then let it fall it to the floor. He moved toward the woman in the center of the room. She breathed in quick puffs. The scent of limewine was sticky on her breath. And something else too. Molassup? When he stepped closer, his foot connected with a soft mattress pad on the ground. He pressed into it further, lowered himself to the ground until he was inches away from the woman.

Was he supposed to grab her? Touch her?

She wrapped warm fingers around Pau's. The cool air pressing into him had all but gone. A slow heat started in his core and began to spread outward.

This isn't ... I can't ...

"Don't be afraid," the woman said. "We're safe here."

Pau wanted to speak, wanted to ask, but he knew he shouldn't. The words came anyway. "I'm not scared. This is ... new." Pau's mind whirled with the possibilities born of the strange setup. He knew of the insertion and subsequent thrusts. They were there for a reason, but for another reason, Pau himself felt immobilized. His thoughts drifted to the man who was in there before him, the confidence behind his smile. "Have you done this before?" Pau asked.

"No. I thought the Dark Room wasn't real."

"You thought the Masters lied to us?"

"Never," the woman said. Pau felt the warmth of her body as she inched closer. "I thought it was only a symbol of something that could help us. I didn't know the act of intercourse was performed."

Pau felt the beginnings of panic. *If the Masters find out we spoke to each other like this, we could be punished.*

"Your body," she said. "It's perfect. Your muscles are harder than osmium." A smooth hand caressed Pau's chest, then moved down. The hand hadn't seen battle, had scarcely even held a weapon, Pau knew. His thoughts grew insistent. *Has this woman ever even left base?* His questions grew louder in his mind. *No! Get this done with and leave. You are a Guardian. That means you uphold the law before all else.*

Pau leaned forward and allowed her hand to reach for his fully erect member. He had never experienced such closeness. A primal terror squeezed Pau's chest, his heart a frantic bird trapped in its cage. Oxygen left his brain in a rush.

Neither of them said another word, and instead did what they had come to do.

Pau's body tingled. He stood naked holding his robe, unable to move.

So that is what they mean by release. It's so different when it's done with another human.

Now, for some reason, something prickled in Pau's brain telling him to get away. A voice inside he hadn't heard before. Not fear or danger. Warnings he couldn't place. He wanted to get away, wanted to be in silence with his own thoughts.

"That was enjoyable. Should we do it again?" The woman's voice was low and sweet.

"Only the Masters decide," Pau said, feeling much more in his body. "Our time is up."

"I want to find you again."

Now, Pau felt danger. People were killed for less. The woman stood up and walked to Pau, as he tried to throw on his robe. Only his voice could be used as defense.

"You go the other way. Where you came from."

"How can I find you again?"

"You can't," Pau warned. "We will forget this." He moved to the door and swung it open, half expecting to see the sandalstone man staring back at him. There was no one. Streaks of light cut into the room, and Pau knew, if he turned around, he would see the woman's shape and face.

"Please, find me again," the woman said. "I'm Jade the Knowledger. I'm staying behind to do research this cycle."

Raw anger made Pau grit his teeth.

She's breaking law after law. We aren't supposed to speak. We aren't supposed to use our names!

He walked out and slammed the door behind him. His breaths were staccato. *No one needs to know. She will forget. I will forget. I can allow this small mistake on account of circumstance.*

Pau walked away, trying to push the experience from his mind, but his body still tingled. A new calm inhabited his body. He felt his frequency vibrate at an even higher pitch. The positive effects of the Dark Room were clear. He could still feel her smooth hands running across his body like water. The warm folds of her body. The gentle swell of her breasts.

Pau walked back from where he had come and smelled another scent.

Sandalstone.

He could smell nothing else.

Pick up these quick, skittering, flightless things, these memories littering the ground. Grind them into dust, unable to be seen anymore by our human eyes.

- from QhaHadur: A History and a Song

7. LUZON THE MAKER

In the Chamber Hall, Luzon stood marveling as the nation-feast unfolded all around him. Flames on the walls flickered, giving light to the darkness. On the balconies above, tribesmen beat on worn drums, rang hand bells, and blew into reed flutes. The steady hum grew. Dust particles jumped and danced in tune. The vast enclave grew like a bubble taking in more oxygen.

The smell of fresh food pulled Luzon's attention away.

Knee-high tables stretched across a cinnamon-red clay floor. Each one was laden with vats of limewine, plates of tamagon hearts piled high, bowls overflowing with racabbage. The scent of tilq came to Luzon in a wave: smoky, peppery, a touch of mint. His nose turned his body to follow the scent, but before he could locate it, the Knowledger greeted him.

Her eyes were wide and alert as she spoke. "What's your item production rate per half-hour?"

"Excuse me?" Luzon asked.

"Sorry," Fenri said. "My question was abrupt. I'm wondering how many items you can make, on average, in a half-hour."

"That's a Maker question. How do you know about IPR?"

"I know many of the cross-discipline training procedures and tests. It's the standard for measuring—"

"I don't like being measured with numbers," Luzon said.

"Anyone can throw together a mud hut in a storm, but that doesn't mean it will stand."

Fenri lowered her gaze. "I meant no offense."

"Oh, I'm not offended." Luzon smiled and tried to catch the Knowledger's eye.

Fenri looked up, swiping black strands of hair from her face. Her neck and arms were a patched-up quilt mended with beige bandages and gauze. Dark rings circling her eyes suggested lack of sleep. "I merely wish to know what all my cyclemates are capable of," she said.

"One day I hope to build a flying ship."

"A flying ... ship?"

"Yes. The same way our ancestors came to QhaHadur. On a ship. I saw it in a sleep-sto—" Luzon trailed off, remembering the Teller's words. *I wouldn't tell anyone about your sleep-stories until you know where they lead.*

"Sleep-stories?" Fenri stood a little taller at hearing the word. "You remember your sleep-stories?"

Luzon could see that Fenri did not remember hers. He wasn't supposed to remember them, but sometimes he did. Was that so odd? That the tilq seemed to intensify them rather than erase them? Surely someone else experienced the same as him. "I ..." Luzon began. The Knowledger leaned forward, breath bated, eyes like moons, as though not telling her the information might bring her instant death.

"Sometimes I do," Luzon said. "I feel like I'm underwater, or in some kind of glass world."

Fenri frowned as if that was not the correct answer. "We don't have the resources to build a flying ship."

"What about the Klonden? What could we do with that?"

"Well, first we have to get it. There is no guarantee of that," Fenri said. She turned her head to the side, revealing its round shape, her small ears. "It depends on how much there is. The Masters will likely use it to expand this base or build another one. I do not think we will see a ship that flies in our lifetime.

A ship going under water, though ..." Fenri's face grew red with anticipation, and the corners of her mouth pulled into a smile. "Could you build a ship that goes underwater?"

"With the right materials, of course," Luzon said. "I could build anything you wanted with the right materials."

She touched a hand to her chest. "I would very much like to search the Electric Ocean next cycle. If there is something that can survive the water's pressure ... I will be interested to learn more about Klonden's properties." When she looked up into Luzon's eyes, he noticed how deeply blue hers were.

"I don't know much about buoyancies, or trajectories—"

"I do," Fenri said. "Physics is not challenging for me. I know every formula and equation. I lack the skills to make something from nothing. But you don't. I have heard positive reports about your abilities."

Fenri's eyes scanned his face, probing it for new information. He had never known a QhaHadurian who cared much about future cycles. Only the present cycle mattered. Survive. Come home. Do it all over again.

Fenri was smiling, taking in the pleasantries of the nation-feast around her. "I must prepare for our departure. I will see you soon, Luzon the Maker." She nodded and was off, into the throngs of tribesmen, muttering something to herself.

When Luzon turned to face the feast, he felt as though the scene had changed. Something—an energy with its own gravitational field—pulled him closer. Hunger pinched his stomach. Tribesmen, their cups and goblets sloshing with limewine, settled into benches at the double-wide tables stretching from one end of the hall to the other. Voices cut the drumming and ringing heard from the balconies in swift torrents. There was laughter, somewhere. Luzon's feet moved before his mind told him to go.

Food.

Limewine.

Tilq.

Everything that had been scarce during Luzon's last cycle seemed to flow without end, but he knew better. They only had access to food that they were able to grow in the Terrarium, or what they collected in the wild. The zeebies' hive populations contributed abundant jars of honey-Q to the mix.

Luzon knew of the materials coming in, of the yields of all plants and animals, how everything was used to power both human and machine. The Terrarium's unique miniature ecosystem and the desert spring on which it was grown allowed them to produce the foods and materials for the plants, animals, and humans to survive.

Luzon remembered the units on food-making more vividly than others. He stopped at a table and grabbed three tamagon hearts. They were warm and smelled metallic and fresh in his hands. He plucked the first one out of his palm and swallowed.

His mouth flooded with the creature's blood, filling him with much-needed amino acids that would build some sort of proteins—he hadn't the slightest idea what—inside his body.

Around him, others reached into bowls and swallowed hearts by the handful. They had steady populations of tamagons at base, but bringing back some from the field was essential too. The last cycle seemed to produce a high yield. Perhaps Luzon said that every cycle. He devoured the other two hearts and pocketed three more. He filled a goblet at a limewine vat, brought it to his face and drank deeply. When he had his fill of the sweet-sour taste, he put his goblet down and was off again.

He quickened his pace, maneuvering around tribesmen as though he were flying. With his arms stretched out to his sides, he realized he longed to be back in his sleep-story. He wanted to experience the sensation again. How could he? How could a sleep-story deliver such a real feeling?

"Luzon! Hey Luzon!"

Luzon turned and saw who had called for him. He stumbled, the limewine starting to take hold, and ducked underneath an archway into an alcove. Immediately the stench of harkine and gulch filled his nostrils, two intoxicants often paired for their similar sweet, dry notes. His stomach lurched. The compact, low-ceilinged room was hazy with smoke and laughter. Luzon squinted to see her.

"Hi Luzon." The voice belonged to the Healer Luzon would be traveling with. Craeya emerged from the cloud of smoke, eyes wild with curiosity, like fire at the end of a smokestick. "Have some." Craeya tilted a goblet toward Luzon's mouth.

He swallowed, wincing.

"Prefer limewine," he said, recalling how differently gulch affected him. The stale, acerbic taste lingered in his mouth.

"How about some tilq?" Craeya turned into the cloud of smoke as she crossed the room. Through it, Luzon could see others, a man and woman, sitting on a clay bench built into the wall. They nodded at him. He nodded back. When Craeya returned, she held out a finger to Luzon's nose. A tri-colored powder speckled her long fingernail, an offering.

"Scorpio's Rainbow," she said, her eyes steady despite what Luzon guessed she had already taken.

"Scorpio's Rainbow," Luzon repeated. "Quite an intense one to start on. We need to leave in two days. You know that, right?"

"Of course I know. It's only a little. You'll feel fine by tomorrow." Craeya inched closer. The space between her body and Luzon's was a hair's breadth. "Trust me, you won't regret this." Her sweat smelled sweet like pressed honey-Q.

How much tilq has this girl done for her to be experimenting with something so intense?

"Do you want some or not?"

Luzon shrugged. He leaned forward, hovered over her fingernail, and sucked the tilq into his body in one snort. A quick burst of fire in his brain, behind his eye, sharp as glass. That same rush coursed through his body like lightning. His fingers tingled. His head warmed. He felt as though the sun were everywhere, lighting him up from the inside.

Had he taken Scorpio's Rainbow before?

Craeya's shape blurred. She looked like she was waving long ribbons in the air.

"Good, right?" Everything was reduced to sound.

"I don't think I can remember anything," Luzon said.

"That's the point."

"Whatever Maker made this batch should be made a Master," came another voice.

"Right now," from the other female.

Luzon forgot how many people were in the alcove. Was it four? Sight returned in a stormy haze. Now there seemed to be more. A flash of pink. On Craeya's head. She climbed onto a table at the end of the room and shook her ribbons again. No, they weren't ribbons. They were her arms. Reality stretched into a starless universe. Luzon's heart raced. He sat on the ground, crossing his legs underneath him. Rectangles and squares protruded from faces, and purples and blues whirled around him in a vortex. He closed his eyes but that only made things spin faster.

He stood up and stretched his arms into the air, feeling his diaphragm expand like a balloon in his belly. Somehow, his hand had found a cup, and the contents of that cup were being poured into his mouth. The gulch was warm and gross, but Luzon didn't care.

He swallowed more gulch. There were definitely more people in the room than before. Craeya said something to him. He wanted to float up to the ceiling.

"Why are there three of you?" Luzon knew it was his voice, but he had no idea how he'd formed words.

"How about some noise, then?" Craeya asked.

Luzon steadied himself. Scorpio's Rainbow was a bacterium, delirium, punching in his gut, climbing, and as he reeled in the pleasure-pain, someone was stretching his brain to make him see things he didn't know existed but would probably like. A deep sigh escaped his body. He could barely make a fist, let alone any noise. How was he supposed to make music when he couldn't even see how many Craeyas there were?

Thanks to the gulch, the edges weren't as sharp and jagged as he stared at them. In the back of his head, he knew there was something he was supposed to be doing.

Craeya stood on her toes on top of the table and looked out, grinning. "Sometimes, I wish I could fly. Just like the dunegulls." She spread her ribbon-arms out, pretending to soar. Luzon didn't know how, but he saw her trip, and in a lightning-quick moment, he stepped forward to catch her.

She crashed into his body, and Luzon felt the weight of an Omega beast bearing down on him. She was a small girl, but the tilq was making everything melty. Luzon held her up under the arms, feeling her blank expression mirror his own. Her pupils were the size of their bigger moon, Kaleem.

"It will look a lot better than that," she said, her eyes focusing on Luzon. The pink streak in her hair seemed to brighten under the dim lights.

Then Luzon saw something in her face. He saw the face of someone else buried underneath. Luzon nearly dropped her. He set her on her feet, and released her, unable to hold her anymore.

"What?" Craeya's eyes bulged.

Luzon shook himself out of his never-ending trance. "Your face ... I—"

"What about it?"

Luzon took a deep breath. What face was he thinking of? He had never met Craeya before. She had never done a cycle before. And yet the details rushed back to him.

"I think I should go," he said.

"What for?" Craeya asked. "Are you okay, Luzon? Scorpio's Rainbow can be strong. It can make us see things that aren't there."

He already knew. He didn't need a novice to tell him the effects of tilq. He had tried all of them and more.

"I need to prepare for the mission," Luzon said, which he was sure came out in a whisper. Then he ran out of the alcove without another word. He weaved through the crowds at speed, moving for the preparation rooms, where he could find everything he needed before departure.

He remembered that he needed to pack his multi-tool with several small knives, pliers, and screwdrivers; a portable toolkit with a hammer, saw, chisel and small wrenches; all his sewing and knitting materials, mesh, twine, bamboo shafts, plexirods, elastic string, feathers, rhodamantium, and a new tool he'd never used before—a digspike.

Luzon tried to concentrate on what he needed to do, but the face came back to him. She was someone he knew. Someone important to him, but he couldn't remember how he knew her. A previous cyclemate? A Master once upon a time? Whatever the case, Craeya's face carried similarities, and it had stirred up … *a memory.*

Luzon hadn't had a specific memory in years. The sensation was new, and jarring, like a sleep-story, but in waking life.

He forgot to imagine flying and instead just ran.

The process for choosing dispatch teams is painstaking and arduous but always fruitful. First, teams are selected based on dispatch mission location, training class, specific skillset, personality maps, and DNA family trees (our Hive devices prevent common bloodlines from being matched). Harvesters are sent to the ocean, Diggers dispatched to the tunnels, Seekers to reefs. When looking at individual units within teams, convergence scores must be analyzed. Members who experience higher levels of convergence are kept apart. Teams should be comprised of members who will satisfy their dispatch missions but also maintain tension. Divergence is preferred. Convergence moves our people closer to memory, attachment, and emotion, thus opening the portal that has been long closed. For these groupings, our intuition and knowledge are nearly perfect. Nearly. Because we are dealing with an impossibly unpredictable aspect of humans, once in every ten thousand choices, an error is made.

- **from *Confessions of the Masters, Volume I***

8. FENRI THE KNOWLEDGER

Peering through the amber candlelight glow of her chamber, Fenri turned over the contents of her terrabag onto her cot one last time. Her map-projector, clamped safely in its indium case, sat on top of her other things: a spare skinsuit, fortified with tamagon and salamanzer cells, folded neatly at the bottom, her visor and sveil, pain-modifying topicals, hunger suppressants, even some of her own tilq. She didn't love it, but she used it whenever necessary, along with her knowledge kit—what was left of it—thermometers, soil meters, pH strips, purifiers, several empty jars, bottles, vials, thimbles, and pouches of food, filled with her cycle allotment: dried tamagon hearts, seakelp, octoghi, rubyrinds, a jar of Honey-Q, and various grains and seeds.

Between periods of fasting, the food allotted to them would have to sustain them, but as Fenri looked at it, worry knotted her stomach. There seemed to be less than last time even though the Masters assured her how good the past cycle was.

There will be some in the field.

Drought happened plenty, but there always seemed to be food if you knew where to look and what to turn over. Without a Seeker or Harvester on the team, they might have a harder time locating sources. Of the members on the team, Fenri would have to lead that front.

She paused.

Her stomach churned. Her intestines contorted like awakening kohbras. She had eaten at the feast, but her hunger still beat at her like a pulse.

Will I ever not feel hungry?

Someone cleared their throat from the doorway, and Fenri turned to see who it was.

A man filled the entire doorway. "Pau," she said. "I was just—"

His piercing gaze stopped her midsentence. His eyes ran over her body like she was an equation to solve, analyzing, processing. "I hear you've done many cycles in the field," he said. "You must be very comfortable on missions by now."

The fire in Pau's eyes jumped out and seemed to burn its way up Fenri's spine, nerve after nerve. Pau was a head taller than her, broader, squared at the shoulders, and leaner. The short-sleeved robe he wore exposed the muscles in his arms, which bulged like peas in a pod.

"Yes, of course," Fenri said. Her bag required her attention again, and she found herself staring into it. There was nothing inside. Everything was on the cot. Pau was expecting experience and knowledge out of her. She recalled her last cycle, tried to conjure up what might help her.

At her bedside table, her larger logbook and her smaller exercise handbook sat alone. Fenri felt the heavy presence of

Pau behind her, still there. He had moved into the dormitory, but Fenri only knew from the way the candlelight cast a slighter, shallower shadow on the far wall. He was nearly silent, neither breathing nor carrying any sort of smell that she could identify.

"Master Qi wanted me to give this to you." The blade Pau held in the cradle of his large palm was minuscule in comparison, like a toy in the hand of a child.

"A durablade." Fenri instinctively turned and quickly knelt by her bag. "What happened—"

"You lost yours on your last cycle," Pau said. "I hear it's with the ocean now."

"I …" Fenri accepted the blade. The weapon felt heavier than expected, crafted from durasteel, a rare mineral found deep beneath the desert sands. Almost every QhaHadurian carried one, marking it as their first official weapon for dispatch missions, a symbol of passage into adulthood.

"Thank you, Pau," Fenri said. She tucked the sheathed durablade into one of her skinsuit's front pockets. "I won't lose this one."

Pau's expression didn't change. "You're an Unable," he said.

"Yes. That's what the Masters told me. You're a Guardian, and this will be your first cycle as Charge Leader."

"Charge Leader or not, I don't show any special treatment, least of all for Unables. You eat the same amount we all do." His eyes bore into Fenri's. Sparks of hazel shone in his irises.

Fenri averted Pau's gaze, swallowed the uneasiness building in her throat. "Of course. Why would you? It's my burden to bear alone. I'll carry my weight."

"Glad to hear you say that because I have some concerns about the team. The Maker is good, but he's got his head up in space half the time, and the Healer … seriously? A first year? To the Quat Zones? *And* an Unable? Who is also a Knowledger?" Pau huffed. "At least you've done a good many cycles and know your way around. I don't understand the point of adding this Stone guy, but hey, I've never understood all the Masters' decisions before. Why start now?"

"You seem to have given a lot of thought to the weaknesses of our team."

"I have to know the weaknesses. That's the difference between life and death every time. Anything else I should know about you and your weaknesses?"

Again, the warmth of fire. On Fenri's arms, climbing up to her shoulders. Where did she begin? The Master's words came back to her. *Never show a beast your back. If you stand there strong, making yourself as big as possible, it doesn't know whether you're predator or prey. The difference is in the beast's mind, and it's up to you to convince it.*

In her mind, Fenri began to list her own weaknesses:

The random paralysis.

The crippling pains of hunger.

Those rare times when her thirst for knowledge became greater than any logical need for sleep, or rejuvenation, or calm, and spun out of control, her brain a breeding ground of firing neurons and unrealized potential.

"No," Fenri said, more confident than she felt. "There's nothing to worry about." But her thoughts drifted to Craeya and the Master's words. Craeya carried ancient dangers. Overactive emotions. Pau would need Fenri's help to quell them, apparently, but she kept the thought still and silent inside her, like a star in the night sky.

"Good," Pau said. "Finish packing and get your rest. See you in the Chamber Hall on the third night at 1500 hours." He turned and strode out the doorway, ducking into the darkness as he went.

For a moment, Fenri could do nothing.

Then, she flew into activity, her injuries and sore areas forgotten or ignored. Grabbing her books off the side table, she thrust them into her terrabag. She returned everything to her bag and buttoned it closed. She lifted it with some boost of energy she must have borrowed from Pau's presence and placed it on her cot. There was still so much to do. Books and reports to read. Knowledge to gain. Blowing out the candles in her chamber, she walked out into the darkness.

Pau would lead them well.

Stern. Direct. Unforgiving.

Fenri knew the selection processes. None of the members of their team were meant to get along.

No. All that mattered was keeping one another alive.

Some will never know this half, this dark part of the world that seeks a different solution. Centuries passed before we learned that a second smaller moon lay in wait behind the first. Centuries passed before this orbiting body revealed itself and changed the tides, the plant life, and the magnetic and gravitational forces at work. Something so far away and so small can seem like nothingness, but it is often the small and far-away things that bring the greatest change.

- from *Confessions of the Masters, Volume I*

9. FENRI THE KNOWLEDGER

Fenri arrived at the Chamber Hall on day three as light faded from the slats and skylights and shadows crept across the vast, echoing space. Fenri assumed that Pau's choice of 1500 hours meant he wanted to review everything before leaving base. There were not many other tribesmen in the Chamber Hall at the time, but the stale scent of spilt gulch and soured limewine lingered.

"In six more hours, the new cycle begins." Fenri turned to see Pau striding forward with Craeya in tow. "I want us leaving early so we're not held up by any other dispatch teams."

Craeya's hair, tied into a loose mess, looked like it had been washed and treated sloppily. Her eyes rushed away from Fenri's gaze.

"Where's Luzon?" Fenri asked.

"I don't know," Pau said, "But he's got five minutes before I go looking for him."

They only had to wait three minutes for Luzon to arrive, and when he did, he stumbled forward much in the same way Craeya had, his terrabag hanging loosely from his back, black mesh cloth drooping out the sides. He threw his bag down on the ground and began stuffing the hanging remnants back inside. "Sorry. I was … making something."

Fenri took in the sight of Craeya once more, saw the indigo skin presenting around her eyes. She took deep, audible breaths, and her body shook at an almost imperceptible frequency. "Are you all right?" Fenri asked.

Craeya looked to Fenri slowly, the veins in her eyes shot red with blood.   "Fine."

At the great door, Pau placed a large hand into the lock and gradually the stone barrier rose off the ground. Light flicked its way inside. The darkness, the dying hum of the nation-feast behind them fell away as it had so many times before.

This one will be different, Fenri thought.

The door closed with a thud.

Outside, Zhao dragged its blanket of light away, leaving only obscure shadows in its wake. The air was warm and dry. Only three days had passed since Fenri had been outside in the field, but it felt longer. Her recovery coming back from the Electric Ocean was speckled with half fugue-like states, skewing her sense of time.

"What were you making?" Fenri asked Luzon.

Luzon, who walked ahead, turned. "What was I making?"

"Yes, that's the question I asked you."

"I don't know. What *was* I making?"

"If you're playing some sort of game, I don't know it."

"Short term memory is severely altered," Craeya said. "He's already forgotten what he said."

Luzon turned and smiled.

"I just wanted to know what he was making," Fenri said.

"I'd venture a guess that he forgot," Craeya said.

Fenri looked from Luzon to Craeya and noticed their unusual gaits. "Does Luzon normally have problems with memory?"

"For ancestors' sake, come on," Pau said. "He's still high. They both are."

The reality hit Fenri, and her thoughts accelerated to a breakneck pace.

Craeya's bloodshot eyes appeared in her mind-map. The veins pulsed, stretched and reached around her irises in a vortex pattern. *Moonblue.* The result of a specific set of alleles pairing, Craeya's two Progenitors each contributing a half. Recessive. Both had to have the marker. Fenri hadn't seen many QhaHadurians with moonblue eyes, but she knew they existed in at least 9.3 percent of their population.

Fenri categorized.

The red-vein and the white. Luzon's vocal tone. Craeya's vocal volume. Craeya's trembling body. Luzon's loss of short-term memory. Categories of tilq fell away in Fenri's mind one by one, like the dropping of stones. They had taken something in the H-class. Hallucinogens. They were both sleep-deprived and dehydrated.

Fenri couldn't smell Craeya, but there was a subtle hint of gulch on Luzon's breath. Showing productivity, not sleeping, engaging in activities. For Luzon that was making *something.*

"Scorpiotynal."

"Yes, that is the one," Luzon said.

"Yeah, Scorpio's Rainbow," Craeya said. "How did you know what we took? I didn't tell you."

"I knew based off your and Luzon's behaviors."

"Figshit," Craeya said, her voice gaining volume. "There are over 750 different names of tilq, and you discovered that by our behavior?"

"And the tilq's interactions on your bodies. Voice Quality. Appearance of eyes. Smell. What I observed."

"Oh please," Craeya said. "You'd have to map out algorithms. You weren't close enough to see my eyes in such detail. No one is *that* clever." She gazed at Fenri.

Fenri looked away.

Did I show my abilities too much? What I did will tell someone a lot about how my brain operates. I don't need to go into such detail.

"Listen," Pau said, kicking at the ground and halting. "I don't care what you ate or drank or snorted up your nose last night, or the night before. I need all of you to be quiet. We are no longer inside where we are safe from the beasts. We are beginning our dispatch mission. If you aren't going to offer valuable information, then it's better to keep your mouth shut until you need to open it to eat. I'll command from the front. Everyone got that?"

Fenri pulled out her map-projector, flipped it on. "We should establish the best route—"

"I know you want to help," Pau said, "but the best route is where I'm taking you. North and east. I know exactly where we're going."

"You haven't looked at the map."

"I don't need to. I have the stars."

"Yes, the stars. But all of that and more is displayed on the map-projector—"

"Let's assume that both of us know where we're going. You have your ways, and I have mine, and seeing as I'm Charge Leader, we are going to follow my way. I don't know if anyone's told you, but knowledge isn't owned by Knowledgers. Guardians have some too. Now, let's silence ourselves. I'll tell you when it's okay to talk again. As soon as we've put some distance between us and base."

Craeya tipped a cylinder into her mouth. She was already drinking her store of water.

Fenri stared at her map-projector. She read the H_2O checkpoints, calculated the distance to the closest one. There was nothing directly on their path. Craeya would need to conserve better. Fenri opened her mouth to say something then remembered Pau's words, and shut it.

"Let's just find this Stone guy," Craeya said. "Listen to the Guardian." She caught up and walked alongside him.

Fenri fell back and said softly to Luzon, "I was thinking, after our talk, about what you said about crafting a flying ship or one to go under the water. That you could really do it."

Luzon matched Fenri's level of quiet. "Yes, I can."

"And have you thought about asking the Masters if you can stay at base and be given a cycle to make one?"

"They'd never grant that."

"If you show them your drawings." Fenri's heart leapt from its place in her chest. She tried to calm it. "They might allow it. Plenty of Makers stay at base to create."

"Yes, but we don't have any materials of our own. We make what the Masters tell us to make."

"They would allow making of a ship. It's only because no one knows how to do it, and you claim—"

"We still need more raw materials. A lot more. I think someday when we do—"

"I'd just need a small one to go underwater." Fenri said. She quietly wondered if she should mention her next cycle to the ocean.

"We have probes for that," Luzon said. "And Divers."

"But they can only go so deep. And the probes can only provide so much data. If we could send a QhaHadurian in a submership we'd learn so much more. I would learn so much more."

"You want to take it yourself?" Luzon peered at Fenri through the encroaching darkness, his thin white pupils bright like stars.

"Yes." Fenri's thoughts accelerated. "Maybe you could build one quickly, and I could ask to take it on my next cycle?"

"During a 72-hour nation-feast, before I go on my next mission. Sounds … impossible."

"They'd delay your mission for you to finish, and maybe mine too. If they believed it was good and well-built and then—" Fenri felt her thoughts going in a thousand directions and tried to slow them. "If it's already made or half-made, the Masters would have to let you finish building it, and then I could use it."

"Fenri the Knowledger breaks rules?" Luzon said. "I'm shocked."

"If it's something that will be good for everyone," Fenri began, not sure Luzon's words matched what she thought of herself. "The Masters are strict, but they're not slow. They'd see the good in it. They'd allow its construction and use."

Luzon laughed. "Alright. I'll ask them. Do you want to go because of the plant you found?"

"Yes." The events of that night rushed back to Fenri, like the waves that had barreled into her. Before they had smacked her into blackness, she had recovered the cold, unfamiliar body with its urchin-like stems. She'd succeeded in doing what she set out to do. She felt something inside her warming, a joy she could not explain. Squeezing the muscles in her stomach as hard as she could, she pushed it down.

"I want to know what else is down there," she said. "I mean *really* down there. Past where the Divers can physically go."

Fenri looked at Luzon, who nodded. She brimmed with energy, trying to name her emotions. Excitement. Hope. Wonder.

With Luzon, I wonder what is possible.

Fenri calculated her team's worth in her brain.

Guardian. Maker. Healer. Knowledger. Later, a Planeteer.

She hadn't gone over savior order yet. Between Healer and Maker, Fenri would save ... well, it was Healer based on utility scores, but Luzon could make a submership. That was definitely something they needed to bring back to base. If Craeya lost her life during the mission, there would be other Healers. The reality was severe, but true.

Fenri analyzed where she would fall in order, building everyone's answer in her mind one by one. Craeya seemed to be the most vital member based on their team's algorithms. Especially since the longer the mission went on, the deeper they travelled into the Quat Zones, she would become exponentially more valuable as injuries, illnesses, and general weaknesses built up over time.

Fenri knew that intellectually, but there were always other circumstances to consider.

Kaleem peeked out from cumulus clouds above, cloaking the desert in a misty everblue light. She turned, took in the sight of Milkali, the second and smaller moon. Though only a quarter full that night, the additional glow was still good for the moon plants and roots.

Ahead, Kaleem lit a path, one that Pau carved with precision. Fenri put her map-projector away and took out her logbook and began writing.

With a churning stomach, Fenri walked on for hours through the night, making entries one by one, all she had learned from the new studies, about the ocean plant she had worked tirelessly to categorize over the past three days.

She moved away from the ocean and a plant that was no longer hers to study, and toward a scorching hot valley peppered with Klonden.

In the early hours of morning, the barren landscape stirred to life. With low winds, Fenri calculated they could walk at that rate for another two and a half hours before she'd need to rest. She moved without trouble. Blood pumped through her veins, sending energy to her heart, allowing her to focus on writing down what she had observed so far about the weather, the air quality, her cyclemates.

The sun was coming up over the horizon strong and bright, its full power soon to be unleashed, and Fenri felt the steady flow of thoughts inhabit her brain as they always did in the morning. She tried to distract herself from those she had not anticipated. Thoughts with sources harder to name. Her eyes caught Luzon's as she turned her head, and she hastily looked away.

Being sent out into the field is a rite of passage. Most QhaHadurians will have at least one chance at a mission. This can be their first cycle at eighteen when all QhaHadurians are expected to finish their youth training. The rate of survival for these novices is low. They have never had to deal with the wild, scorching valley outside the walls of safety they have known their entire lives. Sometimes they experience practice sessions, but even that is not enough. The only way for them to learn is by going out and experiencing those dangers in real time, without the hand of a Master to hold.

- from *Confessions of the Masters, Volume I*

10. Craeya the Healer

"Can we take a break yet?" Craeya had been asking for the past few hours. Zhao was up, and they had been walking through the night. In the desert, behind her slip-shades, her eyes burned with sweat; the light took on a different quality, a terrible fusion of particle and wave.

"Soon," was all Pau could say.

The heat was rising and Craeya hated it.

The tilq she had taken was rushing out of her body, and with it, nutrients, moisture, energy. She smacked her lips, desperate for water.

"What is it?" Fenri appeared from somewhere. Craeya was not paying attention and had lost sight of her surroundings. All she could see was herself at the repair table. He was there too, across the Chamber Hall at another table, lanky with golden-brown arms, deft, knowing. They always knew. Remembering the warmth of his lips on hers in the tunnel, that momentary glimpse into his world, brought Craeya down deeper. She realized Fenri was waiting for an answer, scrutinizing her face.

"Nothing."

"You seem unsettled," Fenri said. "We'll stop soon. If you can just hold out."

Craeya looked to Pau, who trudged ahead, light piercing him at harsh angles and reflecting off the hilt of his sword-chain. The weapon hung behind him, swaying idly. Luzon walked on in silence beside them, tinkering with something in his hands. Craeya caught flashes of ivory white and ebony black.

"I'm okay, really." Craeya wanted to avoid questions that made her think about herself. She walked alongside the Maker. Craeya remembered the look he had given her in the alcove when she gave him the tilq. She had never seen anything like it. Eyes wild with fear. A hint of recognition.

Did he think she was someone else?

Craeya knew the pathways Scorpio's Rainbow took, how it could make people hallucinate beyond what was logical. Words rose up in her then fell. She wanted to say something. The silence was deafening. If sound could cause pain, that was how it began, with its absence. How was she supposed to remain silent for so long?

"What did you see?" she said, a note louder than a whisper. She wanted Luzon to hear her, but not Pau.

Luzon turned, his wide eyes gleaming like fresh figvi. He flashed a quick smile then hid it between his lips. "What?"

"You really freaked back there. What was it you saw? I've seen people use rainbow drugs, but nothing like that. It stirred something up, didn't it?"

Luzon walked further, but he looked at his hands. Whatever he had been tinkering with was gone. He pressed at his callused palms with thin, long fingers. Craeya thought he wouldn't say anything because he was quiet for nearly a minute, but then he said, "I don't know. It was nothing. I don't know."

She sensed his nervous energy and didn't press further.

Craeya threw her terrabag down onto the ground once it was finally time to rest. Zhao was too high and too hot and even Pau knew it would be foolish to push them.

Luzon sat across from Craeya with a clear tube hanging from his mouth. The thin tip emerged from the upper side of his bag, and Craeya watched as he sucked water through it. She searched for her own, put it to her mouth and pulled. The water was chilled, its coolness an impossibility for such a blistering place.

"Go easy on it," Luzon said. "We need it to last the entire cycle."

"What do we do when the water runs out?" Craeya asked.

Pau shot Fenri a glance as if an explanation was outside his job description. He was setting up some sort of tent nearby, dome-shaped with a triangular flap opening in the front. A baracca.

"We need to be using these every day we can." Fenri held up a small box apparatus with three copper wires emerging from the bottom. The opening revealed what appeared to be a palm-sized microchip, gold-plating a miniature field of red balls that reminded Craeya of fish eggs.

"Everyone pull out their gills and let's start moisture collection," Fenri said.

Craeya did. She had seen larger versions of gills near control rooms and in their moisture farm on the north side of base.

Luzon set his own on top of his terrabag. "They won't give us much, but it will delay us running out of water for a long time if we use them every day."

Pau grunted as he struck the ground with a pointed stake, setting up the posts for the frame of the baracca. The cloth he snapped into the stakes flapped in the breeze. The baracca was the color of their planet if you squinted hard—yellow like the teeth of elders, orange like the faded glare of the sun, as red as watered-down blood. As Craeya looked at it, the colors seemed to warp and expand under the light, there one moment, gone the next.

"It's camouflaged," Luzon said.

"How?"

Fenri slid into view. She pulled her dark, neatly cut hair from its bindings, letting it fall an inch above her shoulders. She smelled like peppernut soap, and for a moment Craeya saw a woman who had done much more than her. There were faint lines around her eyes from cycles of walking under the searing sun. She was limbed like a tamagon above, her arms slender and pale. The stem of her wrists bent precisely as she drank from her tube. "Tamagon technology." Instruction was Fenri's delight. Her eyes flashed a deep aquamarine, a bottomless sea of knowledge. "We extract the DNA of the tamagons and thread their cells into the baracca fabric, which helps it blend in with its environment, hiding it from beasts."

Craeya saw it firsthand. At first she thought the tilq was making her see things. But Fenri's information confirmed that the baracca was in fact shifting its hue. "I've heard about that." Craeya lugged her bag over to the finished set-up, examined the cloth up close.

"It's fibrous too," Fenri said, next to her. "That helps reflect deadly UV and RU rays."

"It must take hundreds of tamagons to make something like this," Craeya said.

"Not as many as you would think," Luzon said. "All we do is take the cells and thread them. It doesn't need to be every part per million for the technology to take effect."

"Same with our skinsuits," Fenri said. "The camouflage isn't as effective as it is with the baraccas because they are thicker. We'd need another layer if we wanted that same level of disguise."

"One layer is enough," Craeya said. She fell to her knees and crawled inside. The space was a touch cooler. A draft came through mesh pockets spread through the top that served as vents. Pau had laid down a long, thin bamboo pad to protect them from direct contact with the ground, which was still hot, but bearable.

Pau said, "I'll keep watch. Take a rest and get out of the sun for now. We'll go in a few hours when it's not as intense. A few ticks before nightfall."

The air thickened when Luzon and Fenri entered the baracca. They lay down on each side of Craeya. Everything stuck to her. Her blood ran like rivers of lava through her veins. Steam peeled off her body in waves. She wanted more water but restrained herself. Under the baracca, her thoughts seemed to intensify. A storm brewed, and at the center there was calm, but outside that ring, she saw him again—*Rannum.*

No.

She turned and saw Luzon. Craeya shifted, unable to look into his eyes. Fenri was on her other side, sitting up, writing in a book.

"What are you doing?" Craeya sat up.

"Writing in my logbook."

"Why?"

"I need to keep a log of everything we see and do."

"By choice?"

The question seemed to confuse Fenri. She pondered a moment, computing. "Of course. Logbooks are extremely valuable in helping us learn about and change our planet."

"So not because the Masters ask you to?" Craeya asked.

"Well, I suppose, yes, that's how I started, but I enjoy writing entries in my logbook."

"I don't doubt that." Craeya reached down and pulled her bag into the space between her legs. She opened it, began sifting through. She pulled out her healing kit and examined its contents. Her mind searched for something. She didn't know what, but she knew she wanted something to help her. Her oils, condensed into tiny bottles, congregated in one corner. She grabbed limegrass, unscrewed the top.

"What are you doing?" Fenri asked.

"Inventory." Craeya held the oil beneath her nose, took a great whiff. The lime citrus of the plant left its container in a bubbly wave. Her vision focused. She became alert to the sounds around her.

"Are you nauseous?" Fenri asked. "Limegrass is most widely used for nausea."

"Mostly," Craeya replied.

"Smells wonderful," Luzon said. "Can I—?"

Craeya held the oil under Luzon's nose and he inhaled. "Also for energy," she said.

"Are you tired?" Fenri asked.

Only of your questions, Craeya thought, but she bit down on it.

Luzon sat up. "Energy is correct. It's too cramped in here right now." He left the baracca.

A rush of warmth crawled under Craeya's skin and she wanted to move. But the heat made her want to faint. She leaned over her kit and grabbed another vial, removing jadeflower. She shoved it into her mouth and chewed. Fenri's eyes were on her like fire to petrol. Craeya already knew. She didn't even need to look to confirm it.

"Why did you do that?" Fenri asked.

The jadeflower dragged everything down, kept it neutral. Thank the ancestors it was fast-acting, otherwise she would have killed Fenri with her glare. Craeya crunched on the stiff flower in her mouth. She could almost taste the golden ratio, the nectarine terpenes dampening the fires igniting in her brain.

"You really shouldn't do any more tilq right now," Fenri said.

"Why not?"

"Because it can weaken you."

"I almost never take tilq. But I know how helpful it can be."

"Sometimes, yes. Do you really need more now?"

"Yes, Fenri. I do. That's why it's in my mouth and I'm chewing it. Because I need it. Do you think you're the only one who thinks through decisions? How about you stop telling me what to do?"

"I'm only here to help."

"Being quiet would help." But Craeya knew it wouldn't.

"Tilq should only be used when absolutely necessary. When our emotions or thoughts run too swiftly." Fenri's face fell as she realized what she was saying. She turned to her book, eyes downcast, ultramarine waves easing to low tide.

"Everyone does what they need to do to survive," Craeya said. "Tilq is just one drug. There are many others."

"There are many types of tilq, but they are the only drugs on our planet."

"No," Craeya said, and she felt the effects of the jadeflower connecting dots previously unconnected. "That's not right. There are plenty of others. It depends how you want to classify things." Craeya paused, felt her thoughts stumbling, but she didn't care. She barreled forward. "Knowledge is a drug. Is the way you use it any different from what I'm doing? Feeling sad, or less than. These are all drugs that people use to feel something else." Craeya turned to look at Fenri, who had fallen silent. The look on her face was contemplative, like Craeya had ripped open a hole in the universe and Fenri was falling into it. No one had ever phrased something that way to her, linking psychology with hard science, weaving it with philosophy.

Craeya was happy to be the one.

They went like that for hours: Craeya's irregular breathing, the scrawl of lead on paper, near silence save for the breeze outside. Fenri did not try to tell Craeya what to do after that.

When they moved again that night, Luzon approached Craeya, object in hand. She viewed everything as a cure for her current ailment, and her heart leapt when he handed her some kind of stone.

"Wow, thanks," Craeya said, her tone dry. "Is this for killing tamagons?"

Luzon laughed as they walked underneath the light of the moons. "It's called a yo-yo."

"What's it for?"

"It's a kind of game."

"A game?"

"Yeah, look." Luzon took it from her hand and looped his finger into a hole in a string. Then he threw the stone down with a quick flick of his wrist. The stone spun in place while hanging from the string. "Just for fun." Luzon snapped the stone up to his hand with another flick of the wrist and smiled. "I've seen you fidgeting," he added. "It should help keep your—uh—mind off things."

"Thank you, Luzon." Craeya took the yo-yo and began playing with it, happy to have some kind of a distraction.

At night they moved, and during the day they rested. That was Pau's rhythm. Craeya chewed on more jadeflower. She thought about Scorpio's Rainbow, about taking what little she had left. Nothing had been enough to knock her out of her brain-space, out of her vicious cycle of unwanted thoughts.

When they stopped three nights later, Craeya could no longer bear her agony. She knew what she had to do and couldn't wait to do it later.

Craeya made herself busy in her terrabag. She must have seemed frantic because Pau sighed. "How long before these effects wear off?" he asked. "It's been three days."

"They've already worn off," Craeya said. "I'm just looking for something," She lied, but she wouldn't give anyone an excuse to think that she couldn't do something. The further she got away from base, the sooner she would forget about him.

"It depends when you took them and how much," Fenri said. "You should be late in the excretion phase. It should be gone from your bodies, as long as you stopped taking them."

The sound of water pulled Craeya away from the thing she really wanted to say. She knew what Fenri had meant by it. The water, or rather, the sound of urine being passed into the cracks of the qha nearby kept her from reacting immediately. Craeya turned and saw Luzon, who had his back to them. He let out a heavy breath and cleared his throat. "That's better."

"For ancestors' sake," Pau said. "Do I need to watch over you at the nation-feast next time? This isn't helping us get to this Stone guy any faster."

"Well, excuse me," Craeya said. She knelt on the sand, rifling through smaller items on the ground. "I'm keeping up."

"Not now you aren't," Pau said.

Craeya looked at Luzon, who was also going through his things, though with more deliberation than her. He held up raw ore and examined it. Craeya stole a glance at Pau. He was busy examining his perimeter. Latched onto the side of his terrabag, his sword-chain gleamed in the morning light.

"Here." Craeya lifted a smokestick into the air, examining the thin, grey piece the length of her finger. Relief warmed her. She found a match and lit her smokestick.

"If you're trying to diminish the high and the effects you're experiencing," Fenri said, "it would be better to use calcitrine oil—"

Craeya blew smoke from her mouth. She laughed then let out a loud sigh. "That's so much better! I don't know why I didn't do that earlier." Her body lightened. She had not had a smokestick in months. She didn't love them, but she knew what they did to the body: manage stress and elevate mood, two things she needed in that very moment. Her heartbeat slowed.

Craeya looked at Fenri, and her mind tripped. She had done something, and the knowledge of that grew in the seablue reflection of Fenri's eyes, sharp as shards of ice. Her mind was working out dangers. Craeya followed the gaze. Before either of them could speak, they both saw what Craeya had inadvertently done. On the ground, the fuse on a mini flare shortened rapidly. The flame from Craeya's match had caught it.

"Craeya, your flare!" The words flew from Fenri's mouth.

Pau turned. Luzon turned. Craeya threw herself down, picked up the flare, and held it high in the air as it exploded in a ball of light, creating a deafening screech. Combustion stabbed their ears. A brilliant spark shot up and over all of them, piercing the bright blue sky before peaking and then crashing back into the sand.

Pau's voice came with heat. "A flare! Already?!"

Craeya cowered, her body, her ears, reeling from her mistake.

Pau spun, tried to reel his anger back into his body. Craeya dropped her smokestick and began shoving everything back into her bag as well. The relief was gone, and stress had taken its place. The energy grew frenzied.

Luzon shoved things back into his bag. Craeya knew the sound would attract unwelcomed beasts. If something had heard the loud bang of the flare, noticed the bright light blasting into the sky, curiosity would strike, and for beasts where hunger was a constant, that curiosity would turn into need. Blood rushed through Craeya's limbs, climbing to her neck and to her head, quickening her breath.

Everyone became silent. Only the wind pushed the sand.

Another sound came to them, faint but alive. Some creature stirred, its peace disturbed. Craeya's eardrums buzzed. Far in the distance, behind a thinning cloud of dust and sand, a beast stood completely still.

Pau turned to the group, sudden urgency in his tone. "Do exactly as I say. Get down, and *don't move* until I tell you to."

Craeya collapsed to her knees. She laid her bag on the ground and pressed herself into the scorching qha. She peered up and over the curve of land above her line of sight, heart thumping in her chest like a drum.

All she could do was stare motionless at the beast as it turned its cold, red gaze upon them.

Before our ancestors came to QhaHadur, they would hunt their prey for days. The beasts were much larger than the fauna found in our desert lands. They had claws and talons and thick blankets of fur. Their teeth could sever a human spine or split a skull in two. Much like the beasts we have here. And yet, our ancestors tracked them and killed them. Not because they were larger or more powerful, but because they had an unbreakable, bloodthirsty will. They ate their beasts for survival, for sport, locked them in cages, made them slaves, even domesticated some species as pets. This reality is difficult to imagine. Here, everything is in reverse. Some say that our lives on QhaHadur are punishment for what the ancestors did long ago, that the bloodthirsty will left our bodies and entered the beasts instead.

- from *Confessions of the Masters, Volume I*

11. PAU THE GUARDIAN

In the wide-open expanse of the desert where Quadrant I merged into Quadrant II, four tribesmen lay on the ground still as corpses. Two hundred meters in the distance, a beast clocked their presence.

Hide, run, or fight. Those were Pau's choices. He could not afford injuries or loss so early in the mission. His anger threatened to erupt as he thought about Craeya's mistake, but he pushed it down. Her mistake became his problem, and if he had been more attentive, it wouldn't have happened.

Concentrate. If your mind is somewhere else, you will die. Pau measured his breaths. He squinted against the glare of the sun to analyze the beast.

Alpha beast. Two-headed avian species. Grounded. No known abilities of flight. The pitch of its screech resounded in Pau's ears. Yes, curiosity was there, but something else too.

Fear.

Fear moved creatures in one of two directions: flee to survive or fight to win. The situations beasts and humans found themselves in were often no different. What did the beast want? Pau put on his slip-shades and focused harder through the gold tint of the lenses.

The beast stood eerily still, its two heads sitting atop two stick-thin necks like boulders. Both legs bowed underneath its furry body. Two shrunken wings pinned themselves to its splotchy sides. Long ago, perhaps the creature had flown, but it had since become too heavy and traveled on land. One head alone was twice the size of Pau's—which was large based on human standards—and the beaks jutting out of their heads housed sharp jagged teeth. Its oversized talons could eviscerate any one of them.

"I'm sorry—I didn't see the flare. It's my mistake. Let me—"

"I said *quiet*. We'll deal with that later," Pau said. "We lie here until I say differently. That kind of direction will happen a lot. So listen better, ask fewer questions, and just be good at what you do."

"What is that thing?" Luzon asked. Apparently, none of Pau's words had made any sense to him.

"It's called a greffir," Pau said. "And we're lucky it's an adolescent. An adult would have been here already. And then we'd be in trouble. This one we might be able to trick or escape, or both."

"Not fight it?" Fenri asked.

"That would be a poor choice," Pau said. "Even the younglings can bring death."

The desert fell into a quiet calm. Pau continued to watch, and they waited. Zhao pressed into their backs, and dust storms swirled around in quick flashes of fuchsia and marigold. After some time had passed, Pau pushed himself off the ground and sighed. The day was growing hot.

"It's time to move. Luzon, I need you to make me a rhodamantium-tipped arrow."

Pau knew Makers sometimes carried the materials for such a request. If he was going to get out of the mess, he would need to use his team's skills too.

The others slowly scraped themselves off the hot and hardened qha. They gripped the tubes from their packs with their mouths and drank water. Luzon opened his pack, grabbed several items, and began tinkering.

Ahead, the ground softened and became sand. Dunes and bunches of cactusii rose and fell in winding patterns, coloring the landscape violet and scarlet. If death wasn't around every corner, the land might be pleasing to the eyes.

I need to deal with the mistakes. Already they are exhausting me. Better to set things straight now than to suffer their blunders later.

Craeya walked ahead of them, her head up. Her pace suggested no fatigue, but Pau sensed an overcompensation. He went to say something, but his nose intercepted a strong scent.

"What is—"

Craeya turned. "Did you say something?"

Pau inhaled, took in each of their scents.

Fenri: peppernut oil and moonchoke root and a smattering of other oils and spices Pau couldn't fully separate. Her scent— her Major Histocompatability Complex—was surprisingly complicated. Pau dipped fingers into his dust-pouch and swept his hand underneath his nose to cleanse it.

Craeya: tilq. Layers of it. How much had she done? Her main scent was masked ... something subtle, on the surface, spikes of sweet, citrusy aromas floating off her pores in languid bubbles. Limegrass. Lavender. There was something else there too ... root oils. Of course. She had spent her entire life at base, in infirmaries, lesson-rooms, and healing alcoves. The oils weren't just on her, they *were* her.

Pau cleansed his olfactory pathways again, focused on Luzon. Gulch was on his breath, coming out of his pores, almost gone. What else? Rubyrind. Geriander. Gingitleaf. Citrusy and musky. His smell seemed subtle but came on strong in a second wave.

Pau took all that in, trying to separate each of their scents, one by one. He would need to solidify them in his pathways. Tracking. Anticipating. Saving. Again, he cleansed his pathways with a quick dip in his pouch and swipe of his hand.

Still, there was something more.

There.

Pau inhaled, swept the escaping scent into his senses. He swallowed.

Fear?

Was that the only emotion he noticed? Before he could decide, that raw, prickling scent of fear intensified. Pau picked it up from Fenri, too. The tiniest tug from Craeya.

Even they can feel something.

It was as though they were sensing and reacting to each other.

The smell erupted into a bouquet of pheromones again. Pau stopped, turned on his heel, sent his focus into the landscape behind them. He touched his fingertips together and sniffed the dry air. The smell came a touch stronger.

"Pick up the pace." In three great strides, Pau took the lead.

"Why?" Craeya said, even with him.

"Because," Pau said with finality. "That baby greffir is tracking us."

They stopped to rest at night. Luzon and Craeya collapsed onto the ground, too tired to say anything. Fenri took her time bending and stretching, folding into half her height. She sat still, her legs crossed underneath her. Pau knew that moving during the day was a risk. He had prepared himself for the consequences.

It's odd. It's not only a baby, but it's also ventured far outside of its territory. No beast tracks this far unless they—

"How long can we rest?" Fenri asked. She pulled out her

map-projector and began sliding her fingers across the smooth glass surface.

"I don't know yet," Pau said. "We've covered good ground on the way to Stone, but there's still a way to go."

All ten of Fenri's fingers flew across her screen. Pau had never seen anyone use it that way. "What are you doing?"

"I'm logging the beast sighting." Fenri looked up, met Pau's eyes. "And our current path. Calculating what it would take to get to Stone in time." She said some other words Pau didn't want to break down, like algorithm, and alchemy.

"I thought map-projectors read like actual maps," Pau said.

"Most of them do." She typed faster, her fingers moving over the screen as though playing a reedflute. "I've programmed mine to do more."

The full brightness of Kaleem, the half-silver luminescence of smaller Milkali, skated across her screen, bundles of data reflecting off Fenri's face, glowing pink and caramel. *She is like me in a strange way. She notices everything.*

Pau removed his cylinder from his bag and drank, the first water he had consumed since the nation-feast. The cool, refreshing liquid moved down his throat, and for a moment, it didn't feel like his entire body was on fire. He felt his internal temperature drop a notch.

"It's cold out here," Craeya said, sitting up.

"I can make a fire," Luzon said. He lay on his back looking up at the stars.

"No," Pau said. "No fires. This is not cold. This is mild. Get used to it, Craeya."

Craeya stood up suddenly and began walking away.

"Where are you going?" Pau asked.

"Taking a walk," she hissed.

Pau closed the space between them in two great bounds and gripped Craeya's shoulder, turning her around. "You have a death wish? The beast could still be tracking us."

Craeya shrugged Pau off her. "I need space from all of you."

"*You* need space?"

"Just leave me *alone*," Craeya said, louder. She inhaled a sharp breath and began sobbing.

Fenri looked up, alarmed. "What happened?"

"Nothing!" Pau took a step back. "Why are you crying?

She wastes so much energy, and look at all the water leaving her body now.

Craeya didn't answer. Instead she walked off and Fenri followed her. Pau took deep breaths, trying to remain calm. Everyone was making it difficult. Luzon held a rod in one hand while his other hand traveled across the end of it. Every so often, he would look up at the stars. He had either mastered another level of calm, or the tilq was still keeping him subdued. Pau wondered if he even had another setting.

Again, the smell. Pau sniffed at the air, trying to capture the new essence. He could feel the beast's presence again, somewhere on the perimeter, hanging in the shadows. Pau's head spun. *Am I imagining things? If the beast is that close to us, why hadn't it closed in? Is it waiting for the right moment? What is the right moment?* Master Qi's words came back to him then. *Watch out for Craeya. She feels things differently than the rest of us.*

He didn't always have time to watch out for Craeya. Yes, he would uphold their laws above all else, but he also needed to keep his team alive. That is what he knew better than anything. He questioned how he was supposed to keep such a close eye on Craeya too. Behind clouds, Kaleem flickered on the sand, casting an eerie cerulean shimmer on Fenri and Craeya. Maybe the Knowledger knew how to deal with Craeya better. She knew things, that was sure.

Craeya screamed and fell to her knees. That's when Pau knew they were lost. He spun, scanning the area.

"We need to move!" Pau said.

Luzon took the direction and pedaled himself up. Pau was already on the move. Fenri jumped up. With the help of Pau, they pulled Craeya to her feet.

"I don't know why I can't shake this feeling," Craeya said, crying. She hung limp in their arms.

"Forget about your feelings," Pau said. "The beast is moving. We need to move *NOW*."

They collected their bags and ran. Craeya took longer, but she was moving again. That was the end of the drug running its course. They just needed to get through it, and then they would address everything that had happened today.

Pau leapt ahead. Dunes covered the landscape in sporadic patterns. They needed to get higher. Pau followed a path up as the incline changed, running hard.

Get to the top of this dune. We'll have higher ground.

Pau stole a glance behind them. Finally, he saw it. Milkali gave light to the thing that had been hunting them for the past day. The unknown baby beast that wanted their scent, their fear, their tears, was out in the open making its final move.

"Run!" he said.

He trudged through the sand as fast as he could. If he could get to the top of the dune, he could come down on the beast. He could scare it off. He'd have more time to figure out what to do.

They better be moving like their lives depend on it!

Pau looked again. Craeya kept pace. Luzon moved quicker than Pau had ever seen him move, light on his feet, leaving shallow footprints. Fenri was at the rear, heavier and hungrier.

Pau pushed against the toxic thoughts in his brain. *No, you're not thinking about that right now. All that matters is keeping everyone safe.*

The greffir stretched its legs further and gained on them.

"Fenri, faster!"

He could tell she was trying. *This is it.*

A few more paces and they'd reach the dune's peak. A few more strides and Fenri's head would be in the greffir's mouth-beak.

"Get up here!" Pau reached the top, pulled Craeya to him in one quick yank. Then Luzon. Pau jerked his sword-chain from its holder, swung it around once, twice. He shouted at the beast, hoping to frighten it. Nothing. In a few more steps, it was going to reach Fenri.

"Fenri, lie flat!"

She fell to the ground, and Pau let his sword-chain fly. The chain slid through his hands, giving the sword part of the weapon distance as it shot out, hitting the beast square in its feathered body. Hot red blood spurted onto the sand. The beast screeched and lost its footing.

"Move!" Pau said. "Go down that way." He pointed to a path down the dune, which looked much higher from where they were. "I'll lead it this way. Luzon, I need that arrow!"

Luzon's eyes grew wide with alarm, but he reached inside his pack and produced a rhodamantium-tipped arrow.

Pau reeled his sword-chain back to him. He reached inside his bag, grabbed his sand-spirals, threw them down, and jumped on top of them. He took the arrow from Luzon, tucked it into the side compartment of his pack.

The greffir pushed off the sand and stood up again. Blood dripped from its oversized body as it shot Pau a look, a look both livid and desperate, as though Pau's mistake *would* be his last, then surged in his direction.

"Go!" Pau said, and the others took the path down. Pau slid down an alternate route, carving a path through the sand with his spirals. He was faster, and he had attacked the greffir, making him the easy choice for target.

Sand flew up all around him. Cool air whipped his face. The greffir squawked again, following Pau down the dune. Pau looked east, saw the others bounding down to flatter land. Luzon had his terrabag slung to his side and withdrew items as he ran.

Pau leaned forward to give himself more speed.

Slow the beast down. Stall. Give them time to get away.

Pau turned his hips, spun around, the momentum of his spirals underneath still pushing him forward. He glided backward, eyes fixed on the gaining beast.

He lifted his sword-chain and whipped it at the greffir with a quick snap of his wrist. Two impossibly long legs jumped over the chain with ease. Landing, it sprinted again, faster. Pau reeled the chain in, swung it over his head twice to gain momentum, snapped it again, dragging his wrist to the left to guide it.

Bam! The bulk of the sword barreled into the greffir's body. Faltering, it fell to one of its knees, temporarily stunned. The blow wasn't deep and wouldn't buy Pau much time.

He spun and spiraled down the dune with a burst of power from his left leg, then his right. The landscape evened out. He wouldn't be able to outrun the beast. He'd need to fight it head on.

He clicked his sword-chain into its holster. Now that his hands were free, he withdrew the arrow from the side of his terrabag.

The others were evening out too. Pau could see them fighting to stay on their feet. Pau bent low, snatched the spirals out from under his feet and ran to rejoin the others.

Almost a minute later Pau said, "Get ready for impact!"

He entered their space, gripping the arrow tight. The bamboo shaft was sleek and stiff in his hand. He examined the rhodamantium tip, covered in acidic white powder. *Not bad for a first try,* Pau thought.

He whirled around and saw that the beast was upon them again.

The cool air of the night left his body as the others stopped behind him. A collective bated breath hung in the air. The greffir slowed, seemed to be sizing up the group, where it could attack, what it could win as it zigzagged across the sand, its heavy heads swinging then rearing up to get a better look at all of them. Beasts were strange, alien creatures, and yet surprisingly predictable. *Will it cut its losses and flee?*

He withdrew the plexibow from his terrabag's side case, stretched the thread from one end to the other, and snapped it into place. He took the arrow, pulled it back toward his shoulder into the thread, and eyed the beast head-on as it walked a jagged line.

Focus. Deep breaths. You've got one chance.

The greffir dashed for them.

Pau let the arrow fly.

The greffir's screech pierced a hole in the quiet stillness of the twilit desert. The arrow was lodged in the beast's left head, in the giant white pool that was one of its two eyes. The right head, the right eye twitched in reflex. The greffir crashed to the ground. Sand exploded into the air. Pau put on his slip-shades to peer through the storm.

"Pau, look out!" Craeya called.

Too late.

The beast stood up, thrashing and swinging its left head at Pau like a club. He dodged. Then the right head. Pau lifted his right forearm to block the blow, but it slammed against his gauntlet and he felt hot, searing pain drive through to the bone. Above the elbow his arm went numb. Before he could react, the left head swung again and sent Pau flying through the air.

No!

Pau feared so many things in that first moment of helplessness.

A moment was all the beast needed.

The greffir advanced. Luzon darted away. Fenri froze, staring straight up at the beast.

"Fenri!" Pau said, but his words would do nothing. He had failed.

"No!" Craeya flew into view. She lunged at the beast, at the arrow hanging from the beast's left eye. The wooden splinter turned the beast's head the tiniest of hairs, causing it to miss Fenri.

"Fenri, move!" Luzon shouted. But she didn't. She just stood there.

Craeya threw her weight down, touched her feet to the sand. She brought the beast down to one knee, its eye gushing an impossible amount of blood. Its other head knocked into Fenri, knocking her to the ground.

"Die!" Craeya threw her weight forward, jabbed the arrow further into the eye. "You will die!" She yanked it out in one astonishing pull.

Pau froze at the sight.

Craeya either didn't notice, or adrenaline pumped through her body too fast for her to feel anything, but the greffir's other head snapped into fight mode, wanting to erase the threat trying to kill it. The beast nipped at Craeya at neck-breaking speed, ripping parts of her skinsuit off her body, her flesh, her hair. Pau pushed himself up, wild with fear.

"Craeya!" Luzon called. "Get out of there!"

She wouldn't. Against the rush of the greffir's incensed attack, she stepped forward, thrust the blood-drenched arrow into the other eye. "Die!" she yelled again.

Another screech. Blood vessels exploded in both eyes, covering Craeya in a deluge of salty blood. The annihilation came to a halt. The beast rose to its feet, wobbling. Every ounce of fear in its eyes was obscured by death. Throwing itself up, the greffir ran away, crooked and broken.

"Craeya!" Luzon ran to her.

Pau moved to her, clutching at the pain in his forearm. The damage was like nothing he'd ever seen.

Her skinsuit was half of what it had been. Her body was in pieces. Flesh and shreds of grey suit were littered around them, covered in fresh, crimson beast blood. Craeya heaved, gasping for breath, crazed eyes darting in all directions.

Pau had no idea what to do next. He had protected them to a point, but the greffir … the baby beast had cast him aside like he was a play toy. Their Healer had been the one to take it down. They had suffered injuries. Life-threatening ones. That was exactly where the Healer stepped in to heal and save. But theirs was the one who needed saving.

Doesn't she feel the pain? Pau thought. He examined her and looked from Luzon to Fenri for some idea of what came next.

"What do we do?" Pau asked, looking at Fenri as she pushed herself off the ground. That same fear of indecision gripped him. He had never been in that kind of situation before.

Fenri walked up slowly, her face aghast. "Oh, sweet ancestors," she said, her voice a whisper. "This is bad. This is really bad."

Pau's forehead grew hot. He wanted to scold Craeya for being loud and annoying and out of control. He wanted to help her and heal her too. Fear took its place. He grimaced as his arm tightened in searing pain. Decisions usually came to him with ease, but he was at a loss.

"She will not heal from this quickly," Fenri said. "Even with medicines from base."

"We need to take her back," Pau said. "We can make it back within a day or two."

"How?" Luzon asked. "By carrying her? Look at her. She'll break in two."

The wind pushed at them, skittering across Craeya's body, tiny invisible fingers sprinkling her with grains of sand. In the quiet, it seemed everyone was finally coming to their senses.

She might die. If we turn back, this mission is lost, Pau thought.

"We're not going back," Craeya said, and Pau was shocked that she was able to speak at all. She breathed heavily through her nose. "I can be healed. I won't be able to do the healing, but I can walk you through it."

We never once doubted our decision to spare the life of Fenri the Knowledger, though in those days when she was given life, she was just Fenri. We never once doubted our decision to allow an Unable to walk amongst us. There was something undeniably special about her. All of us Masters saw that. Her own self-doubt kept her honest. She always felt guilty about her condition. We never once doubted our decision to send her to the Quat Zones as part of Project El. The only thing we should have doubted was ourselves, our own blinding blindness. We never knew what Fenri the Knowledger was capable of until it was too late.

- from *Confessions of the Masters, Volume I*

12. Fenri the Knowledger

The scent of fresh blood burned Fenri's nostrils. Her shoulder throbbed where the beast had made contact. She was lucky its barrel-sized head had only grazed her. The pain lingered as a dull throbbing.

Knees ready to buckle, Fenri felt the pull of gravity beneath her, taunting her with the promise of collapse. With one hand, she touched the durablade at her side. She still had it, but fear had struck her dumb and immobilized her. She had never been so close to a beast so massive and so aggressive.

I need to eat something, she thought.

Fenri steadied herself. Blood splattered the sand in haphazard splotches, flecks here and there, like a youth Maker's art exploration.

Luzon and Pau gathered around an unmoving Craeya who lay on the ground.

Obliteration.

There was no other word. Fenri felt a tinge of guilt, then fear, then … a feeling she could not place. She was meant to protect Craeya, and yet she froze when it mattered most.

The attack appeared worse each time Fenri looked. Craeya was a doll, a scarcely put together plaything ripped apart by the sporadic will of a child. No, not a child. An avian beast that had wanted to *kill*. Instinct made Fenri reach for her logbook, but logic stopped her.

No, she thought. *Craeya is in serious trouble. Everything else can wait.*

"What do we do?" Luzon asked, turning to face Fenri.

Pau turned his body a fraction to acknowledge Fenri. Were they asking her what to do? She stepped closer to look.

"Craeya—" the name fell from Fenri's lips. Now that she saw closer, her stomach tightened in horror.

Oh, ancestors. Look at all that blood and torn skin! She may die. We didn't protect her. I was supposed to protect her.

"Saline," Craeya said. "In my bag. And rootwort. You'll need to grind it. Use it as an ointment to stop the bleeding." Craeya didn't struggle to speak at all. "You'll need to wrap the wounds."

She must still be in shock, Fenri thought. *The pain alone should have made her pass out.*

"Get moving, you two," Pau said, his hazel eyes were sharp as jagged rocks, boring into Fenri and Luzon. "It's like you've never done a cycle before. Clearly, she hasn't either, but we need her to live."

Fenri's mind froze. What was she supposed to do?

"You." Pau motioned to Luzon. "Make her a netbed."

"You." Pau glanced at Fenri. "Do what she says. Start making whatever ointments, whatever healers she'll need."

Fenri's stomach growled with hunger. *It's only in your mind,* she told herself. *You just ate at the nation-feast. You're going to be fasting for a good while longer.*

Finding her way to Craeya's bag, Fenri dug out the healing kit and opened it. She had never opened one herself before, but she recognized the layout. Vials, pipettes, mortar and pestle, oils, cloths, gauze, the EM snapped securely in its case. Fenri eyed it, then looked at Craeya. She had convinced Master Qi to give her one even though it was her first cycle, and look at her. Who could need it more than Craeya? Master Qi's words resounded in Fenri's head.

Take care of Craeya. Above all else. She is whip-smart, extremely active, and young. She will learn much from you.

Fenri wondered what Craeya would learn from *her.*

Watch how she works, her decisiveness. You will also learn from her.

Fenri shook down to her bones. The memory of the greffir attack rushed back. Slowly, the shock faded. Some warmth returned to her fingers. What would have happened if Craeya had not stepped in? Fenri couldn't move in that moment. Would she be the one lying there? Would she even be breathing?

Luzon cut bamboo shoots to size, sliding them inside each other, binding them with twine, and arachnasilk. He had been slow before, but he moved with an accuracy and precision Fenri hadn't seen. She felt another pang of something she could not place.

What are you wanting right now?

"Snap out of it," Pau said. "Whatever you're thinking about or analyzing, it can wait."

Fenri realized Craeya had given her more direction.

She grabbed the peppermint oil from the kit and faced Craeya. "Right. I'm sorry."

Craeya said nothing. The light in her eyes flickered, appearing somber under the starry sky.

What sort of training has this young girl had? Is she immune to pain?

"We move as soon as she's been treated and that netbed is ready to go," Pau said.

Fenri wouldn't be caught frozen again. No, she would be excellent at her tasks. She leaned forward, grabbing the vials Craeya told her to and went to work.

Once Fenri had made the appropriate medicines and administered them, they removed Craeya's skinsuit and dressed her wounds. The sand was its own nuisance, but Luzon was careful with his hands, able to clean Craeya's injuries and wrap them before any more sand entered her body.

Fenri dressed Craeya in her spare skinsuit to ensure she could still produce Solaren and convert sunlight into energy. If her second skinsuit was destroyed, she'd die quickly, assuming she survived the greffir attack.

Pau held Craeya in his long arms and laid her on the crisscross pattern of twine suspended between the wooden pegs. Her weight made the net sink down, but her body was still well above the ground. Pau set her terrabag at her feet so she would sink even deeper. She looked like a sick elder, covered in cloths and gauze with very little of her body showing.

The initial healing had taken all night, and the planet lightened like a black and blue bruise smearing yellow. Craeya continued to stare into the cloudless sky. Zhao slipped down over the horizon like a ruby drop of rain. For a moment, the air felt refreshing.

"Will it die?" Luzon asked. "That bird thing?"

"It's called a greffir," Pau said, "and I don't know. With only one eye it might have lived, but the arrow had burning agent on it."

"Too bad it didn't die here," Luzon said. "We could have used its parts."

"Better that the beast is not near us now," Pau said.

Fenri jotted down everything she had seen and heard as fast as she could.

SUBJECT: greffir

Arinx struthitix

Q387*1*6 — We encountered the adolescent greffir approximately forty hectomiles from base, due east and north. The beast kept its distance, about 400 meters from us. After another 10 hours, we discovered it was tracking us. Craeya seemed out of *control from the tilq she had taken at base and possibly attracted the greffir to us with her voice. She fired a flare inadvertently.*

Fenri laid down her leadpen. Craeya still hadn't cried out or indicated any feeling of discomfort. The shout *"Die!"* as Craeya tried to kill the beast echoed in Fenri's ears. Craeya struggled to keep her eyes open. Fenri peered down at her writing. Her log would reflect a mistake on Craeya's part. Was it fair? Did Craeya really attract the beast? Fenri didn't see how else it could have gotten to them.

"Let's go." Pau moved to the front of the netbed and grabbed knotted ends of rope that Luzon had attached to the front. The bed was slim, and Craeya's body fit into it neatly.

"We're moving again?" Fenri asked. "We moved all night. And look at Craeya now. It's going to get hot."

"We need to put some distance between us and this place," Pau said. "If the beast is part of a tribe, others could be nearby. We need to move. Just an hour or so."

"I can pull her." Fenri looked at the netbed, admiring the speed and accuracy with which Luzon had crafted it.

"I'll do it," Pau said.

Fenri closed her logbook and shoved it into her pack, relieved. She felt as though she could hardly move her *own* body, much less pull another one. Pau led, pulling the netbed behind him effortlessly it seemed, while Fenri and Luzon flanked the sides.

"I can make something to relieve the pain more," Luzon said.

Pau projected his voice. "Before that, I need to tell you that what you did was the stupidest thing I've ever seen, Craeya, but since you're practically inches from death, I'll save it until you're better."

"A kohbra strikes at those who wait," Craeya said.

Kohbra. Fenri saw the beast in her head: the giant and hideous snake-creature with severe, midnight-purple fangs like shards of glass that could devour you in one bite.

"Oh, you want your punishment now?" Pau asked.

"What was I supposed to do differently?" Craeya said. "Fenri was about to lose her head."

Pau made a grunting sound. Perhaps he had forgotten that detail.

"You don't need any more tilq," Pau said. "Either of you. That's what got us into this mess."

"Suppressing our appetites and emotions got us in trouble?" Injury had not slowed Craeya's mind.

"Clearly, it did nothing to suppress your emotions," Pau said. "What the hell was that anyway? You know, we could easily turn around and bring you back to base."

"You could, but you won't," Craeya said. "No one here wants to give up this mission."

"It's not tilq," Luzon added. "What I'm proposing is medicine that would help Craeya heal faster."

Fenri's ears perked up. "You make medicines?"

"I've made a few. Nothing as good as the Healers, but I understand creation mechanics."

"Whatever," Pau said. "Make what you need, but I don't need to know every detail of your lives."

"What is it?" Craeya asked, her voice calm.

"Something topical that would amp up the immune system and get into the blood too."

"You've never made it before?"

"No. Technically, it *is* tilq in nature, but it would help you. If I get it right."

"And if you don't?" Fenri said. "Getting into the blood could be harmful. She's so weak right now that I wouldn't risk foreign bodies."

Fenri cleared her throat. *Do they not hear me?* He was a Maker, and she was a Healer. They didn't have the knowledge Fenri had, and yet they acted like they knew everything. A creeping, crawling sensation tickled Fenri's throat. Her chest burned. Fenri swallowed. She watched Craeya and Luzon and her mind processed information at lightning speed.

The human needs appeared in Fenri's mind-map. Craeya wanted safety, protection. Luzon wanted the same thing. He saw that safety and protection in the form of Craeya, in her healing arts. The logic of that thought overtook the mental blocks popping up. Yes, that wasn't so ridiculous. Fenri saw something like that in Luzon too. Not safety or protection but ... *propulsion*. A springing forward into the future. The Electric Ocean. What lay inside. The machines and devices Luzon could build. What he claimed he could build. He was already reaching into his bag, his words as slow and constant as daylight while Craeya listened.

Fenri looked at them. Her and Luzon's eyes met. She looked down at the sand. At her feet, her hands. His hands moved in her peripheral vision. Navy blue veiny rivers pulsed inside them, bulging with power.

Those hands.

Fenri inhaled a deep breath and refocused her attention. Their needs. They were supposed to protect and survive. No one had strayed from that yet. Even Pau wanted his team to live. Of course he did. She wanted to live too.

So then why did I freeze when it mattered most? What do I want?

Slow your thoughts. There is no want. No desire. You do everything for the good of the tribe. If Craeya does something good, it is good for all of us. If Luzon can make a new drug and help Craeya, it is good for all of us. So then—

Luzon laughed loud and true, and Fenri snapped from her reverie.

"Well, I hope you can make it all fit together," Craeya said.

"I always find a way," Luzon said, and a smile passed between them.

Fenri felt warmth in her cheeks, then tiny pinpricks in her chest as sharp as cactusii needles. She tightened. "If you make it incorrectly, it could be toxic to Craeya," Fenri repeated.

But Luzon and Craeya just laughed.

Luzon's hands moved around inside a bowl he held in the crook of his elbow, swift like water, and he began to craft something as he walked.

Fenri's gaze fell on Craeya. She was such a small, fragile girl. Fenri was twice her size in weight and girth. She had done so many more cycles than Craeya. And yet, even wrapped in bandages, she was more noticeable. Fenri recalled how Luzon and Pau had both run to her when the attack happened. *Why does it feel as though Craeya is also one of the beasts? A threat to run from or eradicate?*

Fenri's pulse spiked and her forehead went hot.

Mind before obstacle. The mind powers everything. The mind is limitless.

Fenri slowed her breathing. She focused on herself. If she was being ignored, she would stand where she could be seen. If Craeya outshined her in a certain area, she would improve in that area. There was nothing a Healer knew that a Knowledger didn't. Fenri knew so many things. Sometimes she felt as though she knew so much her brain would burst from being overfull. Now it was about converting what she knew to get what she wanted.

What has gotten into you, Fenri? What would the Masters say and think?

She knew exactly what they'd say. For the first time, she didn't care. Another voice spoke louder. Hers. Reminding her of logical lessons that she had long forgotten but knew every word of.

You get things you haven't had before by doing things you haven't done before.

Zhao rose and fell for the next three days without issue. The desert stretched eternally before them in a sea of ginger sand and swirling figvi red. The heat of the day was always the worst part. Craeya kept still and silent in her netbed, only moving to take antibodies or pain-modifiers or water, or to relieve herself with the help of Fenri. Or to be put underneath their baracca. Fenri's mind began to slow on the third twilit night, the grey tundra of her mind calming from its endless storm.

Pau stopped pulling Craeya and dropped the ropes in the firm-sand. The tawny ground cooled beneath them as Zhao melted away. Milkali was beginning to throw its misty blue coat over the land.

"Do you have enough water?" Pau was crouching, peering down at Craeya.

"For now," she said.

Pau rose. "Everyone else good?"

Fenri tasted burnt sand on her lips and smelled fire. Hunger gnawed at her. She put her mouth on her tube and pulled water from her bag's well. Fenri let the cool water sit in her throat for a moment before swallowing. She wanted more.

"I'm fine!" Luzon said. He sat on a rock, his knees poking up and out, almost reptilian, as he churned something in his mixing bowl.

"How's everyone's energy?" Pau asked. He was checking in more and more since Craeya's injury, a good thing for a Charge Leader to do, but it did not seem like one of Pau's obvious priorities or motivations. He only seemed annoyed. That melted away. In his eyes, Fenri sensed a tinge of fear. Fear that something terrible would happen again.

Luzon looked at Pau from his perch. "Have you slept at all?"

Fenri hadn't seen Pau sleep. That was a skill of Guardians. They went through unspeakable training. Guardian Masters introduced challenges to their youth at early ages, exposing them to pain and suffering, and other dreadful immunity-boosting exercises Fenri could not even imagine. She scanned Pau, new knowledge blooming in her mind about what he was, what he could do. She'd been with other Guardians, but Pau seemed different somehow. He drew the beast away with ease. Had it not had two heads, he might have killed it instantly.

"I've slept," Pau said. But Fenri sensed it was a lie.

"When?" Luzon asked.

"Does it matter?"

"Um, yeah. Kind of," Luzon said.

Pau hasn't read as many books as I have, but he knows the land, Fenri thought. She looked at her cyclemates with new eyes. Her knowledge had gotten her far, but today it wasn't enough. A Healer and a Maker had talked over her even though she knew much more. She knew things, but so did Craeya. That wasn't what had attracted Luzon to her.

Fenri analyzed herself and Craeya in her mind. The two of them ran down alongside each other like transcribing strands of DNA. Fenri took up more space and was heavier. Craeya was smaller, quicker, feistier. Fenri froze on the spot, and it was more difficult for her to get moving. But once she started, it was more difficult to stop her.

Pau's shadow disappeared as clouds passed above and darkness covered them. Fenri shivered. The night was growing cold. She drowned out Luzon's calm voice, Craeya's shrill laugh. They would not be able to help her. She was tired of being pushed aside and ignored. Pau ventured away from the group by a few paces, his nose in the air.

Always so sure of himself. So powerful.

Fenri slid her hand down into her pocket, felt the cold metal hilt of the durablade. Pau had given it to her back at the nation-feast before she knew who he was. Even in ten days, so much had changed.

Fenri approached Pau. He sensed her presence and turned. A gentle breeze pushed Fenri's hair past her ears. She locked eyes with Pau, felt the growing power behind them.

"Something wrong?" he asked in his usual tone.

The words came out without any modification or premeditated thought. "I need your help."

"If this is about asking for extra food, the answer is no."

"It's not about food." Fenri pulled the durablade from her pocket, then the blade from its narrow, shallow sheath. Light from Kaleem gave it a silver glow. A deep focus settled between her eyes. She felt her gaze grow as cold as the sand around her. "I want you to train me. Show me how to fight like you."

What can any of us say about Craeya the Healer? When we made the decision to place her on the dispatch team as part of Project El, some of us Masters had our doubts. We were divided in this matter. We saw the way she grew up and knew her tendencies. She was very young when Project El began. That fateful trip to the Quat Zones was her very first cycle in the field. There are few if any in our tribe that would have been prepared for such a thing. In a way, she didn't need to be. She was our wild card. The girl who was very real, who came to answers in her own unique way, who was full of curiosities we could not explain. We thought we had trained this out of her, but it was just another one of the ways in which our mistakes cost us irreparably.

- from *Reflections on Our Changed World* by the New Masters

13. CRAEYA THE HEALER

Sometime later, a time which Craeya could not begin to guess, consciousness floated back to her, biting into her body as sharp as serrated teeth. The dull buzzing of the EM rang in her ears though she knew she was not back at the Healing Circle. She was not back at base. They had not taken her back for her mistake, for the untimely tragedy she had flung upon them: a dispatch mission without a Healer not ten days into the mission. *How many days* have *we been out here?*

Craeya had no idea. She only knew she was still alive, somehow, barely, lying decrepit in a netbed at the mercy of a body still in shock.

Craeya did not feel afraid, but around her, fear soaked the air like a toxin. She thought for a moment she could smell it, then realized it was only her skin regrowing as Fenri pushed the EM across her body. The sensation felt like a thousand ice crystals shattering on her skin, a sharp, fleeting coldness followed by a dull ache.

"She's awake," Fenri said. The roundness of her face sharpened, becoming more angular as she turned away.

Luzon appeared above her. Then Pau.

"How do you feel?" Pau asked.

The beast wanted to *consume* her.

Too many things were going on inside Craeya for her to know. Her thoughts had trickled to a halt, and the tilq had fully worn off, but she still felt the quiet beginnings of a storm. If the EM was being used, that meant she was moving toward healing. The ointments had at least closed the edges, the various shapes of torn skin. She couldn't tell how many days had passed. Time blended like the golds and reds on the horizon, a union with no beginning or end.

Craeya looked down at her body. Covered in pink and red patches, black and blue bruises, she was the desert's most hideous mosaic. Already she had taken more damage than all of her team combined.

"Is the medicine helping?" Luzon asked.

Craeya's throat crumpled into her stomach. Again, something was off inside her. She closed her eyes, tried to regain the strength to speak. The early-morning heat of the sun pricked at her open wounds like pre-needles, the prickling cactusii appendages that got into the skin but didn't cause much harm. The sensation was almost imperceptible.

"I think it is," Craeya said.

Fenri stared down, and the two of them locked eyes.

Does the Knowledger know something is still off inside of me?

"Then we move," Pau said, disappearing from above. "Two more hours before it gets too hot, then we rest for the day. Stone is still another five days away."

They made good time the next day. Not so much the day after that. Predicting the number of times they'd need to break, to change the bandages, to rest, or to redress the wounds was impossible. The days were quiet. There was not much to say.

"You look worse than yesterday," Fenri said. "Here."

"What is it?" Craeya asked.

"A tamagon heart. You're burning a lot of calories."

"We still need to fast for another few weeks at least," Craeya said.

"*We* may need to, but *you* don't." Fenri reached over, and Craeya opened her mouth to take it.

Every time her patches soaked up her blood, she lost precious nutrients: iron, magnesium, copper. The heart was warm and bloody as it moved down her throat. Fenri unwrapped Craeya's wounds, redressed them, wrapped them again, then tipped water from Craeya's cylinder into her mouth. "Tell us if you need something more."

Craeya stared up at Fenri. "Can you help me move again? I hate being in this bed. I need to walk again soon, or my blood will clot."

"We are moving again." Pau gripped the strap of his terrabag with one hand, the ropes attached to the netbed with the other.

Craeya felt a pang in her stomach. She had been torn apart on the outside, and yet it was her insides that hurt. The pain was dull and heavy, like a large stone being dragged across her torso, with sharp, stabbing throbs as it sank in. She breathed with difficulty. If she could get through the agony, she could work to heal herself. All she needed was her strength back.

The world was full of new realities.

Craeya had never suffered so much before. Yes, there were illnesses. Horrifying cramps. Harrowing nightmares. Everyone in her cohort had them. If a virus found its way into the Healer's Circle, it hurried its way through them. Most Healers knew that their bodies needed to process the ailment naturally, but there were some who used medicines. Did that make them cheaters? Not really. Everyone's body processed differently.

Craeya recalled the distressing weeks of the inflarzine virus, how it swept up Healer Polina in a vortex of multiplying ailments, and no one saw her for days, and all Craeya could see was her wasted body, bones laid out like a ladder, broken and chipped. The virus had touched nearly everyone in the cohort, but it had never touched Craeya.

Now she saw Rannum too, his lean, concave chest, the abnormality of his eyes, the sun-splotch inside, reaching out with orange tendrils. She tried to remember when she had first noticed Rannum.

She saw the tunnels. Rannum removing his skinsuit. Her insides prickled. Her organs twisted. The sun pressed its heat down on her, spreading warmth through her body. She wanted to escape her flesh prison.

Craeya forced her eyes open. To leave the visions in her head. Outside, everything blurred. Voices floated across her body.

"Craeya, are you all right?" Fenri looked down, concerned. "Your chest is heaving."

They had moved on. Fever swallowed Craeya, left her soaking in a puddle of whatever moisture was forcing itself out of her body. The twine underneath the leshblanket holding her in a giant cradle pushed into her like a thousand needles. Craeya tried to slow her breathing. The bone-dry sky hummed with a quiet grey omen.

"I don't know what else to do for her," Luzon said.

Craeya didn't want to see Rannum in her mind, but she couldn't help it. The tilq had only worked for so long. *What am I doing here?* Action in the field was what she had always wanted. That was where she was supposed to use what she had spent her entire life learning. That was the place she would be able to forget.

She squinted the sweat out of her eyes.

She saw him again, clear as any day in the lesson alcoves. Except they were in the Terrarium. Green and yellow surrounded them, and the savory smell of blossoming bloomquests. Craeya lay against the crooked branches of the figvi tree, reaching up. Rannum sat on another branch across from her, the ground underneath them framed by their shadows.

"The tree can grow five or six figvis at a time," Rannum said. "They'll know."

"You don't always have to follow all of the rules," Craeya said. She eyed the mauve fruits budding around her, craving the energy and sweetness inside them.

"I don't always." Rannum smirked, and his smile became the sun, hot and bright. A breeze rushed in through the slats, and Craeya smelled salt water and limewine, a thing she had not yet tasted.

"Hey!" came a voice, and Craeya knew they were caught. "You're not supposed to be here."

Rannum shot her a mischievous glance then leaned over to fall out of the tree. Craeya followed. They both laughed and ran.

"She needs more rest," Fenri said. "And more water."

Craeya came back to the present moment, and Rannum was gone. He was lost to her forever. She needed to accept that.

Craeya fought to keep her eyes open, to focus on Luzon and Fenri. They would help her forget. They would help stop the inner itching and burning. They'd help stop the unseen force trying to rip her from existence.

Craeya coughed and felt her lungs wring against each other with terrible pressure. She squeezed her eyes shut.

Oh ancestors, please. Please don't let me go.

If she could make it a few more days, she could make the cure herself. *What cure? There is nothing to cure.*

"Let's move through the night," Pau said. "We'll give her water when she wakes."

The greffir had ripped at her without relenting. And even though it would die, it had enacted its final revenge. The word *parasite* hung at the edge of Craeya's lips. A word too small to be spoken. A thing that wanted to crawl back inside, down and deeper. But she knew. She knew from the bottom of her

Healer heart that a parasite lived in her body. If the others found out what heinous thing lay beneath, they'd turn back. Craeya squeezed her hands into fists.

"Yeah, let her sleep," Luzon said. "It always helps me."

Another day passed. Maybe two. Time lost meaning.

The metallic scent of tamagon hearts stirred Craeya to life. Something wet touched her lips. She parted them, tasting the bloody heart, and a sweetened touch of Honey-Q.

"That's good. You need to keep your strength up." Fenri appeared again, same as the day before. Her voice carried a dose of comfort.

"What strength?"

Fenri half-laughed, half-smiled, a thing Craeya had rarely seen her do. Night was coming and everything felt cold. "I have *never* seen such a vicious attack in all my cycles, and still you're standing, well, lying, to talk about it."

"I don't want to talk. I want to move. I don't want to have to be pulled along like some sack filled with stones."

"Craeya," Fenri said, her tone dropping an octave. "This is what the cycles are. You don't have to do everything right now."

Craeya knew Fenri wouldn't be able to understand her plight. Lying there was torture. She had to think about her insides more intensely. As far as Craeya could tell, Fenri *enjoyed* being in her head. Were all Knowledgers like her? Were they just troves of information ready to cite any fact or figure at the snap of a tamagon neck? They knew aspects about other classes— Healers, Guardians, Makers—but Craeya wondered what they were actually masters *of*. What good was information when you had a parasite inside you killing you?

Sharp, unseen pain dug into Craeya, yanking her from the spiraling thoughts, burrowing deeper.

Craeya met Fenri's gaze. She looked past her and saw Pau

and Luzon talking about something in the sky. Pau was a full head or two taller than Luzon. Craeya had no sense of depth.

"What's in your healing kit?" Fenri asked.

"What do you mean?" Craeya heard the fear in her own voice. *Does Fenri know? Is she smart enough, intuitive enough, to see the signs of infection?*

Saying the word brought relief, even if only in her head. Craeya wasn't sure if she would feel better if someone else knew what was going on, or worse. *If Fenri finds out, will she tell the others?* Craeya would survive, but she did not want to go back to base.

"I want to know everything that's inside. Can I look?"

"I can just tell you."

"It helps me to see for myself." Fenri didn't wait for permission. She moved out of Craeya's line of sight, and Craeya heard her rustling around, the snapping open of her kit.

"What are you doing? Don't use anything."

Fenri appeared again, her face flushed, pinched pink from the sun. She moved clumps of hair from her face and huffed.

"I'm not," Fenri said. "I wanted to see what you had."

"Why?"

"Because I need to know things. Anything that can help us. Do you have a problem with me looking inside your healing kit? Your hands aren't exactly in working condition."

Craeya ignored Fenri's sass. "Okay, well now you know."

"I can't help it. It goes beyond me just being a Knowledger. It's like I need to know things that have absolutely no importance at all. I used to think everything had importance, but my brain doesn't have enough room for that."

"I get that, but how does that go beyond you being a Knowledger? That's who and what you are."

Fenri took a deep breath and looked away, as though Craeya had said something offensive. After a moment, she said, "I suppose that's what I meant."

"Our class is everything," Craeya said.

"I agree."

"I want to know a lot of things too."

Healer Polina had warned Craeya not to think about certain topics and definitely not to talk about them. But Fenri wasn't Healer Polina. There was nothing Fenri could do that would effect any change. And then, Craeya felt a warmth inside her chest she could not explain, as though she'd taken a swig of limewine. Fenri seemed to understand things other people didn't. Craeya wondered why.

"I want to know about the portals," she said.

Fenri was looking away, seemingly preoccupied with something. "What about them?"

"I want to learn how to open them."

"You of all people should understand how to open them."

"I understand it from a biological perspective," Craeya said. She studied Fenri, how her eyes shifted from her to the horizon over and over again. "But I don't know the other stuff."

"Can you be more specific?"

That was the way to do it: intrigue Fenri with questions until her curiosity made her talk. Craeya looked past her again. Pau and Luzon looked off into the distance, unspeaking. The desert fluttered on, cool and quiet.

"The history of them," Craeya said. "How we developed them in the first place."

At that moment, Fenri's eyes held the sun inside them. A chance to talk about her knowledge, about science, a chance to showcase her true power.

"The portals are vital to our health," Fenri said. "I imagine you've opened one or two before. The latter ones, the intangibles, sound, light, thought—they require more determination and practice to open."

Craeya didn't care about the intangibles.

"The former ones—qha, water, fire—can also be tough to open, and are about safety, identity, actualization."

Craeya didn't care about the tangible ones either. She did, but not then. She wanted to know about the one no one would talk about. Half tangible, half intangible, between the former and the latter.

"What about the fourth portal?" Craeya asked. She was expecting a big reaction, a mouth-gaping, sputtering escape of admonishments and warnings, like the one Healer Polina had when Craeya asked about it for the first and last time.

"We do not speak of that, Craeya," Polina had said.

Fenri remained stoic. Her eyes rested on Craeya, idle like the ocean. "There is no fourth portal."

A similar denial, but Craeya spotted a crack in the lie. Judging by her tone of voice, Fenri certainly knew about it. She was forbidden to talk about it like everyone else. *What else is new?*

"There is. Our ancestors opened it," Craeya said, sitting up.

"Craeya, what is it you want to know?" Fenri said nippily, as if they could get it over with before Luzon and Pau wandered back. Even Craeya knew keeping the conversation confined to just the two of them was in both their interests.

"I mean, what if someone in our tribe reopened it? What if I've opened mine?"

Fenri's eyes darkened, and she shot a look as sharp as lightning. There, the fear. "Hush, girl. No one would or even can. It hasn't been done for thousands of years. Not since our ancestors."

"What about the tribesmen that are put to death?"

"How do you know about that?"

"Just tell me the truth," Craeya said, louder.

"It's impossible," Fenri whispered, but her tone was tenacious. "If you opened it, every beast on the planet would be attracted to you. No one would be alive right now. If one of us has even opened that impossible portal just a hair, none of us would be alive," she repeated.

"Why? Why the beasts? What does a portal have to do with the beasts?"

"There are smells. We've evolved to a certain point. We are what we are because of thousands of years of growth and change.

Because, at best, we have opened *all* the portals, except for the forbidden fourth. And if we did, we would give off new smells. Smells the beasts know well. They are much older, much more evolved. They have been on QhaHadur longer than we have."

Craeya saw the pyre she had built in Fenri's brain.

That was what Knowledgers were good for: keeping knowledge and applying it to the present because of things that had happened in the past. In that way, it wasn't much different from healing.

"If they are evolving, how do we know they can still track us for it?"

The fire dimmed then surged in Fenri's eyes. "We do not need to worry about the beasts, only ourselves. Closing it and keeping it closed is how we survive. Now. No more questions about this topic. We aren't supposed to talk about it."

Now it was Craeya's turn to feel the fire. She felt a rush of energy and swung her legs over the edge of the netbed. "Why? Why can't I ask questions? Why does everyone always tell me that?"

Craeya could see Fenri working out the answer in her head and stopped her. "I'm as smart as anyone else. As smart as you. You want to know things. I want to know things too!"

"You haven't even begun to open that portal because you would definitely know if you had." Fenri hesitated. "The experience is otherworldly. Painfully intense. That is why we don't talk about it or think about it. We would not know what to do once it opened." Fenri stopped talking, out of breath.

For a moment, neither of them said anything.

"And for the record, only those who have opened all the other portals have the slightest chance of opening the fourth one."

That was more than they could ever say in the Healing Circle. That *other* knowledge was where Fenri excelled. Craeya was beginning to understand her areas of expertise.

The strangeness Craeya felt inside her grew. The beast swam into her consciousness, its gargantuan heads towering above her like swollen fruit, thrashing and ready to burst. And Craeya saw it then, an image of too many things at once, created by words that began to sit and settle into her, ringing in her bones with undeniable truth.

The fruit exploded, and when Craeya looked down, her hands were covered in sticky, thick blood. The beast was no longer the beast; it was Craeya herself. The others pressed hands against their ears to shield themselves from the terrible noise. The beast did not attack because it saw them or heard them. The beast attacked because it *smelled* them.

And Craeya knew it the same way she could smell Rannum then, the subtle lavender scent of his body, how even hundreds of miles away she could remember his smell, and she wondered if she'd ever be free of him, of the memory of him.

If the parasite didn't take her, she wondered if more beasts would come and do what they were meant to do. In the deep, dark parts of Craeya's body, in untouched recesses like her heart, the subjugating cavity pumping her full of blood, she knew. Yes, she *knew*.

The others babbled about Stone on the outskirts of camp, about how close they were to joining him, but Craeya didn't care. She only cared for her own healing, only that the feeling would lighten and then disappear before it killed her.

Get it together, Craeya. When the others slept, she would force herself to get up, to make her antidote and expel whatever was inside of her.

She knew of pain intellectually. She had seen it on the repair table countless times, the ways bodies twisted and squirmed, the way their faces scrunched up, unable to bear losing a fingernail, or horrified to learn they'd lose all the contents of their stomach, retching and sputtering until there was nothing left, until they were left breathless and on the brink of death, eyes shot red with blood, holding on.

Yes, Craeya had seen pain, but she did not know it herself, until then, with that inner heaviness weighing on her chest. She breathed in the scentless desert air, gripping the edge of the netbed.

Holding on was the only thing she could do.

Energy takes many forms, gaining speed and power from its original source. On QhaHadur, this is a dangerous thing. Take a Zephnaido for example. A force that powerful must meet another force equally as powerful in order to be vanquished, or it must run its course. Sometimes this course is long and arduous and anything that stands in its way will perish. For us QhaHadurians, just as it is with the Alpha and Omega beasts, these forces cannot be met. They must be avoided at all costs.

- from *Lessons on Survival by the Masters*

14. STONE THE PLANETEER

"Isn't he going to say anything?" Craeya said.

The four strangers had come to Stone the Planeteer in the early hours of the morning, when the sky was milky white with the moons' light. The girl's question was harsh on Stone's ears in the Clayhaze where he had been alone for so long. Inside the voice, Stone heard more than the girl had intended.

Awareness showed him a two-headed bird-beast with sharp talons and a beak pointed enough to shatter bone. It hadn't. It desired flesh. In its way, it would rip it from the Healer's body until she dropped dead. Stone could see it all before him. The Knowledger cast aside for a young, spry specimen.

Quick glances from the Knowledger exposed new emotions. They were raw, unchecked. Stone followed her gaze, the source of her desires, but when she saw him watching her, she looked away. The younger girl with intuitive eyes hid behind a façade of forced toughness.

There.

Stone saw the single-celled organism doing its work, inside her, burrowing.

"Stone," the other woman said. She was older than the first, who was a child compared to her. "Are you okay?" Energy surged forward as the sound waves of her voice expanded, and Stone took a deep breath to brace himself for what was coming.

So much energy. With all of them. Especially this one. In the upper portals, sight and thought. Reckless. She didn't have them in control, but she could. With practice, she could easily see too.

Subtle currents from the others reached Stone as whispers. He saw the older one giving the younger one extra food and attending to her wounds and needs while she slept. The one good with his hands, the Maker, had a racing mind, but there was power there too. Stone's vision slowed, darkening like the sky above when clouds cloaked the world in shadow.

Stone stared at the Maker, his rough, weather-worn hands like tamagon leather, fingernails chipped and hardened, his fingers bent at such angles Stone knew injury had weakened his grip, but no—not him. Somehow, he had found a way to use it to his advantage. His hands were tools themselves, and Stone could smell the nut oils rooting like plants in the fingernails, the shards of metal, the plethora of minerals living in Luzon's hands, lighting up in Stone's awareness like crystals in a cave.

Then there was the tall one. Mystery shrouded his presence. Grounded. Strong. Stone couldn't stop himself from looking deeper. He felt new energies. His mind struggled to find the words ... *real power.*

The visions clashed against each other like surf on stone. Magnetized. Polarized. A sudden, sickening flash of darkness. So dark it gave colors new meaning. Stone pulled away, suddenly exhausted.

"What is his deal?" Craeya said.

"Give him some time," Fenri said. "This is new."

"How long do you suppose it's been since he's gone back to base?" Luzon asked. "Looks like he's been cutting hair from his beard with a durablade."

"How is this guy supposed to help us navigate the Quat Zones?" Craeya said. "He won't even talk to us."

Perhaps she is trying to direct the attention of her own death away from herself. He scanned his surroundings, the quiet emptiness of the Clayhaze, each and every cactusii and shrub he had harvested for food or water for a month, and with abrupt clarity it felt as though he didn't know the place at all. He grabbed his logbook and his planet-tablet and shoved them back into his terrabag.

"Maybe he forgot how to speak," Luzon said. "How long has it been since you've seen another QhaHadurian?"

Such linear inquisitions. So concentrated on visible planes. Time was an illusion they all saw as reality. The amount of time did not matter.

Feeling as though he was ready to join his new dispatch team, Stone stepped forward to introduce himself.

The others continued to stare. He had forgotten what it was like to be around others. *That* reaction.

"He's using his hands to talk to us," Craeya said.

"I see," Fenri said. She knew the language. She used her own hands to respond.

"What's going on?" Pau said. "Why are you both talking with your hands? Fenri, tell us what he's saying. Talk while you do that."

"My name ... is Stone," Fenri said, translating the handspeak. "I have been waiting for you."

"He was born without a voice then," Craeya said. "We learned about them, but I've never treated one or met one up close."

"Our Planeteer is a mute," Fenri said, as if that brought finality to the whole ordeal.

Their language could use some refinement, Stone thought. *I was not born without a voice.* He felt himself falling out of balance. *They will learn that voice is not always something that needs to be heard with your ears.*

They made plans to move. Stone took several deep breaths.

He pressed his heels into the hardness of their planet, the qha that gave him life, and moved to follow their Guardian.

Tiny visions pricked at him.

They need help and I am meant to help them. If I serve no other purpose in my days as a Planeteer, I will serve this one. Stone registered the revelation, but he did not hold it, for it was too hot and too wild to hold for any longer than he had. He merely noticed the thought inside him then released it.

Before dawn, on the outskirts of Stone's awareness, darkness festered, even as Zhao rose. Somehow the combination kept Stone from being able to see. The Master's words from long ago came to him. *You must be able to use all your senses, Stone. Simultaneously. There is no separation. You are one body acting on the universe, just as everything is acting upon you.*

He didn't always need to see. There were other senses to tap into. Others he was neglecting. Instead of seeing colorful patterns, he heard a voice. Her voice. Her worries became his.

She's going to die if we don't find a cure. Base will have what she needs, but we can't go back.

He hadn't heard another voice in so long. Hundreds of days in the arid, bone-dry desert made it easy to forget he wasn't actually alone. Did she know of her power?

"She's not getting better," Fenri said.

Pau pulled the ropes attached to the netbed effortlessly, as though they were stringy pieces of seakelp.

So much strength, Stone thought. And he wondered at Pau's mind. How much of what he had learned did the Masters teach? Stone intuited the answer, found emptiness.

"I'm fine," Craeya said, but her deep cough spoke other truths.

Stone saw his dilemma. Now, their dilemma. His place in it. He handspoke to Fenri.

She will die if the thing is not destroyed.

Fenri showed surprise. *How do you know?*

I have seen death before. I have seen it even closer than it is now. *She is tough. She will fight it. But her body cannot kill the thing alone.*

"What are you two talking about?" Craeya asked, alert.

Fenri hesitated. "About our mission."

"Liar. You're both being intense."

They do not know, do they? Stone handspoke. *The Healer knows it is true, but the others do not know.*

Fenri handspoke. *She's scared.*

What plan do you have? Continue on until she dies? You must turn back.

I know. I don't know what to do.

The further you travel, the more she dies.

It would change the entire trajectory of our mission. It means we'd fail.

Stone saw it then. *You need something. A rare base metal. Why?*

Fenri looked at him warily, eyes wide with surprise.

He continued. *You want to keep her alive. You want to keep her with you. You can't have both.*

I know, Stone. My logic is telling me exactly what we need to do, but somehow, I can't decide. I'm keeping her alive. I will keep her alive.

Do not be foolish in this matter. But even as Stone spoke it, he questioned himself. There were healing arts beyond logic and science that she might have discovered. Stone couldn't see in that direction.

If you don't tell them, I will.

No. Not yet. Soon, but not now.

Fenri the Knowledger did not tell them. She held certain knowledge close to her when it served. Instead of sharing what she knew, she continued to give Craeya antibiotics. Over the next few days, for a week, and longer.

Stone could not sense what happened to the infection because it wore the mask of medicine. He hoped that it was working. His vision required his attention in other areas. The planet had been speaking to him for quite some time, and since the others had joined him, he heard more.

The winds whispered against the hairs of his inner ear. The ground trembled when he walked. The sky bled deep, dark sapphire, but underneath that he sensed other shades. Behind the curtain, aquamarine and jade emerged, reflections he caught from sections of the ocean halfway across their planet. They were going to the Quat Zones, a place he struggled to see.

When the sun grew hot, they stopped to break. Pau set up their baracca as he always did. Stone erected his own so that they'd have more room. When it was up, he crawled inside.

"How many Planeteers are there?"

Stone turned to see Fenri following him inside, her eyes searching his, thirsty for his knowledge.

Stone brought his elbows to the ground then rolled onto his back. There was curiosity in Fenri's voice today, something bright and hopeful. She had been preoccupied with Craeya's illness and keeping it from the others before, but her focus spiraled toward other matters.

"Don't you train with them?" she asked.

They had walked all night and morning. Stone was tired. Sometimes he wished he could communicate to Fenri with his mind. He handspoke, *No. The training for Planeteers is solitary so that it reflects our experience in the field. I have never met another Planeteer before.*

Fenri's face showed shock then intrigue. "You must share information about the planet, though? Have some idea about how many others there are?"

I have an idea.

"And?"

Less than five, I am sure.

Fenri kneeled closer and spoke with her hands. Stone took it as a sign of trust and appreciated her efforts.

Stone, the ocean. I found a flowering plant that I believe is a new species. I wanted to ask you about it. Have you traveled there recently?

I have. Almost three cycles ago today.

Our moons are both in the sky. They're changing the tides. Something in the ocean is changing. It will all be different soon. I'm asking the Masters if I can go back there next cycle. If I return to them with Klonden, they will allow my passage.

What are you hoping for, Fenri the Knowledger?

Fenri blinked slowly. Her mouth twisted, her eyes pinched together in concentration. She spoke aloud. "To bring new answers to the tribe."

Why?

"Because it's what I am meant to do."

The ocean is not the only thing that is changing. Do not lose sight of what is really happening on our planet.

"The ocean holds knowledge that no one has found before. Everyone should have access to that."

Not all knowledge holds the same value.

"That is for the tribe to decide."

Stone said nothing. He waited, watched to see if Fenri would continue. She did not. Her energies were growing stronger. Stone could feel them expanding in the small space of the baracca. *She will go to the ends of the planet to find the truth.* He did not want to say it to her, but the thought invaded his mind. *Knowledge is all well and good, but be careful of truth that shows itself as absolute.*

As if she could read his reticence, she said, "I'm going to go check on Craeya," and left.

Five days passed. The desert opened its mouth wide, and they walked across its bone-white teeth. The ground stretched its body long and flat, a burnt sienna with white streaks where

QhaHadurians had carved paths like muscle striations. But the desert was not bound together tightly. Only the feeling of its instability came to Stone, and Fenri's knowing words: *It will all be different soon.*

But this soon?

The atmosphere sparked, and a well of energy from far away lost its coherence and spilled out in a torrent. Cool, dry air licked at Stone's exposed ankles. A warm draft pressed against the skin around his beard.

Another seven days came and went.

They journeyed deeper into the jaws of the Clayhaze. Their destination, the Quat Zones, crept closer. Stone's uncertainty grew. The air crackled with light and fire underneath the visible plane. Stone swallowed a lump in his throat. He lost his breath. The weather was about to speak to him, but there were other voices.

"Why do we need five team members anyway?" Craeya said. Her health remained neutral, but it was false, and she knew it.

Fenri said, "Do you have any idea how valuable a Planeteer is?"

"No, but I'm sure you'd love to tell me," Craeya said.

Stone stopped to listen to the sounds. They grew louder, more boisterous. Ions reaching out for a dangerous counterpart, a better half. To know what it felt like. To be joined in power.

The antibiotics are running out. We need to make more.

Planetary voices interrupted, the wind, sharp, everywhere, speaking a language he only knew in deep awareness. The Guardian sensed a shift and turned to stare at Stone. "What's the matter?"

Everyone stopped.

Stone nearly had it. The darkness wanted him to look inside, but he knew he couldn't. He could only look from far away. He needed to know what lay on the other side. The winds pushed at him. When he became more aware of his surroundings, he saw that the others were staring at him. *Don't they feel it too?*

Stone pulled his planet-tablet from his bag and scanned it in haste. His eyes shot up. He spun, felt the presence stronger then.

He handspoke to Fenri.

"We need to move," she said. "Follow me! Follow him, I mean. Follow Stone."

Stone ploughed ahead of them at speed. The wind whipped at his face. Heat pulsed through him, starting from his pounding heart and radiating outward, his skin prickling as if fire coursed through his veins. Behind him the others ran. Pau pulled the Healer, one arm grasping the rope, charging forward, his knees driving forward for maximum speed.

Luzon the Maker, light on his feet, jumped skyward like a shrewrabbit. Fenri trudged along behind all of them, carrying extra weight Stone could only feel distantly. She was older than the others, heavy with experience, burdened by her own body.

A single image came to Stone's attention, battling with what he was trying to see. Now he saw her, the Healer, shriveling up in her netbed like a figvi left out in the sun too long. He heard the Knowledger's voice in his head.

She won't die. I can help her.

But Stone wondered how. That didn't matter. His planes of sight converged and that's when he saw it.

A naido.

Stone gasped for breath. Its size alone made him want to burrow underground for protection.

The naido was a giant, the biggest of all three classes. Much slower than the dwarf, and less mobile than the adult, but enormous, godlike in its power. If they found themselves anywhere in its path, they would be sorry.

Fenri saw it too. Pau stopped pulling and turned to look.

Beyond the edge of the Clayhaze, the giant naido twisted in their direction, an otherworldly and unstoppable force that could end them all.

Craeya woke. "What's going on? Why is it so cold and windy?"

She was only cold because of the fever that would kill her. To Stone, the air was scalding.

"This air," Luzon shouted, the furthest ahead. "It's different!"

He was jumping too far ahead.

Stone jumped and let the wind current carry him through the air. He landed hard on his feet and jumped again. A fire burned through him. The strong currents were not a good thing. If any of them made the wrong move, they would be pulled into the storm.

Stone stole a glance back. The giant swirled at a steady pace, its power growing across the hardening plain, a mahogany mass camouflaging the night sky.

The netbed hit a bump that nearly tipped Craeya out of it. "Whoa, watch it!" she shouted.

Stone bounded forward.

Everything after that happened in warp-speed. Stone was so preoccupied sensing paths forward that he missed the danger of his immediate physical plane. The winds pulled Craeya's netbed faster. Fenri caught up to Pau, grabbing the other rope to help him, then she ran for her life. With both of them pulling, they had more control, but the winds grew stronger. Craeya's hair spun in a whirlwind around her head as they flew across the ground, Pau's legs bounding forward, Fenri pounding down with force.

They were much closer to the cliff's edge than Stone had realized. Beyond the veil of darkness in the distance, the Quat Zones loomed.

Stone felt the alarming suddenness of their descent.

Craeya's netbed picked up speed, too much speed.

Pau cursed loudly.

"Pau!" Fenri said, "It's too strong. If we let go, we'll lose her!"

Stone saw it all going wrong. He bounded ahead too late. The netbed collided with a rock jutting from the ground and lurched forward, shooting past Fenri and Pau.

"Fenri, pull back!"

They both did. Pau's rope snapped. He crashed to the ground with force, but Fenri held on. The netbed yanked her forward, and she struggled to keep her legs beneath her.

Stone went to lift Pau from the ground, his knees, face, and elbows scratched and bloody. Air left his lungs in droves, and he gasped. "Where's Luzon?" Pau wiped dirt from his mouth, pained.

Stone looked out, tried to bring in the sight of him. He was nowhere to be found, lost beyond the cloaked abyss ahead. Behind them, the giant picked up speed. Stone faltered, tried to see a path ahead for them. But even that had its limits.

All he could see was the netbed speeding away, Fenri hanging on within an inch of her life, and both her and Craeya at the mercy of godlike winds.

Death is a place like any other. Idling beyond the veil, shifting in polarity from what is real and what is true. Are these bones not real? Is this pain not true? Can you feel that? Feel the heat of death on your skin, for it has come for you too.

- from *Divinations from Beyond the Veil*

15. FENRI THE KNOWLEDGER

With the ocean at least Fenri could time the waves, count from one to the next, feel the pull of the current on her muscles underneath the surface. The wind, the vortex of power Fenri found herself in as she held onto the rope attached to Craeya's netbed, was pulling her along to an end with no return.

These winds will kill us.

Fenri looked down and saw her legs beneath her, but she could not feel them. She held heat in her torso, and she knew she was one mistake away from meeting a painful end.

"Fenri, let go!" Craeya's voice came to Fenri, muted from the wind's roar.

That is not an option. But what plan do you have?

Fenri's feet were a flurry underneath her. A maelstrom of sand and grit pelted her and Craeya from all sides, and yet, somehow the netbed still sped on, pulled by some dark force.

"Fenri, I'm not kidding!" Craeya tried getting up, but the wind was too strong, and she was too weak.

Fenri's brain told her to let go, but her body held on. Her fingers grew numb. There was no separation between her hand and the rope. She couldn't let go. They were melded.

Craeya rose again, her head higher, hands clutching the edge of the netbed. She shook her body the tiniest of degrees. Fenri knew what she was trying to do.

You'll kill yourself, she thought.

Ahead, at the edge of the Quat Zones, the light of Kaleem and Milkali faded to blackness. Fenri could hear the giant naido growing vast in the distance. The bed pulled her faster. She strained to try to hear the others, their screams, but all she heard were the sharp edges of the wind tearing through their world.

I'm going to lose her.

Paralysis gripped Fenri's upper thighs. When her calf locked up, she knew she had lost. "Craeya!" She fell hard.

Fenri only saw black. Thoughts she held onto so tightly inside her mind began to empty. She tasted blood. The ground ripped at her body like ten thousand blades, tearing her open.

"Fenri, let go!" Craeya's shouting was the first thing Fenri heard when she realized her life was still hers. Barely. She was being dragged behind the netbed, slowing them slightly, but still moving at speed. Craeya grabbed the netbed and threw her frail body against the side, once, twice.

Craeya shouted, and she threw all her weight to one side, bumping the netbed off its trajectory in one energized thrust. The netbed bounced. Life drained from Fenri's body as she tumbled, staining the ground a deep burgundy.

The netbed skidded and spun out, throwing Craeya from its hammock. She landed next to it, coughing horribly, sand and dirt falling from her mouth, her hair. She rubbed at her eyes and searched nearby with a frenzied focus.

"Fenri!" Craeya crawled over.

She lay still, one of her arms underneath her.

"Fenri, no, no, no," Craeya said. "Does anything feel broken?"

The word brought Fenri back to the world a fraction. She could no longer hear the wind, only her pain. She didn't see how something wouldn't be broken. Words could not describe the pain, which held an immensity that seemed outside any path to recovery. She couldn't breathe. *What chance do we have?*

Craeya's hands touching Fenri's body was another assault, but Fenri couldn't speak, couldn't move to tell her no. A horrible moan emerged from deep inside her body.

"I know. I'm sorry. I have to turn you onto your back. Oh *ancestors*, Fenri. I can't—"

The rest was a darkened blur. Fenri had experienced pain before. She was always falling or experiencing random paralysis, and had the scars and bruises to prove it, but the all-encompassing pummeling of her body was a new kind of torture.

Fenri gasped for breath endlessly.

"You're in shock. Try to count your breaths. Yes, like that. One, two, inhale, exhale. Just like that."

Bones had broken. Ribs. Something poked at Fenri like shattered glass from inside. Her brain sought understanding, knowledge. She was the one who was supposed to save Craeya, and she was the one who needed saving.

Fenri couldn't see the giant, but she heard it. Craeya had administered something. The air and pain lightened, allowing Fenri to find her breath and voice momentarily.

"Where are the *others*?"

"Save your energy."

"What did you—"

"I gave you some illysium. You need a lot more than that, but it should help. I'm hesitant to give you tilq until we can clean your wounds and find out what the damage is."

Darkness came and went. Pain plunged into Fenri's body in vicious stabs, coursing through her organs and drumming on her bones. She found herself moving on a scratchy bed of twine underneath her.

What?

Craeya had loaded her onto the mangled netbed and was pulling her along. Somehow. Then she was unloading her, and setting her own terrabag on her back. Fenri felt Craeya trying to be tender, but the pain was still unbearable.

"Why is it so quiet?" Fenri asked.

"Don't talk," Craeya said.

"How did you move me?" Perhaps adrenaline stores. So many days on the bed and Craeya seemed ready to engage again.

The infection—

Fenri leaned against Craeya as she half-walked, half-dragged both of them across the hardened qha. Silver gleamed and caught Fenri's eye. A complicated pattern. Cine runes.

"There's a door here," Craeya said, reading the archaic markings. "The Hanil Tunnels."

Of course. We're much further east than we're meant to be. The Tunnels are out of use. Nothing to mine anymore. Still ... we'll be safe inside.

Fenri kept one eye open to a slit to see what Craeya was doing. Her hands flew with dexterity across the door panel. Diggers programmed them. Anyone could open them, but it took time to break down the numbers, the equations to get inside.

Her hands—so sure, so methodical.

Craeya finished the puzzle after a few minutes. Fenri wanted to be surprised but knew she shouldn't be. Healers needed to know cine runes for physical body metrics. The door popped open, releasing a quick gust of stale air, and built-up thioxide. Craeya coughed, readjusted Fenri on her shoulder.

"C'mon. Let's get inside so I can take a closer look at you."

Inside, darkness swallowed them whole. Fenri tried to keep her eyes open to see where they were, but it was useless. A few steps deeper into the tunnels, then a break. Craeya coughed, drew several deep breaths, then moved on again. Fenri staggered. The air was thick with too much thioxide and not enough oxygen. Fenri went to calculate the levels but couldn't.

Her brain demanded her attention in other matters.

Craeya stopped and lowered Fenri to the ground. Behind them the door closed, and the foreign darkness deepened. The constant howl of the wind outside stopped, and new sounds took its place.

Fenri felt her life leaving her. Blood leaked from her body. The cold damp surface beneath her absorbed it. Craeya exhaled, trying to mask her own demise, but Fenri felt both of their pains inside the quiet tomb of the tunnels. Something tapped against the ground. Craeya's terrabag. Fenri hadn't the slightest idea where her own was.

"You stupid bitch," Craeya's voice was hardened and cold.

Moonlight trickled in from a ceiling slat above as clouds cleared overhead. Craeya's jawbone, her already slender structure, Fenri could see, was becoming gaunter.

"You should have let go. Why didn't you let go?"

"My hand was caught in the rope," Fenri said.

"You're a liar. That was dumb. Who taught you that was smart? We aren't supposed to make decisions like that."

"Like what you did with the greffir? That wasn't the smartest idea either."

"Yeah, well it saved our lives, didn't it?" Craeya was rummaging through her terrabag.

"And now you're dying from an infection you don't have the cure for," Fenri said. "We're both dying." The words felt strange on Fenri's tongue but knew they were true. A moment later, bright blue-white light flooded the tunnel. Craeya clicked her flagelight down to a dimmer setting, aquamarine. Craeya continued to navigate her kit in the low light. "I'm not infected ... I'm just not healing that fast."

Fenri gripped her torso and chest, gasping for breath. "AH!"

"What?"

"It's so painful." A moment passed before Fenri could speak again. "You are infected. We used all our antibiotics on you, and you're still not better. Anyone with any knowledge of illness and infections can see that. I should have told the others when I had the chance."

"If I'm so infected, then why aren't I dead yet?"

"Because I helped you. The infection feeds on nutrients. You're only alive because the bacteria had something else to feed on."

"You think I don't know these things?" There was a hint of resentment in Craeya's voice. "You're not the only one that knows things, you know." She paused, looked up from her kit. "What do you mean you helped me?"

Before Fenri could answer, Craeya said, "Food, then. You gave me food. Your food." Craeya made herself busy in her terrabag. "I don't—"

The extra food had saved Craeya, but Fenri's stores were emptier. She didn't even have her terrabag. Her vision blurred.

"Here," Craeya said. "Eat."

Fenri obeyed, taking a tamagon heart into her mouth. The metallic flavor flooded her senses.

Craeya went to work on Fenri while she lay on the ground. She checked every bone, muscle, and organ from head to toe, her hands swift and careful. There was nothing that did not require Craeya's attention. When she pressed against Fenri's ribcage, Fenri started from her half-coma.

"Ow! Not there." Fenri's breath left her. The true damage of what had happened rushed back to her, wrapping her up in a vortex of agony. "Not there."

"You've broken some ribs," Craeya said.

"Well, that's not the worst is it?"

"Open up."

Fenri obeyed, and Craeya gave her another pain-modifier and water.

"There could be internal bleeding. If there is, we need to stop it."

Fenri knew the medicine would take effect soon. Another fog crept closer, and soon she would be blinded by its power. What were they supposed to do in there?

No, Fenri thought, tightening her focus. She had never had much control over her body, but her mind was always her richest, most powerful weapon. On another day, she thought she could rewire her brain to work quicker, to reverse-engineer it. Ignore the pain, fight to come up with solutions. But not that day. The most Fenri could do was keep her eyes open.

Craeya continued to use remedies, oils, and bandages on Fenri's damaged frame. She pulled out her EM, and Fenri could her the dull hum of her skin being regrown as she drifted off to sleep.

Upon waking hours later, Fenri saw the blur of moonblue offset by a pale white. Long, wispy strands of pink hung between the blue. A cold rag licked at Fenri's face, a momentary escape from the internal and external burning. Fenri no longer felt the chill of the ground beneath her. Her body grew hot with fever.

"Where are we?"

"The Hanil Tunnels."

Fenri stared at Craeya, held her gaze. "Your moonblue eye color is rare."

"How are you feeling?" Craeya's face could not hide her exhaustion.

Fenri didn't hear the question. "Rarer than moonblue is agave, and even rarer still, waxe. Have you ever seen waxe?"

"This isn't the time for a lesson. I want to know how you're feeling. The pain-modifiers should be wearing off by now."

Fenri noticed needles in her arms, nearly jerked herself away from them. "How did you—"

"We need to be quick and that means a needle in the vein," Craeya said. "And yes, I've seen waxe before. Healer Polina has them."

The name brought comfort, a person that reminded Fenri of a place. A safe place. She felt warmth in her torso, then cold in her chest.

How will I go to the Electric Ocean again if I die here?

"Moonblue," Craeya said, "is actually the color that first showed us how complicated ocular genes were."

"Moonblue is double recessive. You receive it based on the genes your female and male Progenitors give to you, and it can be traced back to one single ancestor. A mutation that stuck and proliferated."

Craeya grinned. "I agree with everything except for the double recessive part. Eye color is more complicated. New studies have been released."

"Two genes code for eye color." Fenri hesitated. "What studies?"

"The complex eye colorification study. We found new data last cycle. There are actually sixteen genes coding for eye color. It's one of the most complex traits in the human body. You don't have time to read all the studies from all the disciplines every cycle, do you?"

Fenri swallowed a lump in her throat. "No. Not every cycle. What did the study say?" If Craeya was going to counter her beliefs, beliefs she and every other QhaHadurian had held for centuries, she would need to explain herself.

So she did. Fenri listened, watched the way Craeya explained, and noted how different her explanation style was from her own. Whereas Fenri memorized data like her life depended on it, capturing every word and mechanism like snapshots in her brain, Craeya's mind worked in a much different way. Her method was quick, dagger-like, cutting to the heart quicker because she knew exactly where to stab.

Are there areas a Healer knows about that a Knowledger doesn't?

"Anyway, the research is new, but we think the former studies will be countered soon." Craeya dabbed at Fenri's face with a cool cloth. The scent of peppernut oil muted the smell of torn flesh filling Fenri's senses.

"I ... underestimated you," Fenri said, and her words became the master. She found herself out of control. Her thoughts and words spilled out without the usual filters.

"You wouldn't be the first," Craeya said. "And ancestors know, you won't be the last."

There, an ounce of relief. Craeya pulled Fenri's skinsuit up slightly to expose her stomach and began to rub it.

"What are you doing?" Fenri peered down at the circular motions Craeya made with her hands, wondering at the technique.

"Your stomach has knots. There's a ton of energy circulating in this area."

"I'm hungry." But Fenri knew it was more complicated than that.

"Your condition." Craeya looked up, met Fenri's eyes. "It must be tough to live like an Unable."

"Tough is too small a word to encompass such a large thing. Being an Unable is not part of me. It is all of me. And my burden to bear."

"No one should have to bear anything forever," Craeya said. "I could heal it."

Fenri laughed, felt the levity of the pain-modifiers in effect. "It can't be healed. The Masters have tried."

"What have they tried?" In Craeya's eyes, Fenri saw a fire she had seen once before, one that lived in those moonblue pools like a spot of flame on the ocean. The reality of it seemed impossible, but there it burned like magic.

"I ... don't know. I was young," Fenri said. "It's something I've always accepted."

"I don't believe that's really who you are or what you want, Fenri the Knowledger," Craeya said. "I see strength inside you, masked by deeply anxious thoughts. I see a woman who will fight with everything inside her to go to a largely uncharted ocean just to discover something new. A woman who asks questions because she wants something. She doesn't just accept things. No. That woman sees her counterpart, who should probably be left for dead, mere seconds from being swept away by deathly winds and doesn't let go."

Fenri felt a sharp pinch in her chest near her heart. "Craeya," she said. Every logical thought left her head in a flurry. The pinch in her chest grew with a familiar warmth, like she was speaking to a Master who had answers.

"I'm sorry for acting angry toward you sometimes," Craeya said, and Fenri felt another turn happening. Fenri could anticipate what most QhaHadurians would say or do. She knew human behavior, patterns, psychology. Everything was an evolving study inside her brain. Craeya sometimes existed outside of that knowledge.

"My emotions," Craeya continued. "They can be wild. I used tilq at the nation-feast because I thought it would help suppress them. I've used hard tilq before and reacted fine. I think the change of everything was too much for me to handle. I wanted to save you from the greffir, and when I did, it infected me with some parasite. I don't have the cure. I don't know if I'm going to make it. Science would say no. Only base has what I need." Craeya's speech seemed to unwind, become less inhibited. Tears formed in the corner of her eyes.

No, Fenri thought. *We aren't supposed to die in here.*

"We can take you back," Fenri said, and she felt her words were in control again. "We can take both of us back."

"It's too late," Craeya said. "I should have used more logic … like you. You gave me extra food to keep me alive. If I can save you, this won't be a complete waste." Craeya slid back against the tunnel wall, coughed. "Ugh."

"No," Fenri said, feeling a new energy take her. "Craeya, we can … heal you. We need to find the others. They can help us. I've never seen anyone move as fast as Pau. He can—"

"Taking me back ruins everything."

"Not if it saves your life!" Fenri said, and she felt another pinch in her chest, stronger, demanding her attention.

"This is what makes you a good Knowledger," Craeya said. "Your condition. You understand other people's pain because of your own. You don't understand it like that, I think, but that's why. So maybe, your pain hasn't been all bad." Craeya coughed, closed her eyes.

Fenri lost her breath. Moonblue eyes ceased to stare back at her, and in their place, she felt an overwhelming emptiness. All at once, pain seemed insignificant. She pushed through the burning and the prickling and picked herself up off the ground. As she did, she kicked over Craeya's flagelight. The dim light went out, and the environment changed, flushed a warmed, darker hue, bleached by a rosy red light. Above, fingernail-sized lights pulsed on the tunnel ceiling another six feet up.

Fenri took in the sight of them, and her mind opened with new answers.

The Hanil Tunnels, built in Q299 by Diggers and Seekers, housed different types of crystals. Fenri hadn't brushed up on the stalag-life in at least a decade. She dug deeper into her memory stores. The knowledge existed in some compartment. If only the pain-modifiers would stop coursing through her bloodstream. The name came to her.

Hancrystals.

They had a rare molecule inside them that was released once they were crushed.

They can cure Craeya.

Hancrystals were rare but it appeared as though they had grown back in the scarcely visited sanctuary. Another thought crashed into Fenri, slowing her. She kneeled down and watched the crystals' distinct vibrational patterns as her mind raced and catalogued their properties.

She identified their hues and textures, knowing the deepest azure ones held the most healing power. She categorized the crystals into three categories: healing, energy, and null, as she scanned the area, mapping their arrangement, estimating their age, and calculating the optimal way to harvest enough for Craeya.

They were up too high for her to reach them. She looked to Craeya. Climbing on top of one another might help them reach the crystals, but Craeya was without energy. Neither of them was strong enough to hold the other.

"Craeya," Fenri said, lowering to her knees, weakening. She leaned against the wall and stared at the crystals, wondered how they had gotten to the tunnels. She clutched at her torso. Pain tightened around her. She didn't want to go that way. There was still so much to do.

The Electric Ocean. It's only mine if I survive this.

The thought collapsed in on itself.

A loud puff of air exploded from down the tunnel. Fenri turned to see.

Oh ancestors, please.

The door to the tunnel closed with a thud.

"Hello?" came a voice.

Fenri's skin broke out in goosebumps. She knew exactly who the voice belonged to.

In our time as Masters, we educate the tribe to maximize efficiency, impressing upon them patterns of learning so that they are well-equipped for their lives. Nearly all QhaHadurians take to this without exception. There are a few rare ones, however, who do not seem to align with our teaching methods. On standardized tests they do not exhibit any special characteristics. In fact, they seem quite ordinary. These individuals we have found, cannot be reduced to numbers. Their power cannot be described in words. This rare indescribable thing gives them the ability to take a thought in the brain and turn it into something we did not even know was possible.

- from Confessions of the Masters, Volume I

16. LUZON THE MAKER

L uzon stared down the darkened tunnel as low-spectrum magenta light pulsed in the distance. Adrenaline coursed through him with a speed similar to tilq. His chest pounded. The wind outside was behind him, but his ears held the memory of its sound.

Where am I?

Luzon tried to ease his shaking body.

"Hello?" he called again, stepping forward carefully. He had seen the netbed outside the tunnels, bent and broken like a freshly dead arachnid, its legs thrown up into impossible formations. Silence enveloped Luzon in an icy blanket.

They can't be dead, can they?

"Hello?" A voice came back low, desperate.

"Hello?" He sensed the voice's owner and broke into a run. "Fenri!"

"Luzon—"

He ran harder. The orb of light grew. His body was shooting through the tunnel. He saw someone on the ground, but it wasn't Fenri. He knelt down beside her. "Craeya!" He looked up through the haze and saw someone else too. "Fenri!"

"Luzon!" Fenri's eyes were the size of moons, battered, a swollen cobalt blue. "You're alive!" she said.

"So are you!" Luzon's heartbeat thumped faster as he took in the sight of them. "What's happened?"

"She's dying, Luzon," Fenri said. "The greffir infected her."

Luzon hopped to his feet. "Dying?" What do you—"

"There are crystals," Fenri said. She coughed into her hand, clutching her midsection with the other arm. When she removed her hand, Luzon saw blood.

"What's happened to you?"

"It's nothing. I'm fine."

"She is not fine," Craeya said, barely conscious. "She has a better chance of—"

"There are hancrystals, Craeya." Fenri pointed further down the tunnel and told Luzon what he needed to know.

Luzon didn't wait. He ran as though the naido were behind him again, against crosscurrents of wind streaming through the branched pathways. He put on his slip-shades, clicked them to the ultradark setting and saw the outlines of the darkened space, where ceilings, walls, cracks and crevices met.

Craeya's face and moonblue eyes flashed into his mind. Life slipped out of her like crushed limeseed. She curled into herself tighter. A sleep-story danced at the edge of what Luzon could physically see.

There's no time for that right now. Find the crystals.

Clusters of larger crystals began to appear above them, much larger than those in the first tunnel, at least twice the size. The flagelight revealed their specialty, chemical constituents, and quantities. Luzon's intuition and Fenri's explanation told him which ones had the most of what Craeya needed. He'd have to take them and crush them into powder for her.

He gripped the wall with his hands, his callouses a minor defense against the jagged points. His legs burned from his chaotic escape. The muscles in his calves and ankles tightened like rope getting ready to snap. That didn't matter. Digging his foot into a hold, he climbed.

So slick.

His hand slipped off its hold, then his foot. He fell backward but kicked his feet over his head with force, flipping onto his feet.

Too slick.

Luzon rubbed his hands against his thighs to dry them. Time ticked faster. He pulled bamboo shoots from his terrabag and a titanium mold attachment. In half a minute, he held up his finished tool: a bamboo stick with a metal claw at the end. He reached up to the ceiling and began smacking crystals with it to break them loose.

In his mind's eye, he was running again.

The event rushed back to him.

No. Not now.

The alcove. Craeya. The tilq. All of them there. Craeya dancing, falling into his arms. Her eyes. That look. So dire.

No. Not now, he thought, trying to push it from his mind.

He ran harder. Fenri's voice tethered him closer.

"Luzon, hurry!"

He knelt beside Craeya moments later and pulled a mortar and pestle from his bag.

"I thought only Healers carried those," Fenri said.

Luzon pulled out the crystals he had collected and began grinding down into his array. The crystals broke into chips.

"Who do you think makes the tilq?" Luzon said.

"Luzon?" Craeya wheezed. "When did you get here?"

"Save your energy," Fenri said. "Please, Craeya." Turning her gaze to Luzon, she asked, "Will it work?"

"It either will, or it won't. Bodies are resilient. They want to stay alive. They do anything they can to stay alive."

"Some bodies," Fenri said.

Luzon turned and took a good look at her. Caked in blood, covered in dirt and pebbles, beaten down she was a mess, but still she was not broken.

She's an Unable. Her body doesn't work the same as yours, or Craeya's ... but that doesn't always mean the hardware is faulty.

"Your issues center around food. Nutrients," Luzon said. "It's a problem of distribution. Isn't that right?"

Fenri's seablue eyes flickered in the light, and something moved behind them. Luzon felt the intensity of her look, like she was trying to see into him. Luzon looked further, saw into her the way he saw the crystals, their chemical makeup, the inner workings of her *machine,* churning in time.

"Your body is remarkable," Luzon said. "Knowledgers have incredible brains. The amount of information you can hold in there is unfathomable. I wish I had a fraction of that power."

Fenri closed her eyes as though that was difficult information to process, then opened them. "Well, look at you. Look at what you can do." She was staring at Luzon's hands. "All of us Knowledgers are the same, but Makers make very different things. You are not like the other Makers I have known. If you can craft a submership, then clearly you hold information I can't even begin to grasp." Fenri coughed flecks of dark red into her hand that smelled of iron. "For you, it's not about knowledge. It's about application. I probably couldn't even make the lower part of that netbed."

"Our skills are different. That's why we're put on the same dispatch team. To bring out the other's best qualities. I wish I was better at remembering things." Luzon shrugged.

No point in wanting things you don't have.

And then, just like that, he was seeing it again. What he had seen at the nation-feast. Craeya's face. Beside him, she turned as white as the hancrystals. That dying Craeya, the Craeya in the alcove, the other face, they all converged into one pink-white swirl in Luzon's inner mind.

The other face. Who was she?

Luzon found himself sitting outside a safety pod. The head of a woman lay in his lap, limp, eyes shut, lashes fluttering. Her entire body burned with fever.

What is that?

"Bring out the best qualities ..." Fenri said, considering.

Luzon tried to snap himself back to the present moment. He took the white powder between two fingers, rolled it into a compact ball with the heels of his palm.

And some things are better left not remembering, Luzon thought. Still, he wanted to know where the thing came from.

"Is it done?" There was desperation in Fenri's question.

Luzon held up the pill. "Yes." He opened his cylinder of water, nudged Craeya awake.

"Craeya," he said. "Hold on, okay?" He opened her mouth and gave it to her.

"Oh ancestors, Luzon," Fenri said. "Thank you."

"Don't thank me yet," he said, watching Craeya with growing weariness. "Now we wait to see if it works."

As if that was all the blessing Fenri needed, she leaned back against the wall, and shut her eyes. Luzon did the same, and it wasn't long before exhaustion overtook him too.

When Luzon blinked his eyes awake, he sensed a sleep-story beyond the veil of his sleep, dancing at the edge of his memory, taunting and elongating with dark, smoky tendrils. *What did I see?*

Craeya slept nearby, chest rising and falling with the beat of her heart. Fenri's seablue eyes swam into view, tide low and serene.

"Do you ever have sleep-stories?" Luzon asked her.

With effort, Fenri moved her mouth to talk. "I believe I have. All QhaHadurians have them at some point."

"Yes, but do you ever remember them? Do you ever remember what you see?"

"Of course not. Who can remember them?"

"I can. Sometimes."

Fenri's opened the slits of her eyes wider. "What do you mean?"

"I mean—"

Luzon wanted to tell all. He didn't understand his brain half the time. She might though, since Knowledgers knew theories and psychologies from all their reading and researching. Fenri might know about the actual mechanisms of sleep-stories, how they worked. She might be able to tell him why he could remember some of his. Why he had some in waking life too. Something flashed, first strangely distant, then dangerously close. He remembered the words of the Teller. *I wouldn't tell anyone about your sleep-stories until you know where they lead.*

Luzon needed to know everything about them. He ignored the Teller's warning and bared himself to Fenri's knowledge, leaving out Jesimene's final warning.

Fenri took in his words with a newfound hunger. "Sleep-stories are the stories your mind creates while you sleep. Imagined realities. The visual cortex grows hyperactive, and our brain shows us images we may have thought about without remembering when or how."

Luzon watched Fenri light up, how she delivered information like that of a Master. Concise. Articulate. Enlightening. Luzon sensed that they were only scratching the surface of all the things she knew.

"But that's just it. I *do* remember them. And now I hear that that's a rare thing. That we used to be able to do that more, and now we can't. Why not?"

"We can't remember all of them. Our brains only have a limited amount of space to hold information. Memories. Tilq helps mask them, making room for other items. Sleep-stories are insignificant thoughts that don't help us. Our brains evolved to produce less norepinephrine in the cerebral cortex over centuries when our ancestors first came to this planet. When survival was much more difficult than it is now, if you can even imagine that."

Luzon remembered the Teller's words about the flying ship. About the ancestors escaping from their dying home planet, only to land on QhaHadur by accident. There were still so many things he didn't know.

What was my sleep-story this time?

Fenri shut her eyes, wincing in pain. Luzon said, "Can I help you in any way?"

Fenri opened her eyes and stared at Craeya. "I hope it works. I think that … some of my ribs are broken."

"That sounds painful. I could wrap your midsection to brace it."

Fenri gave the smallest of nods. "It hurts to move."

"Do you need another pain-modifier? Craeya has some, doesn't she?"

"There is one way you could help me," Fenri said.

"Anything."

"The submership." Fenri pushed her gaze into Luzon again, a wave crashing to shore. "You should ask the Masters if you can build it."

"Sure, okay. But that's a long way away."

"I know, but—" Fenri's gaze softened. "You have to, Luzon. If you have the ability, you should make it happen. You said yourself, our best qualities are brought out for each other. I had never thought about it that way. Thank you for sharing that perspective." He was seeing a delicate side to her. Not just knowledge or information, but a specific drive, a willingness to go beyond what she was told to do.

"I'll ask them," Luzon said, and his thoughts crashed into others. "If you know the equations and calculations of something going under the water, how to deal with pressure, then can you do the same thing for the skies?"

"The skies? You mean like a flying ship?"

"Yes. If you want a submership, then I want a flying ship."

The corners of Fenri's mouth lifted. "In theory I could. I haven't studied flight patterns of avians in depth, but we could copy the behavior and build something small to start." Her smile grew. "These dispatch decisions are not random. Maybe this is why the Masters put us together. Maybe they wanted us to create—" Fenri stopped midsentence, shut her mouth like a trap.

"What is it?"

"I'm a little out of sorts. I don't know what made me say that last part."

She's afraid of those thoughts, Luzon thought.

She was still paralyzed by what she had said.

"It's okay," Luzon assured her. The thought of building a flying ship, and having someone who knew how to make one with him, made his heart beat faster.

Winds rocked the tunnel ceiling like blades striking down. Pebbles spritzed off the qha in anticipation. Luzon stared up.

It's not going to hold.

Craeya forced her eyes open. "What's that sound?"

"The storm," Fenri said.

Luzon crawled to Craeya's healing kit, found the pain-modifiers and gave them to both Craeya and Fenri. They were strong QhaHadurians in their own ways. Craeya, full of passion and energy, powerful and deliberate with her instincts. Fenri, highly intelligent and determined, dedicated to knowledge and a planet she wanted to develop and explore further.

Pau wasn't impressed with the team, Luzon knew, but he also knew those were the situations that surprised him most. He could build a tiny chip to go inside a map-projector that would give it capabilities well beyond its size.

And that was him too.

He was thinner, more compact than some QhaHadurians, but his mind, all the things he could do, couldn't be measured in the way that Masters or Guardians measured things.

The wind slammed into the tunnel from all sides. At the

beginning of it, the door to the tunnels trembled. Luzon clicked the flagelight to a brighter, aquamarine setting and stood up.

"Stone and Pau," he said. "They're still out there."

"I hope you're not thinking about going outside," Fenri said. "Not with the way the winds are now."

"But—"

There was the grinding sound of stone as the door to the tunnel opened. Wind rushed through the tunnel. Luzon heard nothing but the roar of the giant, hungry for life. He rooted his feet to the tunnel floor.

"My terrabag!" came a voice, heavy with anger.

"Who's there?" Craeya wanted to know.

Pau charged down the tunnel, Stone behind him. They were *alive*. Luzon had run ahead of the winds, carried on currents by sheer luck, being in the right place at the right time. When he saw the giant spiraling for him at a pace he could not outrun, he was lucky to see the tunnel in time.

"How did you—"

The upper half of Pau's skinsuit had been ripped from his body, and his chest heaved with raw power. Every organ, muscle, and vein expanded like a balloon. Thin red lashes lined his face.

Stone didn't look much better with his hair and beard puffed out and all over the place. He stood fixed in his spot next to Pau, eyes searching Fenri and Craeya, then resting on Pau, watching him with wild fascination.

"What about your terrabag? It's right on your back," Luzon said.

Pau ripped it off his back like it was a microbial leech and threw it on the ground. "This one is Fenri's!"

Fenri eyed it but did not move. "I thought I lost it."

Stone handspoke to Fenri hurriedly, and she translated.

"His terrabag ... his skinsuit, skinned from his body like a tamagon. The winds wish to be paid a price."

"What price?" Luzon asked. "How did you survive?"

"I don't know," Pau said. "Stone ... grabbed me. Somehow,

he grabbed me." Pau looked around the tunnel, trying to regain his composure.

Luzon knew that if anyone could survive a god-killing storm, it was his Charge Leader.

"My terrabag is *gone*." The anger returned.

Fenri said, "We can find it once the storm dies."

"It had everything!"

"You still have your Guardian belt," Fenri observed. "Your gauntlets."

"You don't understand," Pau said. "Most of our food stores were in *my* bag. Our baracca was in there."

"We can find more food," Fenri said, trailing off. Perhaps even she didn't believe that was true.

Luzon's stomach turned inside itself. He had been on cycles where food became scarce to the point of nearly starving. Just thinking the word brought him terror.

Then it happened, much too fast for Luzon to understand.

The ceiling ripped open. Smaller rocks on the tunnel floor exploded around them in a maelstrom. Luzon's ears blew out from the wind's roar.

The giant.

No one moved fast enough to secure her. Craeya rose like a leaf, sucked skyward through the tunnel's newest opening. The naido made its next move.

"Get down!" Pau shouted among the confusion. He grabbed the stretch-rope from his belt and snapped it into the air toward Craeya, wrapping it around her ankle. His arm jerked in response. Luzon rushed over and grabbed Pau around the waist. "I've got you!"

The scene was strange—Craeya above, battered by winds, pulled tight, her body stretching out and away, only half conscious. Luzon saw it then. Only the outer edge of the giant sucked her away. The power of the gods lived in its breath. If it cycled back toward them, they wouldn't be able to do anything against it. Even from where he stood, Luzon knew he could be sucked away at any moment. They needed to recover Craeya.

"Pull!" Pau said.

Stone grabbed the last bit of the stretch-rope and pulled. The winds grew stronger. Luzon felt himself and Pau being pulled away too.

It'll be a waste for any of us to go this way. We cannot lose Craeya!

Luzon dug his heels into the ground, yanking the stretch-rope to his core. The chain of rescue slid further down the tunnel.

"Pau! Hold the rope with everything you've got!" Luzon said.

Maybe insanity made him do it. Maybe seeing Craeya up there like that made him throw away his caution. Luzon was small and wiry. He needed to be the one to do it. He climbed through the opening, up the rope. Shards of stone and dirt greeted him. Parts of him tore open. His lips, his cheeks. Damage every second.

That's nothing compared to what might happen.

In his inner eye, he saw it. The lifting and dropping. Falling onto the ground, breaking open like a peppernut.

No. Just climb higher!

"Luzon!" Craeya called.

I cannot lose any of them!

And then, it happened as swiftly as it came. The naido drifted away. Luzon fell, sucked down by the jaws of gravity. He stuck his feet out to catch on the ledge. Craeya was released. She fell into Luzon's outstretched arms, quickly sticking out her own feet to help her landing.

"Are you alright?" Luzon clutched her breathless frame.

"Luzon, what's going on up there?" Fenri asked.

Luzon peered down into the dark tunnel. The cosmic light of the moons threw an ivory blanket onto the cliffs below. Luzon had never seen the Quat Zones, a land of jagged teeth. He wasn't ready to see them.

"Let's go," Craeya said. She half-fell, half-lowered herself through the hole first. Pau caught her from below.

When Luzon tried to move himself, the wind pushed back.

"Pau! Take the rope and pull me back!" Luzon's voice caught in the back of his throat. His eyes were open, but they spun in his head so fast, he only saw black. When he closed his eyes, light clashed against itself like the smacking of blades. He didn't know if anyone heard him. Death became very real in those half-seconds.

If the winds pick me up, that's the end.

"Luzon!" Through the opening, Fenri shouted, her eyes the only light Luzon could see. "Make yourself flat! Get down!"

Luzon obeyed and tried to flatten himself to the ground, but it was too late. The naido was one move ahead. He was lifted easily. Too easily. The sensation terrified him. The rope snapped. Luzon lost control. Dark storms grew around them. He saw nothing but black.

So this is how a Maker meets his end.

The cliffs appeared in front of him abruptly. The winds whipped him around like a stray vine. He was thrown into a vast starry sky he could not see. The giant had gone for Craeya, and then it had him. Apparently, he was not the prize it truly wanted.

The wind lost its grip, and the world went silent.

Luzon fell.

PART TWO
TOUCHED

Going on dispatch missions is only the beginning. As teams reach their destinations, food grows scarce and water depletes. Our star torments us with its heat. Prolonged exposure to team members also carries the risk of opening the fourth portal. Sometimes, survival muddles our minds. The object of our desire and the motivation behind it can cause confusion. When food becomes scarce, we must use things that keep our hunger down and our portals centered: tilq, smokesticks, anything to keep foreign thoughts away. There is no negotiation in this regard. We cannot be late or lazy. Once those feelings hit, they hit. We have been touched. Only doom follows.

- from *Lessons on Survival* by the Masters

THE ENERGIES WE NEVER FELT

QhaHadur, The Quat Zones, Quadrant VII

We never realize another's true worth until they are gone forever.

- from *Diaries of the Ancestors*

17. FENRI THE KNOWLEDGER

201 DAYS BEFORE THE NEW CYCLE

In the valley below the Clayhaze, where the depths of the Quat Zones became their new reality, the team was beginning to accept that Luzon was gone. They had taken a month to scale the monstrous and jagged cliffsides down into their new hellfire.

Cold nipped at Fenri's fingers and toes on the first morning they arrived in Quadrant VII. She was relieved to be in a valley, to not have to travel on cliffsides and precipices in degrees, cortisol spiking every time she moved her duneboot out of line a fraction.

The Quat Zones were a paradox: a sensory overload that somehow felt utterly devoid of life. As Fenri peered across the sprawling wasteland before her, a warning to turn back prickled at her brain.

"Which way do we start looking?" Craeya's eyes were bright with the hope of a new star, back in her body after Luzon's successful hancrystal cure. She was starting to gain some weight back.

Fenri conjured an image of Luzon in her head, his own wild eyes, the wind ripping him from existence. She told herself that savior order put Craeya above Luzon, and that they would be fine without him. She told herself that Pau would deal with Craeya's question, but he said nothing, only looked out into the crimson expanse of their new landscape with tired eyes. Stone's spare skinsuit top barely covered all of him, seeing as he was several inches taller, and much wider in the shoulders than Stone, but without Pau's terrabag, or Luzon and his terrabag, it was the closest fit.

When Pau turned, Fenri could tell that he was suppressing anger. "Next time she gets infected, you tell me right away."

"This again?" Craeya said.

Fenri sensed a fight coming on and thought about what she would say to diffuse it, but no words came out. After a moment she realized that Pau was scolding her, not Craeya.

"This *finally*," Pau said. "I wanted to wait until we got down to talk about it."

"Why keep us waiting?" Craeya asked.

"It's not funny, Craeya," Pau said. "None of this is funny. You were weakened and vulnerable and you compromised our team's safety. And now Luzon is—"

"All right," Fenri said. "It was stupid and selfish," she admitted.

"Selfish isn't even half of it," Pau said. "Clean it up, you two. Teams have died for fewer and less serious mistakes than the ones you've made."

"Why are we assuming he's dead anyway?" Craeya asked.

Fenri glanced at Stone, who sat nearby, searching his face for a reaction. He seemed to always be waiting for something.

"We look for my terrabag," Pau said. "That has food, and the baracca, and a ton of other stuff that will help us right now."

Fenri touched her stomach. Hunger nagged, its weightlessness somehow stone-heavy, enough to make her knees buckle. They had all broken fast on the trek down, and they would need to be prepared for the next feeding.

"Like your gill," Fenri added. "That would help us." Fenri didn't mention that Pau's terrabag was probably buried under meters of sand and that they would never find it, because there was always a chance they would. Guardians were expert trackers, after all.

"Yes," Pau said. "We need to accept that Luzon is gone and move forward—"

"No. I can't accept that," Craeya said. "We should at least find his body."

"The fall would have killed him," Fenri said. "There's no question about that. What point is there in wasting our energy and resources to find his body?"

Fire sparked behind Craeya's eyes. "You just want to look for Klonden so you can have your stupid submership."

How did she know about that? Fenri told herself to keep her thoughts to herself. "Klonden is the whole reason we're down here right now. It is *the* objective of our mission."

That same fire in Craeya's eyes burned in Fenri's stomach.

"Yes, and how do you expect to get any Klonden without any food? How are we supposed to get it out of the ground without any tools, without a Maker to make them?" Craeya paused, looked at each of them in turn. "Do any of you know how to get Klonden out of the ground?"

"The Masters gave us tools for that purpose." *But they're with Luzon.*

Craeya knew that and called Fenri on it.

Fenri tried to summon words from the well of her throat, but it was empty. Her thoughts turned inward, and her mind went into hyperspeed. She didn't want that, but she couldn't stop it.

Looking for Luzon had its pros: he had tools, his ability to make things they needed would come in handy in the Quat Zones, and he was useful in other ways. He was quick, agile, spry. There were cons: looking for him moved them in a direction away from Klonden, both spatially and with respect to time. The longer they looked for him, the more tired, hungry, thirsty, and weak they became. If they retrieved the Klonden and went back to base, they might be able to avoid some of the pain in between.

Fenri felt the weight of the pros in one hand, the cons in the other, and yet she could not sense which was greater. *Who am I kidding? He's dead.*

Her chance to speak, to put her own stake in the ground

slipped away with every new breeze. Paralysis gripped her midsection. She tried to breathe.

What's happening? Say something!

She couldn't. Her mind worked too fast, her body too slow.

It's just a voice. You don't need to use your body to use it!

But apparently that wasn't true either. All the blood and energy coursing through Fenri flowed to her midsection where her condition lived.

It's a problem of distribution, Luzon had said.

A jolt of pain shot through Fenri's chest down into her stomach.

Why now?

Vicious hunger ripped through her. She set her terrabag down, opened it.

Now you move.

There had been internal bleeding, Craeya had found, but no puncturing, and no permanent damage to any of the organs, just bruising. The minimal internal bleeding that Fenri suffered felt like an endless onslaught, but it was mostly healed. Her ribs were mending too. Still, they were sore to the touch, and Fenri had lost her range of motion. She could lift her arms up about ninety degrees but no more.

Fenri dug for food. She still had … tamagon hearts? No, she had given all of them away to Craeya when she thought she would die.

Why couldn't she have died instead?

The thought arrived then fled, quick as a kohbra strike. Fenri pushed it from her mind, but still it felt as though she had been poisoned.

Why are you thinking like this?

Stone lowered to a squat in front of Fenri. His massive beard covered his entire face, overgrown like a tumbling bramble. Fenri looked away, unable to stomach its gruesomeness. He handspoke to pull her back.

You're upset.

I'm hungry, she spoke back, with a quick flick of the wrist that she thought might come off as rude. She didn't care. *Honey-Q is good, but my body craves protein.*

Stone always knew. He had a way of reading things that weren't visible. Naidos, emotions, motivations. *How deep can he look?* The sight of Planeteers was infamous, but Stone had some deeper level of awareness. Fenri was finally in the presence of one, and yet she didn't care. Not then.

Cranky.

Irritable.

Uncertain.

That is what she became when she went too long without food. She stared at Stone. *Looking for Luzon is a bad idea,* she said. *And Craeya's going to get her way, as always.*

This is about something else, is it not?

Fenri caught her thoughts around the midsection, pulled them in with one quick thrust. Around Stone, she sometimes felt as though her thoughts weren't entirely hers. Like they were shared. If she could read voice inflections and body language, Stone could read other things.

Fenri shut her bag and stood.

It's about the safety and wellbeing of our team, she told him. *If Luzon were alive, wouldn't he be waiting for us down here?*

After almost forty-five days? Flecks of amber sparked in the grey ore of Stone's eyes. *You know our planet does not work that way. There are too many factors. Too many unknowns. We find bodies all the time. Beasts do not typically take the whole thing. He could be seeking other shelter. Water. Food. The beasts could have snuffed him out.*

Fenri scanned the long, jagged rock line behind them, the wall of darkness still untouched by Zhao's morning light. She examined its formation, the plateaus and the crags, expanding as its own life form for hectomiles.

Luzon could be somewhere in them. And then, a thought brushed against her, soft as the breeze around her. *Have you seen him?* she asked Stone. *Do you know what happened to him?* She hadn't considered that, with his sight, Stone could see that outcome too.

Stone breathed deeply through his nose, as though trying to summon the answer. *I do not know. But Craeya makes some good points.*

Fenri turned on her heel. Heat came up from her legs through her loins into her stomach. She was angry. She *hated* being angry. Her palms were sweaty and she couldn't see for a moment. Sight returned to her as a flash of light. There was an emotion inside her that she could not name or control.

Pau's gaze was on Fenri when he said, "Fine. We keep Klonden in our minds. Fenri, let us know where the fields are with your map. We move for it, but Luzon is the priority right now until we find out what happened to him."

"Seriously?" Fenri found her voice. She glared at Craeya.

That manipulator. Everyone always gives Craeya what she wants!

Fenri pulled out her map-projector in haste and clicked it on. No one ever considered what Fenri wanted. Luzon's face swam into view, and then all she could see was his dark, hairless hands, the backs veined and hardy, the palms a lighter, puffy cinnamon color. They appeared huge in her mind, but Fenri knew the image was altered.

She thought of the submership, of Luzon, lost. He was the Maker Fenri needed. What other Maker could do what Fenri wanted? She didn't know. Would she have to search the rest of her life for someone like him? Would she even be able to? The thought of finding and asking other Makers, or Masters, for what she wanted suddenly seemed insurmountable.

Fenri's throat tightened. *Why do I feel like this? Why can't I control it? Slow down, Fenri.* She focused on the neon green dots on her screen, noticing congregations of Klonden fields thicker to the East.

Pau was looking over her shoulder. "How does it work?"

"The map-projector responds to satellite crawlers that have pulled data and are now compiling it. Their receptors communicate with each other, sending coordinates. This is all the data we have right now, but there could be more."

"There's a cluster here we could go to," Pau said, pointing. He turned and looked out along the cliff face stretching into the sky back toward base. "It will keep us out of the open desert for now, and we'll have shelter around these reefs and rock formations. Practice caution. Where there is shelter, there are also beasts."

Fenri grabbed her visor and sveil. She set the visor on her forehead and snapped the lacy-thin sveil into place so the climacloth hung in front of her face.

Stone held out his visor and sveil to Pau and nodded.

"This is yours," Pau said, looking down.

Stone shook his head and extended it further. He motioned to his thick beard and full head of hair and nodded. A smile cracked behind the thicket.

"We'll take turns," Pau said, putting it on.

Craeya looked at the map-projector, then Fenri, her eyes softening in a smile. Fenri didn't return the look. She put away her map-projector.

Stone held out a closed hand. Instinctively, Fenri held hers underneath. He opened it and dropped something semi-hard and dry into hers.

She looked up, then jammed the tamagon heart into her mouth without a second thought. She chewed, tasted the tiniest spot of blood at its center.

If you want food, all you need to do is ask for it, Stone handspoke.

Fenri chewed, savored, swallowed. She could feel the nutrients rushing through her body, giving her energy. *I haven't seen you eat anything since we met you.*

It is not a problem for me.

I wish that were true for me.

Even the heat had a smell. The scent of smoke filled Fenri's nostrils, stinging her cerebellum. Sharp lines of cracked qha, onyx and violet in color, split the russet land into a fractured tattoo.

This place carries a quiet kind of doom, she thought.

Zhao climbed higher, reaching toward the Quatzi Range from where they had come, spilling its brilliant golden light onto the land, its blinding sheen sharp like battle lances.

Fenri situated her slip-shades on her face and clicked them to the ultralight setting. Sweat pooled in her skinsuit. She had already changed into her spare shortly after losing Luzon, the first one in her bag covered in blood and dirt, annihilated in so many places from her deadly fall. They had no Maker with them to patch the holes.

If it is not death here, it is over there, Fenri thought.

First, a greffir, obliteration of a different kind. A secret infection. Deadly winds and a giant to end them all. A Maker dead or lost. They were problems of the past, drifting into the present, but they weren't the biggest or greatest. No, for some reason there was something else tugging at the back of Fenri's mind. A question she had heard that needed answering.

Stone's handspeak appeared in a flurry in Fenri's memory and became sound in her brain.

This is about something else, is it not?

No, it wasn't about anything else. It was about fulfilling the mission no matter the consequences. If the submership was no longer a possibility, Fenri could still visit the Electric Ocean and conduct her research. She only needed to return with Klonden.

But her focus faltered.

Craeya's voice, an echo of their previous conversation, halted Fenri's thought process.

What if it's open for some people? What if I opened the fourth portal inside me?

Pau the Guardian, Charge Leader of Project El never gave us any trouble. He performed his duties, played well with others in the ways that Guardians can play well with each other, and he, above all others, realized what it took to keep QhaHadur alive and in status quo. He took his role as a Guardian seriously, and his responsibility as a QhaHadurian even more so. We never suspected he would do anything wrong. He never showed any signs. All of his secret questions remained in his head.

- from *Reflections on Our Changed World* by the New Masters

18. PAU THE GUARDIAN

In the depths of the Quat Zones, Pau found that Kaleem's vast and silver light grew stronger. Above and beyond the Quatzi Range where they had come from, sister moon Milkali felt weaker, a touch colder. Pau glanced down at his slipwatch and counted out the ticks of moonlight remaining. Tomorrow, on their third day in the Quat Zones, Zhao would arrive the same way it always did, proud in its nakedness. Soon they would have warmth again.

Pau stole a glance behind him and took in the faces of his team. Mentally, he checked in with each of them.

Fenri dragged one of her boots as though maimed.

Craeya moved as silent as wind, hanging behind all of them like a delayed draft. Pau found himself, despite his normal processes, wondering at her quietness and thought maybe she was storing energy for when they would need to leave the rock line. He wondered if her thoughts rested on finding Luzon.

I'll need to keep a closer eye on all of them.

Next to Pau, Stone's presence loomed. Words were not the Planeteer's strength. Pau and Stone did not communicate directly, and that thought suddenly struck Pau as odd.

How can someone go through their entire life without a voice?

Pau pictured such a life. He wouldn't be able to perform his Guardian duties if he couldn't tell people what to do. Sand collected at the corner of Pau's lips, and he brushed it away. He swallowed, touched the scratchiness he felt at his neck.

What a burden it would be to lose a sense. It would be harder for me to get what I want.

"Can we rest?" Fenri asked.

"Soon."

"We need to be conscious of the altitude," Fenri said. "It's changed drastically in a short amount of time. I don't want to get sick."

"She's right," Craeya said. "We should go slow at first."

Pau drew a sharp breath, checking his lung capacity. *Has the air pressure changed?* Something down there did feel different, but he couldn't place what because there were so many things on his mind. "We can stop here," he said.

Stone pressed the open palm of his hand against his chest, nodding in agreement.

"Why would we get sick?" Pau said.

Fenri sat onto the qha, folding her legs underneath her. She let out a heavy breath. "Our bodies are accustomed to a higher altitude at base and the surrounding quadrants. They'll need time to adjust. Be careful if you start to feel dizzy, light-headed, or nauseous."

Craeya said, "Not enough oxygen in our blood means higher blood pressure, which can throw us out of equilibrium. We need to stabilize."

In both directions the rock line stretched, casting pointed edges and oblong moonlit shapes onto the ground below. Pockets of shadow grew inward and deep, an endless desert mosaic. Pau inhaled to take in new scents. The recent and sparse everblue fall of rain. New plant growth. Cactusii. Roquee. In the recesses of his inner ear, he heard the skittering of tamagon feet and escaping insectoids.

Fenri had her map projector out and was engrossed in the neon green dots appearing on the screen one by one. "Another two and a half hectomiles until we reach the first Klonden field." She pored over it, her voice wavering with exhaustion. "North and east of here."

"We still have nothing to get it out of the ground," Craeya said.

"I have these," Pau said, pulling one of his grappling claws from his belt. "They're not perfect for digging, but the titanium is sharp and durable. It's the best we've got."

"Once we leave the rock line," Fenri said, "all we have is Stone's baracca for protection."

"We can fit two inside," Pau said. "Two to keep watch. On rotation."

Fenri opened her mouth to protest. Her eyes grazed over Pau, and she seemed to think better of it. They both knew it would be difficult to move that way, but words would not make it any better.

"I'm going to go look for food," Pau said. "And water."

Fenri's gaze was steady. "Thank the ancestors."

Pau scanned his teammates, suddenly feeling the absence of Luzon more than ever. Even though he was always in his head, that scrawny Maker was surprisingly useful.

Pau said, "We need to find a good rock reef. There's been rainfall. Recently." Speaking of the rain felt like an ounce of power, one he could finally use to his advantage.

I need one of them to back me up.

Fenri's eyes were bright with new knowledge, but her body slumped like ragweed, devoid of energy. *No, I don't think so.*

The pink of Craeya's hair glowing bright in the moonlight pulled Pau's gaze to her. He did not notice any trace of injury or infection on her. Like she had never been touched or attacked at all. *Useful, but potentially risky.*

Pau took in the sight of Stone, his tanned weathered skin, grey beard and head of spiky hair like its own rock reef ecosystem.

Pau did not want to know what was living inside. All of it made Stone seem taller and stouter than he actually was. His arms and legs were thicker than Luzon's wiry limbs, but slenderer than Fenri's, like sturdy, matured figvi branches. Stone stood five feet ten inches tall; only Craeya was shorter than him.

Just then Pau saw a flash of something, the snapping of rope.

That monstrous wind-god had ripped Pau's terrabag and the top of his skinsuit from his body. He'd felt its raw power tearing a hole in reality, then a lightning-quick snatch of his ankle and the splitting that followed. Pau couldn't remember what was real and what wasn't. He felt he was only alive because of Stone.

I hadn't remembered that until now.

"Stone, you come with me."

"What?" Fenri asked. "Why can't you take Craeya?"

"Because I—" Pau stopped, suddenly unable to use words to express himself. The reasons confused him. Stone had his own power. There was safety in his presence.

"I want Craeya here with you," Pau said. "In case anything happens."

"And if something does happen," Craeya said. "What am I supposed to do?"

Gouge the beast's eyes out like you did last time.

Pau handed Craeya his other grappling claw. "Use this."

Craeya took the claw, studied it, the metal heavy in her small pink hands.

"The button here shoots a spring," Pau said, showing her the underside of the claw. "It's good for putting holes in things. Save it for our attackers."

Craeya looked up, and Pau saw that same thirst for blood he had seen with the greffir. "You've been holding out on us."

"Just be smart."

"Where are you going?" Fenri asked.

"To look for food."

"I know. I mean, *where?*"

Pau knew Fenri wanted a very specific answer. Coordinates or some area that she could confirm with her map-projector. "I don't know exactly, but we won't go more than two hectomiles out."

To his surprise, Fenri said nothing. She sat down underneath the rock line and made herself busy in her logbook.

The late-night grey of the sky melted to an early morning auburn by the time Pau and Stone reached their first rock reef, which was twice Pau's height and as wide and deep as any training alcove back at base. Mineral-vines tangled themselves around the rocky structure thick as moonchoke. Impossibly strange combinations of stacked stones, funneled formations, and tunnels within tunnels created a labyrinth of darkness so deep sunlight seemed to never touch it.

"None of the rock reefs I've seen are like this," Pau said.

The colors struck him suddenly: purples, and oranges, and reds, and yellows, and mutations of color so far from what he knew he didn't have names for them. Blue and green and grey were the closest he could get. They morphed into new shades the same way the sun changed the color of light on the ocean.

Stone turned, half facing the reef, half facing Pau as the early morning sun bathed him in golden light. His gaze shifted to the reef, and he stepped toward it. The brambles towered over him like a shadowed beast. He went to put his hands on a rock.

"Wait," Pau said, and Stone stopped himself. "We need to—"

Actually, Pau wasn't sure what they needed to do. His nose prickled with new scents. New dangers. He knew about creatures and beasts. How to hunt and kill the former and avoid and fend off the latter. He didn't have any idea about plants and minerals from rocks. At least no more than the basics. Rock reefs outside of the Quat Zones were more barren. Scavengers and Seekers were regularly dispatched to harvest them. With his current team, the hunters, the ones responsible for finding and acquiring food were him and Fenri.

Of course. Now I need her.

Stone lowered himself to his hands and knees and peered into the darkened, winding thicket. He inhaled sharply.

"What are you—" But Pau realized asking was pointless.

I've never spoken to a mute before. How am I supposed to understand him?

Stone had a piercing gaze, a look like he knew something. He crawled forward, coiling underneath the teeth of a particularly hideous rock, a mass of jet black and midnight blue, sick with fungus. Stone shot his hand into the reef lightning quick. When he pulled it out, he held a squirming tamagon in his hand.

Stone opened his hand partially, and the tamagon nearly wriggled free.

"It's huge!" Pau said, unable to hide his surprise. The creature wriggled with unusual ferocity, smelling its own fear as death.

Stone used his other hand and went to snap the neck but stopped himself. From his terrabag, he withdrew a cincher, jammed the tamagon inside instead, and cinched it shut. He took another great breath, locked eyes with Pau, moved his hands in a circular motion then around himself to imitate a bigger version of himself.

Pau watched and waited. *Oh, I see.*

Fenri had said there was more oxygen down there. Pau knew that too, he just thought about it differently. *I need to be quicker. I need to know how and why my environment has changed and what that will mean.*

That was Pau and Fenri's crossover. Taking new information and putting it together to make sense of a new situation. That's why Stone had imitated a larger version.

The oxygen made things bigger.

He joined Stone in the hunt. Pau was an excellent hunter, but somehow after a half hour of searching the reef, he had only found two tamagons, while Stone had tripled that number, as though he had some other sense Pau didn't.

They dripped with sweat. Pau crouched into a dark opening and listened for the tiniest sounds.

Scampering of webbed feet.

Tongues lapping up insects.

Cold bellies sliding across sun-veiled floors.

Somewhere on the other side of the reef, Stone moved, slow and careful.

Are Planeteers trained to be this way? He makes almost no noise ever. Silent as the sun.

The oppressive heat spun Pau's head with exhaustion. If there was life there, and creatures bigger than he had ever seen, there had to be water there too.

Hunger punched through his train of thought. He snatched up a wandering tamagon, snapped its neck, and escaped from the reef labyrinth, huffing. He sat down and began to skin the tamagon with his durablade. He looked up and around the reef, trying to locate Stone. Nothing. Pau cleared his throat. He went to call for Stone but felt a sudden cut.

"Ah alphacka!" Pau cursed, looked down at his hand, his thumb dripping blood. He put it to his mouth, sucked hungrily.

Stone emerged, his head tilted in question.

Pau inhaled deeply, tasting the sweet, warm blood. Stone's image blurred against the sun.

Pay attention to what you're doing. You could have sliced your finger off.

Once the tamagon was skinned, Pau carved a line down the creature's midsection and opened its chest. He ripped out the heart and jammed it into his mouth. He couldn't wait. Maybe Stone could, but he couldn't. *It's my turn for a meal. And water.* The juicy heart flooded his tonguebuds with much-needed iron and niacin. He sipped water from his cylinder and with a gesture to Stone said, "We need more."

Stone nodded. He disappeared back into the thicket.

Pau blinked and saw Craeya and Fenri in a single moment of non-light, sitting underneath the rock line. Several greffirs hovered at the perimeter, waiting. What ever happened to the one Craeya supposedly killed? Did it go back to its tribe and convince them to destroy the humans? Pau wiped sweat from his eyes with his too-short sleeve. The heat birthed strange thoughts. They shifted to Luzon. Was he really gone? Pau had lost all scent of him. There were so many new smells down there. So hot. The heat smelled different. Smoky. Peppered.

From somewhere inside the rock reef, Stone whistled.

Pau walked toward the sound. After circling, he located Stone, his eyes bright with focused intensity. Stone sliced into a tiny cactusii with his durablade and held his cylinder underneath to collect its water. He drank.

Words from Master Qi came to Pau from a place he did not understand.

Watch out for Craeya. She doesn't adhere to our laws in the usual way.

An image came without warning: Craeya gripping the arrow, jamming it into the greffir's eye.

"DIE!" she had said.

So much wild passion. He remembered Craeya's tears, her breakdown just after leaving the nation-feast and wondered if she had used tilq to mask something. Fenri was always on Pau's mind because of what she needed and how he had to protect her, but maybe his focus had been misplaced. Something tugged on Pau's chest, pulling his thoughts deeper. Another image spilled out in his mind.

He saw a woman in a dark room with a mattress on the ground, her voice low, sugary-sweet. Controlled, but in a different way than Fenri. She wanted something from Pau. The room darkened. Not just any room. A dark room. *The* Dark Room. *I've never been to the Dark Room. Why am I seeing this?*

The woman emerged from the darkness, her raven hair cloaking the bone-white skin of her face.

"That was enjoyable. Could we do it again?"

Pau grew hot all over.

Blood rushed to his member.

Stone cut deeper into the cactusii. He withdrew a peach-colored rhizome and emerged from the reef.

Grunting, he held out his hand to Pau.

Two juicy bulbs sat in Stone's palm like radiating suns. Pau took one and sniffed it, inhaling its sugar-sweet fumes as he pushed the fruit into his mouth. Sweet heaven flooded his tonguebuds, a sweetness so intense it became tart and sour in Pau's mouth, but he chewed without hurry, enjoying the meaty texture. The endless juices poured into his body. "How? What is it?"

Stone's face crinkled into a smile as he devoured the other one. Their eyes met. Behind Stone's unkempt head of hair and beard, Pau saw a glimmer of himself. A deeper, darker version. What Pau could become in twenty more cycles. A human that said nothing but made others listen to his quiet, wordless whispers. Secrets of the planet hidden within the Planeteer, who was part of their lands but acted independently, a free-roaming agent, expanded in Pau's mind.

Pau was a body meant to protect, but something was pushing on his mind, making it swell. His need to protect shifted, became a sudden curiosity. Pau wanted to know how Planeteers were trained. He wanted to know what Stone looked like underneath his hair, what his face looked like, how old he was. He wanted to know what Stone looked like underneath his skinsu—

Pau swallowed the fruit still lodged in his throat and turned away from Stone's piercing gaze.

What are you doing? Heat made Pau's knees weaken. He lost his focus. The sloshing and chewing of juices grew louder in his ear. New scents arrived. Dry and honeyed and musky like the first few hours after rainfall. Pau sniffed, wanting to inhale more.

Their eyes met again.

Stone swallowed his fruit, turned sharply, and went back into the reef.

"Stone?"

The heat momentarily confused Pau. For some reason, Fenri was all he could think about. Somehow, she steered his thoughts. In the back of his mind, her voice clattered with knowledge he did not ask for.

She would say something about pheromones activating because of the fruit. Stress levels falling. Becoming more relaxed. That's why the smell had intensified. In it, Pau sensed a tinge of his own scent. A sliver of similar muskiness. Many men had it, Pau knew from his sense training.

Am I smelling his scent, or is it just my own?

Stone emerged again, hands sticky with cactusii juices.

Two more fruit bulbs. Pau went to grab another one, but Stone pulled his hand away. He motioned, drawing a line with his chin beyond Pau.

"For Craeya and Fenri?"

Stone nodded.

"Are there more?"

Stone shook his head. He opened his cylinder, pushed the fruit bulbs inside, and licked the remaining juices from his hand. The sugary nectar coated his mouth. He wiped the rest from his hand on the leg of his skinsuit. Sticking his tongue out, he crinkled his eyes as if to say, *sticky.*

Stone handspoke to Pau.

Pau tightened. His chest grew warm. *Does he think I'm Fenri? That I suddenly learned how to talk with my hands?*

Pau had no idea what Stone was saying, but the language of his body wasn't so difficult to read. He used pointing and finger formations, quick loops and slower cuppings. Pau dripped with sweat. From his cylinder, he took a swig of the newly collected cactusii water. Fenri came to mind and Pau held questions in his head that tried to escape.

Stone walked in the direction of the others and Pau followed, his head swimming with the juices he had just taken in. A surge of energy rushed through him, but the delirium lingered. Another voice came to him.

Please, find me again.

Pau tried to repress the memory that was surfacing.

I'm Jade the Knowledger. I'm staying behind to do research this cycle.

The woman from the Dark Room.

Why did she give me her name? And why do I remember it?

The heat was playing tricks on his mind. He was seeing something that made no sense to him. But then his own anger returned.

No, we weren't supposed to speak.

Silence had its own volume.

Pau's heart thumped like a shrewrabbit moments before slaughter. Thoughts and tiny memories poured into his brain, drops at a time. The absence of sound brought wonder and curiosity, things Pau had always easily ignored. He badly wanted to communicate with Stone. For once, he wanted to talk.

From somewhere else, another thought came. Pau had never heard the voice before, but the sound was clear.

We will, it said.

Pau increased his pace. He passed Stone, passed scents he thought of as his own, lengthening his strides, putting distance between him and the rock reef, between himself and Stone.

He didn't want the voices. Not the voices in his head. For once, he wanted to talk out loud. He wanted answers.

He knew exactly who had the ones he wanted.

The dangerous matter of the love virus (as it was called by early QhaHadurians), later to be integrated into a comprehensive system known as the fourth portal, is that it carries an element of contagion. A QhaHadurian life is precious, but anyone breaking the love law must be put to death to protect the rest of the tribe. The virus reacts to other portals nearby, activating them if there is even the tiniest of cracks. We did not survive such an unforgiving place by leaving cracks unattended. One infection could undo everything we've worked for. As always, we destroy our enemies before they destroy us.

- from *Lessons on Survival* by the Masters

19. CRAEYA THE HEALER

"Why are you being so quiet?" Craeya peered down at Fenri from where she stood, facing the rock line, an endless wall of jagged qha stretching left and right as far as the eye could see.

Fenri scrawled in her logbook. "I'm logging an entry." She did not look up. Her voice was stilted, heavy with heat and the pain of cracked ribs.

"Why?"

"Because if I don't, who will?"

"I can," Craeya said.

Fenri continued to write, the slash of her leadpen rhythmic, almost machine-like.

"Oh, come on, just take a break. You've been writing for hours."

"A few more minutes."

Fenri pulled her words closer to herself, and Craeya felt their cold distance. Perhaps everything was chillier underneath the shade of the rock line.

Craeya stepped out of the shadows into the bright sunlight. Zhao warmed her skin with its invisible glare, and she began to sweat. *Is it significantly hotter down here or am I imagining it?* Everyone had said so.

Craeya pulled the sleeves of her skinsuit up to her elbows, examined her arms. The greffir. The damage it caused had disappeared. The infection, the blistering sun making everything worse, her bloodied skin—all gone. The cure that had coursed through her body, gone. Eradicated and excreted through her pores and urine.

Luzon was gone.

"It's so *hot*."

"We're in a valley," Fenri said. "The heat is trapped and has nowhere to go. I'm sure it wishes it had somewhere to go." She closed her logbook, stood up and stepped into the sunlight too. Her map-projector hung at her side in the belt Luzon had made her.

"You should get some water," Craeya said. "We're losing water."

Fenri said nothing. She typed into her map-projector.

"What are you doing?" Craeya waited for an answer. Sweat covered her. Her armpits, her thighs, even the bottoms of her feet gushed moisture. Combing her hair away from her face with tired fingers, she retied it behind her head. Still, she waited. Fenri was finding new ways to ignore her. Craeya felt something building in her chest, weighing her down. Her feet moved her away before her mind told her what was happening.

"What are you doing?" Fenri said.

"Going to explore."

"No. Pau told us to stay here."

"Did he?" The weight lightened the further Craeya walked away.

"Craeya, stop."

She didn't. She walked faster. Fenri's footsteps sounded behind her, clunky and dense against the qha.

"I said I just need to log a few things."

"You're being hurtful. You're not just logging stuff. There's intent to what you're doing. You're mad at me, and I don't know why."

"Would you just stop?"

Craeya spun. "What? What do you want?"

"I want you to stop walking away from me."

"Oh, now you want my attention? Funny how that works. Doesn't feel good to be ignored, does it Fenri?"

Fenri's seablue eyes dampened, dull under the day's light. "I ... guess not."

"No, it doesn't. And I don't understand why you're being so cold to me."

"It's not you." Fenri nibbled on her lower lip.

"Liar. I can read you like that stupid map-projector. Just *tell* me. I'm not here to play games. If there's something you want to say to me, say it!"

Fenri seemed to be processing. That *was* out of her element. She had no books or training alcoves to fall into. "This is all so new, I guess."

"What is? The Quat Zones? Us fighting?" Craeya paused, feeling an intense warmth wash over her skin. "Not having Luzon?"

Fenri tightened at the mention of their fallen comrade.

"You're a Knowledger with all the knowledge in the world. Express yourself!"

Fenri shut her eyes, winced. "Craeya, I—"

All breath had left Craeya's body. Fenri and the rock line behind her became one whirling image. She steadied herself. The heat was invading every one of her cells.

"Not all things need to be expressed. Some things are better left unsaid."

"That stupid fourth portal stuff again."

"It is not stupid," Fenri said, her voice edged, a blade against Craeya's. They both fell silent.

Craeya found herself thinking many thoughts at once. Her body shook in a state of rage or confusion or passion. Craeya didn't know the word for it. She had never talked to anyone like that before. All at once, she wanted to punch Fenri in the neck and also clutch her in an embrace. All of her thoughts and anger spilled out, and when Fenri felt their wave, her face fell, saddened, ashamed.

Craeya closed the gap between them. "Let's sit down. You need water." Without waiting for an answer, Craeya led them back to the rock line. Her breath was hot and sticky and dry, and her tongue stuck to the roof of her mouth every time she tried to talk. She led Fenri to the shade and sat her down.

"You okay?" Craeya took out her cylinder and held it over Fenri's mouth for a drink. Fenri opened instinctually. A few drops came out and fell onto the desert of her tongue. She sucked them down and wiped the sweat from her brow. "My goodness."

"Finish what you were saying," Craeya said. "Why are some things dangerous to express?"

Fenri leaned back against a rock, holding Craeya's gaze. After a moment she said, "Do you know why our society works?"

"Because we are one."

"And do you know why we are one?"

"Because we follow our laws without question."

"Yes, exactly. All of the Masters have done this before. They've spent their entire lives performing dispatch missions. We bring them back resources and food, and in return they keep us safe, telling us where to go and what to do."

"We keep ourselves safe, or we don't. Luzon is gone. How is that anything the Masters did?"

"If you knew about all the societies that have come before us on different planets, you would see that our society works precisely because of this." Fenri fell into a trance of explanation. "If we just do whatever we want, one by one it all falls apart."

"But it's only what the Masters want," Craeya said. "What

about what we want? You want a submership because you think you can explore deeper, but the decision to make that happen is owned by the Masters."

"If that is their wish, then they have a good reason for it."

"No. I can't accept that. Your wishes may never be met. You and Luzon could change the landscape with your minds. Luzon and I—there's something I think we can invent too that will help all of us. But we need approval, and—"

"What thing?" Fenri's face twisted like a thorn, the strangling of vines fighting for oxygen. "What do you and Luzon want to invent?"

"It's a repair technique," Craeya said. "During training I saw so many people with dismembered limbs or faulty body parts. We can transplant organs for people who need them, but what about actual bones? Knees and hips that are failing or no longer work for people?"

Fenri narrowed her eyes at Craeya. "Matching bones to people is impossible. It can't be done."

"We wouldn't take bones from other people. We'd make our own. Luzon knows how."

"Make your own?" The realization washed over Fenri's face, dark and cold.

"Yes. Out of metal and other pliables."

Fenri fell silent. "Well … Luzon is gone. And if he's not, he's going to ask the Masters if he can have a half-cycle to build the submership."

Craeya went to speak but bit her tongue. Fenri's gaze intensified. Craeya knew how badly Fenri wanted the submership. Not even Healer Polina had the ambition Fenri did. The Electric Ocean and what lived inside was Fenri's future, her current world.

Craeya said, "Of course. That's why we need to find Luzon."

Fenri's face contorted, like her words were about to tumble out, but she held them. Finally, she said, "I don't like it either, okay? I've never met a Maker like Luzon. And I doubt I'll meet anyone like him again."

From behind Craeya, a throaty avian species made its presence known. Craeya swiveled and saw them above: three hideous birds, circling, hungry.

Fenri said, "Craeya, get underneath the rock line."

Craeya stepped out and looked straight up at the creatures half her size, their bodies striped black and grey, splotched with feathers. She grabbed the grappling claw Pau had given her from her terrabag and felt its weight in her hand, heavy as an empty terrabag. She held it high. "They have meat don't they? We could use the food."

"Don't be foolish. Do not invoke their anger," Fenri said. "And they're called pawkwi."

The pawkwi disappeared from sight, behind the rock line above. Craeya clutched the grappling claw tighter. If she could take down a two-headed beast three times her size, she could take down some scrawny birds.

An obscured image crystallized in Craeya's mind for the smallest moment, then blurred again: a boy in a tunnel with his back to Craeya, putting on a skinsuit.

Get out of your head.

On her fingertips, his oil, an overwhelming scent of gingitleaf.

"Stop."

"What?" Fenri turned.

Craeya emptied the memory, shoved it far from her mind.

"Are you okay? You don't need to shout." Fenri's eyes were bright with alarm.

"I keep seeing something."

"Seeing what?

Dark and smooth skin with a caramel glint when he stood in a certain light. His mahogany hair falling down his neck in waves. She didn't want to see his face, so she pushed his memory from her mind and changed the subject.

"I'm not sure exactly," she said. "What did the Masters tell you about your condition?"

Fenri sighed. "I know you think you have miraculous healing hands, but being Unable is not something you can heal."

"What did they try?" Craeya asked again.

"Steroids, mainly."

"That's all?"

"Other concoctions too," Fenri said. "It's autoimmune. My body attacks itself, so steroids help in suppressing my immune system."

"I know how autoimmune diseases work."

"Well, do you know how Unables work? Because I do."

"In theory, yes," Craeya said, recalling the lessons about the rare condition. "There are other autoimmune diseases that we've had great success in treating. Are you taking drugs now?"

"No. After years of treatments, the Masters finally gave up. Now, it either lies dormant or flares up depending on how stressed I am."

"I think I can help you. I want to help you."

"I told you," Fenri said, huffing with distaste, as though her words were an extra stressor. "It *can't* be healed."

"What if the Masters are wrong? They think you're an Unable, and that it's an autoimmune disease, but what if the diagnosis is wrong?"

"Don't be ridiculous."

"I know you think it impossible for the Masters to be wrong. Bless them. But we still don't have the imaging technology to look as deep as we need to."

And Craeya's mind drifted to yet another thing that Luzon would be useful for.

"Being an Unable is still largely misunderstood and underrepresented in our population. There's no reason the Masters couldn't be wrong."

Fenri closed her logbook and raised her chin to peer at Craeya. Craeya had seen Fenri's eyes before, but the edges were pointed, sharpened by intrigue.

"What are you suggesting?" Fenri asked.

"Create imaging strong enough to see what your cells are really doing. Yes, our machines are good, and we have decent answers, but I think our bodies are generally uncharted oceans." Craeya looked at Fenri's thighs, her chafed, pink knees through her torn skinsuit. She looked her age. Craeya didn't know how long Unables lived typically.

"Uncharted oceans. If by that you mean we are both dangers to society, then you'd be right."

"It's not all bad, you know," Craeya said, as she imagined ways she would test her theory. "There are very good reasons for keeping Unables alive."

Fenri's face softened, the red of her cheeks pink. Her curious eyes remained unblinking. She seemed to be holding a breath.

"Think about it. It's not a genetic condition, so it can't be passed down."

"What are you saying?"

"Childbirth."

"What?"

"You're a Bearer too, Fenri."

Fenri stared at Craeya and swallowed hard, her face as hard as granite. "What did you say?"

Craeya watched her and sensed an unraveling of the denial, her own chest opening and lifting.

Fenri touched her stomach as her heartbeat visibly quickened. "I don't—I haven't."

Her fear was *there*, the terrifying look at truth they both felt in words.

"Fenri. Are there any parts of your life that seem completely dark and empty?"

"Of course not. I remember everything about my life."

"That's because that part of your life has been erased. By tilq and other pain-modifiers. All women who give birth experience a kind of induced amnesia. We can't keep those memories because of … well, you know the laws. Familial love and all that. You said so yourself. Our society wouldn't work without it."

Craeya saw how mere words tore open Fenri's universe of knowledge. Fenri's hands trembled against her thighs. Craeya thought Fenri might want to stand, open her lungs, give herself space to breathe. Her breaths came heavier. Craeya gripped Fenri's hand, and she didn't pull away. Fenri shut her eyes and squeezed her sweaty fingers around Craeya's like vines.

It's wrong. Something about this is wrong. But who will listen? To everyone else, Craeya would sound crazy.

Fenri cried. At first, Craeya didn't realize what the sounds were, but when she looked over, she saw Fenri shaking, her face covered in dirt and tears. Craeya squeezed her hand tighter. Fenri squeezed back, sobbing audibly.

"Fenri—"

Above, Craeya saw the pawkwi circling again from the corner of her eye.

"What if our world is a better place with the fourth portal opened again?"

Again, Craeya saw the boy. Now they were somewhere else. A training alcove. Craeya stood alone. She cried about something. She didn't know what.

"It's not better," Fenri said, her tears slowing, her sobs becoming more silent. "It's not, Craeya."

"How do you know?"

"Because I do. Nothing would be better," Fenri said. "The beasts can smell it. There is no place for it."

Zhao vanished behind the rock line as Craeya wrapped her arms around a quivering Fenri. After a moment of resistance, Fenri leaned into her without the usual questions.

The cold sweat iced Craeya's skin underneath her skinsuit, but after a moment she felt a touch of warmth as their interlocked hands brought their bodies protection from the oncoming winds.

In order to eliminate any possibility of familial love or attachment during childbirth, newborns are separated from their Bearers at birth. The Fourth Trimester is non-existent. The Bearer will not see her child, and the child will grow up the same way we all do, as a product of the hive. After giving birth, the Bearer goes through an intensive recovery program. She heals and is allowed rest and remembers nothing of the pregnancy.

- from *Lessons on Survival* by the Masters

20. FENRI THE KNOWLEDGER

Time crawled by in the weeks following Craeya's revelation. Fenri couldn't stop the questions from coming. Like proliferating amoeba, they multiplied and folded in on themselves. Each question tasted bitter in Fenri's mouth, but still she could not voice them.

The group moved slowly, sure to check everywhere for signs of Luzon, his terrabag, or his corpse. Thoughts came to Fenri in quick strikes, from no normal thought pattern she could discern.

Knowledge is power. This is power that is owed to you.

Is it wrong that I need Luzon to be alive for things I want?

Stone could easily manage out in the field, but she questioned Luzon's chances.

The group had rested under the rock line on and off for the past seven days, going out and sometimes coming back with food, some drops of water or plant moisture but mostly more fatigue and unanswered questions.

Under the light of Kaleem, Fenri tried to focus on what lay beyond. Her cold and gentle breaths punctuated the rough, twilit silence. She waited with Pau outside the baracca while Stone and Craeya rested inside. In two hours, Zhao would be up and they would need to move again.

Pau crouched down and looked out, his breathing shallow. Fenri knew the effects of sleep deprivation, of Guardian training. Now she was grateful for it. She leaned against the rock at her back, sat, then pulled out her logbook to write.

SUBJECT: *Quat Zones*

Resources

Q387*42*6 — Twenty-one days have passed since we lost Luzon the Maker. Six days ago, Craeya relayed to me her thoughts about Unables and why Masters keep them alive. It is just her opinion. It doesn't make it true, nor does her supposition about me being a Bearer make her theory true.

I know about the childbirth programs, but I never once thought that I would have been used in them. As an Unable, I've been spared and have always wondered why. Could this be the reason?

The thought had always plagued Fenri, as present to her as the condition itself. She always imagined it was because of her big brain, the way her mind worked, but maybe it was actually because of her physicality.

Above, the sister moons faded into the blanched egg-white of morning. For so long, QhaHadurians knew of only one moon. Kaleem had appeared only in the past 100 years.

The irony. You spend your entire life thinking you're one thing, only to find out you're something completely different.

Unable.

Bearer.

Knowledger.

What other knowledge has been hidden from me?

Younglings. Fenri thought with a sudden intensity. She imagined a female on the delivery table, legs spread wide, Masters and Healers masked and at the ready. Only images in books and concise descriptions told Fenri what to see. The baby emerged, pushed out by the Bearer's undying will, screaming, moaning, blood and fluid everywhere, just for that one little life.

That was me too. I was that child.

Zhao spread its heat onto Fenri's body. Suddenly, she became aware of herself. *I was that child-bearer.*

Fenri had considered so many things in excruciating detail, but not that. Was there a reason for it? Her hand drifted to her lower abdomen, where a subtle pulse of energy thrummed beneath the surface. It was a constant reminder of her condition, a wellspring of power that was both a blessing and a curse. She winced in pain, voracious for food, tasting residual metallic blood.

Fight it.

Fenri returned to her logbook and continued her entry.

We need to find more water. The gills aren't collecting enough, not down here where water vapor in the air is minimal. Soon, we will have to leave the safety of the rock line and venture into the unrelenting heat of the Quat Zones with no cover. If we had Luzon, he might be able to make us something. Could he still be out there? Could Luzon somehow be alive?

"You've been quiet," Pau said. He had turned and was facing Fenri. Sunlight carved chiseled lines into his face. Fine hair lay like patchgrass on his cheeks, reaching up the sides of his face, gathering in a soft bed atop his head. "You're never this quiet."

"Sometimes I can be." Fenri's instinct was deflection, but Pau's voice pressed into her like the sun.

"When Stone and I returned from that first rock reef trip, you were … *shaken.* Now you won't even talk to Stone. You're different."

You would be different too if your entire world was a lie.

Pau spoke in a hushed whisper. "What happened? What did Craeya do?"

She did so much. But Fenri pushed back against that constant thought. *I don't want to talk about this. With Stone maybe, or later, more with Craeya, but not with Pau the Guardian.* Fenri felt the sudden need to protect her thoughts, the things that had happened to her. Her womb had already been touched and reached into. How many times, she had no idea. Fenri turned her legs away from Pau.

"She didn't do anything. We were just talking."

Pau rose from his crouched position and towered over Fenri. "Is it about Luzon?"

"What?" The air grew cold. "No. Luzon is likely dead."

"I think you want him to be alive."

"Well, who wouldn't? He's our team member."

"You look at him differently." Pau stripped a band from his wrist and began rewrapping it. His eyes flicked up to Fenri, and she felt their pull, swift and strong like the undertow. The Guardian, so precise with his senses: sounds, scents, sights— had he seen something in Fenri she wasn't even aware of herself?

"He was a remarkable Maker. Perhaps I peered too far into the future with him. I thought he was the key to moving our planet forward."

"Him and you together, right?"

"If the Masters allowed it."

"You and Craeya *both* wanted him for the future. Seems impossible if everyone goes off in different directions after this."

Fenri's heartbeat quickened, surging with blood at Pau's words. "What do you mean *both*?"

"The Project Proposal."

"Pau, what are you talking about? There is no Project Proposal."

"According to Craeya there is. She said the Masters would approve one project, and she was talking about doing one with Luzon."

Craeya conveniently left that part out.

Fenri jolted up, her legs burning, building a pyre underneath her frame. She stared at Pau because she had no idea what else to do.

If Craeya knew about the Project Proposal, that means a Master told her. Fenri's heart sank into her stomach. She wanted to forcefully shake Craeya awake and ask her why she hadn't spoken about the Project Proposal. *The Masters didn't tell me, but they told her. And she knows, and she was talking about a project with Luzon. Which means, if Craeya were approved, she and Luzon could have worked together on the artificial bones she mentioned.* The idea was brilliant, but it was not Fenri's submership.

"It doesn't matter though." Pau's voice was a blade in the grey tundra of Fenri's mind, tearing through her carefully planted roots. "You know, if he's dead. Craeya talks a lot. I wouldn't worry about it."

The possible truth of Fenri being a Bearer finally slammed into her. All presented by … some child on her first cycle, who had no sense, who ruined *everything*.

They still had to complete their mission. Craeya had always used action to get what she wanted. That was what Pau was teaching Fenri, and there it was right in front of her.

She snapped open her map-projector. The sky lightened with the flash of the device's neon green dots, and with it, Fenri warmed with the excitement that the power of knowledge again lay in her hands.

"The fields will be out in this direction, toward Quadrant Thirty-Seven, twenty hectomiles out." Fenri pointed, and Pau looked over her shoulder. They had been moving deeper into the Quat Zones, finally away from the rock line and its cover. With only Stone's baracca they were at a loss, but they had to move into the Zones eventually.

Pau showed no reaction. "Then that's where we need to go."

"I don't understand. I thought we were still trying to find Luzon."

"We are, but Klonden takes priority now."

Fenri's belly grew hot. Bile rose in her throat. "Why?"

"Because we're moving into Q3, and we need to get Klonden and return with it. I've seen many things in my cycles, and I hate to say it but I don't think Luzon is alive."

"Craeya won't like that," Fenri said, stealing a glance behind her. In that moment, something left her body and she felt lighter.

You're here for Klonden.

You get Klonden, you get access to the Electric Ocean.

That means coming back alive. So what if Luzon isn't alive to make you a submership? It was a long shot anyway. You don't even know if he could really make what he said. No Luzon means no Project Proposal ... for Craeya too.

Pau said, "I've lost his scent. That usually means the person no longer exists."

Fenri swallowed the saliva in her mouth.

Then why can't I stop thinking about him?

Fenri dove back into the map-projector. She calculated routes, tried to reimagine where rock reefs might be based on other signatures and the limited information she had of the space. Fourteen years ago, a mission had been dispatched down there, and they all perished. They had sent some information back, but even then, their technology was limited. Fenri had the locations of a few safety pods, but she was sure they would be somewhat inaccurate.

"How's your blade-work going?"

Fenri looked up from her screen, saw Pau in a fighting stance. "My blade-work?" She felt for her durablade in the belt Luzon had made her and found it secured inside its pouch.

"Get up," Pau said. "Let's see what you can do."

Fenri stowed her map-projector, a jolt of tightness shooting up her hamstrings as she stood. Zhao's golden light unfurled onto the cracked soil before them, a vast, bright blanket pushing away darkness.

Pau pointed the end of his durablade at Fenri. "Assume your stance."

Fenri did as Pau instructed her before. She led with her dominant foot, bent her knees, held her weight balanced between her two legs.

"Good. Blade-hand up. Wrist strong." Pau closed the distance between them in one quick step.

Fenri stepped back, nearly tripping as she did.

"Don't look down."

"What?"

"You're looking down at your feet. Don't ever look down." Pau closed the gap again in one swoop.

Fenri snapped her gaze up and found Pau's blade at her throat, his long arm outstretched an impossible distance.

"That's what happens when you look down." Pau stepped back, pretended to slice his own neck with his blade, making the sound of tearing flesh with his throat and tongue. "Dead."

Fenri stared, grateful it was just practice.

"You seem distracted," Pau said.

"We're using energy."

"Want to stop?"

"When will I ever need to use this?"

"You came to *me* for training. You think because Luzon's gone you don't need to be physical anymore? You need it now more than ever." Pau went at her again.

Fenri backed away and dodged Pau's swipe. Ducking underneath it, she moved on the offensive.

"Good. Use your opponent's strength and momentum against them."

They parried like that several more times. Beads of sweat formed on Pau's forehead. He breathed in the morning air as though it were the best thing in the world. Fenri gulped at the air, her hands on her knees. "Wait."

Pau's stance softened. He wore a curious gaze. "I want to ask you something."

Fenri paused and pulled in all the data before her, how Pau was standing, his body strong and unbelievably tall, his breaths more staccato. Something was different. Something about the request for knowledge was very new for him.

"Go ahead."

"How are Planeteers trained? I mean, how can Stone see things like that? The naido? What kind of training allows him to see things that we can't?"

A cool breeze picked up and chilled the back of Fenri's neck, her exposed ankles. The landscape brightened as a pulsing of light waves.

"Oh, I see," Fenri said, parsing out data for herself. *Prophetic abilities usually develop in the absence of others. Being a mute probably directed him to Planeteer more than anything else.* "It's something that happens when other senses are muted, so to speak," she said. "There's evidence that other senses become stronger. The Masters probably worked with Stone to accentuate them as much as possible."

Planeteers are remarkable. And Stone is a rare specimen. I wonder if the others can do what he can.

Her brain tried to explain the situation with science, but there was something about it that existed outside that realm. History supported the existence of visions. Other Masters who could see the ways in which the planet would move and bend. Stone was one of them.

"What about someone's scent?"

"Excuse me?"

Pau sheathed his blade, lowering his voice to a whisper as though someone would hear. "What makes someone have a certain scent?"

Fenri put her own blade away.

"I mean, how do the beasts smell us?" Pau said. "They track us based on certain smells we give off, right? Smells we aren't supposed to—" Pau's gaze rested beyond Fenri.

She turned to see Craeya and Stone awake. Craeya was folding up her leshblanket. Stone sat cross-legged, blinking sluggishly, his grey eyes adjusting to the hounding sun.

Fenri turned back around to face Pau. He tightened his stance and the muscles in his face.

What is he getting at? Does he want to know how the beasts can smell us? When we do things we aren't supposed to ... Oh my ancestors, even he is curious about this! Fenri started to speak, but Pau cut her off.

"We can talk about it later. Now the others are awake." His

smile turned flat, and he walked away. "Keep us on track with your map. We're going to need it."

The memory of Luzon drifted away further. Fenri was beginning to forget his face, his olive skin, and harsh, angular jawline. How he laughed, cocking his head to one side like some beast examining its next meal. So thin and wiry. In the end, he was lifted by winds that probably snapped him in two.

Beside Fenri, Stone appeared, discreet as a sandmouse. His beard and hair were a tangle of grey with streaks of white lightning. His scent followed. A whiff of his powerful musk climbed into Fenri's nose without her permission.

Stone, she handspoke to him.

You would smell like me if you were out here for almost two cycles too. He grinned.

They walked together side by side, careful to keep pace with the others.

Two days and six and a half hectomiles later, the group encountered their first salt field.

Ahead of them, the glint of moonlight on the lighter, tawny sand showed an untouched land of yellows and marigolds. Colors morphed under the sun, bleeding from one shade to the next.

Hunger and thirst clutched at Fenri's stomach. No one had eaten for several days, and the water collected from the rock reef ventures hadn't yielded much. Fenri slowed, found her mind a step more sluggish.

"Let's camp here," Pau said, stopping next to Craeya, who collapsed into her bag and mumbled something about how cold it was. "I'm going to secure the perimeter," Pau said, stalking away. "Don't move. Any of you."

Fenri pulled out her map-projector and scanned it. They still had some way to go before they found any Klonden. She handspoke a question to Stone. *Could there be some here?*

Beside her, Stone withdrew his planet-tablet and examined the thin metal device. Fenri had not seen him use it much.

What does that show you? she asked.

I program weather patterns, temperatures, orbits of the moons. Anything new and unusual. Stone paused. *I've seen salt deposits before but nothing like this. I think it suggests—*

Stone typed into his tablet cautiously and walked away a few paces, the crunch of sodium beneath him, looking at the fields from multiple angles. He handspoke to Fenri, *There was once water here. A lot of it.*

Are you saying there was an ocean here once?

Stone nodded.

Are there Planeteer reports about it? Quickly, Fenri typed in everything Stone had relayed to her. Her memory drifted to moments long past, quick glimpses of her lessons, rows of bright-eyed Knowledgers in awe of all the things they were about to learn.

For the first time in a long while, so much of what Fenri wanted seemed in reach. She looked up, rested her gaze on Craeya, and remembered how adept she was at getting the things she wanted. Master Qi was right—she *had* learned things from her Healer.

She would learn even more.

The map-projector pulled Fenri's attention back with a quick tug. The screen flashed a sudden neon green then turned dark grey all at once. She clicked the life button but received no response. She clicked it again, held the pin-drop button down to restart it. Nothing.

"No!" Fenri cried. "I *hate* when this happens."

"What happened?" Craeya was peering up at Fenri.

"It stopped working."

"Maybe it's out of power," Craeya said.

"It runs on solar," Fenri said, turning the thing upside down, searching it for answers.

Just when we were about to make progress. Not now!

"Can you fix it?" Craeya asked.

"If I knew how, I would have tried already."

"I thought Knowledgers knew how to do everything." Craeya said.

"Don't patronize me."

Stone handspoke, *There has been activity down here. Recent activity.*

Fenri replied. *Beasts? What activity?*

"What are you two talking about?" Craeya asked. "Stone found something, didn't he?"

Fenri glanced from Craeya to Stone, her body shaking from the cold.

Stone stood there, unmoving. *Human activity.*

It was fourteen years ago that someone came down here, Fenri said.

I'm not talking about fourteen years ago.

"You're talking about Luzon, aren't you?" Craeya crawled out from the folds of her blanket. "Well, what is it? Dead or alive?" Hope glimmered in her eyes.

Stone handspoke to Fenri. *Do you really think he's dead?*

I don't know. I don't see how he could have survived, do you?

Only Craeya wanted to look for Luzon. You were so eager to help Craeya live, but for some reason you don't want to find Luzon. Why?

Fenri felt Stone's piercing gaze again, how it ripped into her mind, searched every nook and cranny. Suddenly, she felt naked. *I do want him to be alive. It's complicated. I'm confused about what I want.*

Are you? Or are you confused about what finding Luzon will mean?

It won't mean anything. What are you asking me, Stone? But even as she asked it, Fenri hesitated, her hands clumsy, her brain sparking with new ideas, the contrast of everything inside her body causing her face to burn with anxious energy. She knew that death lay on the other side for whomever opened the fourth portal.

Is there something you want to tell me? Stone asked.

Fenri ripped herself away from Stone's gaze. *Dear ancestors! How deep is he able to look?* When she turned away from Stone and Craeya, she saw Pau striding back into view. Fenri read his expression as excitement.

"Come on," he said. "Picking up a scent."

"Luzon?" Craeya lifted her terrabag and put it on her back.

The paralysis in Fenri's legs melted away. She scurried after Pau, while Stone and Craeya kept pace beside him, not wanting to lose the scent. They weaved around the salt fields for another half hectomile until they found the thing Pau had smelled. Fenri saw it, perched at the top of a dune like an untouched diamond. They kicked up sand as they climbed the incline.

Pau sprinted up the dune, lifted the terrabag in his hands, and examined it like it could save his life.

"What's inside?" Craeya asked.

Pau opened it and removed items with care. A cincher of food. A cylinder half-full of liquid. Sand-spirals.

"These ... these are my things." The veins in Pau's temple pulsed. He set down metal instruments, looked at them, unsure. "And these ... These look like—"

"They're Luzon's things too," Fenri said.

"My terrabag," Pau said. "With some of Luzon's things." He lifted the bag high, took an immense whiff of the blood covering it like a second coat.

Again, the twisting of Fenri's insides made her want to vomit, and she was unsure of what to do or say. She caught a glimpse of Craeya's new expression—half excitement, half fear. "What does that mean?" she asked. "Is Luzon alive?"

They turned all at once to look at Fenri.

As if she alone had the answer.

As if she alone would know what to do.

PART THREE
CHANGED

We are not afraid of change, per se. We recognize the advantageous things that come from change, all the things we can learn, the evolutionary paths our bodies take. Unables, for example, exist because of a genetic mutation, a minor shift in our gene pool. Is this variation detrimental for us QhaHadurians, or beneficial? If there is a change, we Masters must study it, analyze every last component of it, and decide whether it is suitable for us or not. Although sometimes change can certainly be beneficial to us, we find this to be the exception. If it is something that puts our society in danger, we must stamp it out, quickly and without deliberation. With great confidence, we believe that whatever new situation arises, whatever changes come, we will be prepared.

- from *Lessons on Survival* by the Masters

THE SKIES WE NEVER KNEW

QhaHadur, The Quat Zones, Quadrant X

To go away and come back is the only thing we QhaHadurians know. Retrieve and return. We go back to where we come from. Though the locations of our dispatch missions change, our skies stay the same. We can always find our way. There is only one place we cannot return from, and that is death. Though we found out even that was not true. The members of Project El defied the odds again. What is dead should lie dead. Later, when we found out what happened, we were not prepared for what was bound to follow.

- from *Reflections on our Changed World* by the New Masters

21. LUZON THE MAKER

115 DAYS BEFORE THE NEW CYCLE

Luzon awoke to the blinding light of Zhao and found a pain so deep his mind could only associate it with death. The pain swam up into his veins, clawing at him like a hungry beast.

I'm alive.

Nothing made sense. He heard the vicious rip of wind in his ears and remembered the naido. The tunnels. The Quat Zones. His heart being ripped from his chest as he fell.

But I'm not dead.

Luzon's hands swam into view. He had put them there, but he couldn't feel how he'd made the movement. His shoulders and arms were so numb that he didn't know if they were still attached to his body. Everything ached.

In the sky, Zhao sat steady and unmoving, its glare bright and scorching. A thin layer of rockpowder covered Luzon. He rubbed away the sand and dirt caked into the corners of his eyes. Blinking them open was an effort. He tried opening them wider.

So bright.

In the brightness, Luzon blinked and fell into the darkness of his mind.

He had fallen fast, so fast, and the planet bent and twisted as if made of warped glass, ripping edges from reality, and yet he was alive. *Did I really fall?* His vision blurred and he saw them, Fenri and her seablue eyes, Craeya and her moonblue. They flashed bright in the space of his mind that was opening.

Are they okay?

A searing pain seized Luzon's body, tore him away with the strength of a beast. He wanted to scream out his agony, but even that hurt. He wanted to roll over, but his body wouldn't let him. He had never known such pain.

I need Craeya. She can heal me.

From nearby something rattled. The echo rang in Luzon's ears. His head spun with questions, but he engaged none of them. Thinking of all the ways he could die would only waste precious energy and distract him from trying to stay alive. He looked at his hands again and saw how mangled they were. The backs of his hands and palms were ripped open like some harvested flower, their insides pink and raw with pain. He turned his hands over and flexed his gnarled fingers, examining them like they were tools, machines that needed repair.

Tears came to his eyes.

Sweet ancestors ... my hands ...

The rattling sound grew louder. His gut twisted, anxious with broken agony. He bent at the waist. At his sides, he saw fabric attached to his skinsuit weighing heavier on his frame. *No, impossible.* He looked closer—it *was* fabric, stitched to the underside of both his arms. The climacloth handwoven into the skinsuit, nearly disintegrated, was torn and full of holes.

I made those.

His memories started to come back.

Luzon turned and saw the monstrous precipice that the naido had tossed him from. Zhao blocked some of his view, but he saw the crags of the landscape like jagged teeth, taunting him to come closer.

Did I fly?

Luzon shook off the thought, knowing that he had seen the same thing in his sleep-stories.

But then ... how did I get here?

There was more to do. More to make. Luzon couldn't do it lying on the ground roasting like limenz seeds. With blood-covered hands he pushed himself up. He pivoted and rolled onto his knees. With great effort, he rose to his feet. New pains greeted him. In his elbow, pain grew, sending piercing sparks through his muscles and bones like needles.

Water. Need water.

A silver point gleamed in the sun. First Luzon thought it was his durablade, then decided it was bigger. His terrabag had traveled to the Quat Zones too, and now it was taunting him. Did it fall just as Luzon did? Did it break his fall? Memories trickled back. Each bounce. A slam. Craning his neck to an angle his body allowed, Luzon looked above him at the cliff face his mind told him he had come from.

His mind could tell lies.

Are they a lie?

He saw them again—Fenri, Craeya, Pau, and Stone—and wondered if they were still up there. The wind had separated them, had tried to separate Luzon's cells forever. He wondered if the others were looking for him.

First, my terrabag.

Luzon stumbled and fell to his knees. He realized one of his eyes would only open halfway. His injuries revealed themselves to him one by one. The blistering pain of the sun nagged every inch of his body. Each time he thought he knew the damage exacted, something else would shout to him, demand his attention. Blood caked around his eye made it difficult to see. He touched it gingerly with his puffy fingers. Once. Twice. Thrice.

That one's gonna hurt.

Still his terrabag laughed at him. *You're a loser,* it said.

I am not.

The terrabag laughed even more.

I'm battered. And I'm wounded.

Luzon stood. Wavered. Steadied himself.

I'm on my feet, and my terrabag is right over there. C'mon, Luzon, you're not dead yet.

Luzon snapped the alu leaf in two and squeezed the thick sap into his bowl. He grabbed another branch from the alu plant and began to break open more of the leaves. With a drop of water from his cylinder, he wet a cloth from his bag, then turned his attention to his hands.

These need some work. He scrubbed the dirt and blood from the open wounds. Some fingers were more bruised and swollen than others. When they were clean, or as clean as he could get them, he dipped his fingers into the bowl of alu juice and began to rub the ointment over his open wounds.

Luzon gnashed his teeth so hard he thought they might shatter.

He continued to apply the ointment. The healing sap of the alu would mix with his blood and skin cells and help regrowth. He had used alu before to bind a plexibow when he'd run out of glue and discovered it was soothing. It was not something Makers used often.

He dabbed his eye, removing the mass of blood as best he could with the damp cloth and rubbed ointment there too. His eye opened a little wider, but still not as wide as his other.

The burning seared into his brain.

Find the others.

Fear brushed against the inside of his bones like wind rushing through a tunnel. He did not have his own baracca. Zhao would fry him.

I need cover. I need water. Choking back his dry spit, Luzon snapped off the final alu leaves from the baby plant and pressed them to a dry pulp. With a hollow leaf, he rubbed its outer shell across his body, coating himself with residual juices to help mask his scent. He put the remaining empty leaves inside a spare cincher for later use.

Zhao slid down lower out of the lightening sky. Luzon didn't know what time it was, but he knew that it would help him to know. Everything would help him. He had never been alone before. Not like that.

Rising from his crouched position, Luzon peered back at the rock line a half hectomile away, maybe more. Under the rock line, he'd be protected against the blistering sun. He could spot the others on the way down, maybe. If they'd survived the naido from up there. If none of them were ripped to their deaths. No one had the same suit expansions he had. No one could fly like he could. Luzon knew the thought of him flying was ridiculous, but he had no other reality to hold onto.

Ahead, a jet black blob that absorbed all remaining light like a vacuum grew larger in Luzon's half-blurred vision.

Beast, his mind told him.

Inside his chest, a rush of fear like wind.

Move.

He tripped over the stub of the remaining alu plant then caught his balance. His legs needed repair too. He stumbled out and away from the rock line, away from the safety he so desperately needed. He didn't know where he would go, but he would deal with that later. He needed to move.

Luzon took a deep breath, sent air through his crippled body, and moved as fast as he could. *Did it see me?* He didn't look back to check.

Luzon pricked his finger and was greeted with an aching stab. Cold sweat poured through him. He realized he'd just had a sleep-story. He'd felt a coldness like no other grip his body. He'd seen Craeya, who hurried him on. *Were they back at the nation-feast?* Fenri was there too, waiting, not moving to save him, and a door closing as Luzon ran with all his might, away from a beast, away from a fatal, encroaching darkness.

That felt so real.

Under the light of Milkali, fresh blood trickled out of his pointer finger, a single particle of pain, and yet nothing compared to the rest of him. Loose fabric hung from his suit near his triceps, the new stitching nearly done. He adjusted his weight on the rock he sat on, turned his hips, and continued the patch job to close the holes that exposed parts of him. He paused a moment and fought the urge to shiver.

The darkness around him deepened, the moons high above hidden in shrouds of cloud. He looked at his hands, searching them for damage. He pushed the final thread through the fabric near his tricep with his needle to close it. The naked cold of the night licked at his exposed skin. There was still so much to stitch shut.

Luzon, run!

Craeya's voice rang in his head, desperate, afraid.

Fenri appeared, silent, thinking.

Luzon jolted to his feet. He spun and searched his periphery. *The sleep-story ... was it some sort of warning? Are they nearby? Was Craeya trying to warn me about a beast? What about Fenri? Would she really not try to save me, even if there were danger for her too?*

Luzon knew he could make it. He just needed to run harder, faster. His legs would work again like they used to. He added a splint to his elbow using bamboo, pressing firmly alongside the bone to keep it in place.

The regrowth of his skin assured him that he would heal. His eye still hurt, but he could see. He avoided looking at his hands. Soon Craeya would heal him. A stabbing pain in his chest made his knees buckle.

He thought of Craeya and her wild, fierce eyes, all the things she could do to help him. He would lie on his back, and she would go to work, her own hands adept and full of resurgence. Fenri swam into view, quiet, waiting, watching, worlds of knowledge spinning in her head like its very own solar system. Luzon could fly, but with Fenri … could they really create a flying ship?

Find them. I have to find them, or I'm going to die.

Luzon lifted his terrabag onto his back with caution. The acute pain of his scars and bruises ignited again. High above, behind the flowing herd of clouds, Milkali swam into view. Luzon stared, mesmerized. Kaleem appeared. His vision blurred. Two moons. Now, there were two. The memory of the tunnels gripped him.

Eyes. Fenri's big, bulbous eyes searching him.

Luzon?

Luzon turned, panic pounding in his heart.

He found his voice, finally. "Who's there?"

Only the wind and the shadow of where he once sat, stitching.

No one there. No one is out here with you.

Luzon sensed the strangeness of his thoughts, the deepening of curiosity and query smashed into one formless shape. The clouds cleared, and he saw both moons again, but he hadn't the slightest idea which one was which.

It is said that long ago our ancestors tortured our home world. They killed and molested and did anything they wanted. They slaughtered animals by the thousands and devoured them. They threw their waste on the ground or in the rivers, destroying the environment without any thought for the future. The stories say that our home world was once a very different place. It suffered in the worst ways possible. But QhaHadur is not a dead, lifeless thing. She knows every footstep, every transgression. Like any human, she responds accordingly. Strike someone repeatedly, and they will not just stand there and take it forever. Eventually they are going to strike back.

- from ***Reflections on our Changed World*** by the New Masters

22. STONE THE PLANETEER

Stone's inner vision showed him Luzon, alive, walking the deserts, looking for something.

No. For someone.

Pain pinched at Stone's chest like cactusii needles.

I have tried to see this before. I must see where it leads.

Until that moment, Stone had never known who the man was. In that moment of sight, Luzon trekked away further, peering over a ledge. A hand appeared, and Luzon took it, lowering himself down into the crag. The image shifted, snapping to darkness as the sky blasted open into a storm of horrifying wind and cold. A bruised magenta mass hovered over the area where Luzon had gone.

This darkness.

Someone was crying. *A child? A beast?* The sounds of clashing metal and the tearing of flesh grew louder. The sound came strong, ripping and pulling at Stone, threatening to throw him out of the vision.

Hold on—you have to see this!

In his vision, another man walked up, an everblue drop of truth and hope. A man Stone did not recognize. A man Stone knew better than life itself. The images blurred, became riddled with static. A terrible screeching erupted, a thousand nightbats flapping, calling in ghastly voices. *Help us. Help us.* The winds converged, exploding at the epicenter and turning the sky into an edgeless nest.

Silence.

A naido appeared, a tiny cyclone, growing and flinging its feet in wide circles, sucking in the world around it, an endless gravity. Stone saw—no, he *felt* himself being sucked in.

It was more than a vision. What he saw was real, and he felt himself changing, being sucked away by the energy. Pulling on his face, his hair, his beard, the energy began to separate cells from one another. The pain was quick and sharp, one that built on top of itself.

I'll die if I stay to see what happens.

Stone's throat opened and sound poured out like half-forged liquid metal. By sheer will, he knocked himself out of his sight.

He sat on the rock again, sweating. Three pairs of eyes stared at him.

"You okay, Stone?" Craeya's energy reached out with warm hands, welcoming Stone back into his suddenly chilled body.

Wiping sweat from his brow and breathing out a heavy puff of air, he gave a quick nod.

They took that as sufficient and continued what they were talking about.

"No one ever told me we were changing plans," Craeya said. "Why are you keeping things from me?"

"Oh, you're one to talk," Fenri said.

"I don't understand why we can't just exhaust our options," Craeya said. "Luzon was right here!"

"We're going to keep looking," Pau said. He wore his spare skinsuit, looking more like the Pau Stone had first met.

Fenri swung her gaze in Pau's direction. "I thought you said Klonden took priority now."

"That was before we found this," Pau said, motioning to his terrabag. "We have to look. We need his digspike. We need to find him if we can."

"We're just wasting more time," Fenri said, but her voice trailed off. Stone knew that she was conflicted about finding Luzon.

Pau waved his hands in front of him. "All right. Enough of this. You said you were tired and needed a rest, but if you have the energy to complain, you have the energy to walk." Pau threw his terrabag over his shoulder and strode away. "Let's go."

"I thought your map-projector broke," Craeya said.

"Don't. Just do what you're going to do," Fenri said.

Luzon's efforts to stay alive did not go unnoticed. He had taken all the food, left some water, done everything just right if they were to find the bag, which they did.

Stone felt new truths coming to him. *I will lose one of them soon.* No one gains truth without first giving one of their own. Stone bared his truth so that he could see more.

You must be careful. Do not involve yourself.

Fear speaks in negatives. I am already involved. They need my help. They need to find Luzon. They need healing. I will not be able to travel with them forever.

There.

Stone saw the truth, a quasar of light in a darkened void. *Am I the one that will be lost soon?*

Beyond the horizon, Zhao, a thin slice of rubyrind growing larger, sent waves of heat in their direction. Elsewhere, Stone felt the tiniest ounce of life. A beast. A rock reef. Another QhaHadurian. He didn't know. He focused on Luzon's energy and opened all his senses to try and locate him.

He tried to slow his breath, fighting to bring air back into his body. Even he struggled against the scorching sun. There were no rock reefs in sight, no water to harvest anywhere that he could sense. The jagged edges of the horizon blurred in his vision and became the curves of sand dunes.

Fenri's voice emerged from the sweat-induced cacophony. He did not look at her, but he could feel her sharp gaze on him. "The gills aren't collecting enough at night," Fenri said.

"Here." Craeya offered Fenri her cylinder. "You need it more than I do."

Fenri slowed and lowered herself to the ground so she could sit. The qha-sand was hot enough to burn bare skin, so Stone put his terrabag down so she could sit on the titanyl casing.

Fenri took the cylinder and drank, and for Stone it felt as though she drank the last of their hope.

"I need to go look for water," Pau said. "We can't go on like this."

"Safety pods," Craeya said. "They'll have gathering pools, right?"

"That's right," Fenri said. "Gill technology on a larger scale— gill harvests."

This place tortures us with its withholding of water from the clouds. Stone stared skyward, saw the sheet of red covering the sky, not a single cloud in sight. *It tortures us with its unending sun.* Stone felt his thoughts turning dark. He pulled away.

Fenri was leaning over, wilting almost. "Plants," she said with some effort. "Plants will hold water."

Pau nodded, his eyes bright and wild. "Stone. Stay with Fenri." He handed him his second grappling claw. Stone took it, weighed the lethal weapon in his hand. *I hope I will not have to use this.*

"You're with me this time," Pau said, turning to Craeya. "We won't be gone more than an hour."

A caring and hopeful look passed between Fenri and Craeya. Deep down, each wanted the other to succeed.

Craeya and Pau walked away, two blurred images: a skinny pink stick, hair white and rose, and a thick bronze figvi tree, broad and sturdy, leading the way. They disappeared into a buttery mirage of sun and death.

Stone knelt beside Fenri. Heat came up through his suit into his knees, but it did not burn yet. He pulled the energy of its reaction into his body, storing it in places that held less heat.

Fenri's seablue eyes disappeared under the heavy curtain of her eyelashes. Her tongue emerged from her parched mouth, a slip of pink.

Stone pulled his baracca from his bag and began to set it up. Zhao would be at its most intense in a few hours, which wouldn't give Pau and Craeya much time before they needed to return. Waves of heat pressed thick hands into Stone's back as he helped move Fenri into the baracca, sensing the lingering pain in her ribs as he laid out her leshblanket underneath her. She sucked in a few breaths and coughed. Stone ducked inside and sat next to her.

Without willing himself to, an inner quiet enveloped Stone, and he fell into a vision.

Alcoves bursting with light lined a darkened tunnel.

A woman emerged from an alcove, her hair thrown into a raven-black flurry around her head. Bleeding from gashes that encircled her forehead, she radiated a great power with every step. She held a swaddled youngling whose cries pierced the air.

Fenri.

Fearless.

Eyes of death, wanting.

She had done things she had never done before. New knowledge spun around her as a forcefield. Stone stepped forward to touch her but was blocked by some other force. A man emerged from the alcove. Lights flickered like a million nightbugs. The man looked both ways, his eyes resting on Stone's face. Looking through him. Stone knew those eyes. Different but the same. He had never seen them before. He had seen them ten thousand times. The man turned, his entire body covered in a suit and scarf save his eyes.

Fenri swung her gaze in Stone's direction. Her nostrils flared. Stone sensed something different there.

There.

The face of Fenri, the energy of Craeya, a dual desire to absorb Stone. A sudden fear knocked away his curiosity, his deep sight.

Can I die in this place?

The face morphed and changed. The dark raven hair became pink-blonde. The world convulsed, and a malignant star pulsed into existence. Then, with a sickening lurch, reality inverted. Both Fenri and Craeya, their images superimposed, blending, grating against each other, making an alarming endless sound, became one thing, one churning cascade of light and sound and vibration.

A sound exploded in Stone's ears, and he was ripped from his vision.

He sat in the baracca, gasping for air.

Fenri stared at him with wide eyes. Silence stretched before them.

I think Craeya's opening her fourth portal.

Stone heard Fenri's thoughts, but his own thoughts were elsewhere. The vision. Fenri was there. The younglings. Fenri had a connection to them. A fresh one.

There. The pinched nerve.

Fenri's voice became clear in his mind. *How many have I had? How many more will I have?*

Stone brought himself back to the present, trying to gift himself more time to think. The vision weighed like lead in his heart.

Can I stop this? he wondered. *Can I stop what I feel is coming?*

The blood. The running and the screaming. So much death. *Was it regarding a youngling? Yes, and no. It was more complicated. It was purifyingly simple.*

Is any of this simple?

Stone brought his awareness back to the present, back to Fenri. She was probing at a deep and ancient knowledge, at her past and future. Knowledge was not just her class or her hope, it was her lens for everything. Maybe she thought that knowledge could save her.

Craeya and the fourth portal, he remembered, eyeing Fenri with new understanding.

She's not just any Healer, Fenri handspoke as her entire face fell. She touched her throat, looked to be truly in pain. *I don't think finding Luzon will help,* Fenri spoke, her hands tired and falling, and it felt like a long-awaited admission.

Is Luzon really a danger to us? Stone thought. *If Craeya is opening that portal, is her energy reaching out for Luzon? If we don't find him, will it quell itself, go away before the beasts can smell it?*

Stone wondered at the potency of the portal, what would actually happen if it opened. People had done it, but they were always put to death. Their memories did not survive. The virus was too dangerous to let it live on the lips of their kind.

Stone had opened portals before. He had closed them, blocked them, reopened them, sent daggers of doubt and truth into them, making his system of awareness choke and flourish like the seasons of hot-dry and warm-wind.

We would be put to death, came the thought. *We would have to put an end to it before it spread.*

Fenri was still handspeaking, frantic for knowledge. *If Craeya has activated her portal, then it could trigger it in those around her.* She knew the laws, the research, better than anyone.

Is that what is happening? Stone asked for Fenri to think about it, but he felt the question probing him too. A rare occurrence. He knew himself, and yet he did not know that.

"I don't know," Fenri said.

Stone read her lips.

Her voice was scratchy with disuse. "I feel like I always know what to do, but I don't know now. And even if I know what to do, I can never make anything come from it. All the knowledge in the world and"—Fenri's lips quivered—"Look at me." Her face shook as if she were trying to throw the thought, the feeling, from her body. "I couldn't help Craeya, couldn't stop her from feeling things. I'm the one who knows. I'm the one who was supposed to help her."

Stone thought, *How silly to think her knowledge could stop the opening of a portal.* He reached into his terrabag and pulled out one of his cinchers. The possibilities of what played out next needed to be handled with precaution. Inside the cincher, Stone withdrew the tiniest herb of jadeflower. He held his hand out to Fenri.

Her eyes were daggers of caution. "I don't know if I should do any tilq."

I think we need to.

"Without water?"

This cultivar prevents drymouth. Chew on it. You'll see. Stone broke the flower into two parts, took one for himself, and gave the other to Fenri.

I will give some to Pau and Craeya once they are back.

Fenri placed the flower on her tongue and chewed, her mouth and face twisting in mild distaste. She closed her eyes.

Stone lay down on his bed of penetrating heat, sweat pooling beneath him in a puddle. He'd never imagined that their baracca could burn, but he felt that reality, pressing into him. Then they'd have nothing to protect them. Now Stone could feel the true heat of the Quat Zones, Fenri next to him, burning.

Burning would be the least of their worries.

We lived within a hair's breadth of death. It called to us many times, whispering sweet lullabies into our ears, and yet we fled. We did not answer its call, no matter how close we were. Sweet, unsavory pain! Had I known what we would go through, what the alternative would be, I would have easily taken death's hand. Make no mistake—I would have chosen death every time.

- from *Diaries of the Ancestors*

23. LUZON THE MAKER

Luzon turned on the jets.

He ran as fast as his legs would take him. They felt shorter and more stunted than usual. From behind, four dense legs beat on the ground like a drum. Luzon stole a glance back and saw a beast.

It was hunting time. Dusk.

The beast was gaining on him. Luzon could hear the drum louder in his ears. He ran harder. There were no landmarks in sight, just the cool, dry expanse of desert. No rock reefs, no safety pods, no plant life of any kind. The beast growled, hungry for flesh. Hot breath spread across Luzon's legs like steam.

You're not dead yet. Luzon turned his jets up to full capacity. In certain situations, it was easier to think of himself as a machine. He understood machines.

But his was breaking down, needing a fix, and he didn't have the time to stop and fix it. Other inputs required his attention, but his injuries were causing him to malfunction.

He tripped and the ground rushed up to meet him. He rolled onto his back, every muscle aching.

The beast converged. Luzon squirmed to pull his bag out

from under himself, but the beast pounced, its horrid, skeletal limbs landing on Luzon's chest.

A gnarled, pointed nose sniffed its next meal. Luzon snatched the beast's heinous paw with one hand and craned his other hand behind his back to try and grab his bag. *C'mon—*

Jagged teeth like stalactites moved to engulf Luzon into the darkened cave of the beast's mouth. He grabbed the beast's neck and pushed. Luzon's fuel levels were too low. On his chest, the cave darkened, became an actual physical thing, heavy and pressing.

He pushed the mouth away. A mistake. It only took one.

The beast snapped its jaw down, lightning quick, on Luzon's free hand. He felt a grisly snap and pain that was everywhere. Blood poured out in fountains. His vision snapped into a brighter setting, and when he looked, his hand was *gone.*

His ears blew out.

He understood that his system was going into shock.

The crunch of bone echoed in his ears. The beast spit out its bloodied prize. Ivory teeth sat like towers in its mouth. Everything slowed, and Luzon saw his end, not a bright flash of light, but a dimming into darkness. His systems were shutting down, a sudden cascade of failure. The brute dove in again and went for Luzon's throat, and there was not even a sputter of life left inside him to stop it.

The beast tore into Luzon's neck.

Luzon woke with a start.

His settings shifted with a sudden snap, and he felt like he had left his body to go somewhere else.

A sleep-story.

Sweat drenched his suit. He felt no real pain, only confusion as long, heavy breaths left his body. He scanned himself. His hands were twisted and gnarled like the roots of moonchoke but still attached to him. He touched his neck, which was also still attached to him.

"What was that?" He wanted to see that his voice still worked.

It felt so real. Luzon emerged from his sleeping position and sat up. Zhao's morning heat pushed against Luzon's face like the beast's hot breath. He logged into the system of his body, scanning, standing.

His injuries were healing somewhat. The alu plant he had used relieved some pain, turning his open wounds into scabs. The piercing jolts that ran like electricity from his shoulder to his wrist were becoming less frequent and less painful thanks to the splint. He flexed his fingers, felt fresh blood course through them. Air entered his lungs in a cool rush.

So real. Luzon scanned the perimeter of where he was. There was nothing around him, just wasted death and heat and not a single drop of water, a blurry underwater world of scarlet, maroon, and russet. The open landscape wasn't safe. He needed to find cover. The rock line loomed in the distance, several hectomiles away, a tower of shadow. He could go back there and meet the others. Luzon grabbed his terrabag, threw it over his back, and walked in the direction he had come from.

Luzon squinted at the strange object as it gleamed like a broken fingernail dipped in silver and stuck in the sand. Beasts could camouflage themselves like that. They feigned being a rock, a small sliver of life. When you got close enough, they emerged, the tip only a fraction of their real size.

But there was something unusual and unnatural about the gleam, like it was human made. Luzon stalked closer, head craning forward to see. Caution was his new watchword. The sleep-story still rattled in his brain, still touched the inside of his bones, demanding to be seen.

Five paces away from him, the silver shined brighter. Rays of light came into Luzon's slip-shades, and in that moment he lunged for it, fell to his knees, and dug frantically.

Another terrabag.

Luzon ripped it from the ground with his remaining strength, clapped away the dirt and sand, and held it high. He opened it, examined the contents. Cinchers of food. A cylinder. Tools. A spare skinsuit.

Pau's terrabag. He lost it during the naido storm!

The moment came back to Luzon in a flash and so did the feeling of needing to vomit. His fingers pried into one of the cinchers. The smell of unripe tamagon hearts flew into his olfactory pathways after smelling nothing but burnt desert. He sniffed deeper. His tonguebuds ignited, and his hands shot out, grabbing two and shoving them into his mouth.

Oh, ancestors, thank your sweet minds and hearts. Food!

The nutrients were absorbed into his system, reanimating his brain. He tasted iron and blood. Inside were four more tamagon hearts. He took them all. He gulped from the cylinder then stopped himself. He examined it, felt its weight in his hands.

The food could go bad, but the water would not. He gathered the remaining juices from his lips and swept them into his mouth. Yes, he'd had enough. When the others found the bag, they would need some of the precious liquid. They would need Pau's gill. He took some of his own cloth and stuffed it inside the bag, knowing it held his scent and the knowledge that he was still alive. He weighed what he would need versus what they would need ... assuming they were still alive.

They have to be. If I'm still here, they are too.

The hearts coursed through Luzon's bloodstream, an inner warming. His system was updating. He didn't know all the inputs, but he knew it was improving.

The rubyrinds wouldn't go bad. He ate three and left the others. There was tilq. Jadeflower. A near full cannister of smokesticks. They would help suppress hunger. Luzon took six. He had his own tilq. He wondered if he'd even need it.

Once the contents were mixed to his liking, Luzon grabbed the bag, and walked to the highest dune he could see. Life was so much flatter down in the Quat Zones. His plan would have to do. He situated the terrabag into the sand like an offering on a pedestal.

With Pau's tracking abilities, it was better to leave it for them to find. Then they would know to keep looking.

I miss them.

Luzon walked away from the bag and continued toward the rock line.

Luzon rubbed the sweat from his eyes, unsure if what he was looking at was real. He pinched himself to rule out the possibility of being in a sleep-story. His system was overheating and that made him glitch sometimes, arriving as tricks playing in his mind. Things he thought were close were actually much further away, and things far away suddenly breathed into his face.

The ground dipped into a slight slope before him. At the base of the slope, the land was flat. There it was—*water.*

Water pooled in a small puddle the size of a hand bowl. Pinkish rays flicked off its surface as the skin of the water moved. Soon darkness would cast its nightly spell.

Water!

Luzon ran and fell to his knees, scanning the area before him. The water trickled out from a crack in the ground. He lowered his head to drink, and space and time became lost to him. The water was hot. He drank deeper. When he had his fill, when he felt as though there was enough in his body to fuel his systems, he sat back. More water trickled out, filling the bowl before him.

Luzon set the mouth of his cylinder in the inch-high pool and began to collect. Once it was filled halfway, he took the drinkspout from the end of his terrabag, pulling the tube from the inner lining. He had depleted his terrabag's innervat.

He held the tube in the pool and sucked through the other end then spit the water into his cylinder until it was full. Then he filled two spare vials and an empty bottle. Kneeling down again, he took the tube and drank again. Every drop was a miracle. He imagined he could stay and fill himself with water until he was content. There was always fuel if you knew where to look.

A smile spread across Luzon's face for the first time in weeks. He wondered how long he had been without the others and told himself he would need to start counting days. He ached for them.

The thought quickened his urgency. His pain was still there, still real. His world was real. Not a sleep-story. Not something in his head. Above, Zhao slipped away, and with it pockets of heat left his skin.

Luzon heard a low growl behind him and jumped to his feet. He spun.

Two bloodshot eyes, and a look of only hunger, stared at him. The desperation of starvation, a look Luzon knew so well, lived on its gnarled face, its black-on-black fur and snarling snout. If Luzon came down on his hands and knees, he and the intruder would be roughly the same size.

Luzon gathered his things. The creature was only there for water. Luzon would leave in silence and let the—what was it?— beast-like dog, drink as it pleased. The dog-beast lowered its head, its ears pointing back, stalking closer.

No sudden movements.

The danger of the situation came into Luzon's veins like a memory. The pain of the sleep-story he had experienced erupted inside him like a volcano. His heart thumped in his chest. If the beast wanted to attack, Luzon knew that he would die.

Terrabag on his back, he grabbed a thin aydilite rod from his sideslot, gripping it tightly. The beast had stalked up so quietly. Perhaps that was its watering hole. It didn't matter. It had found another, greater prize.

The beast stopped and stared. A moment of decision arrived for both of them.

Luzon turned to run.

A mistake. He turned his head and saw the pitch-black shape giving chase.

C'mon, Luzon. You will not die here.

The bounding and hungry beast was upon him in seconds. Luzon pivoted on his front foot and swung the rod at the beast's head with a strike like lightning. He connected. Guttural growls emerged from behind, falling away further. Luzon's jets were on. He swiveled again to see. The light of the moons showed a slash under the eye, a stripe of blood, as the beast took a moment to understand the damage.

Silence can be the most dangerous sound of all.

Yellow-daggered eyes grew larger in the abyss as they grew closer. Luzon saw rage building in its face and knew that it would not make the same mistake twice. Luzon was running out of options, of advantages. In his bag there had to be something that could help him.

Now or never.

Now or *never again.*

Luzon wanted to live more than anything in the entire world. *There.*

A rock reef. A small, baby one. Cover. There was his advantage. He needed a trick, something to slow the beast that was five paces away. The rock reef was right there. Three paces away. Luzon swung his rod behind him again and missed.

Serrated teeth plunged into his calf.

Luzon's bones smacked against the ground as he screamed out his pain. The rod came out in a flurry, swinging at the beast at his legs. Luzon connected.

Stunned momentarily, the beast shook its head in a wild swivel as though that would take away the pain before moving to sink its teeth into Luzon again. Luzon grabbed a reef vine hanging above him and yanked himself underneath the structure in one deft move. He slid across the cool rock. The beast crouched underneath the vines, advancing.

Luzon rolled over to his knees and crawled.

No. No. No.

Ahead, the labyrinth of routes ended abruptly, giving way to a tangled mass of darkened vines and jagged rocky rubble.

"Stop," Luzon said. He looked up, saw an opening, and pulled himself up and through. Everything slowed. Moonlight streamed down in lances as he launched himself out of the reef. Gravity and the lack of any remaining strength brought him back down and through.

Darkness was with him.

The beast had forced its way through somehow, a body of brute strength for which Luzon was no match. He froze, and he felt in that terrifying moment that he'd made his final mistake.

The beast lunged and crashed into Luzon, bringing them both to the ground, pinning him. Breathless, Luzon reached out for his rod. He tried to swing. The beast's front paw pinned his arm.

I've been here.

Jaws came down to rip out Luzon's neck. One hand came free. Luzon grabbed a vine and pushed it down in front of his neck as a shield. The beast tasted vine instead of flesh.

There.

Luzon's other hand popped free and swam into his terrabag. A heavy metal thing emerged.

The beast struck again. Luzon pressed hard on his fear, his finger smashing into a button he had never touched before. A chain snapped, and the sharp dagger of the digspike torpedoed out, slicing through the beast's neck as though it were water.

Blood fell torrentially, spurting all over Luzon's neck and face, a hot liquid mess.

Silence.

Then, Luzon heard the beast's near-death gasps for air and final whisperings of hate as life left its body. They were both free. Luzon shoved the weight of the creature to the side with his remaining strength. Oxygen scraped against his raw throat as blood leaked from his torn open calf and new pains greeted him. He had nothing left to give.

The uneven rhythm of Luzon's body slowed. Perhaps his system was failing for good. He stared up through the rock reef's cover as one of the moons winked a cold, silver eye down at him. He did not know what the damage would mean for his body, for the beast's body. Something would be there soon to clean up the mess.

So this is how Luzon the Maker meets his end.

Water wouldn't be enough. It would never be enough. The others didn't need him, but he needed them. Craeya's healing arts. Fenri's knowledge. Pau's protection. Stone's vision. He needed all of them more than ever.

Luzon had always imagined death to be a quick and painless thing, a ripping from the world, and yet there he was, painfully slipping away. He could see both moons through the tangle of vines above him, and he knew he had never seen anything so beautiful in all his life.

In the Alcoves of Knowledge, it is said there are books from our home planet with histories detailing collapsed governments, nations, and peoples. A king, or president, or a prime minister could be benevolent and help the poor, or malicious and cut off the heads of anyone who dared defy them. There are many stories like this—tales of an oppressive government versus a suffering people. A manipulation of knowledge for the sake of power and control. After the rise of Our Changed World, many scholars theorized that this is what QhaHadur was, but they could not have been more wrong. We as Masters did everything we could to help our nation. Everything we did, we did for survival.

- from *Confessions of the Masters, Volume I*

24. Fenri the Knowledger

Fenri was drenched in sweat, and in her mind, she knew it was all wrong.

"Stone?" Her voice was hoarse, and she could hear the beginnings of panic.

Feet shuffled across the ground nearby. She wiped the sweat from her brow, from her eyes, and tried to sit up. Stone appeared in the baracca's slit of an opening, his grey eyes alert behind a jungle of hair.

He handspoke, *They are not back yet.*

How long have they been gone?

Longer than an hour. Stone swung his gaze out into the desert, then turned those grey orbs to peer into the tent. He scanned Fenri up and down, and in them, a strange knowledge lived, a cold, twisting premonition of death. Stone had the sight. Fenri knew what was happening to her body, and the reality slammed into her, like a crashing wave knocking the wind from her body.

Dehydration.

Organ failure could happen in as little as eight hours.

Anger surged through Fenri. She was tired of living a life of mistakes. Tired, so tired, of the knowledge that she could effect change but lacked the permission or resources to do so.

This place is strange, Stone. I can't control my thoughts, my feelings. We're all going to die out here, aren't we? You've already seen it?

Stone crawled into the baracca, his furry shape casting uneven shadows. His eyes fell, dark as storm clouds. *One thing at a time. We still have life in us.*

Fenri touched her throat and went to speak but couldn't. There was a truth somewhere buried deep, and somehow it had blocked her voice, blocked her mind. A moment of lightness, and then she was lying down on her terrabag, feeling sleep pull her into its sweaty embrace. Controlling her thoughts or feelings mattered very little at that point. Fenri just needed to live.

The absence of water within Fenri's body, in her brain and cells, sent her inside herself. In her dark brain-space, thoughts came to her. *If I really was made to bear children, then what else don't I know?* She had lain on those tables of pain and pushed out new life that shared her DNA. She had *made* something.

Will I die quicker than the others because of my body? Because my brain is bigger, will it keep me alive longer?

She recalled her body's makeup, the plague of being an Unable. A double dose of pain. Her brain worked hard to keep her body alive, and it needed more, but there wasn't enough for her.

Fenri wanted to turn her brain off.

If only she could send herself into a coma.

She recalled the ancient stories about the Knowledgers who were able to. So full of power and intellect that they could preserve themselves for hundreds of years by turning their bodies off. Fenri had never known any in her lifetime, but she believed it to be true.

She felt the planet was calling her to return.

She heard voices. She willed her eyes to remain open but felt herself drifting, as though carried away by the surf. A face she knew slid into view. Stone handspoke in a flurry.

Fenri, get up. We're—

Pain stabbed at her, sucking her back into a dark abyss. She lost her sight, lost the sound of the outside world. Only her thoughts remained. If they perished, so would she.

Strong arms lifted Fenri, and she felt herself leave the baracca in a rush. The open air chilled her bones. These were not Stone's arms. They were longer, lighter. Fenri opened one eye and saw Pau the Guardian.

"We found Luzon." Pau gasped for air, and Fenri knew he had been running for a long time.

She tried to make words, but it was too unreal. She had to know more.

"He's got water," Pau said. "Just hold on a little longer."

His voice was strong. So were his arms. If Pau could get her there, maybe she would live.

Fenri would try her best to obey. She didn't know the answer. She couldn't stop herself from thinking the thought.

Oh ancestors. Please let Luzon be alive.

Then the darkness pulled her down.

When Pau laid Fenri on the ground sometime later, rough hands grabbed Fenri's chin and opened her mouth.

"Drink." Pau's knees were under her for support, and he was cradling her head in the palm of one hand.

Water touched her lips and tongue, and she opened her eyes. A single moment of non-pain greeted her. Water trickled from the cylinder and filled her body, her stomach. A ghost-white, night-encroaching silence fell.

She lay there in agony, looking up. Zhao was setting somewhere beyond. Without moving her head too much to either side, Fenri took in her surroundings. They had settled near a rock reef. Stone was there, his eyes wide, still uncertain. He wasn't searching her for truths, he was looking on the ground next to her.

Fenri had wondered for so long, and when she looked over, she couldn't believe what she saw.

Luzon turned to look at that same moment. His eyes opened like the petals of a figvi, a careful unveiling to the world. His face had hardened as if he'd taken on an extra reptilian layer, a bloodied, crusted mess of black, sapphire, and ruby. They stared at each other for a moment. A fire was starting in her basal ganglia as much-needed warmth coursed through her body.

Luzon. Are you really alive? Is this real?

Fenri had so many questions. She wanted to know how he had survived the fall, how he had lived out there in the scorching landscape all alone.

Do not get accustomed to it. He left you, and he could do it again.

Pau held the cylinder over Fenri's mouth, and she drank again.

Luzon had found water. He had the digspike for uncovering Klonden. Just maybe he could fix Fenri's map-projector. Everything was still in order. They could still go back to base. Fenri could still have everything she wanted.

Above Luzon, Craeya slid into view. She was applying peppernut oil to Luzon's calf, a surganeedle in her other hand. Luzon looked up at Craeya and smiled, and air came through Fenri's lungs, cold and wispy, the deep dark of night. She watched Craeya's hands maneuver around Luzon's battered body, and strange thoughts came to her.

The old enemies are not the new enemies.

Luzon and Fenri gazed up at their Healer. Craeya would always be more useful. The darkness tugged at Fenri, a hook in the center of her chest, bringing her down into the depths of an ocean without light.

Nature without urge is stagnation.

Fenri shut her eyes as she winced tears from them. Part of her wished Luzon had died when the naido took him, but she knew that part of her was lying.

We have come to a dangerous place, and we need to get out.

- from *Diaries of the Ancestors*

25. CRAEYA THE HEALER

Craeya kneeled over Luzon. Her eyes grazed over his bruised skin poking through the attempted patchwork of his skinsuit at his elbows and knees. His puffy eyes opened beneath a blackened mass of caked blood, their whites streaked red as he took shallow breaths.

"Luzon, we're going to get you out of this," Craeya assured him, but for the first time, doubt brushed against her chest, filled her up like a balloon, a little bit at a time.

She could smell death. Or something like it. Rotting flesh. Flies feasting.

I could still lose him.

She pressed down on her doubt and steadied her knees into the qha beneath her.

He had fallen hard and fast. Craeya didn't understand physics like Fenri, but she knew gravity well enough and had no idea how Luzon had survived. He swallowed hard when she tilted his cylinder over his mouth to drink, like even that pained him. "I found water," was all he could manage to say.

Craeya was determined to hear more and get him walking again.

Her hands moved down his body. She took great care rotating his right leg to get a better look. Blood dripped from a calf wound Craeya had already worked to clean. His skinsuit was torn open and revealed a bulging muscle sliced open.

Oh ancestors. Please don't let it be infected.

Next to Luzon, Fenri coughed. Her breaths were raspy.

Craeya looked to see a more conscious Fenri. Dehydration was her problem, but there was water, plenty of it, at least for a while. Pau had given her enough, and they needed to conserve. Craeya would also give her plenty of salt and other nutrients to get her healthy again.

On the outskirts of their camp, Stone paced. The bramble of his hair was so thick, Craeya couldn't tell where his eyes were in the escaping light. Craeya exchanged a nervous glance with Pau.

"We need to move," he said.

"Yeah, I know, but we have two team members out of commission," Craeya said.

"Well, it's about to be more than that if we stay."

Craeya followed the trail of blood with her eyes, from Luzon to the rock reef's abyss where they had found him. The ground was covered in maroon streaks. Hydrogen sulfide and ammonia and all the horrible smells of death came to Craeya from the rock reef.

Luzon hadn't been able to give a solid answer on how long he'd been under it, but based on the injuries, Craeya guessed at least two days, maybe three. When he opened his eyes, it looked like he was coming out of a tilq withdrawal. The smell of blood and decay in Craeya's nostrils intensified. Never had she seen anything similar on the repair table.

She pushed air from her nostrils. "Do something with the beast's body. It stinks like shit. Other beasts are gonna smell it."

"It's already rotting," Pau said. "Bigger beasts will be here soon."

"Burn it."

"No fires."

"Bury it then."

"Craeya!"

"What?" Craeya turned from her work to stare at Pau. "I'm trying my best here. Why don't you do something about it?"

"I am." Pau stood. "We're moving. It's our best chance at safety."

Craeya laughed. "You call any of this safety? Luzon can't walk. Fenri can barely stay conscious for more than five minutes."

"I don't like it either. But we either carry them, or you, Stone, and I learn how to fight off beasts. Take your pick."

Craeya returned to Luzon and recalled her training, the most essential tasks that she would need to do in a hurry. She had already closed all Luzon's open wounds and given him injections: one of Vitamin C to strengthen his blood vessels and stop him from losing any more blood and one for the pain. So he could lie there in some semblance of peace. *Sure, peace—we're almost drowning in the stuff.*

"Let me do this and then we can go." Craeya removed gauze from her healing kit.

"Good answer," Pau said. "I'll carry Fenri. Stone will help you carry Luzon."

"How far are we moving?"

"Half a hectomile, maybe more," Pau said. "We just need to get out of this area."

Craeya placed a bloodpad on Luzon's wound then wrapped it. She had to put trust in Pau to protect them. He was a good Charge Leader, and she agreed with his decision-making. When Stone returned to them, he and Craeya lifted Luzon, one under each arm, and they walked. He was shockingly light, and he could at least put some weight on his good leg.

Just get them out of here and healed.

They walked away from the rock reef as Zhao slid off its perch, darkness swallowing the clouded night sky in one bite.

When they laid Luzon down on a leshblanket a hectomile later, Craeya finally felt that they were out of danger. Pau laid Fenri next to Luzon. She fluttered her eyes as though trying to muster the energy to speak, or stand, knowing Fenri. Craeya knew it killed both of them to be down and out like that.

Pau began to set up the baraccas. "We'll need cover for the night. How soon do you think you can get them moving again?"

"Like I said, I'll do my best." Craeya examined Luzon's calf wound again. Stone crouched down beside her to look at the opening. Fenri was awake and curious, and Craeya heard her croaky whisper at her side. "How did he ... survive that fall?"

"I don't know yet," Craeya said. "I've got him full up on pain-modifiers right now."

"Pain-modifiers?" Fenri asked, as though it was the first time she had heard the word. "Can I have some?"

"The kind of pain you're feeling won't be helped. You need rest."

Stone spoke to Fenri using his hands. She watched, tried to speak, but closed her eyes instead. Stone tapped Craeya, pointed to Luzon's open wounds, made a series of actions and hand movements that Craeya only vaguely understood. But even with Stone next to her, she felt a shift in energy. The nightly desert breeze pushed at Craeya's back, moved the hair from her shoulders.

It was going to get cold.

Stone said the same thing again, slower.

"He's not infected?"

Stone nodded. He motioned that Luzon should merely be stitched up.

"How do you know?"

Without opening her eyes, Fenri said, "He just knows."

Without use of a blood panel, Craeya had to trust that he did. She could feel Stone's knowledge whispering into her bones. He had seen the storms before they arrived and knew the ways in which they would move.

Loss of a sense in one area makes others stronger.

And yet there was no way to measure intuition. Craeya stopped herself. She had her own sense of intuition, so she knew that wasn't totally true. She knew that not everything could be explained by science.

Not yet at least.

Above, Pau finished setting up the two baraccas. The moonlight became a faded silver-blue, a body dropping to all fours across the land. Spindly shadows fell across Luzon's body, across Fenri's face. Stone and Pau helped to move Luzon and Fenri inside their cover.

Pau crouched down at the baracca's opening. "How are they doing?"

"Luzon will need time to let the medicines work. It's harder to tell with Fenri. I think she should have enough water now, but it's weakened her. I'll give her all the necessary fluids. They need to rest."

"Good," Pau said, meeting Craeya's eyes. "What about you?"

"I'm fine."

"Good. I'm going out to look for the pool Luzon found."

"Now?"

"Stone will keep watch."

Pau held Craeya's gaze a moment, then he shot Fenri and Luzon quick glances. He opened his mouth to speak then shut it. He paused. "Craeya, you're ... a good Healer. Keep up your good work. I'm going now."

"Why does it sound like you're going off for good or something?" Craeya didn't know whether to smile or swallow the lump in her throat. "I miss when you'd just yell at me."

"No, I don't think you do." Pau moved his tongue in his mouth to hide his grin then left.

Craeya at least thought she missed it. She didn't like separating and going off alone. She knew Pau would be alright, but having the team apart gave her bad memories, ones of Luzon being gone. Him being back warmed a space inside her, a space she was forced to keep closed from others.

She rushed out of the baracca and felt her breaths quicken.

Stone stood there, looking out, a grappling claw hanging from his hand. An eerie quiet stretched across the desert and sucked away all sound. Every now and again, a tweet or chirp punctuated the silence. Desert bats and pawkwi and whatever else lived down in the Quat Zones. Craeya didn't care to know.

Craeya sucked in a mouthful of air and pushed it out just to make sure everything was still working. Her lungs had gotten used to the higher levels of oxygen, and yet sometimes, she felt as though there wasn't enough.

Something flashed in her brain.

A boy, his back to Craeya. Dark and made of flesh. Craeya's own mind oozed with want. A persistent inner heat.

No. Not this.

Craeya found herself inside the baracca, needing comfort, needing cover. The glimpse of what she'd seen was a memory, a very recent memory. One she hadn't been able to forget. She knew she needed to. When Craeya returned to her present environment, she realized Fenri was sitting up, holding her map-projector in one hand, her logbook in the other.

"What are you doing? You need to rest."

"I need to get this working," Fenri said. As though Craeya's question helped her decide which one she would focus her attention on, Fenri laid her logbook down beside her and shifted her focus to her map-projector.

"Fenri, I'm not kidding. You can do it after you rest."

Fenri looked up, her eyes crashing straight into Craeya's. "I've rested plenty. We need to get this working. Thank the ancestors Luzon is back. He might be able to fix it." Fenri's dark gaze slid over to Luzon. She looked him up and down ravenously, as though his knowledge was something she could taste.

"No," Craeya said. "It's one thing for you to be stubborn and forsake your own sleep because you're crazy, but you're not waking up Luzon. He can fix it when he's rested."

At mention of his name, Luzon poked his head up and squinted open one eye, the eye not encrusted in blood. "What needs fixing?"

"No." Craeya moved between them to block the disaster waiting to happen. "I said, NO."

"My map-projector. It broke, and we need it to find the Klonden."

"Give it here," Luzon said. "I'll take a look."

"No!" Craeya said, her insides warming with a heat she could not control. She had never tried to stop an exchange between two people from happening.

Luzon took the map-projector in his hands and peeled open his not-so-good eye to take a look. He began to disassemble it.

"You're both infuriating," Craeya said.

"Says the girl who took on a greffir three times her size." Luzon smirked. He was sitting up, propped up on one elbow, his gnarled hands pressing into the slab, separating parts that seemed inseparable. Craeya went to laugh, to speak, but she was captivated by Luzon at work because he reminded her of someone.

There. She saw him again. His name came back in a wave against the wall of her chest.

Rannum.

That same dark skin. Where Luzon was lanky and swift, Rannum was languid and purposeful. Both appeared, shifted in and out of focus. Luzon, breathing and fixing right in front of her, Rannum, back in the lesson alcoves, potions and cures swirling around his fingers, dexterous as anything she had even seen. They were her hands too. She had become a good Healer by watching to learn.

No. That wasn't right, was it?

Luzon handed Fenri the map-projector. "Some of the inputs were clogged. I freed some space, but you'll need to dump some of it if you want to use it for longer. Should be good for a while though."

"You ... freed some of the space. How?"

"Hmm. Hard to explain. Partitioning is what I call it."

Fenri took the map-projector in her hands, and her eyes fell on it with that same hunger. A smile appeared as she looked at Luzon. "You're a genius, I think."

Craeya watched Fenri as she typed feverishly into her device. Her eyes were alight, as dark and as azure as the ocean. In them, Craeya saw the slight ticks and mild twitches. The realization hit her all at once.

"Fenri, you took some tilq didn't you?"

"What? No. Well, maybe. A long time ago." Fenri's typing slowed as though she was coming to some answer.

"Really? Because you look like you're high."

"So what? Stone and I needed it."

"For what? It wasn't going to help with dehydration."

At that, Fenri looked up. "Why are you wanting to know so badly? You sound like me. It's tilq. I know you've taken it before. I'm sure you know how it works."

Luzon was snoring beside them.

As soon as the map-projector was fixed and out of his hands, he had snuggled up in his leshblanket, and was sound asleep, his mouth half open, emitting hefty sounds that betrayed his small body.

"Come to think of it," Fenri said, and her eyes snapped into focus. "I think it's best if you take some. And Luzon too."

"Why?"

"Because it's that time." Fenri cleared her throat, and the glazed look left her eyes at the snap of a finger, as though she was suddenly over the high.

Good. Maybe she would sleep.

"This is your first cycle, so you haven't had much experience out here. But this is about the time we need more tilq. It's difficult to suppress our appetite ... our emotions, this long without it."

"So there it is. That's the real reason. Emotions." Craeya scanned the new, somewhat out-of-sorts Fenri, her eyes hungry for information, wild even. "Mine are fine," Craeya said.

But even as she said it, she knew it wasn't true. Her emotions were not fine. They were tied so closely to Luzon's wellbeing that every time his breaths became labored, she snapped her gaze over to make sure he wasn't dying. And the thought of that pained her. She already had to live with the thought while he was gone. Now that he was back, it was more real.

"What do you have?" Craeya asked.

Fenri had plenty to suffice. Craeya took what she needed.

Eventually, maybe an hour later, Craeya's mind let go of its hold on Luzon. She found herself slipping into her own slumber. Fenri still sat there, eyes alert and dry, mouth set, writing in her logbook. Craeya found herself wondering strange things.

"It's weird," Craeya said, and she felt her brain and mouth working together, one in action, the other unable to refuse the dance. The words spilled. "I kept thinking what it would be like to never see Luzon again."

Fenri looked up from her writing. "I can't believe he survived. He made wing expansions. He actually flew, Craeya."

"I heard that," she said, the reality of it hitting her from a new angle, sharpening. "Like you spend all this time with strangers and learn all these things, and then they leave you."

"Yes," Fenri said. "It's our way."

"Well, I don't get it." Craeya's thoughts multiplied, almost too fast for her to follow. She tried to pull them all back to her, the tiny skittering of warm light finally unleashed.

"There's nothing to get." Fenri's voice was cold as the night. "This is what will happen. You don't have to imagine it for much longer. After this cycle, we will go on another with new cyclemates. And we'll forget about each other."

"I think that's stupid. I mean, look at the things we've been able to learn and discover traveling together."

"It happens all the time."

"You and Luzon wanting to create flying and floating ships happens all the time?"

"Well—"

There it was, in her voice. Fenri's resistance to the topic. Always such strong resistance. So immediate. So *programmed*. Craeya hated it. She despised Fenri's resistance. Anger came through Craeya's veins and a warmth she couldn't stop. She hated Fenri for wanting to leave and join a new group, for being okay with it. *Why is everyone okay with it?*

Awareness of the other should be balanced by awareness of the self.

Craeya had her own resistances. A thought struck her.

I don't want to go back to the nation-feast if this is what it means.

Her brain was computing at such a feverish pitch, she felt as though an actual fire burned, a pyre suddenly thrown aflame. It burned, oh how it burned, on her first cycle of all cycles in the field, and yet Craeya felt she knew things others did not want to know.

Fenri took a deep breath, shut her logbook, as if the answer had finally come to her. "You can't change it, Craeya. Just take your tilq and live like everyone else."

"So that's your answer? You just give up because it's the way it's always been? You're just going to end up like Rannum. Gone and forgotten."

"Who," Fenri said, "is Rannum?"

"It doesn't matter." But Craeya knew that it did. She knew that the matter of who Rannum was mattered more than most things. Even that far away, she could feel him, she could see him. She wondered where he was, what he was doing. Her mind unfolded, something inside let go, and someone else, *something* else, seemed to be steering. She wondered what would have happened had they been able to spend more time together outside of the lessons, if their years spent together had meant anything to him.

"Maybe I want a different kind of life," Craeya said. "One with real memories. One where we're not drowning them out all the time. There's some sort of pain inside me, and I can't get rid of it." She stared at Fenri, deep into her eyes, and saw her fear. In Fenri's eyes, Craeya saw what she was to her at long last.

"No, Craeya." Where Craeya was fire and heat, Fenri was strike and venom. Oh yes, those eyes could kill if they wanted to. "You are talking about death, plain and simple. The path you want means no Klonden, no base, no Electric Ocean." Fenri sucked air through her teeth when she said the next part. "You're playing with something dangerous. You don't know about it because you haven't lived enough cycles to know what it means." Fenri's chest heaved, but her strength seemed to be back and in full force, her eyes twinkling like black stars in a moonlit sky. "If we come back thinking and acting that way, they'll kill us."

"Then maybe I want to die!"

Fenri raised her hand lightning quick and slapped Craeya across the face.

Craeya touched her face, the sharp hiss of Fenri's hand against her skin still raw. The shock of the move was more surprising than the actual blow.

Fenri glared. "Don't say that."

"It's true." Craeya was ready if Fenri wanted to smack her again. But she didn't. She merely stared back, lips and eyes quivering, then her gaze broke and fell. Craeya thought she saw sadness, swelling like waves within the wells of her darkened features.

So many emotions rolled around inside Craeya. She wondered which ones were real. She needed to know what was real. She wanted to know if what she was feeling had any substance at all.

The tilq was not working.

"The gap of knowledge," Craeya said, pieces of a puzzle moving together in her brain. "It's the same in every discipline. But with yours ... don't you want to know what it would be like to stay with the same people? To let me help you find your cure? To build more than just a submership with Luzon?"

Fenri closed her eyes tight and spoke through the hand she had put to her mouth. "I don't think you understand people very well. I don't think you understand our people."

"I understand that people move toward pleasure and away from pain."

Fenri stood up with effort. "I can't be around you right now." And she left.

Beside Craeya, Luzon stirred. She turned to look at him. He was just a young man who wanted to live. Feeling around in her terrabag, Craeya grabbed the EM, clicked it on, and began to run it over parts of Luzon that were ready to be healed.

Her thoughts slowed. The EM hummed in her ear, drowning out all other thought and sound. Craeya felt energies larger than herself brewing outside the baracca. She felt the tilq coursing through her body. It was working. Or maybe it wasn't.

The wind outside, loud and all-encompassing, was all Craeya could hear.

Just before things became irreversible for the dispatch members of Project El, we sent Stone the Planeteer a message. This message detailed the location of his next mission, which dispatch team he was to meet with, and on what date he was meant to meet them. He should have reached them, as we found out, much sooner than he tried to reach them. What we didn't know about until much later was his hesitation. Stone the Planeteer does not hesitate, and yet he did. We still don't fully understand the reasons for this. Because of what we did to him, he should have been more unfeeling than all of them.

- from *Confessions of the Masters*, Volume 1

26. STONE THE INDECISIVE

On the morning of the cycle's midpoint, a rare message from the Masters appeared on the slick silver of Stone's planet-tablet. Stone read the words once, twice, then put his tablet back in his bag.

"What were you reading?" Fenri spoke precisely.

Stone hadn't noticed her standing so close to him until then. Her thirst for his truth was palpable through the light.

I was ... Stone handspoke, hesitating. *Seeing if I have any data from these quadrants.*

Fenri raised her eyebrows and shot a look like she knew he was lying.

It wasn't a direct lie.

Wasn't it?

Stone considered what the message said and realized that it called for near to immediate action.

Near. Maybe not immediate.

"You two ready?" Pau asked. He had the olive-brown glow of

someone who'd made promises to the sun. His skin showed no pink or red, a hinting at damage that Stone or Fenri or Craeya, the more fair-complexioned of the group had.

Beside him, Craeya was packing her bag, nestling all the medicines and ointments she had been using on Luzon for the past two weeks inside her healing kit. Luzon was better. Still, he limped from time to time, the beast's jaws having damaged his calf, a reminder of how fatal the Quat Zones could be, but he could walk.

Fenri recovered from her dehydration, and Pau had found the pool Luzon discovered, so they had water. Their supply wouldn't last forever, but they were on the final leg of their journey. If they could retrieve some Klonden, all they had to do was turn back and return to base.

Stone sensed unstoppable shifts in energy around him. Something about each of them spoke of new life. He saw it in Craeya's eyes when they lingered on Luzon. He saw it in Fenri's dexterous fingers, her unbreakable determination to find the Klonden they so needed. He saw it in Pau's iron gaze, his jaw set like steel, his no-nonsense attitude. They were healed and moving and ready to fulfill their mission. All five of them.

And yet it all felt wrong.

"You good?" Pau asked.

Stone read his lips and body language. He straightened the visible tension from his body and nodded.

"You look like you want to say something."

Stone froze. Everything inside him ignited, a hurricane of flares. Abruptly, he hated having read the message from the Masters. He hated that he would have to leave them. He hated that he couldn't speak it. He didn't have a voice, but he felt sounds surging up inside him, a past version of himself silhouetting out of his body, wanting to speak and break free. He wanted to speak with more than just hands.

Visions drew him into himself.

His fifth portal, the blue one at his throat, choked and

sputtered. He went to speak, realized that was foolish, but that was what his body was pushing him to do. Inside, the portal diminished, becoming a small orb of charcoal-blue tar.

"Stone?" Fenri turned. Her face was inches from his. "You okay?"

Stone cleared his throat. The portal pulsed open a fraction. He forced a smile onto his face and nodded. *Let us go,* he said, using his hands. His handspeak felt clumsy, but he knew they caught his meaning.

They moved on.

That was your chance to tell them what you need to tell them.

But Stone knew he wasn't the only one who needed to tell things. With that realization, a vision swallowed him, a vacuum sucking in all his light.

Craeya.

She stood there, back arched, peering into a darkened tunnel. Inside, grotesque and vile sounds grew louder. Stone wanted to pull her away from that danger, but realized his presence was not there. He could only see. She turned back, a moment of hesitation in her eyes, then took a step down and inside the swollen pit.

The darkness lessened.

There was some other light. Craeya's light. Portals swirled inside her. Stone found it difficult to look. The power was overwhelming and grated on his other senses, metal against metal. Drums of sound, and brash gong bells pounded into the vision, reverberating, the rattling of bones. The sound twisted, dove underneath the ground, warped into vibrations Stone could not place. He needed to follow, needed to see where the vision led.

Craeya ran through tunnels, her pink-blonde hair flowing behind her, casting its own glowing tail of the universe. Where she ran, the path lightened. She stopped at an alcove and ducked inside. Stone followed, but something blocked him. A body at the door, tall and broad, staring down at Stone.

Pau.

Their eyes met, and inside the look, Stone felt sharp pains in his liver, in his kidneys, and the urge to release a heaviness he couldn't locate within himself blossomed. He felt it as Pau went to his side, durablade gleaming silver-bright under an obelisk in the alcove. Moonlight gleamed down, illuminating other figures.

A dark-skinned young man, lanky with power—*Luzon.*

Beside him, a storm of mind and flesh all swirled into one vague image. Craeya blocked Stone's sight. He pushed deeper, grabbed at a sinking awareness, pulled it up.

There.

Fenri. Something about her seemed strange. She was energy without a body.

No. It can't be.

All of it could be. It was.

Stone wanted to pass, but Pau blocked his path. He glared down. Stone went to speak. He felt energies mounting, too big to be housed by such a small alcove. Then, blades jabbing, tearing flesh, puncturing organs.

No!

Stone saw it within the vision. He couldn't see it with his eyes, but he could feel it.

No!

Now, warm liquid blood splattered fuchsia. His vision blurred. Sudden snapping pierced his awareness, his vision. Screams of death and revenge and unchecked anger bombarded his ears. The energies swirled into hurricane winds, sucked in the glacial moonlight, until there was total darkness.

Stone wanted to leave.

I can die in this place.

He turned to go, but the winds pulled him in. They ripped at him, trying to separate him from his body until he felt a sharp pain in his lungs.

Cannot breathe.

When he looked down, he saw that Pau's durablade was nestled deep in his side, saw blood pouring from his body.

"You should have said something when you had the chance."

Those harsh, metal tones were the last sounds he heard before he was cleaved from the vision against his will.

Stone poured sweat. The cool air of the night brushed against his prickling skin, and he wondered how long his vision had lasted. Everything inside him emptied out. He touched his face, blinked his eyes shut, winced the tears from them. Ahead, three pairs of feet walked in unison, the wink of each step, steady, staccato.

Beside him, Fenri searched his face, her eyes questioning. For the first time in a while, he had no idea what his body had done in the outside world. Clearly, he had managed to walk, to not call too much attention to himself, but he knew he needed to be more aware.

I need to tell them.

You saw something, Fenri handspoke. She always knew. *How? How are you able to have visions? I want to see too.*

And Stone thought, *No you do not. You do not want this curse.* But he said, *Why? What is it that you want to see?* Absently, he touched near his solar plexus, his fire portal, where his lungs would be.

That blade—

Pau had killed him.

They had all killed each other.

Now Stone could see the truth. This would happen. Ahead of him, portals were opening. Within Craeya, a portal Stone did not know at all was affecting his balance. Reality warped and bent around him. His vision blurred. He felt drunk on limewine and all the intoxicating slurring juices.

I want to know all there is to know, Fenri handspoke. *I want to know things no one has ever known before.*

Stone knew she meant exploring the Electric Ocean. He knew what she really meant, though her mind worked differently. She couldn't quite name the thing as Stone saw and understood it.

You want to carry your people forward, Stone handspoke.

What? Fenri replied.

You will be a Master someday. Is this not what you want?

Fenri said nothing.

It is not ego to want to carry our people forward.

I suppose you're right. What is it that you want, Stone?

That same choking feeling rose up in Stone's throat. He criticized Fenri internally but realized other truths with sudden clarity. *Am I the same? I want to carry my people forward, but how am I doing that? I have these abilities, but what are they without synergy, without union? Am I just a researcher, forever fulfilling the Master's wishes?*

He was far beyond the state of just needing and wanting to survive.

Stone realized Fenri was waiting for an answer. *I want our people to be free. From these constant dispatch missions.* And as soon as he said it, he regretted it. He did not want to let Fenri know all of his thoughts. But she said nothing to it, and they walked on in silence.

A burnt orange light was climbing over the horizon when they finally stopped to rest. Stone's senses filled with the early morning smell of insects rustling, plants pollinating, and creatures waking. The team slowed to a stop. Even Pau seemed tired. Stone wondered if there was an end in sight, if they would finally find Klonden and turn around. *If they find some soon, will they turn back and let me accompany them?*

No. It wasn't up to them.

I need to leave them soon.

Fenri searched Stone up and down with those knowing eyes, probing for hidden answers. Her need to know things was all-consuming. She placed her terrabag down onto the ground as Pau began to set up the baracca.

Craeya hovered at the entrance. Luzon tinkered with bamboo and metal in his hands, his fingers twisting and bending like vines. He fumbled and dropped a part then went to pick it up. His body jolted in surprise.

He is not the same.

He picked it up, noticed Stone watching, turned away. "Might be time for a rest," he said, crouching at the baracca's entrance. Craeya turned and kneeled beside him. "Your hands might need a different kind of healing."

"What's that mean?" Luzon asked.

"Here. Give them to me." Craeya took Luzon's hands in hers and pulled him closer to her. "They need some help." She began rolling Luzon's fingers in her hands, pressing and pulling, making the knuckles pop, caressing them with the heels of her palms.

"What are you doing?" Luzon was as rigid as steel.

"It's called massage. It's a healing art. Haven't you ever had it before?"

Luzon shook his head, eyes wide. Fenri looked up from her logbook. Stone could feel Craeya's warm touches from where he stood.

"It feels good," Luzon said. His shoulders dipped, and he fell into a relaxed state, baring himself to Craeya.

Now is the time. While they are thinking about other things. They will not suspect it.

Stone shuffled his feet, wondered how to say it. He looked at Fenri, who was still watching Luzon and Craeya.

The energies were changing, surging even. Quick spurts emerged from Fenri, royal blue and indigo swirling around her head, circling Craeya, then Luzon, desperate to mitigate the scene. Luzon's energies grew then dissipated, a calming of the yellow orb sitting at his solar plexus. With each rub of his hands, he became more subdued. Craeya's energy was growing. Her orange and red rooted beneath her, spreading like vines, staking claim to the area around her.

There.

Stone sensed a thin ring of another color, one he couldn't read. Green.

He sensed his own fear. And Fenri must have too because she

said, "You don't want to do that for too long. You might damage his tissue."

Craeya shot her a tired look. "Okay, Fenri. Thanks for your input."

Fenri sighed and sat next to them. "We're about a day's journey from a large Klonden field. We'll need Luzon's hands. And yours too. Don't overdo it."

"Come here," Craeya said. "You talk too much." She released Luzon's hands and stood. Then she grabbed Fenri by the shoulders and began massaging the dark nest of her head and hair. She pressed into her temples and the divots behind the skull. Fenri tensed, scrunching up her shoulders.

"You're tight," Craeya said. "Reminds me of Pau wearing Stone's skinsuit."

"What?" Pau had finished setting up the baracca. "What are you all doing?"

"Craeya is healing us." Luzon was smiling. "You want one too?"

"I'm good," Pau said.

Craeya pressed into Fenri's head and hair, her ears and neck. For a moment, Fenri's energies calmed, almost fell to nothing. And that's when Stone felt it, a heaviness weighing in his chest he knew he could release if he just said what he needed to say.

I want to be sitting there too. I want to feel what that is like.

Stone looked down at his hands, at the power packed into two heavy fists. The realization that his world was only internal struck him with a sudden sadness.

They only see me when they need my visions.

Now, they needed to see ... needed to hear his greatest truth.

Now is the perfect time. Tell them.

The weight of marble drove into Stone's chest. The thought of meeting a new dispatch team, a team that wasn't his current team, exhausted him. He wanted to be back at the nation-feast then. He would love to bathe and wash himself. To eat. To sleep in a bed. His eyes hung like swollen figvi fruit in his sockets, his cheeks drooped, and all his hair, his ugly bush of hair, weighed heavy like iron on his face.

Get it over with. Maybe after this next dispatch, the Masters will call you home.

Luzon was leaning against Craeya, and Stone felt warmth spread through the middle of his chest. Luzon adjusted himself, sat upright, grinned. The corner of Craeya's mouth pulled up into a smile, and as she pressed into Fenri's head even she opened, her walls of knowledge cracking, revealing Fenri's need to be touched.

Hours passed in Stone's head. In the outside world, Zhao rose higher and higher as they all rested inside their baraccas. Stone wrestled with answers, became naked with certain questions.

Is this the way?

There was a flash of green light in the dark spaces of his mind, and that's when the truth came to him. The message from the Masters meant that he needed to leave immediately. They had sent Stone a message because of a message he had sent them. He had told them of the green aura in Craeya, not knowing what it was. But then he knew.

Craeya has opened the fourth portal, and she is opening it in the others. The Masters know because of me. I must leave before I cause any more damage.

Stone felt as though someone else inside him was speaking. Not the self, but the other.

This will be pain for all of us, but it will be swifter.

Stone stood. His chest closed in on itself, collapsing into ruins. Everything felt wrong. In the other baracca, Craeya stirred. She put both hands on her chest. An impending annihilation, of bones, organs, and blood choking and clogging, was coming.

"Everyone get up!" Pau shouted.

Three slithering shapes grew like mountains as they moved toward the baraccas. Pau stood at the ready, grappling claws in both hands. Luzon, Craeya, and Fenri wandered out from their baraccas, confused and frightened. Fenri looked to Stone, pure terror in her eyes. Stone felt it too.

Kohbras. Three of them.

"Get ready to run." Pau came to the group. The others stood there, staring at him for answers. The kohbras were three feet taller than Pau, broad at the head and neck, with tiny prehensile claws for hands sticking from their scaly bodies, and long, thick, vine-like tails.

We will die here. Unless I do something.

Stone pushed himself into a vision so that he could see. He handspoke to Fenri.

I am going now. For good.

What? What are you talking about?

I will draw them away. You must let me do this for you.

Stone knew he had betrayed them. That is how he would atone for his sins.

What are you talking about? Stone knew he was her greatest ally. There was no choice.

Tell them, Stone said. *Tell them I am sorry.*

"Stone!" Fenri shouted, breaking into half-tears.

Death had come. Stone realized his message might not even matter anymore. Their end may have been nearer than he thought.

With all the strength he could muster, Stone vibrated the chords in his throat. A horrible moan emerged, animal-like. Everyone looked to see, to understand the strange battle cry.

"Stone, please!" Fenri begged. "Not right now."

Yes, now, he thought. *I must draw attention away.* He pointed, signed, waited for Fenri to understand. Then he grabbed his terrabag and ran as fast as his legs would take him, leaving Fenri to deliver his message.

Stone flew against the hardened ground. Heat was a liquid pool floating in the air. He moved through the soup like a laser, glancing back to take in the scene. The kohbras had arrived, all thick black neck and fangs, slithering and hungry.

Craeya and Luzon were running east, and Fenri had gone west. They were divided. Pau ran toward Fenri then noticed Stone and the kohbras following his path. Pau turned.

"Hey! Get away from him! I'm right here!"

Stone turned as he hiked higher up a dune.

One of the kohbras turned back, drawn to Pau's voice. Now two.

No! Stone thought. *I was drawing them away. Do not do this, Pau. You cannot fight them.* Stone's heart crashed like a meteor inside him as the third kohbra turned back for the prize that was Pau. Fenri, Craeya, and Luzon were still sprinting away, maybe even safe. But not Pau. The three kohbras circled, so massive and ugly, filled with the disgusting Quat Zone oxygen.

Everything happened so fast, and Stone couldn't bear to watch, but he had to.

Pau fought. With both grappling claws, he pierced skin, drew blood. Stone heard a screech. An eye fell from one of the kohbra's body, writhing. Another one struck, lightning quick, with an intensity that knocked Pau down and away. He rose, slower.

The kohbras closed in.

Pau fought back again, using sprays and stunners from his Guardian belt to immobilize and then attack. His own flesh tore. The fight would be over at any second if Pau didn't move fast enough. He shot a grappling claw into the heart of one kohbra, and it thrashed and screeched a hideous sound. Pau pulled the chain back to him and the kohbra fell, torn wide open. The beast wriggled off the ground like a vine separated from its parent root then retreated. Now, only two remained. One darted away, hung back, waited.

One on one. The kohbra circled. Pau shifted his stance. He shot the grappling claw again, pierced the final kohbra.

Stone's heart stopped. The other kohbra stalked up quiet as a shadow, as if evolution had prepared it for that very moment, that stealthy kill. Pau couldn't see it, couldn't react. The kohbra would strike and win Pau's head as a final reward. Someone needed to warn him, but Fenri and the others were so far away, they couldn't. Stone couldn't.

The fangs gleamed like diamonds in the sun.

Something inside Stone shifted. Fear forced the action, the eruption of a long-dormant volcano. He didn't know how or why, but his throat produced sound.

"PAU!" he said.

Energies rushed into him with so much force he felt himself blown back. His entire body vibrated, an instrument smashed to pieces, shattered and terribly alive.

He had spoken. And in the space of time that it took to blink, many things happened.

Pau turned around in time. The kohbra missed. Pau jabbed with his claw, gouged out another eye. The beast screeched and slithered away, retreating. Pau fell to his knees.

He had won for the moment, but he had taken severe damage. They had ripped into him too. The way he fought didn't show that, but Stone could see it. He could see so many things.

He touched his throat, tears forming in his eyes.

I ... spoke. How?

He couldn't stop to think about it. He had received the Master's message. He had made his decision. Now, it was time to forget. Craeya's fiery passion and her pink-streaked hair. Luzon's active hands, his spark of a smile. Fenri's constant questions living in her eyes. Her knowing.

And Pau.

His strength. How he protected them. A spark of light warmed Stone's insides. He pushed it away. He didn't want the heat, the burning high above.

He thought about his team members for one last time.

Now I must forget you.

Without looking back, he ran as fast as he could.

A story begins infinitesimally small, a pinprick in time, and grows into a multitude of realities, universes folding in on themselves into an endless saga with no beginning and no end, and every creature will play its part.

- from *Diaries of Our Ancestors*

27. PAU THE PENSIVE

Wind blasted them from all sides. Rocks and debris ripped skin from Pau's body. The naido would tear him away, out into the deep, untouched atmosphere to a quick and painful death. Pau saw Stone's storm-grey eyes, his sturdy hands holding tight, heels like spikes in the ground.

The winds were too strong. They would not relent.

But neither would Stone.

Seconds passed and the gales quieted.

Pau felt a twisting inside him as he returned to his feet. He felt something like comfort, but a growing unease gnawed at the edges. He did not understand why Stone was there, what he was. Pau searched his brain for a word. Any word. *Protector?* No one had ever protected Pau. He knew about beasts and protecting others. The sky, the winds—they were not something he knew how to fight.

But Stone could. He drew breath like a blowfly-fish. Then he ran.

They ran as fast as they could to find the others.

These thoughts returned to Pau in a rush, quick and hot in the river of his veins. He was too tired to force them away. His mind could do nothing but explore them. A weight lifted and left his body.

He startled when he felt someone touch his bare stomach.

Other eyes were staring back at him. A groan escaped his mouth. He hated the Quat Zones. Thoughts and memories drifted back to him.

Stone. *He left us.*

Now there was rage, black and cold as night.

"You're burning up," Craeya said. "Take a little more water."

"I'm fine." Pau pushed himself up to sit.

"Hey!" Craeya said. "No moving. You still need repair."

"What happened?" But Pau already knew. He knew most of it. The naido stole light from its holy source. The kohbras ripped flesh from his body. The sky fractured into pieces.

"You fought off three kohbras," Fenri said, joining them. "And won." Her face was a splotchy rose, leathery and worn.

"Stone," Pau said, unable to stop himself. "What did he do?"

"He left us," Fenri said.

"And he couldn't even tell us," Craeya said. "I expected silence but not cowardice."

They were taking words right from Pau's mouth. Right from his brain. He wanted to speak his mind, his rage, but he found only emptiness.

"I believe Stone received a message," Fenri said. "From the Masters. Planeteers are nomads. They go where they're told to go."

"So he just left without telling us?" Pau wanted to know.

"I think he may have been struggling with a way to tell us," Fenri said.

Pau wanted to know more, like if they would see Stone again and when they would go back to the nation-feast. *These thoughts are distractions.*

He shoved them away. "Klonden. Where is it, Fenri?"

Fenri brightened at the word, looked down at her newly fixed map-projector, and dragged her fingers across the screen. "Not far now. There's a field in the next quadrant, according to these readings."

"Let's go," Pau said, putting his hands down again.

Craeya raised a finger to Pau. "Not yet. More rest for you."

"How much more do I need?"

"I'd normally say a week, but I don't think we can sit still for that long," Craeya said. "A few more days, at least. You've only been knocked out for twelve hours. You almost died, Pau."

And with that word, Pau felt the pain of a thousand suns, pouring into the cauldron of his body. Now, he could feel the damage. He felt his flesh torn open and a sharp throbbing in his right shoulder, like it had been ripped from its socket, then jammed back in. Even with pain-modifiers, Pau felt the pain rising up, demanding to be felt.

Kohbras weren't poisonous, but they could rip you apart with their fangs. They could strangle you with their long, strong bodies. Pau smelled his own wounds, hot and ripe with agony. Blood oozed from every orifice. Craeya had tended to and cleaned them. They burned with crystal clear solutions, excreting dirt and yellow pus.

Pau regarded Craeya for a moment, for what she had done.

They rested. For the first time in a long time Pau slept underneath the protection of the baracca while Luzon and the others kept watch. A week was too long. Pau was up and moving in three days. He couldn't lie down anymore, as it was more painful. Now, getting Klonden and returning home was all that mattered. They had their original team. More than four was just a distraction. Five had always been a distraction.

Pau crouched down. Every muscle tightened inside him. He was not the man he had been at the start of the mission. He wondered if he would be again.

Take it slow. Even you need to be smart about this.

"This way then." There was vigor in Fenri's words and steps.

You're still their Charge Leader. You still need to be composed and lead them well.

Stone's face, heavy as marblestone, pressed on Pau's memories. Their Planeteer disappeared. *Why now? Why didn't anyone know about it? Three beasts came from nowhere to attack us.*

From out of nowhere …

What attracted them there?

Pau sniffed at the air. Did the scent of the beast Luzon killed linger? Or was it something else? Did the kohbras smell a different scent entirely?

He watched Craeya and Luzon, how Craeya's gaze lingered on Luzon. Fenri pushed forward with great strides. Head held high, she was determined to find what they had come for. As soon as they found Klonden, they could journey back. The journey back was based on rote memory and always quicker.

And yet it all felt wrong. Like they were walking into a naido. Would finding Klonden even matter? Where did that thought come from? *Of course it matters. We're going to find some, we're going to survive this mission, and we're going to make it home.*

Pau quickened his pace.

He passed Luzon and Craeya. He didn't want to watch them, didn't want to notice anything that might make him think of his own memories.

"How big is the field?" Pau was even with Fenri at the head of the group. He ignored his own limp and tried to move like nothing had happened.

"Big enough for all of us to fill our packs." Fenri turned to look at Pau. Her eyes sharpened, deep cerulean like shards of ice. "There's … something else there too."

"What do you mean?"

"I don't know. They aren't readings I've seen before. They're not readings from the crawlers."

"Then what are they?"

"I've already asked Luzon, but I think when he fixed it, he changed the programming."

"Just get to the point, Fenri."

"That is the point." Her voice threaded the wind like a needle. "I'm getting readings I've never gotten before. Faulty or novel, I don't know." She pulled out the map-projector to show Pau. "Look. Here are the Klonden readings. These tiny blinking green dots. But here—" Fenri traced her finger in a circle toward the outside of the screen, over coral lights. "This ring gives another reading."

Fenri's eyes snapped up to Pau. "I've already asked Luzon about it, and he said he's never fixed a map-projector before but that partitioning it could have unlocked some data that it was meant to be showing."

"It's something you've done," Luzon said from behind. "That ring wouldn't have appeared with what I did. You've made add-ons, no?"

"Yes, but—"

"Maybe it's something you've *both* done," Craeya said, as if it were the obvious and easy answer.

"I don't care who did it, just tell me what it means," Pau said.

"It could be Klonden buried deeper," Fenri began. "Or another material. One we know about, or one we don't."

Ahead, a ridge tipped with jagged stone arched upward and reached into the sky, wide like a hand, fingers fanning out.

They traveled up the incline, up to the peak of the ridge. Zhao slid overtop down and away, pulling the blanket of its golden light with it. Pau hiked higher. His calves and biceps felt weak from disuse, from the fog of medicines running through his body. They barely masked the enormity of his pain. He focused on the pain in his shoulder and tried to displace it into the rest of his body.

Almost there. And then we go home.

An hour later, they reached the ridge's peak and looked down into the valley, if that's what it could be called.

The ridge opened, its circular structure wide and deep, a bowl for the gods. On the other side, the lip sloped downward again, away from an identical ridge, to other parts of the planet. Pau observed the moons pouring their silvery light into the valley like peppernut milk. No, not a valley.

Something had been there.

"There's a giant depression here," Fenri said. "That is strange."

"What is this place?" Craeya said.

"It's like a volcano was here, and then it was ripped out." Fenri kneeled down, took some of the dirt at the ridge's edge in her hands. She looked at her map projector. "This is the outer ring that showed up on the map. That means there is Klonden down there," she said, pointing.

The decline wasn't too steep, but the pebbles and loose sediment made it slick. A fall could cause serious injury and they couldn't afford any more. Pau ground his heels into the qha, testing his own strength more than anything. He remembered his training: *Pain is only in the mind. I am stronger than my pain.* He stepped over the ridge. Tiny stones skittered beneath his duneboots. He paused to steady himself.

Luzon stepped over the ridge. "Something landed here. A meteor or something."

Fenri rose to her full height. "What makes you say that?"

"Look at the formation. I don't know how old this crater is, but something big and heavy hit our planet and left this mark."

Fenri's eyes flashed, like the sudden crashing of waves. "We don't know for sure."

"C'mon," Luzon said, walking down toward the crater's center. "Let's keep going."

"Luzon, wait!" Fenri said.

Craeya followed. Fenri shot Pau a glance. "This could be a beast breeding ground." Fenri took measured steps, one arm up to steady herself within reach of Pau. "You know beasts. What do you think?"

Pau sniffed the air, tried to pick up on any usual signs. His senses had been shot. Whatever the kohbras had done to him, whatever life they had tried to rip from him, they had weakened his immune system. Pau slipped on some loose pebbles, slid several feet before steadying himself. The Quat Zones and his ailments were sucking life from him. His muscles shriveled, devoid of moisture. He hadn't felt that weak since he was a boy, since the Masters infected him with every sickness imaginable to boost his system. They had given him everything so that later, nothing could hurt him.

The ventricles of his heart thumped against each other like beasts jostling for dominance.

Fenri whispered, "Take it slow, Pau. There's no rush."

He had to keep moving and talking. "There could be beasts here, yes."

"Why did they come like that? Three at once, out of nowhere. I've never seen that before. Never seen—" Fenri caught her breath as they scaled lower. "Beasts that *big* before. Have you? Pau, they were hideous."

"I've seen uglier."

"Is it normal, the way they came?"

"What does normal mean?"

"I think you know what I mean." Fenri's breathing grew heavier. They were descending, but it seemed to be getting harder to breathe. "Is it them? Did the beasts come because of them? I'm worried. Craeya. The fourth portal." Fenri was usually articulate, but her words tripped over one another, like tamagons scrambling to safety. "Pau? Aren't there supposed to be smells? Some QhaHadurians can smell the changes, right? What if—"

"I don't know!" Pau's ears and cheeks flushed with a dizzying heat he could not control. The cool night air licked his skin. "I don't know," he said, dropping his voice.

"You need to know," Fenri said. "You're our Guardian. You're the Oather. If anyone's broken it—"

"So what, you want to kill them?" Pau asked, suddenly sensing the curtain of death all around them, how it could fall and close on them any second. If his mind had not gone into hyper-awareness, if adrenaline did not pump through his body at superhuman speeds, he could have easily lost to the kohbras. They all could have lost. "That's the answer to what you're suggesting. You do know that, right?"

"I'm just saying we need to be careful. With tilq, maybe we can suppress it. But if it happens again—"

And Pau began to realize what Fenri was saying. Even though he knew, he felt the sudden weight of it. As they scaled lower and gravity pulled them deeper into that dark, moonlit pit, he felt her worry tugging him down too. Her words had brought him to that point. He hadn't acknowledged it until then.

Luzon withdrew his digspike from his terrabag. Fenri stalked up with her map-projector, careful to keep a distance from Craeya.

"Here," she said, pointing down. "Klonden readings are strong here."

Luzon stuck his spike into the ground, held the handle with one hand, and with his free hand, pressed a large dial. A spring snapped through the silence. The drill spun out into the rock and pierced a hole. Luzon pushed, dug deeper. He pushed and drilled until they heard a dull, clinking sound.

He stopped drilling. Everyone gathered around.

Craeya craned her neck to look into the narrow hole. "Is that—?"

"Let me see." Fenri pushed her way forward. "Can you dig some more, Luzon?"

Luzon did. He widened the hole so that they could see more. Down deeper, a grey-black ore sat with the stillness and mystery of space. Luzon used a mini spade to knock away rock, exposing the substance. When he pulled out a misshapen rock the size of his fist, everyone stared.

"Is that it?" Craeya asked. "Klonden?"

Fenri eyed it like someone without food for a month would, voracious and hungry for what it could offer. She grabbed it from Luzon quicker than Pau had ever seen her do anything. "I'll need to run a few tests, but yes." A laugh emerged from her throat, and it seemed the air warmed. Tears formed in the corners of her eyes. "I think we finally found some."

As if the planet could feel Fenri's happiness, the ground rumbled in response. Underneath them, the ground shifted and pebbles and loose rocks flipped and scattered then lay still. Fenri steadied herself. Everyone looked at Pau.

"What was that?" Craeya was holding onto Luzon for support.

So many questions without answers. Always. Pau could hear Fenri's even before she asked them. They started soundless, then exploded in a chain reaction.

Pau felt his own.

Home lingered in his mind. With Klonden, they could finally go home. But then, there were other questions. Fenri had taught him that.

Who was Stone? Was he really just a Planeteer sent to help us?

Beneath them, the ground grumbled again, stone grinding against stone.

"Let's move from this place," Fenri said.

Eyes swung to Pau for confirmation. Now they wanted to listen to him. After all that time. Even Craeya was being oddly obedient. Still, she clung to Luzon as they climbed their way back to the top of the ridge.

He betrayed us.

"This place," Fenri said, breathless, trying to keep pace. "It's alive."

Then why do I feel so dead?

Stone's hand movements danced through the air, silent and electric, a ghost vision in Pau's mind.

You should have never trusted him. He never told you the truth for one day. He waited until you were weak and vulnerable and then left without a word about where he was going.

At the top of the ridge, Luzon pulled Craeya up, and she fell into him.

They can't be trusted either. Maybe Fenri is right about them. Maybe Fenri is right about everything.

Pau looked down, saw her trudging up, each step more difficult than the last. Pau thought about reaching out to help her up.

Can I even trust her?

He forced his hand forward, too quick for his mind to tell him no. Fenri grabbed it with sweaty palms, and Pau pulled her toward him. She sat down and stared at the ore in her hand. Her eyes shone in the moonlight, and for the first time, Pau could see tiny flecks glittering on the misshapen rock.

He wondered if it had all been worth it.

This is your dispatch mission. There is no choice.

Does anyone even care that Stone's gone?

When their Planeteer was there, he just *was*. Now that he was gone, Pau found himself thinking of him more. His thoughts twisted like kohbras in the labyrinth of his brain.

Pau stared at Fenri, a grudge building behind his eyes. She had taught him to think of those other, creeping threats. But she didn't return his gaze.

She stared at the mass in her hands, peering at it from every angle. Then with the cold, ugly voice of knowledge, she said, "Klonden," as though it was the most important thing in the universe.

Where does one go when there is nowhere left to go? What does one do when the nation-feast is no longer a safe place? For these questions, there is only one acceptable answer.

- from *Reflections on Our Changed World* by the New Masters

28. FENRI THE FEARFUL

Fenri watched as Luzon smoothed out the rough ore with his elongated fingers, and a magnifier hung from his mouth. Finally. *Klonden.*

"It will be malleable," Luzon said.

"Will be?" Fenri asked.

"I'll need to heat it. Test it in the alcoves to find its true nature."

Beside them, Pau laid back, hands behind his head for support, serene and still. "How much of this stuff do you think there is? How much can we bring back with us?"

"According to these readings," Fenri said, examining her current data screen, "I'm picking up tons of it, enough to fill at least a lesson alcove." Secretly she wondered what the new resource would do for the tribe.

"I want to see how it interacts with other metals," Luzon said.

"Any medical uses?" Craeya asked.

"Sure, probably," Luzon said. "We'll be able to build things with it. I just don't know what yet."

"Weapons?" Pau asked.

"I'd guess it to be harder than carbon steels," Luzon said, standing up, rolling the ore around in his hands like a vital organ, some darkened orb of light. The Klonden gathered light from the moons, and Fenri could see its possibilities reflecting back. "High tensile strength."

The world dissolved around Fenri and her mind went into overdrive.

She wondered about its capabilities: its ability to withstand compaction or size reduction; its resistance to tension or being pulled apart; resistance to deformation, or the strength needed to bend it; resistance to sudden forces without breaking or shattering. All the different terms spun in Fenri's head like a solar system, with Klonden the bright new star at the center, full of opportunities.

All the different strengths: compressive, tensile, yield, and impact, swirled around in her head, numbers at their sides, forming a concrete equation, one Fenri would need to place on the Mohs scale. The equation became endlessly complicated, and she knew her brain was lighting up with new knowledge.

When Luzon's voice pulled her back to the present, she had no idea how long she had been lost in her head.

"Fenri?"

"What?" Her legs stung from standing so long. She shook them out and smacked them each a few times to get the blood moving again.

"I said, will you sleep?"

"Sleep?" Sleep was as far away as the oceans, and she knew she could not find it. Pau and Craeya were already asleep in their leshblankets. Since the injury, Pau had been sleeping. Craeya had given him tilq that caused fatigue.

"Yes," Luzon said. "I said I'd keep first watch."

Fenri sat down beside Luzon, desperate to slow her racing mind. "I'll stay awake too."

"If you say so. We're going to dig in the morning and round up more Klonden."

"And then home." Fenri felt a sharp burst of heat in her chest.

"Yes. Then we journey back."

"How did you survive?" Fenri asked.

Luzon's face fell, his dark features hiding in the crevices of the clouded night. "I barely did. That beast—I had another sleep-story, and this one felt so real. It was the first time ... I actually thought I went into death."

"Into death?"

"Death is a place."

"Perhaps."

"And then when it really happened, I was ready for it. I keep thinking my sleep-stories are trying to tell me something." Luzon turned, and the clouds overhead passed, giving his face the light sheen of freshly washed skin. "I keep having this one sleep-story. About something else." Luzon was looking down into the shallow crater where they had just retrieved the Klonden.

"What is it?"

Luzon set the Klonden down beside him and stood. Fenri felt a shift, the air changing. A bright light hovered beyond the horizon, as though the stars had come too close. Fenri wondered if she even wanted to know what Luzon had to say. Sleep-stories and memories and everything that Craeya and Luzon wanted to talk about only brought darkness. Fenri touched her stomach absentmindedly.

"I can't see, or remember past a certain point," Luzon said, "But … you're there. I can't figure out why."

"I'm in your sleep-story?"

"You're in a lot of them."

Fenri flushed. She wondered what it meant to be in Luzon's mind even as he slept.

"Craeya's there too."

Fenri's intestines twisted in upon themselves. She swung her gaze to Craeya to see if she would react. She rolled over then lay still.

Luzon paced near the top of the ridge. "It's like somehow you are connected. You both are connected to this sleep-story. I found our Teller. Jesimene. And she told me not to tell anyone about my sleep-stories until I know where they lead. But I can tell you."

The Teller. If there was anyone who held more stores of knowledge than Fenri it was their Keeper of Stories. Fenri could not resist the pull of new information. Luzon had lit the flame of curiosity, and not even the Electric Ocean itself could put it out.

"Why would she tell me that?" Luzon asked. "Especially when it involves other people. Shouldn't you know that you're in my sleep-story? I don't know. This has never happened before."

Fenri stood. "What are you seeing in the sleep-story?"

Luzon paced away further, and Fenri followed. "We're making something, you and I, and we're at the nation-feast, except we're not. We're building something for so long that it feels strange. Like we should be going on another dispatch mission. But we're not. And the nation-feast feels empty. Like everyone else is dead. Or gone."

Fenri hastened to catch up with Luzon, as though he had lost all his weight and the breeze was carrying him away. He was talking in a way that reminded Fenri of Craeya. All the rhetoric about starting something new. Didn't he know that they needed the nation-feast like they needed water? That they wouldn't survive a day without it?

"That is a dark sleep-story," Fenri said, finally, feeling the weight of Luzon's words in her shoulders.

"It wasn't though. There was good. Sometimes I can't tell which one is you and which one is Craeya."

"Doesn't seem like a very vivid story. We're very different," Fenri snapped.

"You say that, but you're more alike than you think. I think the story is trying to show me something. Like with the beast, and the wingsuit expansions. Both those things happened."

"What then?" Fenri felt herself becoming hotter, even though the night was quite cool. "What could it possibly be trying to show you?"

"We're meant to make something, just like you said." Luzon spun to face Fenri. They had wandered away from Pau and Craeya.

A breeze touched the sweat at the nape of Fenri's neck with icy fingers. She shivered then warmed when Luzon took Fenri's hands in his. She tried to pull away.

There.

Her paralysis returned in full force, just like that.

"What are you doing?" Her voice still worked. Marvelous.

"I'm looking at your hands." And Luzon rolled them in his own like he had with the ore, examining them with total fascination. His hands were swift but sturdy. Fenri was frozen but could still feel the rough callouses scrape against her own puffy hands, the sharp pricks sending heat into her body, into her stomach, between her temples where a universe of energy lived, churning without any beginning or end. She felt as though she would explode and cover the land around them with amorphous knowledge. She had so many feelings but not a single thought on how to express them then.

"They aren't Maker hands," Luzon said.

Of course they aren't. I'm a Knowledger.

"You are special, Fenri. I think my sleep-story shows me things that I'm not able to see in waking life." He paused, the light of his eyes like the burnt ends of two smokesticks, boring into her. "I think we should try to make that submership," Luzon said at last. "And then the flying ship. With Klonden, we can do anything."

Fenri's throat caught. She had thought Luzon dead, and there he was. She had forgotten him, turned him into a ghost in her mind.

"Don't you want to do that?" Luzon's grip on her hands tightened.

In their new alien setting, thoughts raced through Fenri's mind, warping Luzon's words into something foreign.

"Don't you want me?"

But that wasn't right. Their ideas for progress were about their shared creations, not the individual. Luzon *was* the creation. And yet ... she didn't want him. There was too much uncertainty. He could fall again. He could die.

Everyone always leaves. The only person who stays is you, Fenri.

The mahogany of Luzon's gaze deepened. Tiny yellow flecks

like stars surged in their depths. Fenri's mind was working in hyperspeed, but she noticed her silence was going on too long. Her mind dredged up more buried truths, forcing her to confront them.

This is what you want. This is what you've always wanted. You just need to actualize it.

With Klonden and the Electric Ocean, so much was possible, but with Luzon so much more was possible. She only needed to reach out and grab it.

Words finally emerged from Fenri. "So we'll ask the Masters, then?"

"We could."

"Could?"

"I mean—" Luzon released Fenri's hands from his grasp, turned, and swung his hands around in a sweeping motion. "There's so much Klonden here. Think of everything we could do. If we bring it back, the tiny amount that we'll be able to fit in our bags, then what? Look at what it is. It's new! You think the Masters are just going to forfeit it? Let me and you use it to build something that will probably sound ridiculous to them?"

"Yes, they will—"

Luzon lifted the ore in his hands, held it high. Fenri didn't even know he had brought it with him. Silver specks breathed life as the moons touched it with their light. "Fenri, don't be fooled. The Masters will take it, just like they did your plant. They'll do what they want with it."

Fenri choked on her words. She felt her breath leave her. The desert lost all sound. That was not the path she had expected. Those words were not from Luzon. "You sound like Craeya. You've been talking to her, haven't you?"

"Is that such a bad thing?"

The warmth of being near Luzon changed and morphed into the dark cold depths of the ocean. "You're going to make something with her too."

"I hope to."

That was why Fenri didn't get attached to anyone or any idea. Nothing was certain. Home was certain. Answers from the Masters were certain. *But that? The Klonden and those empty proposals?* Fenri was furious at herself for believing Luzon's return was a good thing.

"At least Craeya is open to possibilities. She's not rigid and uncrea—"

"There are no possibilities!" Fenri said.

Luzon scoffed, and all at once, Fenri noticed how he had changed. Clouds overhead slid through the night sky, casting them in shadow. They gazed at one another for a hot, deep moment. That is not what Fenri had expected when they found Klonden. She was the Knowledger meant to simplify, clarify, and keep her team on the path.

Stone's gone. Craeya's drifting. And now Luzon too ... All I have is Pau. Fenri stopped herself. *No. I have no one. No one is here to save you, Fenri. The only one who stays is you.*

As if to confirm all her beliefs, Luzon stalked off toward the others. "Don't let what you have go to waste. Don't waste your life on unfair laws that stifle your genius."

And Luzon was gone.

Fenri could move again. She crossed her arms over her chest, grabbed her shoulders, and squeezed herself tight. As though she could rid herself of the icy air. As though the steam inside her would dissipate in time. If she stood any longer, she knew she'd become lost in a dark place. She needed to move.

When she rejoined Luzon, she wrote in her logbook. All that mattered was getting words on the page. Nothing else. After an hour, her mind felt lighter, but she had no idea what she'd written.

She looked up, and at the same time, Luzon looked up from what he was doing. They avoided each other's gaze. Fenri closed her logbook. She didn't know what made her do it, but she crawled onto the ground next to Pau with her terrabag and curled up into it, her mind suddenly exhausted. She hoped sleep would take her. She hoped tomorrow would be better.

"Are you going to rest?" Fenri asked.

"No," Luzon said, his voice easy and calm. "You go ahead. I'll keep watch."

Fenri slumped back into her spot and sighed. She ran over everything that had happened for the eleventh time. Minutes became hours. Sleep finally came. For how long, she had no idea.

Voices woke her. New pains lived inside her. *A sleep-story?* Voices lingered at the edge of her memories. She rolled onto her back and stared straight up at the passing clouds, their silver and sapphire flimsy streaks. Still, she heard the voices, and she knew they weren't in her sleep-story.

Fenri sat up.

Nearby, Luzon no longer sat on the ground, legs crossed underneath him. He no longer caressed his ball of ore. Fenri pushed herself up. She scanned her surroundings. He was nowhere. Maybe she had upset him. She caught sight of Craeya's leshblanket, a heap of cloth bundled up.

Empty.

Fenri's thoughts raced. Fear pushed her to move. She ran to the edge of the ridge and looked down into the pit where they had found the Klonden. A breeze moved through, lifting the dirt off the surface like one giant blanket. The wild breathed its own life.

There.

In the pit. Luzon. Craeya. Their voices again. Craeya saying something, her body tightening in resistance, a compact ball of energy. Luzon trying to reason, advancing, arms out and wide. Fenri read the inflections, the gestures, though she could not hear the exact words.

She spun around. Pau was sleeping. The injuries from the kohbras still plagued him. *No time to think about that, Fenri.* The panic returned. Voices rang in her ears. *What are we supposed to do if a beast stalks up?* Luzon had left his post. Craeya was a danger to them again.

"Pau!" Fenri's voice was loud with power. "Wake up!"

Pau sat up at the waist. Rubbed his eyes. "What? What is it?" He was on his feet in an instant, sliding into his duneboots, kicking into the heels in one deft move. "Fenri?" Pau scanned their camp, confused, rattled. "Speak!"

"We need to do something about Craeya."

"What are you talking about? What's happened?"

"What the Masters told you. Told us. About Craeya. It's happening." Fenri turned and was gone, down into the pit, toward Luzon and Craeya. Her chest and thighs burned.

And yet, it all felt so cold.

The ground underneath Fenri shook as she descended into the pit. Ahead, Craeya stood in a crouched position, and Luzon approached her gently. Fenri came closer, heard the words.

"I can't help it," Craeya said. "This horrible place is cursed."

"It's okay," Luzon said, stretching out a hand.

Craeya didn't seem to care or notice. Her face was wet with tears. "I can't go back now. Knowing what I know. You can all just leave me. Leave me like Stone left us. I can't go back."

Maybe this is the answer. The new thought seemed selfish and wrong, but it grew and Fenri couldn't stop it. Craeya was a danger. Without her, Luzon would be free to do what he wanted. Then he and Fenri could request a half-cycle, maybe even a full one to make the ship. The exploration was still in reach. Luzon's words rang in Fenri's head. She could still take him up on what he wanted.

He stepped toward Craeya, as though approaching a baby beast, cautious and gentle. Double-crossings were done slowly then all at once. Fenri watched his languid movements, all he had done to survive, and her affinity for him came forward in the moment when it mattered most.

"Leave her, then."

Luzon turned. "What did you say?" His mouth twisted into a frown.

"I said leave her. If what she's feeling is true, then we can't take her with us."

"See, Fenri gets it," Craeya said. "They'll kill me. Those beasts came because of me! I can't stop what I'm feeling. I can't!" And Craeya shot up, stood high on her toes, her breathing staggered. "Leave me alone, Luzon. You don't want to die because of me."

But her words didn't work. Luzon advanced further.

"Luzon, no," Fenri said. "She's been compromised. She's just admitted it."

"She doesn't know what she's saying."

Fenri saw her opportunity slinking away. Soon Luzon would thin out, become only vapor and gas in the air. That wasn't how it was supposed to go. Fenri treaded forward. "Luzon," she said, her mind-map assimilating data at breakneck speed, working out possibilities and algorithms. She needed definite answers from Luzon. A yes or a no. Right then he was hanging in limbo, unsure what Craeya's words actually meant. The beasts *were* because of her.

I want him.

Fenri pushed the thought away, disgusted by it.

No, Fenri! This isn't what you want. The virus hasn't touched you.

But for the first time she was unsure of her thought processes. A foreign threat had arrived in her brain, a superbug invading through a different structure, powered by something else. Fenri felt Craeya's words deep in her chest. She couldn't control it either. She dove deeper into her thoughts to try and fix the brokenness.

"Just come with me," Luzon said, just feet away.

"I told you I can't," Craeya said. "I'm not going to risk all of your lives for mine."

Fenri saw it slipping away. Pau arrived beside her, breathless, frantic. "Craeya, just calm down. We can talk about this."

"No, Pau, we can't," she said, her arms up and out like she was ready to fly.

Let her fly then. Let the beasts take her. Don't let them take Luzon.

But they were only thoughts. They couldn't make Craeya do anything she didn't want. Luzon drew closer, and before Craeya could dart away, Luzon grabbed her wrist, yanking her to him in one nimble movement. She writhed against him. "Stop, Luzon!"

He didn't.

Pau stepped forward, paused. Fenri was unsure what to do next. *Is Luzon trying to talk her down? Will he let her go?*

"I'm not leaving you," Luzon said.

"Luzon, think about this," Pau said.

"I have."

Craeya relaxed and curled into Luzon tighter. Her deluge of tears fell like rain. Then she pulled away and looked out, her mouth and face twisting, words hanging loose at the edge of her lips.

She'll ruin everything!

Before anyone could say another word, the ground beneath them rumbled. Underneath Luzon and Craeya, the blanket of dirt shifted and stuttered, and without warning, the ground opened up, creating a hole big enough for them to pass through, as if the planet had finally swallowed them up for their transgressions.

Craeya screamed as her arms shot up in a blur, and then they were gone. Only Pau and Fenri remained, and the naked silence of the desert.

PART FOUR
HUNTED

QhaHadurians are trained in highly technical ways. Knowledgers must hold so much knowledge in their brains, for example, that they cannot possibly attain the skills of a Maker. A Maker cannot hope to gain the vast amount of knowledge of a Knowledger, but he or she has a training period that is just as intense. They are like Alphas and Omegas—they cannot be compared. Healers and Guardians and Diggers and Seekers—our pasts and skillsets are colored by our training. When in danger, however, all that falls away. We stare through the darkness with the same eyes, peering into the same waters with the same objective. When we look inside and truly know ourselves, all see the same thing. Every time, a Hunter stares back.

- from *Lessons on Survival* by the Masters

THE LOVE WE NEVER HAD

QhaHadur, The Quat Zones, Quadrant XXXVII

It is said that Ast was an extraordinary being with mystical powers. He came from another dimension, another universe. QhaHadurians believe he was the first Maker, able to create potions, arrowheads dipped in magical ointments, and deeply entrancing aromatherapies, all with the same purpose: to make others fall in love with each other. When our ancestors settled on QhaHadur, they were already under the spells of love. Very quickly the world fell into decay. Love became an entity so dangerous that our ancestors evolved out of its deadly grasp in order to survive. When Ast came to visit QhaHadur again, he made no potions and shot no arrows. On our world alone, he saw the damage he had already done.

- from *Reflections on Our Changed World* by the New Masters

29. Craeya the Cursed
99 DAYS BEFORE THE NEW CYCLE

In the center of Craeya's chest, pressure built with the power of a volcano. Her blood boiled so hot she imagined she was all steam inside, expanding to a state that could no longer be contained by her body. Craeya knew what had caused that. She knew why it was there, and she knew it was her fault.

Now, she would kill all of them.

She wanted to be alone. Dying down there would be the best thing for everyone. The planet offered her a chance, and she wanted to take it. But there was someone else with her. Someone that would die because of her. She thought of running. She truly wanted to die.

Darkness covered her like a leshblanket, total and suffocating. She couldn't see her own hands in front of her. She wanted to move. Her knees were scraped and bruised, her skinsuit torn.

And yet, she felt nothing on the outside. All her pain lived inside.

"Craeya?" Luzon's voice echoed nearby. "Are you all right?"

"No, I'm not." Her voice was weak from dehydration.

"Where are you?"

She had no idea. She had fallen through the ground. "I'm right here," she said.

He touched her. Hands larger than the dark grabbed her fingers, her hand, pulled her into him.

"Why'd you do that?" she asked.

"Do what?"

"Try to help me. I'm doomed, Luzon. I'm dead. You shouldn't be here. You're only going to make this worse. Get out of here while you can." Craeya's ears were hot coals. Her throat was a flame, burning with unspoken words.

Luzon squeezed Craeya, his arms like endless vines, covering her. "Stop. You're acting hysterical. We're going to slow down and talk about this."

"No!" Craeya said. "I don't want to talk anymore. Didn't you hear me up there? This is my fault! I am the one who brought the beasts. I've opened the fourth portal, okay? Now you know. Get away while you can, or you'll die too." Craeya tried to wriggle away from Luzon, to fall to her knees. The weight of her feelings pulled her down, down into the ground, wherever the hell they were.

The air hung heavy, thick with the smell of mildew and a suffocating warmth that pressed on Luzon like a physical hand. Luzon released her from his grasp. A light flashed on, and Luzon's sharp, dark features swam into focus in what seemed to be an elongated tunnel. He held his flagelight above his head and swept it around them in a circle.

"We slid down some sort of chute, I think." Luzon shone the light on his own body, on his legs and knees, his skinsuit ripped open from the fall. He nodded in the direction they had come from. "There's a ladder."

Sure enough, Craeya saw it, encrusted underneath the rock wall they had presumably slid down. Metal bars shone through like teeth.

"What is this place?" Craeya asked, feeling its sudden alien nature.

"I think—" Luzon spun, eyes growing wide under the light of sudden revelation. He revealed more of the area with his flagelight. The ceilings stretched high, double their height, and the tunnels were wide enough to fit all four of them comfortably if they walked side by side.

Four of them?

Two.

One. Craeya couldn't bring them down with her. And the impulse to flee gathered momentum in the balls of her feet. Her brain buzzed.

Luzon noticed and grabbed one of her arms. They locked eyes. He steadied her.

"Let me go."

Luzon was making things harder than they needed to be. Craeya knew she had to lose him.

"I can't. It's just like you said. I can't now, not after everything I know. You're wild, Craeya, but you know things others don't. I couldn't just let them kill you."

"Then they'll kill you too."

"They won't."

"Luzon!" Craeya tore her arm away from Luzon's grasp with all her remaining strength. Having control again felt good, and she realized some of her power was trickling back into her body in pieces. "You're not listening to me. I've opened the portal and if you stay around me any longer, you'll open yours too."

Luzon's face slackened. His irises dilated to an impossible halo-size ring, as though he was understanding Craeya's words for the first time. "How? How did you do it? How do you know that you did it? There's no test for it." He paused, unsure of himself. "Is there?"

"The beasts smelled us!" Craeya had felt the changes happening inside her long before, and the attack only confirmed her suspicions. That same inner heat appeared, sparking in her chest. Warm electric vibrations coursed through her body. There it was. *No, not here.* She was thinking of him again.

Craeya wept, a sudden unleashing of storm-rain. Her feelings could not be contained anymore. They were in her hands, wet, out of control.

"I loved him! I'll always love him." Her throat tightened at her words, the sudden onslaught of tears blocking her like a plug. She swallowed with difficulty, squinting through her teary mess.

"Who are you talking about?"

Craeya had never used the word *love* before, but she knew it was right. She knew everything about it was right. How she'd never see him again, and if she did, she wouldn't be able to stop herself from wanting him. It was better to not see him again, to push him away, think him dead, *want* him dead. Those options were easier, less painful.

Craeya sobbed into her hands, mute with shock, the name begging to be released from her body.

"RANNUM!" she said, and as soon as she did, she felt the weight of the tunnel close in around her. She had released it, spoken a truth she'd carried inside her for longer than she could remember. Her mind tried to locate the moment it had begun. If it was something recent, or something that had been building, happening all along, resisted because of a tribe that would not allow such foolish things.

The spiral sucked her down.

She tried to hold on to the physical world. Any semblance of truth or normalcy. Something that could ground her. The words spilled out like magma, unstoppable.

"I hate these feelings. I miss him and want him, and yet I know I shouldn't, so I take tilq to forget, to numb myself and become quiet, but not even tilq works. Nothing works on me. *Nothing,* Luzon."

"It doesn't need to work on you," Luzon said. "You're unique, Craeya the Healer. You should never see that as a bad thing."

He *really* wasn't getting it.

Craeya's chest heaved. *If this is love, it's exhausting.* She could finally see why her ancestors eradicated it. She could finally see that Fenri was right. Luzon didn't know because he hadn't opened his portal. He didn't know the raw pain, the thousand openings of the same wound, how blood poured out from her, and yet she lived.

"I saw things," Luzon said. "In my sleep-stories."

No. That wasn't the way.

She couldn't stand there and let Luzon weave himself into the messy fabric of her life. He lowered his gaze, and his hand slipped from Craeya's wrist for the tiniest moment. Craeya saw her opening.

She ran.

"Craeya, wait!"

She flew like the wind, her feet barely touching the ground.

The flagelight blasted streams of light around the curvatures in Craeya's path. Alcoves appeared on both sides of the tunnel, winding back and away in different directions.

Craeya ran, the air in her lungs the only thing moving her. That was the only way. If her body burned up all her nutrients, maybe she could die that way. Maybe everything would hurt a little less.

Shadows emerged from the tunnel and clashed against the light. And then Craeya saw another darkness—the memory appeared in her mind—that same dark, olive-brown skin.

He had run once. Away from her. Rannum.

Now, it was Craeya's turn to run away. The memory of it threw her mind into the battlefield she had been trying to escape. She loved Rannum, and all he could do was run. He didn't want her. Luzon chased Craeya.

She peeled off into an alcove. Her knees knocked against the ground. She sobbed. To want and to be wanted and to not really have either of those realities because everything was so messed up were the only thoughts pressing into her. For the first time, Craeya felt as though the world was the ocean and she had never even seen its pearly-blue waters.

Bright flashes of sunlight flickered through the slats. She smelled the honey-sweet aroma of figvi fruit as her skin pressed against the rough bark of the tree. She felt his safe, sure hands, and a breeze coming through. The memories shot through Craeya like a powerful injection.

Her mind spun. Whatever was inside her came out. She vomited midnight-purple foam that gurgled like acid. Her forehead pounded with ugly heat.

This place. There is no escape.

Luzon appeared in front of her, heaving several weighted breaths. He lifted Craeya's chin to look at her. She wiped away the spit from her mouth with her sleeve and glared at Luzon.

When he caught his breath, he said, "My sleep-stories, Craeya. They're becoming more vivid. I'm remembering them."

Words escaped Craeya. She couldn't move and felt like she could collapse at any moment. That was how the virus began: an annihilation from the inside out. She finally saw its horrible shape. There were no books, no amount of knowledge in the world that could save her from this.

Luzon held his flagelight high into the air to examine the alcove. The room brightened, revealing its size and depth.

"Oh my ancestors," Luzon said. "This place. Look at what this place is."

Craeya snapped to attention and scanned her surroundings, as if predatory beasts could somehow jump out and attack. She had never seen anything like it.

Luzon moved to a wall with machines built into it: buttons, and screens, and complicated panels Craeya did not know.

"Literally," Luzon said. "The ancestors. Our ancestors."

Craeya didn't understand how Luzon could be smiling at a time like this. She stared at him in a daze.

"This is where they landed, Craeya. This is their ship."

"What are you talking about?"

"The Teller told me about this place. I didn't know it still existed. Our ancestors landed in the Quat Zones, and we haven't been back since."

"Luzon," Craeya said. "I don't care. I don't care about any of that. Please, just make it stop. My suffering. As quick and as clean as you can." Craeya looked up at him, the veins in her eyes crying out in pain. "I'm begging you. There is no way out of this hell except for death."

Luzon turned, and when their eyes met there was a crackle of light in his. "What if there was a way out? Other than death, I mean. Would you hear what I had to say?"

Only death can save us from the unknown.

- from *Songs of the QhaHadurians*

30. LUZON THE LUCID

Under the orb of his own flagelight, Luzon stood in a ring of dust and bacteria in the misty darkness. Craeya stared at him with those wild eyes. Tears carved lines down her face. Her hair was thrown around her face in a fiery, pink storm. "What could you possibly say that would change my mind?"

Luzon didn't know. He only knew that he wasn't ready to lose Craeya. The words hung at the edge of his lips as he had once hung at the edge of the Quat Zones, unsure of where to go or what would happen next. Something in his sleep-stories had led him there. They always did. Now all he needed to do was *remember*.

"Craeya, will you trust me?" He held out his hand.

The word sounded strange in his mouth. *Trust* was a notion embedded in their society, though they rarely spoke the word aloud.

Voices echoed from above.

Craeya swallowed hard. Fenri's voice sounded down the hall, desperate, frantic. Pau bellowed something at her.

"They're coming for you," Luzon said. "For us."

"Save yourself, Luzon. Tell them you tried to help but you couldn't."

Luzon held his hand out stronger, firmer. Their window was shrinking.

"You can all just leave me here."

"They won't. They won't let you live. Are you ready to die?" Luzon pointed his words at her like a durablade. He knew it was the only way.

Craeya searched Luzon's face for answers, surprised. As though she hadn't considered this before. Craeya the Healer did not simply die. She would never let it happen. Lifting her gaze to Luzon, she took his hand. "I trust you."

They ran out of the alcove they'd been in. Another light streamed down the tunnel.

"Luzon, Craeya, wait." Fenri's voice had a strange power in it, and it immobilized Luzon for a moment. He turned back and saw them. Fenri, heaving from the climb down, Pau behind her, his shadow tall and broad and grim on the walls. Fenri put her hands out for ... pause? Peace? "We didn't plan for this."

No. Everything would be different now.

"Come back with us, and we can figure out what to do next."

That wasn't Pau's fight. He only knew and thought of what Fenri told him. He couldn't recognize the virus any better than Luzon could. That was a thing only the tribeswomen of their party knew.

That's not right.

Luzon knew something of it. When he looked at Fenri, he felt a strange mix of guilt and shame. He didn't want to leave her either.

She had made her choice. She wouldn't shift her worldview, even just a little bit, even for inventions and discoveries that she wanted more than life itself. Luzon turned away from her. That was his choice. When he squeezed his hand around Craeya's tighter and ran, he knew he might regret it later. He ran faster.

"Stop!" Fenri called.

They kept running, Craeya at the lead.

The light of the others' flagelight shrank, and Luzon heard the heaviness of distant breaths. With his inner eye he saw Fenri, her hands on her knees unable to take another step.

They put distance between themselves and the others.

Luzon stepped into another alcove to catch his breath. The alcove stretched high and wide, twice as big as any lesson alcove at base. He saw metal stretching into the hazy distance with steel eyes, poking through the qha it had crash landed into, and he finally began to understand the immensity of the colossal vessel they were exploring.

Luzon swept the light around them in a great, arching circle. The entrance was also their sole exit as far as he could tell.

Capture would be their end.

They could outrun Fenri but not Pau.

The fear of being killed shot into Luzon's chest like a digspike. Craeya was leading them behind a control panel of some sort. She eased herself down onto the ground. Luzon clicked the flagelight to its ultradim setting and the light withdrew into itself, a soft and rusted onyx. They could hide there.

Craeya's moonblue eyes shone starkly against the backdrop of faded blonde, pink-streaked hair and Luzon saw the universe, all of its possibilities. The world shifted from its physical plane. In Craeya's eyes, Luzon saw *her* again.

That woman.

On his lap, dying. The memory kept surfacing, like a sea-creature sipping precious oxygen, then vanishing as quickly as it came. Luzon held on. His mind was a nutrient-rich sea-sponge absorbing connections he had never known.

There.

The memory unfolded, and he saw he and his team members standing outside the safety pod all those cycles ago. During his first cycle, she had died. There was ice in her moonblue eyes as she lay completely still.

"It was her," Luzon said, finally. "You have her eyes." The memory rushed into Luzon's processing systems, and he felt cool wet drops on his face.

"Luzon? What is it?"

"She died. In my arms." Luzon was trying to connect how that even mattered. His senses flooded. His heart thumped in his chest like a drum. "That night at the nation-feast, when I met you. It was like I was seeing her."

"Who? What are you talking about?"

"I think that—" Luzon didn't know how to talk about it. Sharp flashes of light inside his brain disrupted his thought patterns. The woman stood in the grey twilight of his memories, fading, then appearing. That place was forbidden, but he went because his mind was taking him there. He'd seen her many times in his sleep-stories. "They're trying to show me something."

"It hurts, doesn't it?" Craeya said.

"I can't fully remember. It doesn't feel good to not remember."

"It can hurt to remember too." Craeya put her arms around Luzon and squeezed him. He warmed underneath his skinsuit. A drop of sun swam through his veins.

"You helped me forget about him," Craeya said. "For a time." She pulled away from the embrace, held Luzon's hands in hers. "I don't know what any of this is."

"I don't either."

Patience could yield extraordinary results. Everything was manifested in time. Luzon always found a way for things to fit together.

Craeya's moonblue eyes stared into his deeply, wondering, waiting.

Luzon had no idea what made him do it, or how it was a thing his body and mind could make him do, but he leaned forward and fell into her, their lips crashing and melding together like a weapon forged in fire. They were fire and metal becoming one. Luzon tasted her sweet lips in his mouth. Time lost its way.

When they pulled away, their breaths were heavy with new life. They fell into each other again, and Luzon grabbed the back of Craeya's neck and guided her into him. They tasted each other longer then. Craeya's kiss was not water or food or medicine, the usual things Luzon put into his mouth for life, it was more than that.

Luzon inhaled, his chest rising against Craeya. A spark ignited as their lips collided again and again in a hungry exchange that left them breathless and yearning for more.

Luzon knew that was done in the Dark Room sometimes.

Not always mouth to mouth, but other places as well. Luzon had spilled his seed before. He knew the pleasure points. Craeya seemed to as well.

They stripped off their skinsuits in a hurry, as though their bodies burned inside them. The flagelight tipped over, went out, and the alcove swallowed them in darkness. They didn't stop. Luzon saw things in his inner eye, how it all fit together.

A new way forward.

Craeya pushed Luzon down and climbed on top of him, strewing her limbs across his body. She had thought about it before. Maybe not with him, but somewhere in her subconscious, she knew how it worked. Heat burst into Luzon's belly, the sudden explosion of a tamagon heart, spreading down into his legs, into his thighs.

Oh, ancestors.

Their act wasn't wrong.

The Masters haven't sanctioned it.

It was far too late for any of that.

Only in the Dark Room, and only with permission.

They were in a room, and it was dark, and they had given the permission to themselves.

To consider the love virus, one must also regard both memory and nostalgia, for the three are intertwined. Memory and nostalgia have long been linked to the opening of the fourth portal. Memories that carry emotion must be expunged. This has created controversy among some of the Masters, but most agree that some memories are too powerful, and should remain untouched. There are certain memories, that if accessed, would destroy even the most trained among us.

- from *Confessions of the Masters, Volume I*

31. STONE THE FAR-SIGHTED

For the tenth time that hour, Stone touched his throat. He ran his fingers down the length of his trachea, probing as though it were a flute.

Impossible.

He opened his mouth to speak, but no words came out. He cleared his throat as he had always done, but then reached deeper into his awareness. Sound emerged as a moan.

I spoke.

And when he said those words in his head, the memory returned to him: a surge of light, then darkness, flitting around his brain like a sudden flash of lightning. The memory warped, blackened. He wondered if he had even been there at all with the four of them.

No. Do not think of them.

Stone had been walking in the heat. Mid-morning sun lasered into him like fabric that would burn. The entire weight of his body sank into the semisand beneath him. He carried new burdens. His scent became sour, a medley of sweat and missed chances.

I did not tell them I was leaving. I left him to die. He is dead because of me.

Stone rallied against the thought, tried to quell it before it spread.

No. I cannot think in that way. They are behind me. I did what I was meant to do. Lead them to the Quat Zones. Now I must join my new team.

The thought of a new team choked him, and he saw the terrible shadow of the kohbras again in his memory, closing in, ready to squeeze away precious life.

Dunes rose up like the knuckles of a god in the distance, pointed and taunting. Stone pulled out his planet-tablet, examined the details of his next mission, and saw that it would take him at least thirty days to get there.

Normally, that was his operation. He'd travel great distances without another human, carrying the barest resources, living off a sturdy mind and endless sun, tricking his metabolism so that he could live, *always*. He had done so a hundred times. He would do it a hundred more. And yet, for the first time … he didn't want to do it.

Stone lost his will to do anything, and his planet-tablet crashed into the sand beneath him. When he bent to pick it up, he glimpsed a past-Luzon, picking up his own tools.

Stop seeing them.

His planet-tablet shook in his hands. The neon red dots filled his mind, vibrating at a low frequency. The slab of metal shifted in his hands. He saw Fenri's map-projector, its smaller oblong shape, the silver screen scratched from overuse. Her seablue eyes stared back at him.

Stone!

Stone was running before his mind told him to.

The only way to be rid of them was to travel away further. But his control, his inner peace began to shake loose, grains of sand slipping through a narrow vacuum.

A time-sieve.

A new vision.

A costly death.

I left them to die. I sent a message that will be their end.

Now someone else was running. Craeya. Running through tunnels. Holding her hand, Luzon. Running from a dark threat. Something Stone had done? The dark hands squeezed Craeya's, and fear came into Stone's heart hard and fast, the strike of a match on sandalstone.

Fire could burn forever under the right conditions.

Stone glimpsed another dark hand, smaller, and a boy with vicious, knowing eyes. He upheld the laws, but he had ideas of his own. Stone's vision began to shift, like their planet around its axis. Visions crashed into him like shooting stars.

There.

Pau. Striking at three kohbras with grappling claws, jabbing with sting-rods, blasting terrible, noxious sprays. He was some sort of beast. Horns and pincers pierced the silence of the sky, defending, battling, winning.

Losing.

Pau fell to his knees and looked up into the sun, and Stone drank him in, his veins and muscles pulsing with power, his body glowing. If gods were real, he was the manifestation of one. The sky opened above, bright and blue and vast, stretching endlessly beyond comprehension.

Pau fell. The kohbras struck all at once, and the Guardian was crushed, like a star smashed to black.

I killed them.

Stone ran harder and faster, knowing it was the only way. The ground pounded beneath him. Pain prickled through the marrow of his bones. He ran until he heaved for oxygen, until their faces swam into view.

Forget them or die.

Stone vomited as his knees crashed onto the ground. He wiped his mouth and noticed a sole tamagon heart drenched in sticky, white foam lying still in his vomit, no longer beating.

Stone clenched at his heart. His third eye twisted and sent pain rippling through his entire body like the beating of a thousand drums. His hands shook unbearably.

This, again.

Ripping. Like the naido. Something tore at his cells, wanting to separate all his parts, deconstruct him into an organism with no volition. The cells moved. Inside he felt dangerous changes taking place. He knew that he could die there.

Maybe death is what I want.

Maybe death is what I deserve.

But death had its own agenda and teased with tantrums and torture.

The marrow inside Stone's bones condensed. All his cells expanded then compressed, like a yufish out of water, taking its final sips of life.

Let this power take me and kill me.

Everything Stone was, everything he had done, came into his awareness with a crystal-sharp focus. The deep meditative trances and the opening of his portals was all work that he had done. Above his third eye, two neurons collided and pressure exploded in his crown, its power radiating outward.

He heard someone's else voice. *It will kill you.*

Stone fell through a shaft of light. Lower, deeper, brighter. Blinding light.

He lay on a metal table. The icy surface pressed against his exposed arms and legs. Fear weighed his body down. He couldn't move.

"This will only take a minute," came a voice.

Spindly white fingers reached toward his face, toward his throat. He opened his mouth in obedience. He was a tiny fragile boy who had scarcely used words. The fingers reached inside the mouth, spread the cheeks open with a clamp. Five intruders climbed inside, insects invading a foreign hive. He felt the sharp sting of a needle then intense pain in his neck as the lights dimmed to near darkness.

I must see this.

Stone held on.

He wanted to speak, wanted to stop the hands from imprisoning the sweet sound of that boy's voice. The probes crawled inside deeper. They clamped onto the vocal cords with metal teeth.

The boy awoke sometime later, groggy with sleep and heavy with the non-knowledge of an event pricking at him like a thorn he could not locate. His feet dangled from his chair. A man stood in front of him. Strange symbols and letters on a stone tablet hung from the wall. The man turned and began to *handspeak.*

The boy had never seen it before. But he would learn. He would learn many lessons, and fast. He touched his throat. A vision came to him. A vision within a vision. The boy saw orbs, dark and cold, metal underneath, silvery death. But the vision collapsed. He couldn't look in that direction. Not then.

"You will not see that," came the voice. "You will see many things, but you will not see that."

Now Fenri's voice: "Losing one sense gives unknowable strength to another."

"We will make the trade. He is the one meant to see."

I left them to die.

All voices pressed in. His crown cracked, stone split asunder.

You will die here.

Too much pressure.

You left them to die.

You will die here.

"STOP!" Stone's eyes opened and the world exploded into a pallet of colors. The sky bled maroon. Clouds expanded like smoke, violet and indigo and gold and grey. His single word echoed through the desert, alone like him. There was no one else there. Agony, a warning to others had come. The truth exploded inside Stone, a crash without sound.

They took my voice from me.

The sunburnt landscape revealed cracks in a world he had

never noticed before. They were always there, and in that moment he could see them. New senses opened. He smelled the first page of a new book. He was the first one to open it.

"I ... have a voice." The sound was strange. Another person he had never known was living inside him. The voice belonged to that person, not Stone. But he was Stone, and Stone was him. *Is that not right?*

Stone wept. Tears washed dirt and grime down and away.

He pulled his durablade from its sheath and stared into its long, metal face. Stone's storm-grey eyes stared back at him. The light of the sun gleamed down, showing him another face.

I sent him to his death.

Awareness pulled Stone up and out and away. He wiped the tears from his eyes and looked out.

The world cried out with new colors.

Flitting in the light of midday, three tiny blurs: two orange and one red slid across the sand with ease. The image of Pau was sucked away by a cold and distant undertow. In the intense heat, the three figures shifted in and out of focus. Fear came into Stone like a wave, and he couldn't breathe.

I called them, and now they are finally here.

When you create a society of Gatherers and Seekers, you
must not forget that a Hunter too, resides within.

- from *Poems* by Haldur the One

32. FENRI THE FIGHTER

L uzon and Craeya had disappeared from sight, and every
moment was black, stretching into a starless void. Fenri
eased forward, Pau behind her. The place couldn't go on forever.
Eventually, they would have no more tunnels or alcoves and
only dead ends. Fenri fingered the durablade in its sheath and
considered what came next.

She held her flagelight high and dipped it into the next
chamber. The light spread like the light of Kaleem on the
ocean, swift and vast, and unbridled by clouds. Her eyes took
in everything that the light showed her. There were chairs and
machines, oddities she had never seen before. Pau stepped past
her, sniffing the air.

"They're here," he said. "Or they've been here."

"We need to find them."

"What is this place?" Pau asked, looking up. The ceiling was
at least three times his height.

"This is human made."

Reality crashed into Fenri, triggering a mental explosion, and
her thoughts of Luzon and Craeya became lost in the shuffle
of her growing knowledge. She noted the ladder they had come
down, the chute Luzon and Craeya fell through, the long and
winding tunnels, expertly crafted, and the machines, drooping
with decay, rotting with an ancient evil. Their new location
wasn't the work of Makers or Builders, and nothing appeared in
Fenri's mind from literature she had read.

Truth came to her in pieces.

The radiation.

Fourteen years had passed since a dispatch team entered the Quat Zones. *Why? Why radiation for the entirety of our planet's history? Why is it safe now?*

Fenri rolled the thoughts in her head within the span of a second, and more questions shot through the expanse of her brain's unfathomable depths. Neurons fired. Axons and dendrites sent information to one another, burning at both ends. There would be fire. Fenri tried to slow it down, but she couldn't.

Pau turned, frowning. "Fenri, where in ancestors' name are we?"

"This is where they landed," Fenri said, her voice a whisper. And as soon as she did, she knew it was true. Other thoughts spilled out. *How many Masters know this is still here? How could something so big not appear in the texts? Why is this place forgotten?*

"Where who landed?"

"The ancestors. When they came to this planet."

The flagelight flickered, sent shadows spitting through the stale air.

"What are you talking about? Came to this planet?"

"Yes. We didn't begin here. We ended up here generations ago. We escaped from our home planet. Everyone should know that. Why does no one know that?"

Pau shrugged, as though the information had no meaning to him. He walked toward some sort of control panel in the center of the chamber, waist height. He looked behind it, bending at the waist, sniffing.

"They were here. They've gone deeper."

Fenri found herself at the front of the chamber, staring into glass. *These windows were for seeing a course through space.* They were buried deep beneath the ground. Above the vague sheen of glass, Fenri spotted wires snaking down the wall. Something had been ripped from them. Her mind went to her map-projector. She knew the tribe had devices: medical, seeking, researching, all fashioned after technology from the ancestors. Everything had been taken from there, reformatted, reprogrammed, parts and pieces hanging at her side, embedded in a device she had known more than half her life.

It was taken from here.

Fenri touched buttons on the panel in front of her, its crevices encrusted with dirt. A place frozen in ancient time. Fenri felt its strange, creeping presence, nearly alive. Underneath the panels, there were shelves. Her hand found its way to a book below. She pulled it out and stared at it.

Oh my ancestors.

Desire moved underneath her skin, slithering toward the light. She flipped the book open to see inside and coughed when a cloud of dust emerged. She tried to speak, tried to clear the sand and grit from her throat. Every moment was precious. In the back of her mind, she knew she needed to find Luzon and Craeya.

"What is it?" Pau appeared beside Fenri.

Fenri skimmed the pages. They were written in another language. An ancestral one. Fenri searched her bank of knowledge for the name of it, for the books she had read covered in its symbols and markings.

Farsi.

Why? Why this language?

She remembered that the ancestors had come from many different places on the home planet. With hundreds of different cultures, languages, shades of skin. She felt her own ancestry deep inside her bones, but simultaneously, she became aware of how different they were.

"It's some kind of logbook." But they weren't recordings of elements. There was no study inside the words. No research. Only confession. Interpersonal relationships. Fenri flipped through more pages. Translation lessons were so long ago. There was only so much her brain retained, but that knowledge was inside her somewhere, she just needed to access it. The other word came to her.

"*Diary.* It's a diary."

"A what?"

"Someone writing their own story."

Fenri flipped through with a Knowledger's tenacity. She ingested every word, every paragraph as though it were real food.

"Is this really the best time?"

Fenri ignored him.

She read stories of the ancestors, of a person. There was talk of a system running down the body's center, nearly on every page. There was a man of interest. The man was more than just a man. *Some sort of ... god?*

Minutes passed. Fenri felt herself being ripped in two directions: one of that treasured past and the other, a present that desperately needed her. She learned many things. She recognized the system as the portals, but the language describing them defied translation. Other languages brightened in her mind, and she pulled from different disciplines to see if she could find one that fit.

I need to know. Always.

The answer did not come to her.

In the pages, tattooed lines stared back. One in particular caught her attention. She translated.

I feel him as I feel the sun, unrelenting and ever-present. To me, he is everything I need. Like food, water, the promise of returning back to our ship unharmed. A safety I can only feel when I am near him. If they are to call this love defect a virus, then I am terribly infected.

Knowledge came into her then, traversed her skin with the heat and speed of fire. Thoughts alone could not stop what was coming. She set the book down.

"What is it, Fenri? What does it say?"

"It's in another language."

Fenri found that language beautiful in a way she could not explain. Like looking into the sunset and knowing that thousands of systems contributed to forming a world that Fenri could experience in real time. In the places where Fenri's mind had gone dark, it flickered with light.

Luzon stared at her at the nation-feast, talked about how he could not be confined to systems and tests with numbers. Fenri remembered asking him how many items per minute he could make.

She shook her head, as though to be rid of the question's foolishness.

He was there, walking beside her, dark, elongated fingers crafting a thin strap that would soon be Fenri's belt. He was there, staring down at her, holding onto Pau's stretch-rope as the naido sucked him into oblivion. That moment hung in Fenri's memory for a moment. Everything she had dreamed of—the Electric Ocean, submership, advancement—had all been stolen from her like the sudden snapping of a whip.

She squeezed the muscles in her stomach to push it all down.

He appeared again, beside her, both of them lying on the ground, Fenri drying up like a figvi, Luzon battered and caked in blood. She had no real answer as to how he had survived. He had flown. *What kind of QhaHadurian can fly with their bodies?*

A pyre was building in Fenri's mind, and all it needed was a spark, one match to get the fire to burn.

Luzon appeared, but he was frowning. He was proposing something to Fenri, but the words twisted in the air, speaking of death, bringing with them fear and uncertainty. Fenri had declined his proposal because it existed outside her knowledge of what was acceptable.

She saw *her.*

The girl with the pink-streaked hair that everyone loved, that procured EMs from Masters, even though it was their first cycle. The girl who could recklessly take on vicious beasts and win. Win against them, against infection, and seem brighter and stronger than ever before.

"It doesn't matter," Fenri said, recalling Pau's question about the book. She took it, shoved it inside her terrabag. "We need to find them."

She held out her flagelight and left the alcove, going back out into the tunnel. The shaft of ivory light cast shadows. Beneath them, memories coursed like veins and Fenri remembered. In another tunnel, Craeya had almost died of infection. Luzon had been ripped away from them by the wind.

"What do you plan to do?" Pau asked as they moved forward.

Fenri knew it was the opening of the fourth portal.

Punishable by death.

"Who must be the one to draw the blade?" Fenri asked, calling on ancient texts.

Pau sighed. "Are you sure that you're right about this?"

"If I'm wrong then take my life too."

"Usually it's the Charge Leader, or the Guardian," Pau said.

"I'll do it," Fenri said, and when she did, a new power rose up through her chest into her throat. She felt as though she could do anything.

"Both of them?"

There was no doubt that Craeya had opened the portal, but Fenri wasn't sure she could swing the blade that would rip Luzon from the world.

"I don't know yet."

Luzon was salvageable. Craeya was the blockade to everything Fenri wanted. She was the only thing that stood in the way of making all her dreams come true. She was the nuisance of an infection. She *was* the infection.

I will kill her.

"What about us?" Pau's voice carried emotion, the beginnings of fear, a sound Fenri had never heard before. "What if the virus has reached us?" Pau asked. "The longer Craeya is out there, alive, the longer Luzon is exposed to her, the higher the chances that we become infected." There was uncertainty, but Fenri saw that Pau had the same understanding.

She lightened.

Kill Craeya. Save Luzon.

Finally, the power to do what she had set out to do, building momentum in her chest, propelled her forward. She would make this thing happen even if it killed her.

I am a loyal QhaHadurian. I always follow our laws. Craeya is young and already the Masters are suspicious of her ways. They will believe whatever I say. She is the betrayer.

Fenri heard voices. The fire in her brain and the burning in her heart reached out to touch each other, the two becoming stronger as one. Bites of sound, memories of Craeya's voice drove Fenri further, faster. She ran.

"Fenri!" Pau called after her.

Magenta lights flickered in an alcove ahead. Finally, the deed would be done. She flew into the alcove, hair wild about her face. Pushing it away, she held her light high.

"Fenri, stop," Luzon said.

He stood tall, his own flagelight dimming, its energy draining to nothing. Craeya stood beside him, her eyes bloodshot, face exhausted and worn. Something had happened, a turning point for them too. Fenri felt it like she felt her own.

"It's too late to stop," Fenri said. "She made her choice."

"I did not," Craeya said, and her voice was calmer, more measured than it had been. "I could never control this. And whoever thinks I can is insane. I never made this choice!"

"Then you do not belong in our society," Fenri said, and the words felt right coming from her mouth.

"Clearly, I don't!" The fire returned in Craeya's eyes, and Luzon clutched her hand in his. Their wick was burnt to its end. Too tired to hide, to run, to trick Fenri and Pau into letting them live, or pass, or just ... be. No, it was far too late for any of that.

"You ruined everything." Fenri brandished her flagelight at them. "Receive your punishment, and we can take Luzon back."

"I'm not going back either," Luzon said.

Fenri had expected those words, but not the edge of Luzon's stare. His eyes were cold and resistant, and in their reflection,

Fenri saw that she was an enemy. The ball of yarn was beginning to unravel faster than she could track. Her mind acted of its own accord.

"Then I'll kill you too," she said.

"Fenri," Pau said. "Just calm down."

"I'm sorry, Fenri," Craeya said, her eyes watering.

It's a trick. It's always a trick. I'm not trusting her. I'm not trusting anyone.

"I don't know what we're doing." Craeya took a tentative step forward. "But I know this is right for me. You can just let us be."

"Or join us," Luzon added.

"What you suggest is impossible. It doesn't make any sense." Her anger swelled in her forehead, dizzying her. "Stop saying, *join!*"

She's weak. I can kill her.

Fenri had never wanted anything more.

Craeya got what she wanted by doing. Fenri had yet to actualize anything she wanted, on that mission, and others. She was tired of being just barely.

Her life appeared in her mind as a vast stretching image, laid out flat. No peaks, no valleys. Solid, but uninteresting. Inside, where only she could see, it was a world like no other. Her world had cascading waterfalls, snow-peaked mountains, and deserts with actual beauty, with oases, and giant palms and creatures, everything from her lessons, from books of old forming a swirling image in her mind: beautiful, and wondrous, and full of possibilities, but none of it hers. None of it would be hers, ever. And the pain set in and sat in her stomach like a stone.

Fenri choked back tears, held their weight in her throat.

I'll always hate her. As long as she's alive, she will always be my curse.

Fenri stepped forward to do the deed, but Luzon moved between them.

"I don't want to hurt you," he said. He was taller in that

moment, body stretching from floor to ceiling stalk-like, rooted, arms out like pointed stems. His own durablade gleamed silver under the flagelight.

"I'm not after you," Fenri said. "We can still save you."

"Pau, help," Luzon said. "Call her back. We can talk about our options. You are our Charge Leader—"

Before Luzon could finish, many things happened at once.

Footsteps, swift and light flew down the tunnels. Fenri waved her flagelight in the direction of the sound. A man appeared at the entranceway. He stepped inside, tormented from lack of breath. He heaved, took in the sight of everyone all at once. Everyone took him in. The strange newcomer with his hair buzzed short, face clean and washed, smelled of smoke, and his eyes were like a storm, brewing with power.

Pau sniffed to learn his scent, and Fenri studied.

Her mind connected to his, like it had before.

I am sorry, he said.

"You?" Pau asked. "Why?"

The others soon realized that Stone, a new Stone, washed and shaved, younger by at least ten years stood in their presence.

Why has he come back?

It didn't matter.

Stone stepped forward and Pau startled. "Fenri, stay back!" He stepped in front. Fenri moved to go for Craeya, but it was too late. They had seen the opening and taken it. Craeya and Luzon ran. They danced around Stone at the entrance and then shot into the tunnel, the pounding of their feet becoming more distant with every passing second.

They were gone.

Fenri shoved Pau away with all the strength she could muster. "Move!"

Pau tackled Stone and they rolled onto the ground.

On another day, Fenri would have stayed for their fight. She would have tried to stop it. Stone was an ally once. He and Pau writhed on the ground like kohbras fighting for dominance. Now, she wasn't sure what Stone was. It didn't matter. There were more pressing needs on her mind.

Fenri returned her durablade to its sheath and ran out of the alcove in the direction of Luzon and Craeya and their dying footsteps.

The idea of never seeing them again touched a deep part of her heart, but she pushed away its pain.

Then she ran.

There is one class hidden from the others for purposes that cannot be relinquished in written text. They are known as Assassins.

- from *Confessions of the Masters, Volume 1*

33. EIDER THE ASSASSIN

E ider recalled them in his mind as he had been told about them:

Fenri the Knowledger.
Luzon the Maker.
Craeya the Healer.
Pau the Guardian.
Stone the Planeteer.
Leave none alive.

Eider didn't plan to.

To his right, a soundless Quei shifted on his belly, sand curving around his long body like a tomb. To his left, Maej pushed red grains away from her mouth with small breaths. Zhao was beginning its ascent ahead of them, dressing the land in a blanket of golden light. Eider drew a deep breath and narrowed his focus on the tiny blots on the ground hundreds of yards away.

"There's no one there." Maej's voice was devoid of emotion in the Assassin way.

"They've left their camp." Quie's mouth barely moved as he spoke.

"It could be a trick," Eider said. He would not approach unprepared.

"What do we do?" Maej said.

"We wait," Eider said.

He warmed under the sun's silence. The upcoming execution made him thirsty. Eider the Assassin had not been in the field for at least three cycles, maybe more, and the events of his last journey were hazy at best. Blood brewed inside of him, crawling underneath his skin, his reptilian need to move.

"What's our final report?" Quie asked.

"We take them down quickly," Eider said.

"As if that isn't obvious," Maej said. "The question is how, Eider?"

"Take down the Guardian first," he said. "He'll fight till his last breath, and even after that. You'll know which one he is."

"They have a Knowledger?" Quie asked.

"Yes," Eider confirmed. "She won't know how to fight, but she'll be dangerous in a different way."

"Meaning?" Maej shifted to look at Eider with her piercing eyes. Her auburn skinsuit lightened under the sun's glow. She became one muted beige color on the ground.

"She must not know who we are. No one can survive, especially her."

"There is a chance," Quei said, "that some will survive?"

He is new to this role, so I'll permit his ignorance. He's never spilled blood before, hasn't been changed yet. He's mastered theories and techniques, now all he needs is integration.

Eider inhaled air through his nostrils as he thought about the integration of his durablade and human flesh.

"There are more of them than us, but we will succeed."

"We will succeed," Maej and Quei sounded in unison.

Wind brushed at their backs with soft bristles, bringing the smell of seawater and citrus. Eider drank the scent in deeply. That was his forte, smell. At the camp's edge, the unmistakable scent of fear rose into the air. Maej's specialty was sight, and she was squinting from behind her sveil, nothing but cold, alien-grey eyes underneath. Quei was quick. Quicker than anything Eider had ever seen, a sandy blur in training sessions, a flash of cosmic light. Soon he would be again.

"What of the others?" Maej said.

"The Guardian is mine," Eider said. "I'll take down the Knowledger as soon as I am done with him. The Planeteer we followed here. We have all seen how he moves. Quick, decisive, like his life may end at any moment. He is rattled."

"He is the one who sent the message," Quei said.

"Yes," Eider said. "It seems his indecision grows. He is the oldest and the wisest. The closest to becoming a Master. A purveyor of planets, a wise man of weather patterns, but fighting will not be foreign to him. Quei, he will be your first kill."

Quei breathed in the information, exhaled a stilted grunt.

"That leaves the other two, Maker and Healer," Maej said.

"The Maker is crafty and quick. I'm unsure if he knows how to fight or kill, but do not underestimate him. Sink some of your starblades into him to slow him down, and then bring down the knife. Follow suit with the Healer. She will be trying to attend to her teammates. I've heard she is quick and has the gift of youth on her side."

"Youthfulness breeds stupidity," Maej said.

"None of them will be stupid," Eider said. "We are no better than any one of them. We have merely come here to perform our mission. The last two are yours, Maej."

Maej and Quei sounded their agreement again.

They are good companions. Loyal and tough and stealthy. They will make excellent killing machines.

It was Eider's first mission with others of his class. All of his missions had been performed solo. He had never eliminated an entire team before. And his mind went to places that it often did, thinking of reasons and origins. He was not encouraged to know about such matters, but he hated only seeing the surface of an object. He needed to roll it around, see its shape and girth, feel its texture to understand. He could not always quell the curiosity of his soul.

They have done something unforgiveable.

Adrenaline welled up in the walls of Eider's chest like

fast-acting poison. *So many years of training for a moment so small it could fit into a grain of sand. Squash this evil before it can spread any more.*

"Do not touch them, and do not respond to anything they say," Eider said. *Which ones have caught the virus by now? All of them? Are none salvageable?* The dichotomy rose up in Eider's throat as a tangle of unspoken words. On the one hand, he wanted to taste their blood, but on the other, he wondered if any of them could be saved. His need to know where things belonged became a series of intangible lists in his head. *If they have names, I want to strike a line through them at the end of the day. Killing is not a senseless act. Their stories live on in me. There is a reason we have come to this crossroads.*

"And what if we fail?" Only Quei, a first-timer, could ask such a question.

The query slammed into Eider's back with its suddenness, pressing down. Eider felt the blood-red of his suit dim and become one amorphous shape with the ground beneath him.

His need to kill was changing him.

"We will not," he said. "We will defeat them and when we do, we return home greater than before."

I must tip the scales of self-actualization and fear. They must feel both strongly.

But the spike of new smells entered Eider's olfactory pathways, the tiniest spot of doubt, a mix of gingitleaf and moonchoke.

"There are more like us," Maej said.

Eider drew his headscarf over his mouth, allowing only his eyes to show through the cloth's opening. He took in the setting, calculating all means of escape, every danger he would need to know, the curves of the dunes, the weight of the wind, the heat of the sun. He sniffed the air to detect more information.

"We have all the assassins we need right here," he said.

The traitors appeared abruptly, climbing out of a hole in the ground. Eider's heart thumped with longing, a wild fear. A woman climbed out first, tiny-bodied and pale like bone, her skin tinged red and hair streaked pink. A man with thin, lanky limbs and dark eyes, skin, and hair in varying degrees emerged next. The olive hue of his body and the girl's bone white stood in stark contrast.

The descriptions are accurate. Healer and Maker.

Once they had climbed out of the ground, they grabbed each other's hands.

Yes, you should run.

Another woman trailed close behind. Heavy and lumbering out of the hole, breathless, crazed. Their Knowledger, Fenri.

There is inner strife.

Eider didn't want the mission to be any easier. He wanted to be the one to see the last light in their eyes go out. He waited to see if anyone else would emerge. They did. First, *him*.

The Planeteer.

He lifted himself out of the hole, rolled onto his side. Tried to stand, fell. Eider knew by the way the Planeteer was clutching his side that he was gravely wounded.

Finally, their Guardian emerged. He flew out of the hole and shot into the sky like a zeeby from its hive. When he landed, he swept the area with his gaze. The Planeteer stood, and they faced each other.

From where Eider lay, he could feel nothing but warmth at the thought of extinguishing them. The starblades concealed within his suit pressed against his chest, cold from disuse, then warm, warming. *They will fly truly.*

The new technology, the two small circular explosives strapped to Eider's shoulders would be used wisely, he knew. If necessary, as a last resort. *No matter how quick or clever they are, they won't be able to survive the blow.*

Quei's voice speared the deafening silence. "Now?"

"Wait." Eider pushed his hands into the ground and raised himself a hair's breadth. The heartbeats of his companions quickened in unison beside him. Eider had grown accustomed to his teammates and their company for the last quarter-cycle. He knew their strengths, their weaknesses. They were cold, clean-killing machines, but not invincible.

Every Assassin has a weakness.

The sun pressed into them like a scalding foot, pushing down. Wild danger came up into Eider's throat, and he knew that it was time. "Now."

Without hesitation, the three of them sprang from their spots on the ground. Eider dipped low, silent as wind, arms back, head tilted forward, sprinting.

They moved in like tamagons across the sand.

When the members of Project El were faced with the darkest of all questions, they chose what was forbidden. Imagine undoing eons of progress in a single moment. Perhaps we made too many mistakes, and this was our punishment. Perhaps they believed they had no other choice.

- from *Confessions of the Masters*, Volume 1

34. STONE THE RENEGADE

When Stone emerged from the underground tunnels, the sun was high over the meridian, and its heat could kill. An empty and cloudless sky bore down on them. Light poured into the basin, a terrible blinding thing, enough to cauterize the eyes. Stone staggered and tried to regain his footing. His throat clogged with a world of too many things unsaid.

Touching his side, he felt the gash in his skinsuit, the open flesh where the blade had gone in then out. Only once, but the wound was true.

Pain, a dark tide, threatened to drown him all at once.

And Stone deserved it.

He fell to his knees.

"Stone!" Fenri appeared next to him, and he felt another presence, circling. Pau moved closer, his mouth and eyes twisting in surprise.

"I'm sorry, I didn't know—"

"You," Fenri said, examining Stone's side, "*stabbed* him?"

The blood pouring out could have filled a goblet.

"He betrayed us," Pau said, but the conviction died on his lips. "I'm sorry," he said quickly. "I was confused—"

Fenri swallowed the lump in her throat. Stone could still see

Luzon and Craeya at a distance, standing there, sweeping the horizon with their gazes, uncertain, afraid.

Their world was falling apart.

"Can you help him?" Pau asked, and there was kindness in his voice. Remorse. He was sorry, and so was Stone.

It is okay, Stone thought. *This is my punishment. I wish there was time to tell them everything.*

All the things Stone had seen and felt in the past week since deserting them begged to be released. He thought he had sight before. Now he knew he had only seen a muted, colorless canvas. There was more to see. And soon death would blind him.

This is how I go.

"Stone, I—" Fenri trailed off, and Stone felt her mind grow tall and wide with unease. She stood, and without hesitating, shouted, "Craeya! Please help us!"

Craeya turned from where she was thirty yards away, Luzon at her side. They stared. "It's too late. You'll get what I have."

"He's dying!" Fenri said, her voice strained.

Craeya slackened. A moment of calm overtook her. Stone felt her mind expand to an overwhelming degree, the ground around her suddenly thrown open to quicksand. But she was not sinking. She was thinking of betrayal and trickery. She was considering if healing was possible at that point, or if Fenri called her over so that she could stick a knife in her back.

Stone wondered the same things.

He hadn't been around them for more than a week, but it felt longer. It seemed so many things had changed. Pau and Fenri were together in that moment, and so were Luzon and Craeya. Lines had been crossed and new barriers had been built. And Stone wasn't anywhere. He was bleeding the last of his life onto the ground, leaving the world with nothing but his mistakes. Zhao, a relentless storm of sunlight, engulfed him.

Stone tried to hold on.

He looked into Fenri's crazed eyes, saw her determination for his recovery, wondered at their truth. He wanted to tell her his past, so many of his memories, of voice clamps, and icy cold metal tables. Pau leaned over, his golden-brown face blanched white. The force that was Craeya shifted from its axis, ran for them without a second thought. She arrived and looked down at Stone, her hands already at work examining the death-wound.

"Shit, Stone! I need saline! And a gauze, and some pain-modifiers," Craeya said. "BRING ME MY HEALING KIT!"

Luzon disappeared from view and returned seconds later. Fenri and Craeya glared at each other, their eyes sharp enough to cut flesh.

The sky darkened. Stone wanted to speak. He opened his throat to try.

I am so weak.

"What happened?" Craeya asked.

But no one answered. She poured sweat as heat pressed into her. They needed to be under a baracca. They would lose too much moisture. Sharp pain seared into Stone's side, nothing like that initial plunge, but still agony, creeping through his veins, tapping on his bones. Craeya touched the wound, and Stone felt a spot of warmth where her hand lay. Something entered him at that moment, a thing he could not see or name, swirling through his body, into his center, up through his throat, his forehead, expanding as heat at the crown of his head.

He did not know if he would live.

But that is not why I came back.

The sharp pain became a thousand needles in his side. His arms fell, became heavy like lead. His eyes worked tirelessly to remain open.

There.

They had finally come.

If he did not use his voice, he would kill even more of them. Maybe there was still a chance he could do something to help.

"I am sorry." His voice was crumpled and infantile from neglect.

Their eyes and faces showed surprise. Pau had not told them of Stone's act.

"Stone? How can you—" Even Fenri did not know.

"It does not matter. I am sorry. And now they have come for you." Stone felt his breaths leave him in a hurry, desperate to escape his body. "You must make your choice now."

Stone heard their swift footsteps in the sand, the quiet pitter-patter of fatality. The killers' godlike power to extinguish life was in their stratosphere.

Craeya cleaned Stone's wound, then wrapped it with gauze, placing a large pad-cloth underneath to slow the flow of blood. "Stone?"

Pau stood, straightened. The others turned to see. Stone could see between the gaps of those standing before him.

They have come to pass their judgment.

Three newcomers fanned out like a bright and caustic crimson feather.

Two in orange, one male, one female, flanked the one in the middle, a male, taller than the others, his suit a deep, dark, blood-red, festering with death as its source. They showed nothing of their bodies, of their skin, except their eyes.

Stone hung his head. Pain jabbed at him like a zeeby's zinger. He did not need to see. Not with his eyes. He had seen all of theirs, piercing and dripping with venom and demise. These were not typical QhaHadurians.

No, Stone did not need to see.

He knew how it would end.

The body ages at a rate we understand. The heart and the mind do not.

- from *Reflections on Our Changed World* by the New Masters

35. Fenri the Forsaken

Rage came into Fenri's body like a storm, and she was at its eye.

Her anger was raw and wild and hot, like nothing she had ever experienced. She was angry at Pau for stabbing Stone, angry at Craeya for ruining everything, and angry at Luzon for choosing wrong, for not choosing her.

I've failed again, she thought, and all of her anger for the others turned inward, a floor suddenly collapsing.

There was no time to linger on it. The three strangers before them coalesced into one tall flame, burning a vivid ruby and gold. Fenri touched the durablade at her side. *Who are they? QhaHadurians, but different.* They stood still as death, weight leaned ever so slightly to one side. Fenri wanted answers, but she was sure she would not get them. They didn't seem to be in the talking mood.

Their eyes were weapons themselves with the way they stared. If Fenri stood there long enough, she thought their eyes could kill her faster than she could kill them with her blade.

Exhaustion was another enemy. Fenri had survived the weather, and beasts, and dehydration, but she'd never faced the threat of her own kind.

Is this how we go?

She couldn't move.

Her eyes clashed suddenly with the piercing gaze of the man in red. His presence staggered into her unwelcomed, and Fenri almost crumpled into herself. He was tall like Pau, though not quite as, and lanky like Luzon, but firm, more robust. He was all that Fenri could see, the other two orange figures melting into the expanse of the sun behind them. She thought he would speak, but he said nothing.

Even Fenri knew they were beyond words.

The red-suited man's hand shot to the side of his skinsuit, but Pau was ready. His grappling claw hurtled through the air, and the three killers dispersed in a wave of heat, sand and sunlight swirling around them like wild flames.

Stone groaned and Fenri looked to him. His face twisted under the weight of his fatal wound. His face was new and unfamiliar. Fenri only knew those grey eyes, but even underneath the jungle of hair, Fenri felt she had known Stone her entire life.

What will happen now?

Another voice came back. *Take cover.* Stone's handspeak, in her head, was filled with urgency. She grabbed the biggest thing she could find nearby—her terrabag—heaved it up to her chest and jumped in front of Stone. Metal hurtled against the titanium backside, clinking against the bag, then there was silence.

These killers were not loud like some Guardians Fenri had traveled with. No. Their strength was in their stealth, in the way they moved unseen, in flashes of dizzying speed.

The storm raged around her. Pau had expanded from the circle and was parrying with the man in red. Pau battled with his grappling claws, using them independently like mini blades then together as a shield. Fenri had to look away. She did not want to see anyone strike Pau down.

Their opponents wouldn't stop until all of them were dead.

Craeya and Luzon cowered underneath the shadow of the killer in orange, the female. Her sable hair hung down from her cap, over her scarf. She slashed at Luzon's terrabag as he backed away, then parried against Craeya's swift jabs.

Fenri searched for their third, the male in orange.

Metal gleamed in his hands. He held some sort of throwing weapon. *Starblades.*

Fenri had read about them, but she had never seen a

Guardian use them. She had no idea her tribe made them, and she had no idea who those people were. Gaps in her knowledge filled her with fright. She tried to fill it at once. These people were trained in their own class. The word came to her.

Assassins.

The starblades came once more, quick and heavy as hail. One lodged itself in Stone's shoulder.

He moaned and collapsed lower. Fenri dropped to her knees and held the bag up in front of them to block. They were trying to put holes in them to bring a slow and painful death. There was the other Assassin, the orange female, sinking her own metal into Craeya and Luzon. They both fell.

We're losing.

Fenri spun, saw Pau. She wanted to call for help. Her body trembled.

Blood covered the ground near Pau's feet in a sudden splash. A blow tore a gash across his chest, splitting his skinsuit in two. His dark skin was flaming-red and fresh with pain. Pau screamed, but it emerged as more of a battle cry than an admission of loss. The red man advanced again, slashing with his stiletto, the thirst for blood bright in his eyes.

With one knee on the ground, Luzon ripped a starblade from his thigh and cried out in pain. Craeya was on her feet again, and Fenri could see it as clear as lightning in a dark sky. The crazed determination Craeya possessed with the greffir came over her again. She was alive and did not want to die on something, *someone*, else's terms.

The Assassin seemed startled by her behavior, perhaps unable to anticipate such ability from someone so young and fragile. Fenri knew the feeling. To them she was just a Healer, but beyond her class, she was some other thing with her pink-streaked hair blazing bright under the sun and eyes glinting.

Fenri's arm stung, and she cried out. Blood trickled from the starblade wound. Stone lunged, and somehow, with the accuracy of the Assassins themselves, caught another starblade before it struck Fenri between the eyes. The effort was too much, and Stone crashed into the ground. Fenri could do nothing. The Assassin was already upon them, blade high in the air, ready to come down on Stone's head.

Snap!

Pau whipped the Assassin with his stretch-rope, tearing his skinsuit open, ripping the flesh underneath. There was a sharp intake of air through his teeth, and the killer fell back. Stone regained his balance. He tried to stand.

"Craeya, look out!" Pau said, and he ran off to help the others.

The fight was happening too fast for Fenri to comprehend. Her anger had dissipated, and in its place, there was fear, moving into her like a plague. She wanted her anger back. She had never made that trade. Even in the midst of those potential final moments, her mind looked ahead. The end had come anyway. All of them were compromised. After that, there was nothing. And yet, when she looked over at Pau and Craeya, she saw that they were still fighting.

Luzon was down. The man in red was getting up, and he came to settle the score with Pau, skulking like a tamagon across the sand.

"Pau, he's coming!" Fenri found her voice. She turned. Another Assassin was inches from her face. Again, Stone's hand came up to intercept. He struggled against the killer's brute force.

Kill him, said a voice in Fenri's head.

She hesitated and then didn't.

With a quick snap of her wrist she grabbed her durablade and drove it into the Assassin's side.

But she was too slow and only grazed him, slicing a thin strip from his body. He grunted, the first audible sound Fenri had heard any of them make. A fist came from the left like a bludgeon into Fenri's skull. She hit the ground, and the blackness of the sand swallowed her.

Fenri heard metal clashing against metal. Sharpening. Grinding. Was it battle? The world was blurry. There was pain, plenty of it. Everything from one side of the horizon to the other burned. The sky bled scarlet. Fenri felt like she was looking through her map-projector, but someone had damaged the tint.

Fenri had no idea how long she had been out.

Stone lay nearby, his stormy eyes wide but still. He breathed with difficulty. Fenri pushed herself up to her elbows, saw Pau, hands on his knees, heaving, with Craeya at his side. The three Assassins closed in on their group.

This is truly the end.

The Assassins held all the power. They were trained for that. Fenri wanted to believe that Pau could save them, but not even he could hold them off. Craeya was a help, and Fenri had seen her fight hard, but she was young, and weaker than her opponents. They'd had a good cycle. They had found Klonden. Fenri had tried. She had tried to follow the laws, but the portal opened within some of her teammates, and she knew it had come for her too. The sensation was strange. She turned and saw Luzon trying to get up. Something warm rose in her chest, filling her lungs with air.

I want to live, but is it even possible?

The fight to stay alive meant going against the Masters.

Everything Fenri wanted since the cycle began swirled in her head: new plant life from the Electric Ocean, building ships that could go under the water or through the air, working with someone like Luzon who could push them forward as a tribe, working with someone like Craeya who had a mind for cures and possibly Fenri's cure. Maybe one day.

That day would never be hers if she died.

Have I done my best?

The thought weighed heavily in Fenri's chest. She wanted to be rid of it. She tried to stand.

The man in red went for Pau in that moment, knocking him down with a swift, barreling charge. Pau fell to his knees. He lifted his head for the final blow, but it never came. Fenri noticed, and a new fear came into her then, mixed with relief.

A beast had come hurtling forward, its four legs pounding on the ground, as tall as Pau, body wide like a kohbra but with thin, wiry limbs.

Galapus: dog like a horse.

Jagged teeth shone like diamonds in the sun. In one fell swoop, the beast came down on the man in red, crunching into him. The galapus snatched him by the torso with its mouth and ran off into the direction it had come. Two smaller galapuses followed their leader's attack. One went for the female in orange, the other bounded over to Luzon.

The man in red was gone, and in his place, the tiniest spot of hope blossomed.

We could live.

Pau stood and lunged at the man in orange, cutting him down, but it wasn't enough. The man rose again. They slashed at each other, both their lifebloods spilling onto the ground. Pau cut him down again then fell on top of him, knees and all. In one fluid motion, Pau drove his durablade down into the Assassin's heart. Pau slumped over, laid still.

Closer to Fenri, the other galapus snapped at Luzon with its vicious knife-teeth. Luzon blocked the blow with his makeshift terrabag shield. He slung it over his back and tried to run. The galapus's jaws closed over the bag and lifted Luzon into the air, ready to tilt back and swallow him.

Fenri's heart leapt. *No, not him.*

Luzon squirmed. He threw up his arms, and slid out the top of his skinsuit, as though his body had been covered in peppernut oil. Only the terrabag and the skinsuit hanging from it remained in the beast's mouth.

Luzon fell to the ground, clutching a flare. He lit it with a flick-lighter and aimed it at the galapus's face as it spit out the bag and lunged for Luzon again. The flare cracked and lit, the spark of crimson a fizzling tail, and shot straight into the beast's mouth, taking part of its face clean off. Luzon swayed, drunk with exhaustion.

The final beast faced off with the last Assassin, and Fenri felt the hope inside her grow. She could smell victory, one that stunk of blood and death. Before the beast could make its move, the Assassin ripped a circular device from her shoulder and punched a finger into it, causing a blink of pink light. She threw it.

The device exploded in a blinding flash, cleaving the open air and leaving behind a churning vortex of smoke and debris.

Fenri's ears rang. She shut her eyes hoping it would stop the pain. When she opened them, she saw that the beast was gone, annihilated into a thousand pieces. Warm blood showered her.

Some sort of bomb?

Fear slit the throat of hope then.

What kind of weapon is that? One with enough power to erase a beast in seconds? If they had weapons like that, Fenri and the others didn't stand a chance. The female killer in orange was the only one on her feet. She clutched at another device on her other shoulder and ripped it off.

Another device!

Craeya stood with the quickness of youth and charged. The Assassin saw her coming, dodged, and slinked underneath Craeya's arms.

"Die!" Craeya said, with that same desperation she'd had when she ended the greffir. She spun, went to attack again. Again, the Assassin was prepared. She lifted her foot and kicked Craeya in the chest hard, sending her careening backward onto the ground. Craeya held her chest, gasping for air.

A thousand waves crashed through Fenri's brain at that moment. Each one different and more powerful than the last. *What comes after life? What happens when there are no more chances left?*

The female pressed the button on the device, then flung it at Craeya. The explosive slid and bounced over the ground, landing close enough to where it would annihilate Pau too. No one stirred. Fenri was calculating how many seconds she had before it exploded like the other. Would a knife in her own heart be less painful when the female came to end her? Would Craeya and Pau's deaths be quick and painless?

If this love defect is a virus, then I am terribly infected.

Craeya was infected, but what did it matter? That word, *defect,* had a strange effect in Fenri's brain, living as more than just a word. *Defect* was Fenri's past, her future, and she realized in that moment that seemed to stretch into eternity that she and Craeya were no different.

Now.

Fenri pushed herself off the ground. Seconds ticked in her head, a countdown to destruction. She sprinted for the device knowing it might go off before she got there. *No.* She scooped it up, turned on her heel, and as she did, it was as if the entire world tilted from its axis too.

She hurled the device back at the Assassin with a strength that did not seem hers.

The last thing Fenri saw was the bright white of the killer's eyes wide with fear as a stream of light ripped reality in two, sending limbs and blood and bone through the air in meaty chunks and foamy spray.

Fenri fell to her knees. Fire ripped through her body. She was scared that her own spark could grow and combust and stop her heart. She looked around at her team, strewn on the ground like lifeless playthings.

They had won, but it didn't seem to matter. The smell of blood and death rose stronger, and they didn't have much time.

We were so worried about the love virus and what it would mean that we were completely blind to all other contagions. What an uncanny combination. The members of Project El were all great in their own ways ... and we lost every one of them.

- from Confessions of the Masters, Volume I

36. CRAEYA THE COMFORTER

I n the Quat Zones, in Quadrant XXVII, it was late afternoon, a time so sticky with heat Craeya imagined she had died.

She couldn't move.

She would die if she didn't move.

She had to move.

She forced her eyes open as the sun pressed into her skin with unseen fingers. Underneath her, the qha was hot; it boiled her stomach, burned her inch by inch. She moved to her elbows and took in the sight around her. Death-blood splattered the ground in puddles. Dismembered limbs, both human and beast, littered the land. Everything smelled of death.

Time was precious.

Craeya knew some of them would die if she did not act. She pushed herself up off the ground. She felt metal weighing her down. One of those shiny throwing stars had lodged itself into the back of her thigh. She probed for the weapon, found it, and yanked it out. The blood flowed. Craeya staggered and steadied herself.

We beat them.

But the fight seemed far from over. Craeya's mind swelled. When she decided that she wouldn't go back to the nation-feast, she never expected that others would fight with her. *For* her. Craeya scanned the area, trying to see through the soupy and tepid air to find her teammates. Pau lay on his back, holding his chest, his breathing labored, staring straight up into the sky. Stone lay face down, unmoving. Luzon was crawling to his knees. Fenri was down and barely breathing.

Craeya's chest surged with a sudden desire, and she knew a battle was raging inside her about who to attend to first. Her vows pushed her one way, her heart another. She chose her vows as a Healer and ran.

Pau first.

He had taken the most damage and was sliced open like a cactusii for its rainwater. The kohbras had done a number on Pau, but the Assassins, mainly the one in red, had tried to slow Pau down by cutting him open in as many places as possible. Craeya grabbed her healing kit, then knelt down next to Pau and went to work. As long as she did not recognize her own pain, she could heal Pau and make it to the others. She tended to Pau quickly, wrapping him with her remaining gauze and whatever skinsuit pieces she could find in her bag and in the surrounding area.

Stone came next. His stab wound had already been tended to, but Craeya reapplied peppernut oil and redressed the wound. She searched for any metal stars in Stone's calloused and rocky body, but he seemed to have avoided all of them.

Craeya jumped to her feet, and blood rushed to her head, leaving her dizzy and parched. She steadied herself and tried to keep herself from toppling over. She wiped sweat from her forehead and pushed her hair out of her face. *The sun is so awful all the time, why would now be any different?*

Craeya heard a moan and was brought back to where she was standing.

Fenri.

Craeya found her closer to the hatch they'd fallen into. They'd been in the weird underground ship hours ago, but it felt like days. There was no time to think about that.

What about water?

Craeya knelt down and breathed in dry air that sat heavy on her tongue. *Oh dear, water.* They all needed water. Craeya rolled Fenri onto her back and scanned the bloody mess. There was metal lodged into her left shoulder and another piece in her lower stomach. Fenri groaned, no power to her voice. Her eyelashes fluttered, a meager attempt at filtering out the blinding sun.

"Fenri, can you hear me?" Craeya's voice was childlike, powerless.

Fenri's face didn't move. Only her eyes showed signs of life. She forced one open, looked at Craeya, and mumbled something.

Craeya peered back at the others. No one stirred. If one of them could help her get the baracca up, they could save what little precious energy they still had and not get roasted to death. Craeya returned her focus to Fenri.

"You're hurt. Is there any more metal in you?"

Fenri coughed. Her eyes opened and closed sluggishly. Words emerged from her mouth. "You're hurt," she said.

"I'm fine," Craeya said, but she knew she would need rest too. Without asking Fenri anything else, she morphed into Healer mode and did what she knew how to do. She removed the metal from Fenri's shoulder and belly. She tried to stop the blood from leaving Fenri's body with padcloths and gauze. She had a few leftover hancrystal antibodies so she gave them to Fenri to help ward off infection. The metal hadn't pierced any major organs. *Thank the ancestors, one less thing to worry about.*

Craeya pulled Fenri's skinsuit off her stomach to look at her wound. The rivers of red ran deep. Craeya pressed a cloth soaked in saline into the wound to clear out the dirt.

"Ow!" Fenri clenched her teeth, bit back the pain. "Is it over?" she managed to say.

Over.

Craeya knew what Fenri meant by her question, but it brought other answers to the forefront of her mind. Craeya allowed the future of that moment to lie before her. She didn't know what it would mean. She had opened her fourth portal, that was sure.

There was no way any of them could go back to the nation-feast, not after fighting against the people who had come to kill them.

Not after killing in their own way.

Craeya's thoughts began to come apart, disassembling like molecules too hot and denatured to remain what they were. The light on her back was so strong, and everything was leaving its original state. Craeya lost herself in the light, felt distant from her body, a combination of particle and wave.

Fenri reached out with a trembling hand.

"I don't think so," Craeya said, bringing Fenri's hand into hers and squeezing. "Do you still want to kill me?"

Fenri drew a deep breath and stared into the sky. She swallowed a painful lump in her throat. "No. I don't think I do."

Craeya laughed despite herself, but tears began to form in her eyes. Delirium was not far away. Hell, it was already there. She had no idea what was happening, or what would happen.

Luzon appeared at Craeya's side. She felt the warmth of his body, smelled his sweet sweat. Being near him was life, even in the midst of murder. His wet hair hung over the edge of his head. When he looked at Craeya, she felt her lungs expand, so full she thought she might burst with a light brighter and hotter than the sun.

She had only ever thought about being on top of Rannum, but he was gone forever. Luzon was here, right next to her. And he was enough.   Craeya noticed that Fenri was watching them. The small smile she'd worn faded from her face, and she looked away. The warmth and air filling Craeya's lungs tightened, and her heart thumped out a new rhythm.

Nothing would be easy.

Craeya squeezed Fenri's hand again, held her tight in her grasp. Fenri responded in turn. She turned to look back at Craeya, and there was deep sadness in her seablue eyes, tides pulling her down and under.

"Are you all right?" Craeya asked.

Fenri's face changed and became like the explosives, full

and whole one moment and then ripping through the air, its parts rattling, separating, and then exploding into a million pieces. Her lips trembled. The space above her eyes shook like the ground coming apart. Then she broke.

Fenri wept.

Craeya held onto her. There was renewed strength in Fenri's grasp. She wept, and it was a cry Craeya had never seen before, an ugly thing, senseless and feverish, like a patient just before death. But Fenri was not dying. Craeya leaned over and held Fenri tight, and her own tears flowed. Craeya let go of any control she imagined she had. They both wept in each other's arms.

Above, the clouds converged into soundless grey shapes. Craeya felt drops on the back of her neck before she knew what it was. The spray of blood had been so constant, that for a moment, she believed she was still in battle. The sky opened without a sound, like handspeak between Fenri and Stone. The rain drizzled onto the ground, mixing with Fenri and Craeya's tears and dirt and blood. And the red flowed away like pain, washed away down into the qha, until it could no longer be seen.

Redemption exists in the minds of many QhaHadurians. Coming back to the nation-feast each cycle is a sort of redemption, one we can all know and experience. Even those who do not go into the field can feel it. We feel it as a tribe. The value of each of us is tied directly to the other. Our abilities are accentuated by the roles we assume in society. We return because we have done good. Yes, every QhaHadurian will know about redemption and how it feels, even if they can't always name it.

- from *QhaHadur: A History and a Song*

37. STONE THE SHREWD

On the morning after the Assassin's arrival, everyone tried to gather the bits and pieces they had lost in the bloodbath. The rain had washed much of the death away, but decay still hung in the air. The limbs of the female Assassin littered the land like charred twigs. The body of the male in orange lay still, frozen by death, damp with rain.

Rain. After, all that time, finally … *rain.*

Stone sat up for the first time that day. He touched his side and a tenderness consumed him from his toes to the crown of his head. The knife had gone in, but not deeply, as though Pau had changed his mind halfway through. He wanted to hurt Stone and make him suffer but not kill him. Stone's stomach was a black hole of pain sucking all of his energy away. He was a broken, chopped-up thing that had come back to help his fellow team, the team he was ordered to leave.

Did I do the right thing?

Wondering about such things was a waste.

Time to move forward.

Stone felt Fenri's presence before she knelt beside him. Her movements were slow and needled with pain. The sun was coming up over the meridian, somewhere across the stretch of land that never ended, away from the nation-feast, its heat trickling into Stone's body. The water and moisture all around them held off Zhao's true power.

Fenri did not use, did not need to use, handspeak.

"Did you know that all of this would happen?"

Stone considered the question. He sat silent a moment. When he spoke, his voice, the new sound of his, pierced the air, high, shrill. "I saw many things," he said. "I did not know which future was the real one."

"How can you see that way?"

"It is not something I can describe well in words."

"Try."

"It would be better to show you sometime."

Fenri turned and their eyes met in a quiet calm of cerebral energy. She reached out for that power, for the *knowledge* of that power. Stone would help her hone it, if he could. The weight of it was too heavy to bear alone.

"There is something else on your mind," Stone said.

Before them, Craeya and Pau were picking up all the starblades on the ground, like avian species yanking out worms.

Fenri studied Stone's face, her eyes filling with curiosity, he knew, at his new, freshly shaven look. What had been hidden was open and bare. "What is the point of talking if you already know everything?"

"I sense the thing, but in this case, not what the thing is. It is like that many times."

"We can never go back now, can we?"

Stone stared at her. With his eyes, he traced the long sickle-mooned scar along her cheek, the slash of crimson. The mess of her hair sat tangled and clumpy, like a nest on her head. Stone felt no need for words for the question.

"Are you satisfied with your decision?" he asked.

Fenri moved to sit. She held her knees close to her body, squeezing. "I don't think I had much of a choice."

"You always have a choice, even if the Masters tell us the one we are meant to make."

"I don't know what it means." She shook her head.

"We do not need to know right now. This will be new. For a long time."

"So we just live out here without anything? We have nothing. No resources from the tribe, no water, no food, no medicine. It will all be gone soon. We'll die within the year. No, before the midsummer solstice."

With Fenri, such things needed to run their course. If Craeya was headstrong about getting her way, then Fenri was the same way about getting answers. He knew the emptiness would plague her.

"But," she said, the tone of her voice softening. "Maybe we can succeed. We've made it this far."

Silence fell over them.

Beyond their camp, Luzon was digging into the ground, looking for pieces of metal and stone and ancestors knew what else. To Stone's right, he felt the smallest of tugs from Fenri. In the center of his chest, fear and excitement sluiced through him, a combination he was not familiar with, surging inside him with a persistence that approached pain.

Will this thing Craeya has done end all of us in time, like it did the ancestors?

Stone fell into a vision that lasted less than a second, but he had seen glimpses of future moments. The thing he had seen possessed the dark, unique shape of Luzon, all limbs and joints and knuckles.

Finally, I can see him.

Luzon was on their side, as far as Stone could tell, but he sensed a trouble he could not name. When he looked over to Fenri, he felt the tug again. In her eyes, he saw a heart battling to open.

"I was scared to die," Fenri said finally. "I didn't want anyone else to die either. Even though Craeya did what she did.

"I didn't think I would ever betray the Masters," Fenri said. "I never imagined I wouldn't go back to the nation-feast. Will they come for us again? I don't want to die."

"There are things more painful than death."

Fenri looked at Stone, and he noticed a shadow flicker behind her eyes. Then it was gone, replaced by an oceanic light. She leaned forward, eyes fixed on Stone's throat. "May I?"

Stone hesitated. The memories of his vision rushed back to him. Physical pain lingered on the horizon of those memories. But Fenri had a knowing presence about her. Her curiosity quelled his resistance.

"Okay," he said.

Her hand was warm. The warmth of her touch brought him unexpected ease. Wide, seasoned fingers traced the bulge of his throat, pressing gingerly. "How?"

Stone swallowed. No hands had touched him in … he couldn't recall how long. Exchanging items or briefly brushing against someone were small and rare moments that offered the grace of another human's touch.

The images shot back into Stone's awareness.

He saw the Masters holding him down, strapping him in, shoving a needle into his neck to numb the pain, to knock him out. No. They couldn't knock him out. Not forever. Fenri's fingers probed as though his throat were dough, trying to find its true shape. "They did something to you."

She acknowledged his pain, and it was enough to open him.

Stone's nostrils flared as he took in as much air as he could for what was coming. His throat unlocked, chest pumping one, two, three times, and then his own onslaught of memories unleashed themselves. Fenri rested her hand on Stone's knee.

Yes, this is new.

There were things not even the Masters taught. In order to gain sight, something else had to be offered in exchange.

Stone wept.

He wept for all the years he wanted to speak but couldn't. He loved the Masters, but they had stolen something from him that was not theirs.

When he finished crying and wiped the tears from his cleanly shaven face, he looked at Fenri. She embraced him.

Hugging someone else was a strange gesture, but Stone welcomed the warmth and closeness of Fenri's body. Stone held onto her. He loved her too, he thought. He could not explain the feeling of who or what Fenri was to him, but he allowed himself to fall into it headfirst, for once, rather than fight against it. He had fought against so many things for so long.

When they pulled away, silence fell around them in a veil.

After some time, Fenri stood. "There's so much we need to do." She walked back to the old ship they had found and disappeared into the opening in the ground.

They would spend their days in and out of the ship, escaping the sun as much as they could, and then nights out in the desert, until they could figure out more about what was in the ship. Their texts taught them they'd left their home planet hundreds of years ago.

How could something survive that long?

If anyone could figure it out, it was Fenri.

After Luzon and Craeya cleaned up the battle arena, they retired to the ship as well. Pau remained outside, looking out into the blood-red of the horizon. Zhao was coming up hot and bright.

Pau walked over to Stone. They had not spoken since the day Stone left them, and he felt the immensity of his decision in that moment, in their neglected interactions. Yesterday, they had wrestled and punched each other, and then Pau had driven a knife into his side.

Pau sat beside Stone. His words emerged slowly, measured. "More beasts will come then? If what Fenri said is true."

"They may," Stone said.

Pau was silent. Speech was not his strong suit.

"I am sorry," Stone said. Perhaps it was his turn to speak.

"Sorry for what?"

"Sorry for not telling any of you. For leaving you to die with the beasts."

"I didn't die," Pau said.

Stone inhaled the damp qha and crisp air of the past rain all around him. A heaviness hung in the air, idle, waiting. Stone wanted Pau to hear his words, but he would not even allow this apology. "You could have."

"I didn't."

There was stillness, and for the smallest of moments, Stone thought he might receive his own apology. All Pau had offered was that he was confused when he pushed the blade into Stone's body.

"Why did you come back?" Pau asked. His questions were direct, already formed.

Stone considered his answer, how he could help Pau understand. "At first, I did not want to. I tried to forget all of you."

"You should have."

"I could not forget. I saw things, Pau." Stone said Pau's name for the second time, and the sound of it in his mouth was like drinking the juices from a cactusii, familiar and simple. "I saw what they did to me. To my voice."

"Is anything you've said true?" Pau asked.

"Everything I have said is true."

"I don't know if you'll change your mind again." Pau's words were like daggers on his tongue. "Or why you're even here. To get something out of us? I don't trust the Masters anymore, and you've been sent by them. You answer to their call. How can we feel safe around someone like that?"

None of Pau's words were amiss. Safety and guardianship always helped him find the right words, it seemed. Stone considered all of that. "I am here because I want to find a way forward with all of you."

"Do you think there is a way? Forward?"

"I would not have come back if I did not believe there was."

They both fell silent again.

The sun rose higher, and they both began to sweat, but neither of them seemed bothered.

"There is a saying among us Guardians," Pau said. "It goes: no one is a Guardian until their hands have tasted the blood from those that would kill." Pau looked down at his hands. They were weathered and sliced open, bandaged, healing.

He turned and Stone met his gaze. "I understand," Stone said, nodding. "I will show you that I can be loyal." *I will be his Guardian. I will protect him always.*

"It's good to hear that," Pau said, standing. "I guess we'll see what you will do." And he walked away.

Stone sat there for a long time after that, watching Zhao climb higher. Everything was utterly still, from the cloudless sky, to the deep brown qha. Day became night, and days rolled along like loose bramble. Stone listened to the quiet signaling sounds of the desert that pressed into his ears like music he had long forgotten the words to.

They tell you a heart can break by losing something. Or someone. That it can break because of grief, or pain, or love unfulfilled. They never tell you the bursting part can be just as painful. They never mention being so loved and wanting to love so much, about having a heart so full that it bursts. No one told us those things, and no sort of training could ever bring us back to where we were before the moment of change. We could never again be students in a society that would not accept us. There were no more books for us to read. Instead, it was time to write our own.

- from *Reflections on Our Changed World* by the New Masters

38. LUZON THE LUCID

Tamagon hearts covered the tables of the nation-feast by the time Luzon arrived. He salivated as he watched the Masters arrange each spread. He hadn't been home in so long. He warmed as sunlight streamed into the hall, felt its glow spread into his fingers and toes.

A voice came from behind him, puncturing his concentration. "I wish you good fortune and plentiful spoils with your new team." Luzon turned and saw Fenri, her eyes wide with all the knowledge in the world. There was beauty to her, something about the way she stood in her skinsuit. Luzon had not thought about her as beautiful before, but he was thinking about it then. The sun had touched her in an irreversible way, turning her skin a light bronze. Her seablue eyes reached out like the tide, pulling Luzon in.

These thoughts are forbidden.

Luzon paused. He looked around the Chamber Hall. No one was watching. "New team? What are you talking about?" When he focused back on Fenri, he found that she was gone.

There was a strange contradiction in that place, veils of reality superimposed upon one another. Luzon walked with a slowness that made him feel like he was underwater. He moved along through the chambers, not because he wanted to, but because his body was making him.

Not for the first time, he felt like an unwanted bystander in his own body.

Moments passed. He moved through the vast hall and after some time, passed Pau and Stone. One followed the other, and neither spoke to Luzon except for a slight nod of the head. Seeing the two of them together, seeing Stone at the nation-feast at all, was strange. Luzon watched them for a while, until the pair found seats at a table. The Chamber Hall shook with beads of light, and sound seemed to come to Luzon unevenly, obnoxiously loud one moment, eerily quiet the next.

"Luzon!"

Craeya appeared from an alcove without warning. That was always her, arriving like a spark of fire, sudden and warm. She held the length of her long and beautiful hair in her hands, like she would a drying-cloth and threw it over her shoulders. "I guess we won't be seeing each other again." She smiled.

New cycles meant new team members.

This feels wrong.

"Maybe you can relax more next time, since you won't have to take care of me," she said.

Luzon smiled at the sweetness of her voice, the spreading sound of light it made. Her words sank in, and his smile faded. The sudden need to touch her, to pull her into the heat of his body took him. The impulse bordered on unbearable, but Luzon couldn't move. Craeya smiled back, her eyes kind and soft, one hand resting on her stomach. "Take care, Luzon." She leaned over, planted her lips on his cheek for a moment, and then she was gone.

Luzon tried to call for her, but the words never came, and she became lost in the crowd. He stood on his toes to see above the gathering of heads, to see if he could spot the pink-streaked hair.

Where did you go, Craeya?

Luzon turned. There were too many people. He'd never seen so many people at the nation-feast. He had never seen so many people ever. The stream was endless. People exited alcoves, bunching together like honey-making zeebies, multiplying. He didn't recognize anyone. When he looked to the table Pau and Stone had gone to, they were gone too.

What's happening? Why didn't I stop Craeya when I had the chance?

Another thought followed, interrupting the pattern of Luzon's subconscious, the quick strike of drumstick on drum.

In three days' time, I'll never see any of them again. After that, they'll be gone from my memory forever.

The thought took hold of Luzon by the ribcage and held his discomfort in place. He stood rooted to the spot, icicles forming in his brain. Solutions to his problems taunted him as distant memories shifted and swayed like the surf.

A Master dressed in impossibly long brown robes walked toward him. Luzon stopped her. His voice was feverish and brackish with dread, but he didn't care. *What are we supposed to do?*

"The same thing we do every cycle," she said. "Survive."

"But this isn't survival," Luzon said, but his words came out differently from the ones he could hear, muted and grey. "We aren't living anymore!"

"That's exactly what we're doing," the Master said. "Do you have a better idea?"

Luzon left her and ran.

Ideas swirled in his head like storm clouds, heavy, all-consuming. He always had ideas, but for some reason, they felt distant, unreachable. He didn't like the notion that he wouldn't be with Fenri or Craeya anymore. That he would never see Pau and Stone again, and if he did, they'd give him nothing more than a nod of the head.

And something stronger was pulling him along.

Another voice, one Luzon could not locate, sounded in his ears. "You came back to the nation-feast. That is the way it goes."

"Then," Luzon said. "I don't want to be back at the nation-feast." His words were as loud as thunder, but no one could hear him. He realized the hopelessness of what he wanted. There was life at the nation-feast, or there was the thing he was thinking about, another, unobtainable, impossible thing that twisted inside him like thorns around his heart.

I want both. I want Fenri and I want Craeya and I don't want this!

"Greed has no place in nature," came the voice again. "You cannot have both. You must choose one."

But everyone is gone.

"Not everyone, Luzon. Look and see for yourself."

Luzon awoke then. Panic coursed through him like tilq.

The panic deepened, dug into his skin even as the baracca shielded him from Zhao. He rolled out from his protection, looked up and out over the horizon. Early morning light trickled into their camp in tiny waves. He clutched his chest and spun.

Craeya was up, staring at him, eyes wide, unblinking. "What is it?" She was looking around for something too. At the same time, her eyes, and Luzon's, landed on Pau. Like a rock, Pau stood there before them looking out, body tired, loose with unrest. When he turned, Luzon knew it was all wrong. Craeya let out the smallest of sighs, and that's when Luzon felt an emptiness he could not name.

Luzon had seen it in his sleep-story: a nation-feast muted and faded as though underwater and voices ringing in his ears telling him things.

"Where is she?" Craeya asked. The intensity of her stare, of those moonblue eyes, a cosmic gravity pulling everything in, had an opposite effect then.

Empty.

Luzon lost his breath and he became a soundless, guileless thing.

"She left last night," Pau said, easily, as though speaking a name.

"Why? Craeya asked.

Only silence.

"When is she coming back?" Craeya asked.

Somehow, she had seen it too. Her questions were too sharp, too pointed with conclusions for her to not have thought about how the situation might end.

"She's not coming back," Pau said. His voice was thick with the misery of a man who'd walked hundreds of days and still lost someone at the end.

"Did you know?" Craeya asked. "That she would leave?"

Pau nodded.

Craeya tightened and shook her head. "You just let her go!"

"I didn't—"

Craeya ran. She sprinted past Luzon, past Pau to the west, nothing but the soft, pink bottoms of her feet flickering back at them.

Luzon ran too. He would not lose Craeya. His legs ached from the fight with the killers. His thigh slowed him, but he pushed onward, running, running.

"Craeya!" he said. "Stop!"

She didn't stop. She ran faster. Luzon ran faster too. His legs were longer, his strides greater, but she had more energy then, bursts of flame stored inside her from sleep. They ran for a minute like that, and then Craeya stopped. She reeled over in pain, feet scraped and bloodied from an unkind landscape. Her face twisted with anger then fear. Luzon moved to her, pulled her into his body, but she pushed away.

"Craeya." Luzon was trying to hold her to him.

Her breath caught in her chest. Tears rushed down her face.

Dots connected in Luzon's mind-map rapidly. Fenri's behaviors had changed since the battle. She was still her curious

Knowledger self, but she resisted interactions with Luzon and Craeya, not separately, only when they were together. Fenri would drift off, and Luzon finally knew why.

"It's painful," he said, and Craeya broke a little more. Pieces of her chipped. Jagged edges fell at her feet as tears.

He never imagined he would lose someone to an entity other than death.

"Why would she leave us?" she asked. "After everything?"

"To survive, I think."

The crying, the longing, was new. In Luzon's mind he saw the land before them unfold. The copper-hued qha peeled back its many rough and layered edges, showing its true face.

"What about us? Doesn't she care about what happens to us?"

"I think she does," Luzon said. The strangeness of beginning a new creation seeped into him. Because a new reality existed, more paths could be created. The end of one thing was the beginning of another. "We've invented something new, Craeya."

"I wanted all of us to make something together."

"I did too."

"She's alone. She'll die. She's not—"

"She didn't leave on a whim. I know that. She will have a plan." Something had been on Fenri's mind, something she could not contain. Craeya was quick and impulsive. Fenri was analytical and thoughtful.

Both had visions of a new world.

Craeya possessed the unrelenting force of fire, constant and wild. Fenri was the twin moons, silent and vast, vigorous and lasting. They had wanted different things. And Luzon only had one of them. He wondered if he had done the right thing.

She will come back. I hope she comes back.

Craeya leaned into Luzon's embrace. Their chests thumped against each other, bare and uncaged, like freshly cut tamagon hearts from dying bodies. A dull ache formed beneath the beating, and Luzon fought to breathe.

He clutched Craeya tighter, felt as though he could feel the pain oozing through her skin. They held each other a while longer until the tears dried, until only the early morning sounds of the desert whispered to them.

Their new life wasn't perfect, but it felt okay for the moment.

Luzon turned and looked back toward camp. "C'mon. Let's hear what Pau has to say."

Dispatch of the Assassins into the Quat Zones to eliminate the threat that was Project El required no deliberation. We took Stone the Planeteer's message as truth and acted accordingly. It was possibly our gravest error. Had we not interfered, the members of Project El would have likely perished. They would have killed each other or died after so much time away from base. By sending the Assassins, we delivered them an enemy. They should have died, but they chose life for reasons we can easily guess. Too many of them had been infected by then, and we know the virus acts strangely on our bodies. If they had stayed together, we could have dealt with the problem in another way, but again, they did not. They split themselves into groups. That is the moment when our planet changed forever.

- from *Reflections on Our Changed World* by the New Masters

39. PAU THE TRUSTWORTHY

Hours before Luzon and Craeya awoke to the news of Fenri leaving, Pau stood watch like most nights, his ears open for sounds of intrusion, his eyes sharp for signs of movement. Something stirred behind him.

Fenri appeared.

Instinct brought Pau's hand to his durablade. He hesitated, taking in the sight of her. Her dark hair was drawn back tightly against her neck, her eyes were bright and alert, like she hadn't slept at all. Her terrabag hung neatly on her back, fully packed.

"Fenri?"

She drew a deep breath as she passed Pau. "C'mon. Let's talk. I don't want to wake the others." Tonight, she moved with authority.

Pau turned, opened his mouth to speak, then closed it. With reluctance, he followed, stealing a glance back at the baracca. No trouble had arrived since their battle a week before. Bones and bodies had been buried. The rain had washed away the blood, the smell of death. Water grew new life and there was plenty of food for beasts in their own habitats. Intruders would arrive again, but for the time being, there was safety.

When they were far enough away, Fenri turned to face Pau. The light of the moons fell on her face and shadows fled.

"I'm leaving." Fenri held Pau's gaze. "I wanted to tell you before I went."

"What do you mean you're leaving? For what?"

"I'm going back to base," she said, and Pau's first thought was of betrayal. Fenri's gaze held steady, and he realized she meant something else. "I have too many questions. I can't stay here."

"They will kill you," Pau said.

"They will not find me."

In his mind Pau saw a past version of Fenri, knuckle-white grip on her durablade, feet set apart awkwardly, like a fish sprouting legs. She couldn't even catch and skin a tamagon, how could she possibly use any stealth? "I don't understand," was all Pau could bring himself to say. "After everything we did to get here. You want to go back?"

"It doesn't make sense to me either, but there are things I need answers to." Fenri exhaled a deep breath. "I will come back."

But Pau was not sure he believed her. Life lived in her eyes, but in the great, unrelenting beyond, death lived in many more places. Pau imagined Fenri alone, and fear came into his chest like a nightbat swooping into a cave.

"Do the others know? Did you tell Stone?"

"I didn't tell Stone, but I think he already knows. I can't hide things from him. Luzon and Craeya—" Something moved behind Fenri's eyes when she said their names—dark, swift, the scuttling of a sandmouse—and then it was gone. "They would have tried to stop me."

"And I would not try to stop you?"

Fenri turned away. "Pau. I have learned so much from you."

She was diverting the topic away from Pau's question. A very Knowledger thing to do, he had learned.

"I need to do this." Her gaze fell. She looked at her trembling hands. "There are things I don't understand right now. And I need to. I need to understand them, or I'll die. I need to be away right now." She looked up, and that same shadow, that dark, unwelcomed creature was swimming beneath the surface of her eyes. She wanted to escape, and for a moment Pau thought he understood.

"There's more I want to ask you," he said.

"Remember them. Ask me when I return. You'll likely answer many of them yourself."

Fenri smiled, and Pau didn't know why or how, but he stepped forward and stretched his long arms around Fenri, behind her terrabag, and pulled her to him. Against him, Fenri's breaths slowed. When they pulled away, Pau said, "Wait here."

Moments later he returned. He held out both his hands.

"Your grappling claw?" Fenri looked at it as though it was death itself. "It's so heavy."

"You're strong, and you need a weapon."

She took it and put it in her terrabag. Pau handed her a cinch bag. "And food. There are fresh hearts in there."

"There are a lot in here."

"We can find more."

"Thank you, Pau."

"You really shouldn't go."

"Don't try to stop me."

Pau sighed. "I'll always want to protect you, but I'm no longer your Charge Leader."

They stood in silence a moment longer. "Look at you now," he said. "Hold on to your durablade this time, okay?" Pau felt her departure creeping closer, and with it, an angry fear, subtle, dreadful and unknown.

Fenri failed at trying to hide her smile. "I never imagined we'd actually like each other."

"I still think you think too much."

They laughed.

Pau wanted to say more, but before he could, Fenri was gone.

Time became something else then, senseless and cruel.

Pau stood alone.

He held his breath, then released it, recalling the echo of their final moments together. He stood there for a long time lost in the waves of his thoughts, until Luzon and Craeya woke and discovered the news, until they ran off, tears taking them, grief and confusion rising like it had for Pau. He stood there for a long time, picturing the shape of her body, of her lengthening shadow coming back to them.

Life came to those who knew how to grab a spear and throw it.

A day passed and another after that. Fenri was further away, but thoughts of her grew closer to his chest, tighter, more intense. Luzon and Craeya resented Pau for what he had done, but they wouldn't have done anything different in his position. *I had to let her go. Didn't I?*

On that third day, when sleep was impossibly unkind and his mind grew tired with the same old patterns of thought, he came to Luzon and Craeya. They were sitting down tinkering with Klonden that Luzon had broken into smaller pieces.

"I'm going after her," Pau said.

Craeya looked up, eyes glued to Pau. "You are?"

"I thought she told you not to," Luzon said.

"I don't care anymore. She won't survive out there alone." Pau sighed. "I'm tired. I made a mistake in the moment. I see that now."

"I will go with you." Stone appeared from somewhere. Behind Pau, beside him, he had no idea. Stone had been going off alone lately, walking around with his eyes closed. "All of us are tired, and all of this is new. It is okay."

Pau looked at Stone, and cold, storm-grey eyes stared back,

unblinking. Seeing his face without all the hair was strange. His face was chiseled, youthful even, not as old as Pau had originally thought.

"Fine. It shouldn't take long," Pau said.

Stone walked away to gather his things, and Luzon and Craeya stared at Pau, wonder and hope bright as new knowledge in their eyes.

He could still see Fenri, her jaw set, eyes dry, hair tied back tight and secure. He could still smell her. Honey and iron and fresh rainfall.

I'll find her. I have to.

The new world lived beyond the horizon, and it was waiting for us all along. The old world was nothing but a shattered memory.

- from *Reflections on Our Changed World* by the New Masters

40. FENRI THE UNACCOMPANIED

Fenri peered down into the valley below her and recalled those she had traveled with, Luzon and Craeya, their bodies next to each other, sleeping and warm. *What would have happened if I'd stayed? I would have become more confused. Take some time to understand what the virus is doing to me. Out here, away from them, my portal will diminish, and the beasts will not smell me.*

She hoped.

Stone's endless grey eyes swam into view, his freshly shaven face, young and handsome. She still felt him inside her head somehow, watching where she went. Pau was likely keeping watch and sleeping very little. For a moment, Fenri envied him, that he had not yet opened his portal. In the presence of the others, maybe it would happen in time. But until then, he did not have to deal with the strange, aching pain.

The Masters always told us how dangerous and confusing the virus can be once it infects us, and now, I think I understand. The feelings I have for Craeya, Luzon, Pau, and Stone are all different. The fourth portal is complex and has more than one entry point.

She thought of her own … children, the ones she bore without her knowledge of it, and a strange sensation different from all others, blossomed inside her.

Fenri clutched her chest.

She looked up.

The second, smaller moon carved a white-blue sickle into the vast black sky like a scar. The larger moon sat to its right, glowing and bulbous, a fruit yet to be discovered. Fenri pushed wispy breaths from her mouth as she watched stars press through the blanket of night with yellow eyes. She was not totally alone. Her planet had a way of guiding even the most lost. Turning, she peered down into the valley one last time.

I will see you all again someday. This I promise.

EPILOGUE

Love is the root of all evil.

- from *Lessons on Survival* by the Masters

MASTER QI OF THE YORBAST TRIUNE

Master Qi stood above his newest patient, pressing two fingers to her carotid artery. Upon his touch, she opened her eyes abruptly, startled by the cool depths of Qi's fingertips. She blinked awake, then focused on Master Qi.

"Hello, Jade," he said. "How are you feeling?"

"I'm—" Her hands came up to her face, touching gingerly. "Alive." *Somehow, yes.*

"Alive and well. You've been quite sick."

"What happened?"

"Nasty virus sweeping through the tribe."

Jade pressed the back of her hand to her forehead. "Virus?"

"Don't worry. Not *that* virus. This one was airborne. We've dealt with it."

"I can't … remember anything. How long have I been lying here?"

"A few days. You're finally coming out of it." *She survived. Incredible. I think we are finally understanding how to keep both of them alive. This one is special too.* "I wanted to make sure you were okay. You gave us a scare."

"I guess I'm okay," Jade said. "If I'm here, that means … did I complete my cycle?"

"You did. Here at the nation-feast. You conducted research, don't you remember?"

"What type of research?" Jade's eyes sharpened the tiniest of degrees.

Master Qi stared at Jade without blinking. "New species and their habitats. Surely you remember that."

"I don't," Jade admitted, lowering her eyes. Moments later, she looked up again, and her smile was bright. "I'd like to see what I did. Maybe it will spark my memory."

Knowledgers and their curiosity. Their need to know will be the death of me, I swear. "Your research has been turned in to the Masters for formulation and categorization."

"I see." She had enough memories to know how those matters went, at least.

Again, she swept her gaze up and over Master Qi, and when their eyes met, Qi thought he felt something from her. *Desire? Resistance?* He didn't have the time to ponder it. There were more important matters to deal with, but he wanted to check on Jade the Knowledger, the anomaly that she was. *Child bearer and child, both alive. All memories of the event will soon fade.*

"Now that I see you're feeling okay, I'll take my leave."

"Master Qi," Jade said, grabbing his hand before he stood. Qi looked at it. Her hands were unusually warm for being asleep so recently. "Thank you for coming here. I look forward to remembering more." She lifted her chin high, and the inflection in her voice, whether she was aware or not, hinted at persuasion, a challenge even. *Did I teach her that?* Her seventh portal—thought—was strengthening in the Knowledger way.

Master Qi responded in turn. "It is nothing. I only wish to make sure my tribesmen are healthy."

"You are an excellent Master," she said.

They stared at each other another moment. Jade's dark eyes and Qi's hazel clashed at each other like a cloudy sky filled with thunderheads. Master Qi took his hand away, keeping his thoughts and words to himself. Then he turned from the room and was gone.

Master Qi returned to the Chamber Hall where the tribe waited in near silence. A reverence fell over the tables like a plague, killing sound in the tribesmen's throats, keeping their eyes dry and focused forward.

Master Qi saw his place at the head of the tables. They did not often speak to the entire tribe all at once, and never in such a manner. Before he reached his place, a familiar face swam into view, walking into Qi's path.

Long, unkept hair fell down her face like a curtain. Behind the streaks of grey, her eyes were dark moons, every story in the world hidden somewhere in their depths. Master Qi stopped to look at her.

"I will speak to them if you wish it." Jesimene's voice was smooth as it glided into his ears.

"What could a Teller say right now? You know the seriousness of the matter. This isn't a time for stories."

"Stories are the bedrock of life. They remain in people's minds better than commands."

"Indeed, but they need not see a storyteller's face right now," Qi said. "They may take the message in the wrong way."

"I understand. I only meant to offer my help."

Qi inhaled the muskiness of the archives coming off her pale skin. She was getting old. Older than Qi. Her face sagged like the robes she wore, unwashed and soiled. A tiny bald spot at the top of her head shone white through the grey like a horn. "It is appreciated, but I think directness is best here. I need them to understand the gravity of this. I cannot risk them interpreting a story incorrectly."

Jesimene bowed in deference. "You will speak well."

Master Qi strode away, feeling every set of eyes on his back as he walked toward the raised platform at the hall's apex. He stepped upon it, spun, and took in the sight of the nation-feast. No food had been set out yet. A chilling quiet stole voices, coughs, whispers. Every time they sat in that place, there was food. No one yet knew why they were there otherwise.

The food will come. First, this.

"Children of QhaHadur." Master Qi kept his voice just below a boom. "Welcome back to the nation-feast after another productive cycle."

The quiet was everywhere. Master Qi looked at some of the other Masters in the crowd. They had voted on which of them would deliver the message, and Qi had won. His skin crawled. He hated it, but he would rather the words be his than someone else's. He knew precisely how to deal with the situation.

Then why does it feel so hard?

"Terrible things have happened," he said. "Not all of you have returned here. This happens. We go out, and the planet takes lives as it always does. Except this time—"

The quiet rippled. Tiny bursts of bated breath and held whispers bubbled up like the nastiest swamp.

"This time, the planet has not claimed everything." Those were not the right words. *How am I supposed to explain such a thing?* "We are all in danger," he said finally. "Laws have been broken. Oaths have been shattered. Tribesmen among us have done the unthinkable." Master Qi faltered in his own mind. He did not even know how they had done it. *Was it one of them? All of them?* The Planeteer's message had been so quick, so sparse. He had given them away.

The Assassins were dispatched at once, but after months of no contact, no return from the fastest, deadliest beings on the planet, he knew that they had perished. Fenri's map-projector was still online, and so was Stone's planet-tablet.

They were *alive.*

The Assassins, all three of them, Master's Qi's brightest and best, were defeated at their untrained, non-killing hands. How?

The quiet broke a little more, and Qi heard the whispers, but only because he was attuned to such things.

"Traitors."

"Who are they again?"

"I hope they meet painful deaths."

Is this what we taught them? To wish for the deaths of their brethren? I know the consequences of what has happened, but we are still one. Qi went to speak again, but he felt his voice breaking.

Aren't we still one?

He said the thing he knew he had to. "Because they have broken the law, they must be eliminated. Before the virus spreads and wipes us all out."

Cheers of approval echoed through the hall.

If the beasts are not the biggest threat, it can be them. Fear is the strongest motivator. "You know our words. Love is a horrible virus that cannot stay."

The tribe cheered.

Qi's heart tightened in his chest, shriveling, reaching out for air. He tried to collect himself. *They* became the loudest thing in his mind. Their specialties and weaknesses crashed against him like waves, pounding into him like the raging, double-mooned surf.

They were truly QhaHadurian, through and through.

Something twisted in Qi's chest, and a sudden fear seized him: *Can they reach me, even here with their virus?*

He pushed away the absurd thought.

They couldn't.

They were alone and in the Quat Zones, and they would likely meet death soon. That would make things much simpler.

"Do not engage with them if you find them out there. They will not survive against the beasts for long. Remember that the beasts are attracted to the virus. If you happen to run into them on your missions, do not speak to them. Give them no chance to drag you down. Kill them upon first sight."

Applause erupted into the hall like thunder, like a storm Qi had never heard before, thirsting for sustenance, and drowning in its suddenness. His speech seemed to be over, rushed off into the waves of excited chatter. The tribe had something new, a challenge, a new enemy to keep them in order.

Master Qi knew when killing a QhaHadurian was necessary, and they had reached one of those times.

Then why is it so hard to breathe?

He turned away from the tribe. His face burned. His jaw tightened, and he winced away tears. *What is happening?*

Their faces swam into view, bright and silent, faces he had sent into the field exactly one cycle ago. He hadn't the slightest idea which of them were still alive.

"Ancestors please help us," Qi whispered to himself.

There was a long moment of silence in his mind, and then: *Fenri ... Luzon ... Craeya ... Pau ... Stone ... What have you done?*

END

SHARE YOUR SUPPORT

Your review helps more readers discover this book. Please share your thoughts by leaving an honest review for *The Fourth Portal*. Scan the QR code below to activate your sound portal and leave a review.

Thank you so much for your support!

ACKNOWLEDGMENTS

First off, I want to thank those who read early versions of *The Fourth Portal*, when it was still called *Saudade*. Your notes and feedback helped me give shape to a somewhat amorphous story. Alana, thank you for providing such in-depth feedback. Adrian, thank you for treating my story like a real book, even back then, and for providing sci-fi fantasy infused advice at every step.

To my friends who made my final year in South Korea much brighter, when I was going through my own saudade sickness and missing home so bad it ached. Lorna Rose, our writing sessions in little old Boseong remain one of my most fond memories, and I still think of you and Brenda often. Pete Lucarotti, thank you for listening to me ramble about *Saudade* when the idea first sprang to life, for asking thoughtful questions, and for being my friend. What a lovely, strange, and unbelievable time that was.

Rachael Ritchey, I can't thank you enough for everything you've done for me. Your thoughtful feedback, empathy, and generosity have helped make my stories better. You're a beacon of light and one of the greatest people I've met in my author journey.

Blayne Milburn, thank you for deep diving with me about the nature of love, its evolution through time, and all things learned behavior. I admire your brilliance and gusto for life. Thank you for world-building with me and bringing my story to the next level, adding historical, psychological, and philosophical aspects to *The Fourth Portal*.

Sunjay Sethi, thank you for helping me approach my story from an immunological perspective, adding layer and depth to the love virus. Your feedback and suggestions were invaluable.

Grant, thank you for reading my story and believing in it, even when it was downright wild and strange.

Gergs, thank you for seeing potential in my work. I still remember when you said, "You have the bones." I remember the late nights, the phone calls, and organizing notecards to track timelines and storylines. I treasure our shared love for sci-fi and fantasy. Thank you, brother, for everything. My story wouldn't be where it is today without you.

To my editor, Jean McConnell, thank you for all that you do. Your encouragement is always appreciated, but it is your tough love and no nonsense attitude that elevate my stories even more. Thank you for never going easy on me, and for expecting such a high standard. I can't thank you enough for gently nudging me toward taking things into my own hands, and for challenging me to fight for what I believe in.

I want to thank my beta readers, ARC readers, and street team, who have helped breathe life into *The Fourth Portal* even more. You are the real heroes. Thank you for taking time out of your busy days to believe in me and my story and share it with others. I'm grateful to be part of such an amazing community.

I specifically want to thank some beta readers by name. Katherine K., thanks for believing in and loving my story with so much enthusiasm, I almost couldn't believe it. Jenna M., thanks for providing thoughtful feedback and for believing in this world and wanting more. Suzy, thank you for keeping me honest in the world-building department and for bringing a different perspective to the story. Shauna J., wow. Your support and enthusiasm sometimes brought tears to my eyes, and your kind words were always so well-articulated.

Chris, thank you for everything you do. Thanks for believing in me and my dreams, for seeing me, and for reading all my stories. You are only ever encouraging and supportive. Thanks for reminding me to breathe, to open my fourth portal, and to enjoy life. No win or celebration is too small for you. I love you with all my heart, and I can't wait to celebrate more releases with you.

To Kateryna, thank you for the incredible book cover and for bringing my vision to life. I'm still amazed every time I look at it. Thanks to my proofreader, Katherine S., and my typesetter, Jose P. You helped me in the final stages and pulled everything together when it mattered most.

Thank you to my family for supporting and encouraging my writing, especially my Mom and my younger sister, Mary. The summer after I graduated college was magical. I stayed up until dawn writing because you both begged me for more chapters. Thank you for nourishing and igniting my creativity and providing a space where I could keep on writing.

Thank you Marta, for reading so many of my stories, and for your loving big-sister guidance throughout the years. Growing up with you and Monica was such an incredibly fond experience, and in many ways, you are the heart and soul behind some of my characters.

Thank you to my younger sister, Mary, who deserves more recognition than I can fit in these pages. I treasure your feedback, sharp literary eye, and kind words, always when I need them the most. In *The Fourth Portal*'s final hours, when I had already exhausted my editor with my questions, you came to my side, and helped me work through the final elements of the story. Year after year, the knowledge and wisdom inside you grows even greater. You are limitless, and I'm so lucky to have a sister like you.

Thank you to the rest of my family for inspiring me every day with all that you do. There are pieces of you in all my characters.

To Mom, Dad, Josh, Jake, Jeremiah, Mollie, Marta, Monica, Jude, and Mary: although full of challenges and hardships, we had an incredible childhood filled with adventure, space to run and play, and a family that loved and fought for each other when it mattered most. I hope we will always fight for each other, no matter our differences.

Finally, thank *you*, reader. Thanks for picking up this story and giving it a chance. I write with you in mind, and hope you enjoy the story and universe I've created. I'd love to know what you think of *The Fourth Portal* when you finish. Cheers.

ABOUT THE AUTHOR

J. A. Merkel specializes in fantasy and science fiction that explores multiverses and themes of redemption. His stories feature complex anti-heroes, love as magic, and tragic reversals. For Merkel, writing is an enchanting universe with endless possibilities, offering readers a chance to immerse themselves in extraordinary journeys, filled with joy, discovery, and the search for home, wherever that may be.

Subscribe to J. A. Merkel's newsletter at jamerkel.com/newsletter for free content, updates on new releases, and early access to special giveaways!

GLOSSARY

CHARACTERS:

Craeya: Healer, blonde-white hair with pink streak, moonblue eyes, emotional, 18, nicknames "Craeya the Wild Card" and "Craeya the Curious"

Eider: assassin, man, strong sense of smell, red suit

Elan: stocky, long hair, dark, deep-set eyes, high cheekbones, Charge Leader, Guardian, middle-aged, muscular

Fenri the Knowledger: seablue eyes, pale skin, black hair, round head, small ears, Unable

Gaia: Jesimene's Teller apprentice, wild hair, pointed ears

Hasil: man, black hair, Healer

Healer Polina: waxe eyes

Jade the Knowledger: Pau's companion in the Dark Room, dark eyes, dark hair

Jesimene the Teller: bulbous nose, round face, wild salt-and-pepper hair, dark eyes

Luzon: rough olive-toned skin, wiry, hairless limbs, Maker, misshapen hands, angular jaw

Maej: Assassin, woman, gray eyes, keen eyesight, orange suit, dark hair

Man in Dark Room: black hair, oval head, sickle scar on cheek, one brown eye, one blue eye, toothy smile

Master Ghen: Master Guardian, member of the Mimenza Triune, yellow robe, green eyes

Master Qi: member of the Yorbast Triune, hazel eyes

Master Yaa'ga: member of the Oragami Triune, orange robe, russet hair, young, highly intelligent, low voice

Neren: man, wounded in Chapter 1

Pau the Guardian: lean, large bald head, 6'4", hazel eyes, Charge Leader for the mission, dark skin

Quei: Assassin, man, moves fast, orange suit

Rannum: tall, thin, olive skin, dark eyes flecked with orange, thick eyebrows

Stone: Planeteer, mute, dark, deep-set eyes, russet beard, grey and amber eyes, grey hair

Unnamed messenger boy: Chapter 2, thin

SETTING:

*21-hour time is used

Books: *Lessons on Survival* by the Masters, *The Elegy of Survival, Diaries of the Ancestors; Songs of the QhaHadurians; Confessions of the Masters, Volume I; Poems* by Haldur the One, *QhaHadur: A History and a Song; Reflections on Our Changed World,* by the New Masters; *Divinations from Beyond the Veil*

Chamber Hall: reddish-brown clay floor, site of Nation Feasts

The Dark Room (room for sexual encounters)

Electric Ocean

Kaleem: sister moon

Leeg Peninsula

Milkali: sister moon, revealed after centuries of lurking behind Kaleem, changed the tides on the planet

Portals: qha/earth, water, fire, air (the fourth portal), sound, light, thought

Project Councils

Project El: two decade-long project

Q: stands for QhaHadur their planet (time designation)

Qhahadur: referred to in the feminine

Quat Zones: divided into quadrants

Quatzi Range

Terrarium

Yorbast Triune

Virus L (the love virus)

Zhao: sun

WORDS:

Aguavi Alpha beast alphacka: curse word alu ammonia Analyzer: contains data *Arinx* *struthitix* Assassins Ast: considered to be the first Maker, made love potions auto immunes: medicine aydilite	baracca: leather dome Bearer bird-beast blade-work bloodpad bloomquests blowfly-fish body-blood brain-space	calcetrine calcium bulbs castusii Charge Leaders cinch bag cincher cine runes Clayhaze claystones climacloth cyclemate cycle-partner cylinders	diggers digspike Divers drinkspout duneboots dunegull durablade dust-pouch	Electro Moleculizer (EM) Engineers everblue
figshit figvi firenz flagelight	galapus: dog- like horse Guardians gawkil geriander gill: device for collecting moisture, small box with three copper wires gingitleaf gnatfly greffir (Arinx struthitix): bird creature in the desert grey growroom gulch	hancrystals: contains a rare molecule handspeak: sign language Hanil Tunnels harkine Harvesters hauntaray healing kit (not capitalized) Healing Alcoves Healing Circle hectomile Hive homecomer honey-Q hyperspeed	illysium indium: material inflarzine virus innervat IPR: item production rate for Makers	jadeflower: neutralizing medicinal Janga drums jaw-cave

kelester: fabric ketones kiloleen Klonden: rare base metal with changing properties, silver specks, referred to as an ore Knowledgers kohbra: black-purple fangs, large, broad heads and necks, tiny claws, scaly bodies, long, thick, vine-like tails	leadpen leshblanket lesh: soft plant material used to make blankets lesson-alcoves lessonmates limegrass limenz limeseed limewine: sweet-sour taste logbook	Major Histocom patibility Complex (MHC): component of immune system Makers map-projector marblestone Masters Messenger meter Mimenza Triune mind-map mineral-vines molassup moonblue: special eye color moonchoke Mountaineer mute	naido (short for Zephnaido) nation-feast netbed nightbat nightbugs norepi nephrine	Oather octoghi Omega beast Oragami Triune osmium: hard substance
pain-modifier patchgrass pawkwi: black and grey stripes peppernut milk/soap photovoltaic skinsuit pin-drop planet-tablet Planeteer plankti (pl. planktii) plexibow plexirods plushgrass pre-needles pre-sweat	qha qha-sand QhaHadur QhaHadurian	racabbage reedflute repair table: in the Healing Alcove rhoda mantium rockpowder roquee: plant rootwort RU rays rubyrinds	salamanzer: material salt-sand sand-spirals sandalstone sandmouse Scavenger Scorpio's Rainbow (Scorpiotynal, form of tilq) seablue seakelp Seeker semisand shrewrabbit sideslot skinsuit: converts sunlight into	tamagon Teller: the tribe has one Teller in training at a time terrabag thioxide tilq: drugs titanyl tonguebuds

Project Proposal (always a proper noun) pado beans			energy using Solaren sleep-story: dream slip-sandals slip-shades: gold- tinted lenses slipwatch smokestick Solaren stalag-life starblade streamsand stretch-rope submership sun-veiled surganeedle sveil sword-chain	
ultradim Unable	valley-bowl	walking dragon waxe: color	youngling yufish	zeeby Zephnaido zinger

PRONUNCIATION GUIDE

Craeya the Healer: KRAY-uh

Eider the Assassin: EYE-der

Elan the Guardian: EE-lan

Fenri the Knowledger: FEN-ree

Gaia, Teller's apprentice: GUY-uh

Hasil the Healer: HAH-sil

Healer Polina: poh-LEE-nuh

Jade the Knowledger: JAYD

Jesimene the Teller: JEH-sih-meen

Luzon the Maker: LOO-zon

Maej the Assassin: MAYJ

Master Ghen: GEN

Master Qi: KEE

Master Yaa'ga: YAH-guh

Neren the Seeker: NEH-ren

Pau the Guardian: POW

QhaHadur: kah-HAH-dur

Quei the Assassin: KWAY

Rannum the Healer: RAHN-um

Stone the Planeteer: STOHN

www.ingramcontent.com/pod-product-compliance
Lightning Source LLC
Chambersburg PA
CBHW060243030726
47493CB00025B/1577